CASSIE EDWARDS
THE SAVAGE SERIES

**Winner of the *Romantic Times*
Lifetime Achievement Award
for Best Indian Series**

"Cassie Edwards is a shinning star!"
—*Romantic Times*

SAVAGE SURRENDER

"Your full freedom will be yours again," Iron Cloud said, turning his horse back in the direction of Fort Calhoun, "after you accept your life as one of my people — and your new name, White Willow."

"If you strip me of my true name, you will not only be stripping me of my freedom, but also my true identity," Damita said, her voice quavering. "How much am I to be forced to accept? That I am a captive is enough!"

He drew his reins tight, stopping his horse. "When you kissed me, you did not play the role of captive," he growled. "Let us see again how you react to my kiss. Tell me then if you feel as though you have been stripped of so much."

Before Damita could protest, Iron Cloud turned her around so that their lips could meet in a fiery kiss. He held her so tightly that she could not squirm free. The spinning in her head told her the fright was lessening within her. There was pure magic in his kiss!

Other *Leisure Books* by Cassie Edwards:

SECRETS OF MY HEART
ISLAND RAPTURE
EDEN'S PROMISE
WHEN PASSION CALLS
ROSES AFTER RAIN
TOUCH THE WILD WIND

The Savage Series:
SAVAGE PERSUASION
SAVAGE PROMISE

SAVAGE MISTS

CASSIE EDWARDS

LEISURE BOOKS NEW YORK CITY

With endearing love, I dedicate SAVAGE MISTS to my son, Charles, his wife, Sheryl, and my adorable grandson, David.

ALSO
With much warmth I dedicate this book to my cousin, Helen Dowling, and her husband, Ed; my Aunt Aggie Osborne; and my longtime friends, Jack and Madonna Collinsworth.

ALSO
I dedicate SAVAGE MISTS to BRIAN'S PLACE, our family business in Mattoon, Illinois...Brian and Charlie know why.

ALSO
I dedicate SAVAGE MISTS to my good friend from Nebraska, Nancy Demuth.

CASSIE EDWARDS

I see the lights of the village
Gleaming through the rain and the mist;
And a feeling of sadness comes o'er me,
That my soul cannot resist.
A feeling of sadness and longing,
That is not akin to pain,
And resembles sorrow only
As the mist resembles the rain.
     —*HENRY WADSWORTH LONGFELLOW*

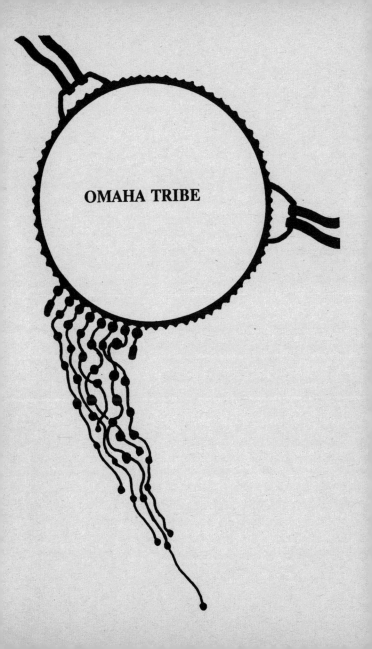

OMAHA TRIBE

Chapter One

Although it was June, normally a time of endless days of sunshine, a slow mist falling from the gray sky made the office of the Indian agent even more gloomy than usual. A pot-bellied stove sat cold and dull gray in one corner of the room. A kerosene lamp cast its dim light across a desk stacked high with ledgers and strewn with papers.

Chief Iron Cloud stood tall and wide-shouldered over the desk. His hands were doubled into tight fists at his sides and his midnight-black eyes flashed angrily down at Jonathan Jacobs, the Indian agent who sat behind the desk, an arrogant, smug smile on his narrow, pock-marked face.

His body sheathed in fringed buckskin, his shoulder-length black hair sleeked down with bear grease and held back from his handsome copper

11

face with a beaded headband, Iron Cloud had come to speak for his people, who were receiving shoddy clothing and spoiled provisions from the United States government. The end of the Civil War had brought no improvements in conditions for the Indians. Under the slovenly administration of President Grant, the Bureau of Indian Affairs had fallen into the clutches of a heartless set of plunderers whose only god was gold who robbed both the government and its Indian wards with happy impartiality.

Iron Cloud saw this Indian agent at Fort Calhoun as one of the worst of the lot. He was making enormous profits at the expense of the Omaha Indians, taking kickbacks from suppliers who were furnishing him with inferior provisions.

"Am I to understand that you will not release my people's annuity goods to them unless I give you presents of horses, robes, and valuable beadwork?" Iron Cloud said, his voice tight as he continued glaring down at Jacobs.

"*Maha*, that's it in a nutshell," Jonathan said, casually running his fingers through his thick ash-brown hair that had a tendency to curl up at the ends. Then he ran a finger around his stiff, white shirt collar, becoming unnerved beneath Iron Cloud's set, angry stare.

"You insult my people when you call Chief Iron Cloud *Maha*, proving your laziness in not saying the name Omaha with accuracy. And I will remind you again that I am not my father, whom you tricked time and again with the tactic of blackmail," Iron Cloud said, his voice smooth and even, void of any emotion. "While I rode with the United States cavalry during the Civil War as a trusted scout, you took advantage of my ailing chieftain father and his people."

Iron Cloud rested the palms of his hands on the desk, allowing him to lean down into Jonathan's face. "You gave our people only sick and bony cattle for beef, and the cheapest of shoddy clothing," he said in a low hiss. "Even now, anything good you receive from the government for my people you sell to traders. I have heard that you have netted some three thousand dollars profit in less than three years by cheating the Omaha! That profit should have been my people's!"

Jonathan backed his chair up and rose slowly to his feet, his right hand resting on a holstered pistol at his waist. "Just because you rode scout for the United States Cavalry during the war doesn't give you the right to come in here and talk to me like this," he said sourly. "*Maha*, if you know what's good for you, you'll back up real easy-like, then head the hell out the door. When you've cooled down, come back and we'll talk business. Do you understand?"

Iron Cloud stood his ground, and when he straightened his shoulders and the shadow of his six-foot-four height fell over and dwarfed Jonathan, who stood five-feet tall in his stockinged feet, Jonathan swallowed hard and took a quick step back from the Omaha chief.

"Get outta here, Iron Cloud," Jonathan said, his

hand nervously clasping and unclasping the handle of his pistol. "No Indian, not even a chief as powerful as you, comes in here throwin' their weight around."

"My father died a disgraced man," Iron Cloud said, his heart aching as he recalled his father on his death bed, his eyes void of pride. "His people are now my people. They will never again be forced to trade buffalo robes for scraps of food!"

Jonathan laughed sarcastically and sank back down in his chair, placing his fingertips together before him as he looked up at Iron Cloud. "You Indians are all alike," he said, his blue eyes gleaming malevolently. "You stretch the truth until it becomes a bold-faced lie. You know damn well that your people were never forced to eat scraps of food."

"*You* are a liar. It is a truth that even though our people were loyal to your government during the war, even lost several of our beloved warriors while riding alongside the white pony soldiers in the capacity of scouts and guides, the United States government still regard the Omaha as unfit to be treated as white men are," Iron Cloud said. "Little by little, treaty by treaty, your government has bought up Omaha land. By a treaty of March 1865, the Omaha sold more land to your people, a portion of the payment for this land to be expended for stock, implements, blacksmiths, and farming implements. The promises have yet to be fulfilled!"

"You are wasting your time telling me about

broken treaties and promises," Jonathan said, shrugging. "Go to Washington. Tell your troubles to President Grant." He smirked. "I'm sure he'd take the next train out here to hand out food and clothing single-handedly to each of your people."

"You are an evil man with a dark heart," Iron Cloud snarled, his nostrils flaring, his eyes filled with fire. "My father was once a proud chief. You broke his spirit. But never will you break mine!"

Iron Cloud glared at Jonathan a moment longer then turned and moved with slow dignity to the door. Just as he placed his hand to the knob, the door swung quickly open, and he found the softest blue eyes imaginable gazing up at him, momentarily taking him off guard. The young lady was tall, slim, and fair-skinned, with long golden hair.

Though not a breathtakingly beautiful woman, he saw a gentle innocence in her facial features. She was taller than most women Iron Cloud had ever seen, so that his first impression was that she was like a willow tree, and the name White Willow came to him in a heartbeat.

"Excuse me," the young woman said. She shifted her feet nervously and seemed to sense that he was as much at a loss for words as she.

But she *had* appeared suddenly at the door. And he must have seemed in a big hurry to leave the agent's office!

When one of her hands went to her hair and she combed her fingers through the wet tresses, Iron Cloud was drawn out of his reverie and made quickly aware of how wet she was. He could not

15

help but move his eyes over her again, this time noticing how her wet travel suit was clinging to her figure, revealing the gentle curves of her breasts and hips.

And then he became aware of the young man who had been standing at her side when he stepped around Iron Cloud and half-ran into the agent's office.

"Timothy!" Jonathan said, rushing across the room to bend down to give his fifteen-year-old cousin a hefty hug.

Then Jonathan stepped away from him. "My Lord, but you are wet," he said, wiping his hands on his breeches. He looked past Timothy and stiffened, realizing that Iron Cloud was taking too much time to make his departure after Damita made her sudden appearance.

Jonathan's voice behind him made Iron Cloud stiffen. He did not wish to have another altercation with him today, so he gave the girl one last intense gaze, then stepped around her and rushed on outside where he found his friend, Lieutenant Brian Davis, dismounting at the hitching rail, another soldier standing in the misty rain beside a buggy piled high with all assortments of travel gear.

After twisting his reins around the hitching rail, Brian went to Iron Cloud and embraced him, both ignoring the slow mists of rain as they then stepped away from each other and exchanged troubled gazes.

"So you've had words with Jonathan again, have you?" Brian said, glancing past Iron Cloud

16

at the agent's cabin, then back again at Iron Cloud. He squared his broad shoulders and smoothed golden wet tendrils of hair back from his brow, then clasped his hands behind him. "Iron Cloud, I had hoped Jonathan would treat you better than he did your father. But nothing is going to change that bastard. Jonathan is greedy as hell, not caring about anyone but himself."

"Nothing belonging to the past now seems stable to the Omaha," Iron Cloud said, a haunting sadness in the depths of his eyes. "Only the familiar landscape remains to remind us that we are still in the land of our fathers. It seems that the very ground is being cut from under our feet— that we are forsaken by all in whom we have ever put our trust. Even the government that we have always respected has betrayed us."

"You know how sorry I am about all of this," Brian said, placing a hand on Iron Cloud's shoulder. "My complaints to Washington have been ignored. I can try again, but each time I do I take a chance of Jonathan finding out. You know that he would stop at nothing to ruin me, and I see myself as perhaps the only link to your people's chances at being eventually treated fairly in Nebraska. I care, Iron Cloud."

Brain paused, running his fingers through his hair. "Aw, to hell with Jonathan," he suddenly blurted. "I'll travel to Washington tomorrow and be your spokesman, if you think it'd help."

"No, that is not necessary," Iron Cloud said, his voice void of the emotion that he did not want to reveal, just as he could not reveal his true plans to this friend who had been his confidante for years—who had even ridden with him during the war, as though Iron Cloud were white, not red.

The two men had few secrets from each other, but now it was time for Iron Cloud to keep a most valuable secret from Brian. Even though Iron Cloud realized that Brian could read his moods, as though he and Brian were of one mind, he would chance Brian never discovering that Iron Cloud had chosen that he and his people would break ties with all whites and live off the land as his ancestors had done. This meant forgetting his best friend, also.

"Iron Cloud, I can sense that something is different today in the way you are speaking and acting," Brian said, frowning at Iron Cloud. "What are you planning? Please don't do anything you will regret later."

"Whatever I do will be in the best interest of my people," Iron Cloud said, sighing deeply. "Chieftainship in the old meaning of the term is quickly losing its power. Too many governing powers have become centered in the United Stated Indian agent. *I* am the leader of my people. *I* am their chief! Steps must be made to assure that no one will ever forget that!"

Iron Cloud turned and gazed at Jonathan's cabin, embittered again at the memory of the agent's insults and insinuations. Iron Cloud knew now that he had been wrong to join the whites, trusting them, hoping this would be best for his people. He now realized that with only a few exceptions, all white people were liars. His people had all but forgotten the ways of the Omaha because of the white people's treaties and lies, but he had decided that his tribe would be reminded again of how it had been—and how it would be again! He was going to lead them far away from the white people, and even the other tribes of Omaha who still wished to take instructions from the United States Government.

His people would live apart from everyone but themselves. They would live in peace in the old tradition of the Omaha. They would learn to live off the land again.

They would ask for nothing from anyone!

Also, he would find a way to answer his need for revenge against this evil Indian agent, Jonathan Jacobs.

His heart leapt when he caught sight of the white woman in Jonathan's cabin as she walked past the window, and then was gone again. He turned to Brian. "Who is the woman and young man?" he asked, glancing at the buggy filled with luggage.

"They are Jonathan's cousins," Brian said, glad that the rain had stopped and that the clouds were rolling away overhead. "They have traveled far. Their parents were murdered in Boston. Damita and Timothy weren't with them, so they came out of the mishap physically unharmed. Jonathan is their only surviving relative, so Damita and Timothy have come to live with him. I escorted them from the railhead in Omaha."

"Cousins?" Iron Cloud said, his lips tugging into a slow smile as an idea formed in his brain. "They are now *waho-thi-ge*—orphans?"

"Yes, orphans, and Jonathan is their cousin," Brian said, nodding. "But that is all I can tell you. Neither Damita nor Timothy seemed in the mood to talk on the journey here. The rain dampened their spirits somewhat."

"As it would anyone's," Iron Cloud said, rubbing his chin thoughtfully.

"She is quite lovely, don't you think?" Brian asked, smiling at Iron Cloud.

"In an innocent sort of way, yes," Iron Cloud said, then went to his blue appaloosa. He took his reins from the hitching rail and quickly swung himself into his saddle. "Pity her having to make residence with the agent we all despise."

"Yes, a pity," Brian said, patting Iron Cloud's horse on the rump.

"I must go," Iron Cloud said, wheeling his horse around. "My people await my return." He placed a doubled fist over his heart and locked eyes with Brian, then turned his eyes straight ahead and rode away.

Iron Cloud smiled to himself, now realizing how he was going to achieve his vengeance! Jonathan had taken much too much from Iron Cloud and his people. Iron Cloud would now take from Jonathan something perhaps as valuable to him—the woman named Damita, Jonathan's cousin! She would be Iron Cloud's first captive.

Chapter Two

"Damita, you've not changed all that much. You're just as tall and skinny as the last time I saw you," Jonathan said, although his eyes showed his approval as they roamed over her gentle curves. "Yet, it seems you've grown into quite a lady." His gaze met hers. "A very *pretty* lady."

An uncontrollable shiver grabbed at Damita, and she blamed it on the ride in the misty rain from the railhead, which had chilled her to the bone. She gave Timothy a worried look as he came and stood beside her, shivering, his clothes just as wet as hers.

Then she looked at her cousin sourly. "Jonathan, why didn't you meet us at the railhead?" she said, her blue eyes flashing. "Why didn't you send a covered buggy to fetch me and Timothy? Surely you knew that rain was expected."

Jonathan slipped more comfortably down in his chair and propped his booted feet up on the desk. "I had more things on my mind than rain, and I couldn't leave my duties to someone else," he said with an annoyed frown. "When President Grant appointed me the Indian agent at Fort Calhoun, he handed me many responsibilities." He glanced at the door. "From time to time, some of the more stubborn Indians get out of hand. It's up to me to put them in their place."

"I suppose that Indian who was just leaving your office when Damita and I arrived was one of those Indians?" Timothy said, his dark eyes anxious. "Jonathan, he was awful tall and he looked upset. Did you put him in his place?"

"I sure as hell did," Jonathan said. "He's just one of the many who come to me with complaints. I've learned to listen with only half an ear, and even less heart. There ain't no need in getting too wrapped up in the Indians' troubles. It doesn't do any good. The government sends out their annuties, I hand them out. The Indians can't ask for more than that from me, now can they?"

Damita pursed her lips and gave her cousin a wary look, suspecting that Jonathan was not at all what the government was paying him to be. She knew that her cousin had his devious side, to say the least.

And she hoped that she was wrong. She was being forced to live with her cousin. She did not want to have to look the other way if he was truly involved in illegal activities. She was honest through and through, and she would surely be forced to turn him in to the authorities if he was doing the Indians wrong in any way.

"That Indian who was here before our arrival," she said guardedly, "*did* appear to be quite upset as he was leaving. I could see it in the set of his jaw and the fire in his eyes. Why was he angry, Jonathan? Who was he? From which Indian tribe is he?"

She realized that she was asking questions about this particular Indian for more than one reason. When their eyes had met and held, there had been something silently exchanged between them. At first it had frightened her, and then she had become intrigued by it. She wanted to know his name, for she hoped to see him again.

"He was angry, but most Indians are when they leave my office," Jonathan said, shrugging. "It's beyond my power to give them everything they want. So I sit here and listen to their complaints, then send them on their way. I tell them that if they want to get answers, they should go to Washington and meet with President Grant."

"But you know that the Indians don't have the money to travel clear to Washington to lodge their complaints," Damita said, seeing through her cousin's tactic to put the Indians off. She glared at him. "Jonathan, that's why *you* are here. To assist the Indians. You are paid well to offer those kinds of services to them."

"I will never grow rich being an Indian agent," Jonathan said, jerking himself up from his chair.

He picked up a ledger and held it out for Damita to see. "Sometime when you have the time, take a look at this ledger. You'll soon see where the money goes. It sure as hell doesn't go in my pocket."

He sat back down and glanced at a bottom drawer in his desk. He carried the key to the lock safely with him at all times. In a ledger in that drawer there was enough to condemn him, and perhaps place him before a firing squad.

Never would he allow anyone access to that drawer!

"Well, I imagine your salary is enough to allow you to live comfortably or you wouldn't *be* an Indian agent," Damita said, stiffening her upper lip.

Jonathan gave her a sly glance, knowing that she was going to be surprised to see just how he did live. He knew that she would be absolutely apalled by where she was to make her residence until she managed to get a wedding band on her finger to take her away from the world that she had been catapulted into upon the deaths of her parents. She was used to comforts of the affluent, for her father had been a well-established physician in Boston.

Here in Nebraska, things were different.

Jonathan lived poorly now, knowing that things would be different in the near future. He was stashing away monies right and left for himself, and when he accumulated enough, he planned to flee the country and perhaps live in France, a man of distinction and wealth!

"Jonathan, you never did tell me who the Indian was, or what tribe he is from," Damita said, her thoughts being taken time and again to the handsome Indian and the troubled look in his eyes. She did not want to feel pity for him, for something told her that he would not appreciate being pitied by anyone.

He seemed fiercely proud, fiercely independent. Surely he was a powerful chief!

"Let's not talk about Indians any longer," Jonathan said, evading any more talk of Iron Cloud. He had seen how Damita and Iron Cloud had stared at one another for much longer than he would have liked. One thing he did not need was an Indian chasing after the skirts of his cousin!

He rose from his chair and stood between Damita and Timothy, snaking an arm around their waists. "Let's talk about you two," he said. "I'm sorry as hell about your having to be uprooted from your home in Boston to live with me out here in the middle of nowhere. But since I am your only surviving relative, I understand there was no other way."

Damita slipped away from Jonathan and went to the window. She stared out at the sunshine that was now pouring from the sky in golden streamers. It was drawing moisture from the ground, creating a dazzling, dancing haze along the land.

"Jonathan, there is only one reason why I am here," she said. She turned slowly and their eyes locked. "At age twenty, I am certainly old enough to care for myself. But Timothy needs a man's guidance. I could not supply that. So you were the only other recourse."

She paused and inhaled a quavering breath. "But now that I am here with you, and I see that you haven't changed one iota, I feel that perhaps my decision was wrong," she murmured. "Yet, I did promise Papa that should anything happen to him and Mama, I would bring Timothy to you to raise since you are all that is left of our kin. I have kept my promise. Now the rest is up to you. If you prove to be unworthy of papa's trust, then I shall find a way to raise my brother, alone."

"Ah, yes, there is the matter of money," Jonathan said, moving back to his desk, sitting down on the edge. "I believe there was a substantial sum left me in the will? I trust you brought it with you."

"Yes, I have it with me," Damita said, glowering at her cousin. "It's hidden at the bottom of one of my trunks. Now, if you don't mind, Jonathan, Timothy and I would like to be taken to your house and shown to our rooms. We both need to change into dry clothes. And I would like to be left alone to take a nap. The journey was very tiring."

"I shall apologize in advance for the smallness of my house," Jonathan said, looking from Damita to Timothy as he moved back to his feet behind his desk. "It ain't what you're used to."

"Right now I wouldn't care if you took me to a tent and said that's where you lived," Timothy blurted out. "I'm cold, Jonathan. And these wet clothes are itchy."

"Then let's go to my house and make things much more comfortable for you," Jonathan said, slapping an arm around Timothy's shoulder and walking him toward the door. "Come on, Damita. We'll have your clothes changed before you can bat an eye."

Her clinging, wet clothes also itching her almost unmercifully, and her hair tangled as it lay across her shoulders, Damita followed Jonathan and Timothy from the cabin. The evening sun was slipping behind the mountains in the distance, creating a lush sky of oranges, pinks, and golds. The soft cooing of a mourning dove drew her eyes around and upward, where she discovered the dove perched on the roof of the cabin. There was something comforting about the peaceful call of the dove.

Then her thoughts went again to the handsome Indian, who had seemed anything but serene and at peace with himself.

She turned to Jonathan to ask him again about the Indian, but he had just stepped up to the soldier who had obediently stood guard by the buggy, where Damita's trunks were stacked in the back. She was embarrassed for the soldier as Jonathan began handing out orders, telling him in a most unkind fashion to get the trunks unloaded.

She looked around for the lieutenant who had brought her and Timothy from the railhead— Brian, she believed was his name—thinking that he would not be the sort to allow Jonathan's undermining of the soldier. He would surely step up in this meeker soldier's defense and put Jonathan in his place.

But he was nowhere in sight and the stern, cold voice of her cousin as he ordered the soldier around sent chills up and down Damita's spine.

She feared being treated in the same way.

She looked quickly at Timothy, seeing the dread in his eyes and realizing that he too was wondering about how Jonathan would treat them. Damita and Timothy's father had been a strict disciplinarian, yet it had been done with much love and caring, in such a way that neither of them had felt anything but respect for him.

But a cousin was much different from a father.

Respect could be lost quickly.

Damita went to Timothy and took his hand possessively. "Things will be all right," she whispered, leaning close to his ear so that only he would hear. "I'll always be here to look after you, Timothy. Never forget that."

Timothy gave Damita a sidewise glance, then looked back at Jonathan as he came back to stand between him and Damita.

"Now that that's taken care of, let's go on to my house," Jonathan said, watching the soldier as he grunted and groaned ahead of them, dragging several trunks behind him, stacked atop one another.

"I could have carried one of the trunks," Timothy said, wincing when the top trunk slid and landed on the ground with a loud thump.

"Never you mind," Jonathan said, glowering as

the soldier scampered around to get the trunks righted again. "There'll come a time when you'll wish you didn't have so much to do. So don't go asking for chores you might regret later."

Damita sighed and shook her head slowly, regretting having to be there in the company of her cousin whom she had detested from the time she was old enough to realize there was such a thing as liking and disliking someone.

When she was five and Jonathan fifteen, he had enjoyed tormenting her when they went on family outings in the park. He had chased her incessantly, poked her with sticks, and teased her about being so tall and lanky.

Later, when she had gotten older, she had hated it when he had said that she looked more like a boy than a girl!

Until recently she had been self-conscious of her height because of her tormenting cousin. But of late, she had seen that the height did not matter, not as long as the girl filled out adequately enough in the right places. And she had.

And she knew 'pretty' when she looked in a mirror, and she was pretty.

Of course, pretty was not 'beautiful'. But who needed to be beautiful? The world was filled with more pretty than beautiful girls, so she felt she fitted in quite well with the world and its offerings!

Damita began searching with her eyes for her cousin's house among the few cabins spread along the land, just outside the walls of the fort. She quirked an eyebrow, seeing none that fit her cousin's scheme of things. All of them were mere log cabins, and quite small.

Her mouth went agape as she watched the soldier go to one of the smaller cabins and carry the trunks inside. An Indian squaw came from the cabin, wiping her hands on an apron as she walked briskly toward Jonathan.

Jonathan broke away from Damita and Timothy and met the squaw with a big hug and kiss, then placed an arm around her waist and took her to Damita and Timothy, who had stopped to gawk openly at the affection shared between their cousin and the Indian.

"This here is Yellow Dove," Jonathan said, smiling from Damita to Timothy. "She's my woman. She's one mighty good cook." His eyes gleamed as he winked down at Yellow Dove. "And that's not all she's good at."

Damita blushed, knowing what he was referring to and wishing that he would not be so bold in front of Timothy. He was not used to any open intimacies. Their mother and father had kept such talk and actions behind their locked bedroom door.

Damita stepped forward, wanting to change the mood of the introduction. "Yellow Dove, I am very glad to make your acquaintance," she said, trying to hide her shock over so many things that were being unraveled before her eyes.

Her cousin lived in a cabin that almost could

have fit into the living room of her parents' palatial mansion.

Her cousin was married to an Indian!

And her cousin seemed to have lost his social graces after leaving Boston!

Damita continued her introductions. "I'm Damita and this is my brother Timothy. I hope we won't be of any inconvenience to you. I—I had no idea my cousin was married."

"Married?" Jonathan said, laughing boisterously. "Who said anything about being married? Yellow Dove ain't my wife. She does everything expected of a wife, but who needs signed papers out here in Nebraska when you want to take a woman to your bed?"

Damita gasped and paled. She glanced quickly over at Timothy, who seemed not at all disturbed by the news that his cousin was actually living in sin.

But he was a child, and thus far innocent.

Little by little, the discoveries became more and more shocking to Damita, yet she knew that she must conform to many things in her new way of life, especially for Timothy's sake. He was the one who mattered now that her parents were gone.

Her feelings came second to his.

Yellow Dove looked humbly to the ground, then slowly rose her dark eyes to Damita and smiled at her. "You are hungry?" she said softly in fluent English.

Timothy stepped forward. "I'm starved!" he said, sniffing as he caught the aroma of stew cooking over the fire inside the cabin. "I could eat a *bear*!"

Jonathan chuckled as he went to Timothy and placed an arm around his shoulder, walking him on toward the cabin. "Now if that's what you really want, that could be arranged," he said, causing Damita to pale considerably at the thought of eating bear meat.

Chapter Three

The calumet pipe had been passed around the circle of Omaha warriors who sat in council with Iron Cloud beside a fire in the council house. Dressed in only a brief breechclout, his hair falling free and long down his back, Iron Cloud inhaled a great puff of smoke from the pipe, then exhaled it slowly as he looked from warrior to warrior. Their eyes had never left him since their arrival for this special meeting.

Resting the pipe on his bare knee, Iron Cloud squared his shoulders, realizing that most were partially aware of why he had called them to this meeting. The word had spread among his people of his restlessness with reservation life. They knew that he had made plans to change things, yet none knew exactly how.

As he began to speak, they leaned forward and listened intently, their expressions changing from wonder to shock the more they were brought into the realization of exactly what Iron Cloud had planned for them all.

"My warriors, today I received the same arrogant answers from the white agent at Fort Calhoun," Iron Cloud said. "We are a fiercely proud and independent people, and we cannot grovel before the white man any longer. Do you not realize that because our forefathers stood up against their persecutors, they were singled out for more than their share of measures designed to break their spirit? We are living today on a reservation because our forefathers fought to retain our dignity! The spirits of my chieftain father and grandfather were finally broken. I am now chief! Never shall that happen to me!"

He laid the pipe aside and rose tall above his warriors. He spread his legs and folded his powerful arms across his chest. "It is I, Chief Iron Cloud, who demands changes for our people," he said, his dark eyes glittering. "I demand a return to how it was before the white man's interference in the lives of the Omaha! I no longer trust them. Their word is not true! Our village must leave the reservation—break away and become a separate entity from the other Omaha tribes. Our people will move to another land far away. We will adapt the ways again of the old, and live off the land, away from the influences of the white people. By doing this, our tribe will survive best of all the Omaha tribes!"

Gasps wafted around the circle of warriors.

Black Coyote, one of Iron Cloud's most restless warriors, stood up and boldly faced Iron Cloud, his face etched with anger. "What you suggest will harm, not help our people," he said. "Everything for our people now comes through the United States government. Must we turn our backs to such offerings? Must we be forced to hunt for every bite of food we feed our children? Must we do without clothes that are now given to us? Our people will be forced to do without, while others— the Sioux—will be glad to see us gone and will come and take what was rightfully ours!"

"You shame our people by admitting that you are solely dependant on the white man!" Iron Cloud scolded. "With the coming of the white people, the Omaha were no longer obliged to make all articles required for their use, and the time formerly occupied by the long and wearisome tasks of the past is now wasted. The stimulus for acquiring skill in oldtime industries has been withdrawn."

Iron Cloud looked Black Coyote up and down, seeing him as Iron Cloud's same age, having been on this earth now for thirty winters. "You have visions of lazy days ahead by depending on the white people to provide you with food and clothing!" he said, his words almost a hiss. "You are one whose spirit has been stifled by the white man. You are one who needs to be transplanted to another land, where you can learn the art of hunting again—where you can learn the ways of your elders! It is only right, Black Coyote, that you be forced to do these things with your people. If not, you will no longer be allowed to call yourself an Omaha!"

Black Coyote's shoulders slumped, and he looked ashamedly from side to side, recoiling when he discovered fierce looks directed at him. He slowly crept back down to the mat before the fire. His struggle to agree with Iron Cloud was evident in his expression, in the way he focused his eyes somewhere above the heads of his fellow warriors, distancing himself from everyone and from what was being said.

Iron Cloud ignored Black Coyote now, and when he talked, he talked to everyone else, making sure never to settle his eyes on Black Coyote again. He knew that Black Coyote had much to sort out in his mind, and this was something each man had to do for himself, in the privacy of his own thoughts and dreams—and desires.

"My warriors, do you not realize that the white man is cunning?" Iron Cloud said in a lower, subdued voice. "They have succeeded in weakening the powers of our ancient beliefs, introducing new standards to our people, commercial in character. We must not let that happen any longer! From the beginning of time, the Indian has lived on the fruits of the earth."

Iron Cloud settled back down on a mat among his comrades, crossing his bare legs before him. "This is true when he feeds on the animals, for all draw their nourishment from mother earth," he went on. "Our bodies are strengthened by animal food, and our powers can be strengthened by the animals giving us of their peculiar gifts, for each animal has received from Wakoda, the Great Spirit, some special gift. If a man asks help of Wakoda, the source of all things, Wakoda will send the asker the animal that has the gift that will help the man in his need. And so shall it be for us in this new land we seek in which to live in isolation from everyone else."

An older warrior leaned forward, his eyes locking with Iron Cloud's. "Wakoda teaches us that our words and our acts must be truthful so that we may live in peace and happiness with one another," White Owl said. "Truthfulness in word and in action is fundamental to the scheme of ethics taught among the Omaha. Wakoda causes day to follow night without variation and summer to follow winter. We can depend on these regular changes and can order our lives by them. It is so, Iron Cloud, that we depend on you, our chief. What you say, we will do. Now where is this land you wish to take us to?"

"I have sent scouts out to find us a most suitable place for our new village, and they found land in the forest haunts of what is called Illinois that is scarcely populated by whites or Indians," Iron Cloud said, smiling at the elder warrior. He then gazed slowly around at the others. "It is in the southern half of Illinois. There are many trees, fertile land, animals and rivers. It has all that is required of the Omaha to live a happy, industrious, free life."

White Owl sat down to be replaced by another warrior, who offered a new sort of objection to Iron Cloud's plan. "Illinois is far from where the Sacred Pole is kept," he said, his quavering voice revealing his concern. "The Omaha take their troubles to the Sacred Pole, where they make offerings and requests of Wakoda. True, it resides now in another village of Omaha, in the Tent of War, watched over by the Keeper of the Sacred Pole. But it is not more than a half day's ride to get there. If we move far away, it will be impossible ever to see the pole again, much less take our troubles to it."

"It is true that the Sacred Pole, which symbolizes the power of the chiefs, will be far away," Iron Cloud said. "But we must make sacrifices to have this new life that I have planned for you. We will learn to make offerings to Wakoda without the Sacred Pole."

There was a great silence, and then Iron Cloud put his idea to the true test. "Those who do not wish to travel with our people, rise and leave the council house," he said, frowning from warrior to warrior, his eyes momentarily locking with Black Coyote's, awaiting a possible negative response from him, perhaps even a decision to leave, to set out on his own, even to become a renegade.

When Black Coyote offered no response, nor rose to leave, Iron Cloud's gaze left him.

"Those who cannot conform with my new vision of life, go quickly from our village with your families and never look back," he said evenly. "From that point on, you will not be of our tribe."

He smiled then, from warrior to warrior. "But those who wish to stay and be a part of the new adventure, disband now and begin dismantling your dwellings. Get prepared for travel. Ours will be a secret departure. We will soon be rebuilding our village in the forest haunts of southern Illinois!"

To his dismay, everyone joined in to take turns embracing him and praising him for his unique plan.

And then he told them one more step to his plan that he had left to last, not wanting to be questioned about it.

This was another secret—but not to be shared with anyone—not yet.

As they all left the council house and gathered around Iron Cloud outside, where the stars were flecking the sky like a million sparkling jewels, he raised a hand to silence them. "My people, I will accompany you for one day of the journey, to see that you are well on your way, and then I must leave you to do one last task that involves people with white skins," he said, ignoring the quizzical stares. "I will then return to proudly lead the exodus to a new land—a new life!"

There was a moment of subdued silence, and Iron Cloud could see in his people's eyes that they wanted to know more about his planned mysterious departure, but none asked. They went on their way and Iron Cloud watched as his people busied themselves dismantling their dwellings.

He was glad to hear an anxious, cheerful chattering flowing through his village. That alone gave him the courage to go on with this plan. He had never wanted to let his people know that he had doubts that he was doing the right thing for them.

But his father had sat by, doing nothing for so long. Iron Cloud could not do that!

Iron Cloud had to make things work for his people!

And *now*.

Iron Cloud's thoughts wandered to the tall, slim white woman. "She will soon join our exodus," he whispered to himself.

White Willow.

Yes, he thought, smiling to himself, that was an appropriate name for her, one that she would be forced to accept, just as she would be forced to accept the fact that she would never be allowed to live with the white people again! Once he abducted her, he would never let her go. Until Jonathan Jacobs died, the evil agent would regret having ever maligned the Omaha Indians so viciously!

Iron Cloud doubled his hands into tight fists at his sides. "Especially Iron Cloud!" he said in a low hiss that to a passerby would have sounded more like a snake that was ready to strike its unknowing victim.

In her cotton nightgown, Damita drew the thin, patchwork quilt closer to her chin and squirmed on the small bed, trying without success to get comfortable on the lumpy mattress.

She gazed slowly around the one-room cabin, dismayed by the conditions in which her cousin lived and had invited her and Timothy to share with him. In the dimming glow of the fire in the fireplace along the one wall, Damita could see what was to now be called her home—a crude, sparsely furnished house.

She gazed wistfully at Timothy, who was sleeping on a pallet on the floor close to the fire. There was no bed available for him.

She glanced at the rickety narrow ladder that led to the loft overhead, where her cousin and Yellow Dove slept in their private hideaway. She cringed and worried about Timothy when the activity overhead became sexually explicit. She hoped that her brother would not be awakened by the heavy breathing and bodies coming together so noisily.

She glared at the loft. Wasn't it enough that she had to know that her cousin and the Indian were living in sin, without having it acted out for her within earshot?

She yanked on her quilt and pulled it up over her head, turning her back to the loft. She was filled with regret for having brought Timothy to such an undesirable environment, yet she had had no choice!

She had promised her father!

Yet, if things worsened, she would have to find a way to get herself and Timothy out of this situation.

She regretted now having turned down the many proposals of marriage that she had received these past several years. If she were married, her husband would provide Timothy with a positive male influence.

As it was, she had placed her ambitions before any sort of private life. She had planned to work at her father's side for many more years, until she had absorbed all the knowledge required to become a doctor in her own right, with a practice of her own. After achieving that goal, her next was to find a man who did not mind having an independently-minded wife.

But these plans were now only pipe-dreams. This was real life, and her aspirations were no longer of prime importance. Her brother's welfare came first. He was her total responsibility.

And she could never allow herself to forget how important it was for Timothy to have the guidance of a man in his upbringing. "But surely not just any man," she whispered to herself. "Surely not my cousin!"

Filled with despair, and sorely tired of worrying over how she had found things in Fort Calhoun, Damita tried to focus on something more pleasant—at least more intriguing!

The Indian.

Chills of pleasure ran up and down her spine at the thought of his eyes locked with hers, in their depths such a gentle kindness, whereas only moments before she had seen such an anger!

She had known that she was responsible for the

42

change in his mood, and she could not help but feel flattered.

"And I do not even know his name," Damita whispered, finally drifting off into a restful sleep, the Indian there in her dreams as though he were truly there, touching her cheek, caressing her long, golden-blond hair....

It felt wonderful, the attentions from this Indian with the large, piercingly dark eyes that seemed to look clean into her soul—most surely into her heart!

Chapter Four

Three Days Later.

The wailing of children in the crowded agent's office unnerved Damita, making her heart go out to the Indians of various tribes who had come for the annuities that the government had promised them.

In their eyes she could see misery and suffering and hunger.

In their slouched postures, she could see defeat.

Damita was ashamed to be a part of such a process as this that took the soul—the very spirit—from such a proud people.

Her thoughts went back to the handsome Indian and how he had come, alone, to speak for his people, surely not wanting to see them disgraced as these people were being disgraced today, as though they were not even human.

Handing out clothes and food to the women and men was not enough to erase the shame that Damita felt, for she knew that she was not giving them enough supplies to last for long. Worse, most of the clothing was shoddy, and the food was less than acceptable in her eyes.

Again she thought back to the handsome Indian. She was proud of his stand against her cousin and the United States Government and wished she could find a way to tell him of her feelings!

She glanced over at her cousin, realizing that every time she asked for the warrior's name, Jonathan very decidedly evaded the question, as though speaking the name of the Indian would contaminate him!

"Bigot," she whispered to herself, then her face grew red with embarrassment when the Indian woman standing next in line asked, in excellent English, what she had said, obviously thinking that Damita had been addressing her.

Damita smiled awkwardly down at the lady who was much shorter than she. "I'm sorry," she murmured, picking up another stack of clothing and offering it to the woman. "I was only . . . thinking out loud."

The woman smiled up at Damita as she accepted the clothing into her arms. But Damita noticed that her smile faded quickly as her gaze shifted to Damita's clothes.

Again Damita was engulfed with shame, knowing that the woman was comparing the clothes that she wore with those forced upon her and her family.

Self-consciously, Damita looked down at herself, at the expensive dress that had been bought in one of Boston's most exclusive stores. It was a fully-gathered, pale orchid silk garment, trimmed with delicate white lace at the collar and the cuffs of its long and graceful sleeves. The bodice was pleated to the waist, curving beautifully over her generous breasts.

Her hand then went to her hair, touching the satin bow that she had used to tie her hair back from her face while she assisted her cousin, realizing that the Indian woman's gaze had stopped there, silently admiring it.

Without further thought, Damita untied the bow and handed it to the woman, tears suddenly burning the corners of her eyes when she saw the pride in the woman's eyes that made her refuse the ribbon.

"Please," Damita encouraged. "I want you to have it. I—I have many more."

Damita wanted to bite her tongue when she realized what she had just said. Of course she had many ribbons! Did that not make this Indian woman even see more seriously her own plight?

Again Damita handed the ribbon toward the woman. "It would please me so much if you would take the ribbon," she murmured. "If not for yourself, perhaps for your daughter? Do you have a daughter?"

"No, no daughter," the woman said, squaring

her shoulders as she peered over at Timothy, who was handing out shoes to some young Indian braves. "Sons. I have several sons." She turned her gaze back to Damita. "The boy who fits my sons with shoes. He is your son?"

Damita gazed at her fifteen-year old brother. If she ever had a son, she thought proudly, she would want him to be just like her Timothy! So much about him reminded her of their beloved father—the blondish-red hair, the freckles that crowned his face, the twinkle in his golden-brown eyes, and the smile that went with it.

And he was such a knowledgeable young man! So eager to learn, and so easy to teach! She regretted that he would not be able to attend Boston's schools any longer. She had watched his interest in schooling and how he had soaked up all of the knowledge that his mind could hold.

Today, in his dark breeches that hugged his legs, and white shirt with a trace of lace at the collar and cuffs, he looked the business person he was pretending to be while helping his cousin.

Timothy had adjusted quickly to the loss of his mother and father—or so he perhaps pretended to have done, Damita suddenly realized.

"He is your son?" the Indian woman repeated, her English quite sharp and intelligible.

Damita looked quickly away from Timothy and smiled down at the woman. "No," she murmured. "He is my brother." She glanced over at Timothy again and saw the pride shining in his eyes as two young Indian braves walked away from him, hug-

47

ging pairs of shoes to their bare copper chests.

She smiled at the Indian woman. "And I'm very proud of him," she murmured. She lifted the ribbon for the woman to view it again and nodded toward her. "It would make me very happy..."

The woman returned the smile and without further hesitation took the ribbon. "You are a good woman," she said, then walked away, admiring the ribbon as she held it out before her for her two sons to see as they scampered to her side.

A sudden presence at her own side drew Damita around in a jerk, and she found herself looking down into Jonathan's angry eyes. She had to momentarily ignore the other woman waiting for her share of clothes, for Jonathan had grabbed Damita by the arm and had taken her aside.

He peered sharply up at her, unnerving her at first, then making her feel awash with anger.

"Don't do anything as stupid as that again," Jonathan hissed.

"Are you talking about my giving away a mere ribbon?" Damita asked, stunned by his reaction to her small gesture of friendship.

"If you give them things they don't deserve, they will begin to expect it all of the time," Jonathan said, leaning up into her face. "Not only the one that you give free handouts to, but everyone else. Word spreads. Everyone would know what you are doing. So don't do it again, do you hear, Damita?"

"That's absurd," Damita said, stepping back from him so that she would not have to breathe his vile breath, which was laced with tobacco and alcohol. "You don't give the Indians much credit, Jonathan. You think they are mindless idiots! You think they are beggars!"

"After you're here long enough, you'll get as tired of their shenanigans as I am," Jonathan said, glowering as he looked toward the waiting Indians. "If it's not one thing, it's another. Gripe, gripe, gripe. That's all I hear. Just a lot of bellyaching!"

"I've been here all morning and I have not had one person complain to me once," Damita argued. "They just stand there, politely accepting what I give them, even if it isn't adequate enough to last them for any length of time."

"That's today," Jonathan said, shrugging his shoulders. "Just you wait until tomorrow."

Damita looked sadly at the line of people. "I'm not sure I'll be here tomorrow," she said cheerlessly. "I don't think I have it in me to—to be a part of such deceit." She turned and glared from her taller height down at her cousin. "You know they aren't getting enough provisions. Is that your fault? Or the government's?"

"Never you mind," Jonathan said, taking her by the wrist. He led her back to the Indians who were waiting in line, clear through the opened door of the cabin to the outside. "And don't get any notions of not helping me. Now that you and your brother are here, you've got to do something to earn your keep."

He swung a hand in the air, gesturing toward the Indians who were crowded inside the walls of the fort. "Hell, this is as good a way as any," he said sourly. "You'll keep a lot of their bullcrap away from *me*."

He leaned up into her face again, his blue eyes squinting into hers. "I suggest you behave," he threatened. "There ain't one good Indian among these you're catering to today. Become too friendly, and they'll take advantage of you, and when you get tired of their stink, and they realize it, your blond hair would make a pretty scalp in some northern lodge."

Damita paled and gasped as she stared disbelievingly at Jonathan, now certain that she had to find a way to get away from him and his evil ways—most certainly from his vicious threats!

Yet she could not help but worry over where she would go.

And how?

Timothy was only fifteen. His whole lifetime lay ahead of him—a lifetime of learning.

And they had hardly a cent left after paying their passage to Nebraska. Although their parents had lived well, it had been largely pretense. After Damita had paid off her parents' debtors, there had only been enough money left for Jonathan in her father's will to look after Damita and Timothy, and enough money for Timothy and Damita to get to his residence.

She gazed at Timothy, sad for him, yet seeing again how well he adapted to change. No matter what she decided, surely he would be all right.

She went back inside to the waiting Indians and smiled at each one as they stepped up to her, their eyes eager as she sorted through the clothes to find the size that each of them asked for. Whenever she saw young Indian women who appeared to be her same size and age, Damita's thoughts would go to the many unopened trunks in her cousin's cabin, in which lay her beautiful clothes—too many ever for her to wear, especially out here in Nebraska where she would not have the opportunity to dress for parties or outings of any sort, it seemed. She so badly wanted to take the young women by the hands and show them her clothes, to let them sort through them and choose whichever they liked for themselves.

But she knew that her cousin would stop her before she got two yards from the agent's office. He would humiliate not only her, but also the Indian women. She had no choice but to stand there and do her duty until she thought of some other way that might better benefit herself, Timothy— and perhaps, somehow, the Indians.

A soft cough drew Damita's thoughts back to the present. She found herself gazing down upon a tiny bundle in the arms of a frail Indian lady. Again she heard the soft cough and realized it was from the child wrapped in a blanket in the lady's arms.

Damita bent low, bringing herself eye to eye with the Indian, in case she did not know the English language as well as the other women she had talked to. She spoke slowly, enunciating her words carefully. "Is your child ill?" she asked, hoping to offer some assistance even if her cousin would be angry. This was a different matter. This was a sick child. Her father had been a physician with whom she had worked for sometime before his untimely death. She knew many diseases—and their cures.

The Indian mother nodded, and when Damita offered to take the child, the woman allowed her to.

Holding the child in the crook of one arm, Damita raised her fingers to the corner of the blanket and slowly drew the thin buckskin fabric back so that she could peer down at the tiny copper face. Damita paled when she realized what her discovery had unmasked—a child very ill with measles!

"Measles!" she gasped, knowing well enough the dangers of the disease. Not so long ago, back in Boston, as well as all across the country, many had died from a measles epidemic. It was one of the most contagious diseases that she had read about while studying to be a doctor. With Indians, whose immune system was not as strong as the white people's, a whole tribe could be wiped out in only a few months.

"Did I hear you say something about measles?" Jonathan said, quickly at Damita's side. He became quite shaken and his face drained of color when he saw the measled child. He gasped with horror when he realized that Damita was holding the child, exposing herself to all sorts of misery, and possibly even death!

In one lunge he had the child out of Damita's arms and had thrust it back into its mother's. "Damn it, Damita, what were you thinking?" he said, his voice rising in pitch as he shoved the mother and infant through the crowd of Indians toward the door. "Christ, Damita, you're the daughter of a physician. Don't you know the risks involved here? Damn it, the minute you saw the Injun had the measles, you should've run the damn squaw and her diseased brat outta here!"

Damita stood her ground for a moment, watching with utter disbelief at how her cousin was behaving toward the frightened mother and ill child.

Then she broke into a run and grabbed her cousin by the arm, stopping him and stopping the mother. "You can't just send her away," she cried, facing her cousin with a firm jaw. "The child needs help. Perhaps the whole tribe that she was from needs help. Is she Sioux? Is she Omaha? Which is she?"

"She's Sioux," Jonathan shouted back at her, despite the fact that all the Indians were turning and glowering at him. "But what does that matter? We've got to get her out of here. She was stupid for even coming!"

"Not stupid!" Damita argued, running her fingers frustratingly through her loosened hair. "In trouble! Aren't you here to help those Indians who are in trouble? Aren't you?"

"This ain't any ordinary sort of trouble brought to my desk for solving," Jonathan said, turning to the frightened mother again, finally succeeding at getting her through the crowded doorway.

Damita followed them outside, into the blazing sun of afternoon, and knew this was a battle that she could never win, so she watched, anger rising in her, as her cousin handed out orders to a soldier.

"See that this damn squaw and her brat get far from Fort Calhoun," Jonathan said, shoving the mother toward the soldier's horse so that she almost fell, the child clutched hard within her arms.

Jonathan stepped up to the soldier after the soldier had mounted his gelding. He spoke softly, so that only the soldier heard. "See that she doesn't return to her reservation to spread the disease, either," he grumbled. "I don't want this sort of catastrophe on my hands."

"What's she got?" the soldier asked, cocking a thick red eyebrow as he looked down at the mother and child.

"It's not what she's got," Jonathan said, "It's the child. It's got the damn measles."

The soldier paled and stared at the Indian and child, then gazed back down at Jonathan. "I'll make sure they don't get near me, nor anyone else," he said, only loud enough for Jonathan to hear. He placed a hand on his holstered pistol. "I know the only way to rid the land of contaminations like this."

"You've been taught well what's expected of you," Jonathan said, grinning slyly up at the soldier and slapped his horse's rump. "Now get on with you. There ain't no need in delaying this any longer. I've things to tend to."

Damita had tried to hear what had been exchanged between her cousin and the soldier, but they had talked too softly.

But she had to believe that the mother and child would be taken back to their people, where they would be separated from the others until the child either died or got well. She did not expect it to be the latter, and hoped that this child was the only one of that Sioux tribe that was afflicted. It was true that it could cause quite a catastrophe if the disease got out of control among the Indians!

She stiffened when Jonathan came back to her and glowered up at her from his five-foot height. She gazed angrily at him as he began his tirade.

"Get in there and get Timothy, then both of you go down to the river with two brand-new bars of lye soap and scrub until your skin is raw," Jonathan said in a rush of words. "I didn't invite you clear out here to have to nurse you out of the measles—or die from the disease, and forever feel to blame."

"I'd think you'd be glad to be rid of us," Damita dared to say, placing her hands on her hips. "You've got enough of my papa's money now to last you a lifetime. I'm sure you truly wouldn't care if we died. Your only fear is that you might get the disease yourself should we get it." She leaned down into his face. "There are three brand-new bars of lye soap lying on the table in your cabin, Jonathan. Perhaps you'd best join Timothy and me at the river and take your own bath. You were just as near the baby as we were."

Jonathan placed a hand to his throat and swallowed hard, his eyes widening. "I never thought about that," he said, then scurried away from her

Cassie Edwards

toward his cabin. Damita watched him leave the cabin in only a matter of minutes with a towel and a bar of soap, hurrying toward the river.

She laughed to herself, knowing from her father's teachings that nothing, especially not a bar of a soap, was going to stop someone from catching the measles once they were exposed. She went casually back into the cabin with the Indians and continued sorting through and handing out supplies. She could not help but be frightened over having been exposed to the dreaded disease, yet she could not stop thinking about the poor child and its mother.

She trembled at the thought of what their true fate might be.

Chapter Five

The moon was high in the sky and wolves howled on a distant butte. Sheathed in his fringed buckskin attire, Iron Cloud was sitting boldly on his blue appaloosa on the outer fringes of the forest, his eyes never leaving Jonathan's cabin. He smiled to himself when the light at the window dimmed to nothingness. He would wait a little longer to be sure that everyone in the cabin was asleep, and then he would go and abduct the white woman, the evil agent's cousin. It was not what he wanted to do, yet he saw this as perhaps the only way to send a silent message to Jonathan Jacobs that he must change his ways.

His smile changed to a deep frown when he allowed his thoughts to dwell on Jonathan. Although it would delight him to place a knife at the agent's throat, just to see the fear in the depth of his pale, cruel eyes, Iron Cloud preferred to envision the agent's frustrations when his beautiful cousin was discovered missing!

Again Iron Cloud smiled, knowing that he and the girl would be far away once the abduction was discovered. And too many people—too many Indians—hated the agent for him to single out only one to blame! Jonathan would learn to be wary of everyone—and treat them with the respect and dignity they deserved.

He would know that worse things than an abducted cousin could happen to him if he did not.

"Yes, this is the only way," Iron Cloud whispered to himself. "And it is up to me to do this. I will see that nothing happens to the white woman. It is best that I do this deed, for another might see the hated agent's image in his cousin and kill her out of pent-up frustrations against the evil the agent has committed over the years!"

Feeling that enough time had elapsed and that everyone should be asleep by now, Iron Cloud dismounted and tethered his horse to a low tree limb. He moved stealthily away from the trees, then ran panther-like across the open field that was white with the splash of moonlight until he came to the side of the cabin.

He pressed his back against the logs close to the window that was covered only by a buffalo hide, his hand resting on a holstered pistol at his waist. He leaned an ear close to the window, listening for any sounds that might indicate that someone was still awake in the cabin. When he heard nothing but a faint rumble of snores wafting through the buffalo hide, he smiled.

Now!

Now was the time to make his move!

Should anyone try and stop him, he would not hesitate to shoot. He only hoped that the woman would not cry out in her struggles to be free. She was the last person he wanted to harm. In her, he had seen a gentleness—a caring. Without exchanging a word, they had shared something in their first lingering look.

Taking a wide step that took him around the corner of the cabin directly to the door, he reached a hand out and began pushing it open, ever so gently, relieved that doing so created no noise.

When he finally had the door open enough to move into the cabin, he took a soft, quick step and found himself in a room dimly lit by embers burning low in the fireplace. Yet it was enough light to make out everything and everyone in the one-room cabin.

He saw the loft overhead and was quickly aware of the snoring again, as he had been while waiting outside the window. He assumed that was where Jonathan and his woman slept.

He shifted his gaze downward and saw the young man asleep on a pallet on the floor beside the fire.

He again shifted his gaze, and his heart warmed strangely when he saw Damita asleep on a bed against the far wall.

It was at this moment that doubts assailed him—doubts that his decision to abduct her was wise. If something went amiss during the next few moments and she was harmed in any way, he would forever regret being the cause.

Yet, he had come this far.

He was only a heartbeat away from Damita.

There was no turning back.

With moccasin-padded footsteps, Iron Cloud crept across the room and stood over Damita. Something seemed to grab him at the pit of his stomach when he saw her innocent loveliness in her deep sleep, her golden hair spread out on her pillow like sprays of sunshine.

His gaze moved lower, seeing how in her sleep, the patchwork quilt had been kicked aside and her gown had slipped up past her knees, revealing her long and shapely legs. As she tossed suddenly over to her side in her sleep, his heart lurched when one of her breasts became partially exposed where the gown had come unbuttoned in front, leaving a wide gap at the bodice as the gown pulled beneath her. Iron Cloud had to draw on his reserve of willpower, when everything within him wanted to reach out and caress her soft, pink flesh that lay so open to his feasting eyes.

But when one of Damita's hands reached out in her sleep, subconsciously aware of her discomfort in her twisted gown, and jerked it from beneath her to rearrange it, Iron Cloud feared that he had waited too long to make his move. He expected her eyes to fly open at any moment and find him there—before he had the chance to gag her.

He held his breath and stood stiffly quiet until

she relaxed again, her eyes closed in what appeared now to be a peaceful sleep. He started to reach for the gag that he had thrust into the waist of his breeches, but stopped, again staring at the thin cotton nightgown she wore. He frowned, knowing that was not proper travel attire. He searched with his eyes around the room and found her dress draped over the back of a chair, a shawl on a peg on the wall, and her tiny slippers beside her bed. He also spied her undergarments neatly arranged on a trunk at the end of the bed, and a hairbrush.

When his gaze found a canvas bag on the floor beside the trunks, he quietly picked it up and methodically filled it with all of her clothes and her hairbrush, then went back to her bed and set it down on the floor. In a flash he had Damita gagged. Her eyes suddenly opened wide as she peered up at him.

But she did not have time to struggle to get free, for he quickly tied her wrists together in front of her.

Damita looked desperately up at the handsome Indian who had been on her mind so often since she arrived at Fort Calhoun. He was abducting her! Even though she was innocent of any wrongdoing, he was going to take his anger out on her over what her cousin had done!

She tried to jump off the bed, to get away from him, but he was there just as quickly, a firm hand on her shoulder, stopping her.

He leaned down close to her face. "Go quietly,"

he whispered. "Or someone might get killed."

A mixture of frustration and fear swept through Damita as she took him at his word and looked at dear Timothy, thinking of what might happen to him should she make enough noise to awaken her cousin Jonathan. She did not want to believe that this proud warrior would harm a child, yet his beliefs and anger had already led him to do what she would not have thought him capable of only yesterday.

For Timothy's sake, she followed Iron Cloud's instructions, yet dreading to leave her brother under the supervision of Jonathan without her there, making sure that he would be treated fairly. Now, it seemed, all of her plans to protect her brother had gone awry.

She glared up at Iron Cloud.

Because of him, she thought bitterly. Because of the handsome warrior, nothing she had wanted for her brother would ever come true.

Yet she weakened in her anger toward the Indian, knowing that the true blame lay upstairs, in the loft.

If Jonathan had treated the handsome warrior and his people humanely, the Indian would not be there now, separating her from her beloved brother!

She flinched when Iron Cloud lifted her off the bed and into his arms, then she looked at him wonderingly as he grabbed the canvas bag and forced the handle into her hand. What else had he stolen tonight besides her?

But she did not have much time to wonder about this, concentrating on getting out of the cabin without waking her cousin. That would have been the worst of dilemmas for Timothy. She knew that—and for herself.

Jonathan would be the sort to grab his shotgun and begin firing, and Lord only knew who would end up alive—or dead!

Her cousin did not seem to have the brains to think through anything before acting. How he had become the agent at Fort Calhoun was a puzzle to her. She had come to the conclusion that he had friends in high places—or knew who to bribe.

She clutched the bag as Iron Cloud carried her gently across the room and then outside into the shadows of the moon. Not being able to place an arm around his neck to support herself with, she felt clumsy in his arms as he ran across the open land toward the forest.

Her heart pounded as she spied his horse through a break in the trees a short distance away and the reality of what was happening began sinking in.

She was going to be an Indian captive! She might never see her brother again! Was she going to be used for ransom, or was this just out-and-out revenge?

When Iron Cloud placed Damita's feet to the ground, her first instinct was to run. Surely, if she made any noise now, it would no longer endanger her brother or awaken Jonathan. If she got loose from the warrior and could get back to the cabin in time to grab a gun before he got there, she could teach him a thing or two about abducting people!

If she must, she *would* shoot him!

The instant Iron Cloud reached for his reins to untie them from the tree, Damita took the opportunity to start running back in the direction of her cousin's cabin. With her mouth gagged, she found it hard to breathe, and with her wrists tied, she felt unbalanced, threatening to fall if she ran too quickly.

And then none of this mattered. Iron Cloud was there, his muscled arm grabbing her around the waist, stopping her so abruptly that it crushed the wind from inside her.

For an instant, she blacked out. When she awakened, she found herself sitting on the ground beneath a tree, the gag gone and her wrists freed.

"That was foolish," Iron Cloud said in a low growl. "Do you think I risk my life to take a captive to let her get away from me so easily? White woman whose beauty matches the gentle loveliness of a willow tree, do not try that again. Next time I will be forced to not be as gentle. You are my captive. Now and forever more. Never forget that."

Damita rubbed her raw wrists where the rope had cut into her flesh when she was jerked into Iron Cloud's arms. "But why?" she murmured. "Why did you abduct me?"

She searched his face for answers, finding only a bitterness in the depths of his eyes and etched onto his handsome, copper face. She recalled how seeing him the other time had affected her. It was no less now, except that now she had cause to be afraid of him.

Iron Cloud ignored her question. He picked up the bag and thrust it into her arms. "Your clothes are inside the bag," he said flatly. "Get dressed. The forest is too cold and damp for your sleeping garment."

Stunned over his having thought of her welfare while abducting her, Damita opened the bag and stared down at what he had brought. She pulled out one garment at a time. She reached for the hairbrush and gazed up at him.

"You even brought my hairbrush?" she said, clasping its wooden handle.

"Hair care is important to the Omaha," Iron Cloud said flatly. "I am sure it is the same for white women who have hair the color of wheat. The hairbrush. Take it with you as we ride farther into the forest. Or I shall make you one later of stiff grass."

While she stared disbelievingly up at Iron Cloud, he had to look away from her. Looking into her lovely eyes reminded him of all the reasons that he should not have abducted her.

She was innocent of any crime. She was devoted to her brother, whom she had been forced to leave behind.

And she was too beautiful to be mistreated in any way!

He prayed to *Wakoda* that she would not force him to behave differently than he had planned!

Anger replaced Damita's amazement that this

Indian had been thoughtful enough to bring her hairbrush. He had abducted her. A hairbrush did not make his crime any less!

She rose to her feet, clutching her clothes to her chest. "I remember you from my cousin's office," she said, her voice firm. "I thought you were angry with my cousin Jonathan that day. Now I know that I was right, and how angry you truly were! You abducted me because you are angry with *him*! That's not fair. Do you hear me? Not fair! Take me back. I can't be separated from my brother!"

Iron Cloud turned quickly back to her. He placed a hand to her shoulder, firming his fingers into her flesh as she tried to jerk free. "Yes, I was angry," he said. "Your cousin has done my people wrong for as far back as time is counted on a white man's calendar. My father's spirit was broken by your cousin and men like him! My father is now dead. I am now chief! No one will break my spirit! Nor my people's. I not only abduct you to avenge all wrongs done by your evil cousin, but my people have left this land to seek a new life elsewhere. You are going there with me. You will adapt to the ways of the Omaha, as the Omaha have for so long been forced to adapt to the ways of the white people!"

The color drained from Damita's face as his words sank in. "Again I say that you are not being fair," she murmured. "I am only one person. Do you think that abducting me and making me live with your people will solve anything? It won't. Please reconsider!"

"Having you with me has already brought much peace into my heart," Iron Cloud said, dropping his hand from her. "Knowing that Jonathan will awaken tomorrow and find you gone is reason enough for inner peace."

Damita stood with her mouth agape and her eyes wide, realizing that talking to him was like talking to a wall of stone! Nothing she said meant anything to him. His mind had been made up before tonight, she was sure—more than likely since the moment he had seen her in her cousin's office, he had known how he would achieve his revenge against her cousin. *That* was why he had stared at her that day. It had had nothing to do with a strange, quick bonding between them. He had not seen her as attractive, but as someone he could use.

"Get dressed," Iron Cloud said softly. "We have a long way to go. My people anxiously await my return."

"If I must, I must," Damita said. She placed a hand on a hip. "But I won't while you are standing there watching!"

"I will turn my back so that you can dress," Iron Cloud said, turning slowly around so that his back was to her. "But do not think this will give you the chance to escape. I would not allow you to get far. And if you choose not to cooperate with me, I will gag and tie you again. That is not a pleasant way to travel through the forest."

"I'm not planning to try and escape," Damita said bitterly, yanking her gown over her head.

"Not now, anyhow," she whispered to herself, smiling at his back.

"You will be treated well while you are among my people," Iron Cloud said, twisting the horse's reins around one finger. "They are good and kind. It was wrong for the white people to treat them so badly, as though they were no better than animals. There will come a time when all white men will see the wrong they have done to the Indian nation—the wrong done to Chief Iron Cloud and his proud band of Omaha."

"Who is this Chief Iron Cloud?" Damita asked, slipping into her last shoe.

Iron Cloud turned and faced her. "Chief Iron Cloud?" he said, amused that she did not know with whom she was traveling, yet somewhat hurt that she had not asked her cousin the day they had briefly met without proper introductions. He could still feel the strange, quick bonding between himself and this woman when their eyes had met and held. He could feel it even now, as though fate had brought them together for other reasons than his need for revenge.

Completely dressed, her shawl draped around her shoulders and her hairbrush clasped within her hand, Damita took a step toward him. "Yes, Chief Iron Cloud," she said, firming her chin as she looked up at him. "Who is he? Is he one of your best friends?"

"The best," Iron Cloud said, chuckling. "You see, White Willow, I am Iron Cloud."

She was momentarily taken aback, then she felt

honored to have been chosen by him to be his prisoner. Surely to him she was special.

He was to *her*, she hated admitting to herself!

"I thought you were a chief that day we first met," she said, then their eyes locked. "You called me ...? What did you call me?"

"White Willow," Iron Cloud said, smiling at her.

"But why?" she asked, thinking the name beautiful, but wary of being given a name other than her own by this powerful chief. She was afraid of losing her identity altogether if she parted with her true name. But perhaps that was what he had planned for her!

"You remind me of the willow," he said, but offered her no more explanation now. "We have talked enough. We must now ride. We talk more when we reach my caravan of people. They will be easier once they know I am among them, their leader."

Tears misted in Damita's eyes.

"You are going to cry?" Iron Cloud said, forking an eyebrow. "You find my company so unbearable that you have a need to cry?"

"It is not you that I am crying over," Damita said, the tears now rushing down her cheeks. "These tears are for my brother! He has only had me since our parents' deaths. Please let me go. My brother needs me."

"Your brother will get by," Iron Cloud said, placing his hands to her waist and lifting her onto his horse. "He will adapt, as you will. You are never going to be returned to the white community. Ever!"

Damita became silent, the fight lessening within her. She tried to envision Timothy when he awakened and found her gone—and her cousin's reaction. How would he treat Timothy when she wasn't there to defend him?

She tried to imagine herself in the Indian village, doing daily chores alongside the Indian women.

She squirmed to get herself comfortable in the saddle as Iron Cloud settled in behind her, then sighed heavily when one of his arms snaked around her waist to hold her against him as he rode away into the darkness.

"I must find a way to escape," she whispered to herself.

For Timothy, she must!

Chapter Six

The ride through the forest on horseback was frightening for Damita. Yet even though she was a captive, she could not help but be glad that Iron Cloud was there, holding her securely around her waist, protecting her. He could have brought her to the depths of the forest, abandoned her, and left her to die. He had nothing ugly planned for her—at least nothing that she knew about. He had seemed sincere when he said that she would become a part of his village and learn the ways of his people. As long as he kept that plan, she would be alive—at least until she found a way to escape!

The trail wound like a tattered ribbon through the trees. Iron Cloud's appaloosa weaved in and out of the thickness of the forest and around the trees and knee-high weeds. The shine of the river was now evident through the break of trees up ahead, the moon reflecting on it like millions of fireflies lit up beneath the surface.

Iron Cloud snapped his reins and urged his horse toward the river, then drew his steed to such a sudden stop before he reached it that Damita was jerked almost from his arms.

She questioned him with her eyes as he placed her quickly to the ground and dismounted just as quickly himself. She did not have time to ask him why he had stopped, or why in such a rush. He had gone to a spot where the tall grasses had been crushed flat and had fallen to his knees, looking at something.

Afraid, but too curious to just stand there, Damita began edging toward him, and when she finally reached him and saw why he had stopped, the reality made a lightheadedness sweep through her.

Iron Cloud looked quickly over his shoulder at her. "Go back to the horse," he said flatly. "What I have found is not a pleasant sight."

He stared up at her for a moment, then moved to his full height over her, no longer blocking the view of the dead woman and child lying in the crushed grass. "Yet perhaps it is best that you do see the ugly works of the white people," he said, taking her by a wrist and moving her closer to the scene of death. "The child and its mother have both been shot through the head."

With a pounding heart and weak knees, Damita stared down at the bodies, finding it hard to imagine how anyone could kill such innocent people. The mother was still clutching the small, naked baby to her bosom, even in death.

And then something grabbed her at the pit of her stomach, giving her a sudden urge to retch. The leaves in the trees overhead were blown aside by the wind, allowing the moonlight to shine through. And what it revealed filled Damita with great splashes of fear—fear for her dear, beloved Timothy who was now completely at the mercy of her cousin!

"No," she cried, placing a hand to her throat. "My cousin wouldn't have—"

"What are you saying?" Iron Cloud said, turning her to face him. He clutched his fingers to her shoulders. "Tell me. Do you recognize the woman and child?"

Damita cast her eyes to the ground, ashamed, a keen revulsion for her cousin seeming to cut through to the core of herself. "Yes, I know who they are," she said. She winced when Iron Cloud gave her a shake.

"And how do you know them?" he said, his fingers squeezing into her flesh, hurting her.

Tears near, Damita raised her eyes slowly to his. "They were at the fort," she said softly. "I saw them there. They had come for their annuities. My cousin . . . he . . ."

It was hard for her to find the words to tell him the full truth, for telling him would seem to condemn herself in his eyes. Her blood kin had surely ordered the killings! That was what Jonathan had been whispering to the soldier after he had told the soldier to take the mother and child away!

73

She was horrified by the thought that her cousin had ordered the killings to eliminate problems for himself by keeping the measles away from the fort.

"Your cousin," Iron Cloud said, jerking her closer, his eyes filled with rage as he glared down at her. "He is responsible for this?"

"I believe so," Damita murmured, becoming more and more afraid beneath his cold gaze.

Iron Cloud released her so abruptly she almost stumbled to the ground, but she quickly regained her footing as she saw confusion replace the anger in Iron Cloud's eyes.

"Never have I known the Indian agent to kill innocent women and children," he said thickly. He knelt beside the woman again, touching her long, dark hair. "It is so senseless. Why would he do this? The Indians only go to Fort Calhoun for supplies because this sort of life has been forced upon them by the white man treaties. They go, stand and wait for hours, and then look like beggars as they take the white man's goods. Your cousin kills for this? Never can I understand why. Never!"

"Although a senseless, cruel thing to do, I know why he did it," Damita said, bending to her knees on the ground beside Iron Cloud. "And I cannot believe he could be this heartless. But there is much about him that I do not know. He is not a man I know, or respect."

"You say you know why," Iron Cloud said, looking intently at her. "Tell me so that I may understand the evil workings of this madman's brain."

"The moon is not sufficient light for you to see the red splotches on the child's skin," Damita said, realizing that the longer she and Iron Cloud stayed with the contaminated child, the more chances they took of being exposed themselves.

Yet there had to be time taken to explain this to Iron Cloud, even though telling him would not lighten the guilt of her cousin, who had acted out of hate, not pity.

"Splotches?" Iron Cloud said, leaning closer to the child. Damita placed a hand to his shoulder and urged him away. He looked at her with a raised eyebrow.

"It is not wise to get any closer to the child," Damita said, drawing her hand away from him. "The child's body was ravaged with measles. The disease is quite contagious. This is why my uncle chose to hand down the death sentence to both the mother and child."

She rose to her feet and hung her face in her hands. "I'm so sorry," she said, tensing when she felt him rise beside her. Then she was awed by his gentleness as he took her by the hand and walked her back to his horse.

"You stay here," he said, gazing down at her with his midnight dark eyes. "I will cover them with grass and twigs so that their bodies will rest in peace. They are not from my tribe. If I knew which tribe they were from I could send word."

"They are Sioux," Damita said. "That is all I know. Which band, I do not know."

"I thought she might be Sioux," Iron Cloud said,

glancing at the woman. "I have never seen her at any of the Omaha gatherings."

He gazed intently down at Damita again. "You will be all right?" he asked, having seen the trauma this had brought upon her. He had abducted her, but he wanted nothing to cause her unhappiness! She was blood kin to her evil cousin, but she was not one with his heart and soul.

She was different.

She was kind. She had compassion.

And there was no doubt that she was slowly stealing his heart away!

Damita wiped a stream of tears from her cheek and smiled up at him. "I will be fine," she said, holding back another deep-throated sob. "And I am amazed, Iron Cloud, that you would even care. After seeing the woman and child, and knowing who surely killed them, I would think that you would hate me."

"You are not the sort of woman one can hate all that easily," Iron Cloud said, then turned and went back to the woman and child. "And you are not to blame for this atrocity. Your compassion would never allow it!"

Damita was stunned by what he had said and his revelation that he had feelings for her. Then, when she saw him lift the mother to another spot beneath the trees that would not be so evident to passersby, and even risked his own life by taking the baby to lie with her, she turned her eyes away and let the tears flow freely.

Oh, how she was torn with feelings! She knew

that she should hate the Omaha chief, yet she couldn't. He was fighting for his people's very existence! Taking her with him was a way to prove a point to her cousin.

Yet she felt so helpless, not so much because she had been abducted, but because she could not help the handsome Omaha chief in ways that would truly benefit him.

But no one who cared about the plight of the Indians had ever truly found ways to help them. And there were too many others who saw them as savages and wanted nothing to do with them, except to trick and kill!

"It is done. Their bodies are covered," Iron Cloud said, returning to Damita's side. "I should turn right around and ride back to Fort Calhoun and tell the commandant what your cousin did, but to do so would delay my return to my people. It would also draw attention to what my people are doing. So your cousin will get away with another atrocity, it seems."

"Then you believe, as I do, that he is guilty of this crime?" Damita said, looking past him at the mounds of leaves and twigs partially hidden behind a thick cluster of bushes.

"There is no doubt in my mind that he is," Iron Cloud said, following her gaze. He felt a keen sadness for the deaths, even though they were Sioux, long-time enemies of the Omaha. This had been out-and-out murder. When the lives of the Sioux were taken during a battle, that was a different matter. And dying in battle was an honorable end.

Damita allowed Iron Cloud to lift her onto his horse and arranged herself as comfortably in the saddle as she could. "If they hadn't had the measles, my cousin wouldn't have ordered the killing," she said, yet not in defense of her cousin. It was just a statement of fact. "And pity any other Indians who might come to the fort bearing the marks of measles. I am sure he would not hesitate again to see them dead."

As Iron Cloud swung himself into the saddle behind her, again anchoring her against him with his muscled arm, a sudden, horrifying thought sprang to her mind. Her eyes widened and she gasped as she spoke the name of her brother.

"Timothy!" she said, turning an alarmed look to Iron Cloud. "Oh, my God. Iron Cloud, the woman and child exposed both me and my brother to the measles. If Timothy should come down with the disease, will Jonathan rid himself of that problem in the same way? Will he order one of his soldiers to take Timothy into the forest and kill him?"

"I would think so," Iron Cloud said, looping the horse's reins around one hand, yet not sending his horse into a gallop. He sensed that White Willow needed to rid herself of her worries by talking them out. He would let her talk, then they would continue on with their journey.

Damita placed a hand to her mouth, stifling another gasp as she turned her eyes from Iron Cloud. "Timothy," she whispered. "Lord, Timothy. What am I to do?"

She turned desperate eyes back to Iron Cloud. "Please take me back to my brother," she cried. "He's not safe with my cousin. Should he get ill, he will need me. I—I must be there to care for him, and to protect him from Jonathan!"

"You do not know that he will become ill," Iron Cloud said matter-of-factly. "The white people are not as susceptible to diseases as the Indian. You know that. So we will continue the journey, White Willow. Forget your brother. You are not going back!"

Damita jerked herself free of Iron Cloud and jumped to the ground, falling to her knees in the process. When he was quickly there, his hands at her waist, pulling her up before his angry eyes, she was frightened again, yet stood tall and stubborn before him.

"You must have family," she said, trying to keep her voice from quavering. "Surely there are bonds among you that make you understand the bond between me and my brother. Reach into your heart and understand why I must go back to him. I am all he has. His future is bleak without me, especially should he become ill. My cousin has no true feelings for me or Timothy. He'd let him die. One way or the other, he would be free of Timothy."

"I listened, you have spoken, and now it is time to go," Iron Cloud said. He tried to lift her on the horse again, but this time she was too spirited. She yanked herself free and began running away from him.

He shook his head, sighing deeply, then bolted after her and soon had her wrestled to the ground. He turned her over so that she was on her back and he straddled her, holding her wrists to the ground, over her head.

"You do not listen well," he growled out. "No matter what you say, you are not going back to Fort Calhoun. Now do I have to tie you to the horse so that we can travel onward? Or do you come without further complaint?"

"I see that begging you is useless," Damita said, sobbing. "So there is just one other thing I am going to ask of you. Please listen with your heart. It is not an impossible thing, and it would make your travels much easier, for I would never complain again about your plans for me."

"What is it?" he asked, his gaze going slowly over her face, its loveliness, its innocence—and then lower, at the swell of her breasts that were pressed against the inside of her cotton dress, revealing their generous curves, even the shape of her dark nipples.

He was weakening in many ways, and this was dangerous.

He wanted to kiss her! He wanted to hold her in his arms and tell her that everything would be all right! He wanted to tell her that forevermore she would be his, and then kiss her until she promised that she wanted this as badly as he!

His heart was pounding, his loins burning, wanting her more than even his next breath!

So suddenly taken was he by her loveliness and

his need to kiss her that he only half heard her as she poured her heart out to him.

And then finally her words sank in, and her plan did not seem at all that bad. It even seemed that it would fit even better into his plans.

"Will you do it?" Damita cried, tears splashing from her eyes. "Please? For me?"

"What you ask is simple enough," Iron Cloud said, releasing her wrists, then smoothing a fallen lock of golden hair back from her tear-filled eyes. "Yes. I think it can be arranged."

Damita's breath was taken suddenly away, so surprised was she that he had actually said yes without further argument.

She was even more surprised when his lips came to hers and he gave her a kiss that did not offend her at all, but instead caused a wondrous melting within her.

She twined her arms around his neck and returned the kiss.

Chapter Seven

Alarm set in as Damita felt herself being drawn more and more into the spell of this handsome Omaha chief and his way of affecting her. Although she had enjoyed the delicious feelings that washed through her when he kissed her, she knew that it was wrong to let it continue.

She must never forget that she was his captive! She should hate him, not be falling hopelessly in love with him.

And what of Timothy? she worried to herself.

Gently, she shoved at Iron Cloud's chest. She drew her lips from his, turning her face away from his seeking mouth. "Please," she whispered, her pulse racing, knowing that she was speaking that which her heart did not agree to.

Never had a man affected her in such a way. Never had a kiss turned her insides into something warm and beautiful!

But this was not the time, the place, or—surely—the right man for her. Although she did not have harsh feelings toward the Indians, she knew that everyone else did, and that relationships between an Indian and a white woman were forbidden!

And, again, her brother had to be foremost in her mind. Iron Cloud had agreed to her plan. She must do nothing now to jeopardize it!

Iron Cloud gazed down at her for a moment longer, understanding her rejection of him, more than he understood himself for wanting her so much. He had his pick of women among his tribe of Omaha. There were many who had voiced aloud their desire to be his woman!

Up to now, he had taken women to his bed only to quench his desires of the flesh.

Up to now, he had placed the welfare of his people before his own needs.

But after tonight, and the way White Willow had responded to his kiss, he knew that she would be the woman warming his bed until the day he died!

But he knew he had to move more slowly with her. He knew the attitudes of the white people about white women marrying Indians. He knew that he could never change the world's viewpoint about this.

There was only one person who needed convincing.

White Willow.

And the process of teaching her had just begun....

Cassie Edwards

Iron Cloud rose to his feet and offered Damita a hand. When she hesitated, her eyes locked with his, he reached down and took her hand and eased her to her feet before him.

"If I am to go back for your brother, it must be done now, and quickly," Iron Cloud said, placing his arms around her waist, unable to stop himself from drawing her against him. "White Willow, I would not do this for anyone else. Only you, whose voice is soft as a thrush's. Do you understand?"

His lips only a heartbeat away and his mighty arms holding her next to him threatened Damita's train of thought, and her willpower against them became all too weak again.

She stood there for a moment longer, mesmerized anew by his midnight-black eyes. Then something seemed to snap inside her, bringing her back to her senses.

She wrenched herself free and turned her back to him, breathing hard. She placed her fingers to her lips, which still throbbed from the passion exchanged in that kiss.

She felt dizzy with desire, yet she forced her thoughts back to her brother and his safety.

Turning to face Iron Cloud, she swallowed hard and looked him square in the eye, fighting back the sensual feelings she felt for him. She did not even understand where they were coming from. Usually she had more control of her feelings.

Yet she had never been introduced into feelings of passion before, either. That was the difference.

"You are very kind to agree to go back for my

84

brother," she murmured. She had decided that her brother would be safer with her, no matter where she was—or with whom. "Timothy will be happier with me. I know that my cousin would soon see Timothy as an encumbrance. If not that, he would only tolerate his presence because he could force Timothy to work for him. And, Iron Cloud, I so fear what might happen if he comes down with the measles!"

"I will go back for the lad, but if he becomes ill with the measles, you both will be separated quickly from my people," Iron Cloud said firmly. "You will still be a part of us, but will stay your distance until you are well again."

"I understand," Damita said, nodding her head anxiously. "I would not want to bring any disease to your people. And I would make sure it did not happen."

Without much thought, she flung herself into his arms and hugged him. "I knew you would do this for me," she said, clinging to him. "You are a kind, compassionate man. How could my cousin treat you so unjustly?"

He eased her from his arms and led her back to his horse, lifting her onto the saddle. "There are many things in life that remain a mystery," he said. "But there is no mystery about your cousin. He is greedy, cruel, and unjust." He placed a hand to her cheek. "Men like him don't last long. I would wager a bet that your cousin won't be alive more than two more winters. Men like him are courting death when they treat others without respect and compassion."

"While in Boston, I was not around people like my cousin," Damita said softly. "My father and mother were very soft-hearted people, as were their friends. Those are the people my brother and I were raised among. Being with my cousin just one day brought me and Timothy face to face with what we had been protected from. We had never been around greedy, evil people. It was hard to accept that our cousin had those traits. I . . . I had even decided to find a way to leave him." She smiled awkwardly down at Iron Cloud. "It seems that has been taken care of for me without any planning on my part."

"And so then you should be able to accept that what I have done is in truth a favor," Iron Cloud said, chuckling as he swung himself into the saddle behind her. "Now if you will just accept your new status in life, you will see that you are much better off."

She glanced at him over her shoulder. "Perhaps if I had not been abducted in the night like—like something used for bartering, I might be able to see that my future is brighter at this moment, away from my cousin," Damita said softly. "But the truth is that I am a captive." Her eyes locked with his. "I am a captive as long as you force me to stay with you. How can I truly agree that I am better off with you, if my freedoms have been taken from me?"

"In time, your full freedom will be yours again,"

Iron Cloud said, turning his horse back in the direction of Fort Calhoun, "after you accept your life as one of my people—and your new name, White Willow."

She frowned up at him. "If you strip me of my true name, you will not only be stripping me of my freedom, but also my true identity," she said, her voice quavering. "How much am I to be forced to accept? That I am a captive is enough!"

He drew his reins tight, stopping his horse. "When you kissed me, you did not play the role of captive," he growled. "You played the role of a woman who was pleased to be with a man! Let us see again how you react to my kiss! Tell me then if you feel as though you have been stripped of so much. I am offering you more than you realize!"

Before Damita could protest, Iron Cloud turned her around so that their lips could meet in a fiery kiss. He held her so tightly that she could not squirm free. The spinning in her head told her that the fight was lessening within her. There was pure magic in his kiss! She could not help but respond again, her heart pounding so hard she thought it might burst from the excitement of the moment.

And then his arms loosened around her, giving her the chance to move away from him. But she did not want to stop kissing him. She placed her arms around his neck and drew herself even more tightly against him, blinded to what this sort of passion could lead to. That she was with him, thrilling inside with his kiss, and the way his hands were now stroking her so caressingly down the full length of her back, made everything else seem unimportant.

But when one of his hands crept around and cupped her breast through her dress, this shocking, wondrous sensation caused her to bolt from his arms and stare with a throbbing heart up at him.

"Now tell me that you do not want to stay," Iron Cloud said huskily, softly running a finger over her swollen lips. "If you want to be set free, I will let you go. You will be free to go back to your cousin, where you and your brother can live in fear. I know that you said you were going to find a way to leave him, but a woman in this world of men does not get far alone. And a young brother is not enough protection from men like your cousin who are everywhere, looking for pretty victims like yourself to use—and to ruin. Leave if you wish. But it would not be a wise decision. I will treat you like an Omaha princess. Your brother will become one of our young warriors and be taught the ways of the Omaha. He will one day ride alongside the others, a great warrior himself."

What he offered Damita, should she stay with him, was a great temptation. She saw him as an honest man, working hard to better the lives of his people. And she felt that she could trust him. There would be no reason for him to lie to her. He was offering her eventual freedom—once she had proved that she was worthy!

And he had awakened such desire in her! She did not want to turn her back on that—or on him.

"No," she murmured, awash with sensations again as his hands slowly caressed her back again. "I don't want to go back to my cousin. I will stay with you. I believe that you will treat me justly. I only hope that Timothy won't be frightened of the idea."

"Once he becomes involved in challenges with boys of his same age, he will never want to be anywhere else but with the Omaha," Iron Cloud said. He framed her face between his hands and drew her lips close. "You have made a wise decision. White Willow, you will never want for anything. I will cater to your every whim and desire!"

She melted into him as he kissed her hard and passionately, but was glad when he released her and they resumed their trek through the forest. She was again thinking of her brother. Also, she was just beginning to worry about the danger in what she had asked Iron Cloud to do. He had entered her cousin's cabin once without being detected. But could he do it a second time? What if Jonathan awakened?

She shook her head, not wanting to think of that possibility, and leaned back against him as they moved onward. When she realized they were near her cousin's cabin, she glanced back at Iron Cloud as he drew his horse to a shuddering halt.

Her heart pounded out her fear for Iron Cloud and Timothy as he lowered her to the ground, then dismounted quickly himself.

But her mouth opened in astonishment when he came to her with a rope and started binding her hands together at her wrists.

"Why are you doing that?" she gasped. "Didn't you hear anything I just said? Or was I foolish to believe you even cared? Were you just playing games with me?"

"I listened well to what you said, and I was touched by it," Iron Cloud said, tying the last knot. He gazed intently into her eyes. "I hardly know you. How do I know that you were being truthful? Do I have a reason to trust you? If I allowed you to ride back to your cousin's house, how do I know that you would be quiet—that your fears about your cousin's treatment of your brother was not all pretense just to get me to return you to your cousin?"

"You're wrong!" she cried. "I meant every word. I don't trust my cousin. After seeing the woman and child, I am terrified of him! His next victim could be my brother!"

"You have said enough," Iron Cloud said, taking her by the wrists, and guiding her to a tree. "I will leave you here and return soon with your brother." He gave her a steely gaze. "Trust must be earned. In time, I hope never to have cause to doubt you again."

"I have given you no cause now!" Damita said, wincing with pain as he placed her wrists against the rough grain of the tree and started tying a rope around her and the tree. "Please don't do this. I promise not to make a sound! I want Timothy to be safe! If I caused a fuss, he might be shot in a crossfire! Please! Don't leave me here like this!"

He turned away from her and began walking toward his horse. "I won't be gone long," he said, giving her a quick look over his shoulder. "Soon your brother will be safe." He turned his gaze to his horse and quickly mounted it and rode away before Damita had a chance to plead her case again with him.

She was too angry and humiliated to cry. With a tight jaw and harsh breathing, she worked with the ropes, trying to get herself free. But too soon the ropes were cutting her wrists and she recognized that she had to accept what fate had handed her.

She peered into the darkness, slowly moving her eyes around, waiting breathlessly for Iron Cloud's return. What if he got caught and was murdered? No one would ever find her!

For what seemed an eternity, she watched for any signs of movement. A tremor shook her at the slightest sound—the unexpected beat of a wing, an uneasy shifting among the leaves above her. She knew that she was at the mercy of any creature that came along—on two legs or four.

How could Iron Cloud have been so thoughtless? Surely he knew the dangers of leaving her alone like this, unable to protect herself? If he did have feelings for her, he had strange ways of showing them, she thought angrily.

Soon the sky began to lighten through the umbrella of trees overhead. She knew that Iron Cloud should have been back by now if all had gone well with his second abduction of the night! Her insides quavered at the thought of what might have happened to Iron Cloud and Timothy. Perhaps they both were dead!

The sound of an approaching horse made Damita's heart skip several erratic beats. And then she heaved a great sigh of relief when through the semi-darkness she could see Iron Cloud, and on the saddle in front of him, Timothy!

Trailing behind Iron Cloud's horse were two others, surely stolen from her cousin's corral and meant for her and her brother for their journey to meet with Iron Cloud's people. Iron Cloud's mind never rested, it seemed. He was always thinking, always scheming.

"Thank the good Lord, you are safe!" Damita cried, wanting to dash forth and greet them both with eager hugs. But the damnable rope still held her immobile, as if she were an enemy.

She saw a look of utter shock and fright sweep across her brother's face when Iron Cloud drew rein close to where Damita stood, tied to the tree. And when he jumped from the horse and came to her, she saw a sudden anger flashing in his eyes as he turned and faced Iron Cloud.

"You said that my sister was not forced to leave with you!" Timothy shouted, doubling his fists. He raced to Iron Cloud, pummeling his chest with them. "You lied! She's tied up! She is a captive!"

Iron Cloud grabbed Timothy's wrists and held them. "What I told you was part truth," he said. "Yes, she is a captive. But she is now willing to escape from your cousin. I told you her fears. They

are real. She did send me for you. Go to her. She
will tell you this is so."

He released Timothy's wrists and, boldly reaching for the knife sheathed at his waist, offered it
to the angry young man.

"Go," Iron Cloud said, nodding toward Damita.
"Set her free."

Timothy took the knife, clasping his hand
tightly around the handle. His heart pounded,
knowing that this was an opportunity to use the
knife on the Indian. Yet, the Indian seemed sincere. And it had been exciting to leave with him,
to go to his sister! As they had traveled back to
where Damita was waiting, what the Omaha chief
had said that he had planned for Timothy's future
had been so wonderfully etched out in his mind
that he could no longer chance its never happening. It would be fun to mix with the young warriors. It would be exciting to be challenged by
them! He wanted the chance to show them that
his strength and bravery matched theirs!

He turned on a heel and ran to his sister. In an
instant he had the ropes cut and she was holding
him in her arms. "I was so worried," she said,
combing her fingers through his thick, reddish-
gold hair. Then she held him out away from her.
"How are you feeling? Are you well?"

Timothy cocked an eyebrow. "I'm fine," he said,
shrugging. He then lunged into her arms again.
"I'm glad you are all right. When I realized that
you weren't in the cabin, after Iron Cloud awakened me, I don't think I've ever been as afraid."

"I'm fine," Damita said, looking past Timothy's shoulder to Iron Cloud. She smiled at him, no longer angry at him for having tied her to a tree. He had kept his word. He had gone for Timothy. And now their future was his, it seemed, for better or worse.

But she could not see how it could be anything but wonderful!

She encouraged Timothy to sit down beneath the tree. She explained the situation to him—why she had been abducted and why she had felt it so important for him to be taken as well.

She assured him that it was all for the best.

"Don't worry about anything, Timothy," she murmured, speaking to her brother, yet looking up at Iron Cloud. "Iron Cloud is a man of honor."

Timothy turned his head and gave Iron Cloud a sidewise glance, then nodded and turned back to Damita and gave her another hug.

Then they all mounted their steeds and rode away into the vast expanse of the sunrise as they broke free of the thick, overpowering darkness of the forest.

Chapter Eight

Sitting beside a slow-burning campfire, Damita was sorely tired from the long day's journey and was glad that Iron Cloud had finally stopped and made camp. It was not yet dusk. Above her, the last of the day's sunbeams were catching in the wings of many violet-green swallows in their wheeling, circular flight. In the forest beyond, the weakening sun's rays danced, and shadows formed, moved, and disappeared again.

Damita peered harder into the forest, in the direction that Iron Cloud had taken in his search for food. An uncontrollable shiver enveloped her, causing her to draw her shawl more snugly around her shoulders. The country looked mysterious to her and not easily traversed. Wildly flung rocks, dark forests, close thickets, swamps and rapid streams seemed to be everywhere. So far, they had not come across another person, yet she could not help but be wary every time she heard a faint sound, or thought that she saw slight movements midst the trees.

Her gaze shifted to the pistol that lay beside her, which Iron Cloud had left for her and Timothy's protection while he was gone. Then her gaze shifted to Iron Cloud's tethered horse not far from where she sat. The appaloosa was grazing peacefully, temptingly near.

Her heart pounded, knowing that she would probably never have another chance to flee. And that Iron Cloud had given her the chance made her think that he knew, as well as she, that flight was not what she wanted!

Damita gazed down at Timothy as he slept soundly on a blanket spread atop a bed of soft moss. She could see that he was just as exhausted as she, and she could tell by the growling of his stomach in his sleep that he was also as hungry.

Lovingly, she leaned over her brother and gently smoothed her hand across his brow and kissed his freckled cheek. Then she straightened her back and looked slowly around her again, wondering what was taking Iron Cloud so long. It seemed to her that he had been gone for hours. Through the day they had only stopped occasionally to feast on wild berries, then had resumed their travels through forests and meadows, on their journey back to Iron Cloud's people.

Not wanting to give in to her urge to join Timothy in a much needed nap, Damita rose slowly to her feet and went to stand at the embankment of the creek they had made camp beside. Never had she seen anything as beautiful—as peaceful. The creek rushed between two white shores and plunged into a dark chasm of almost black spruce. The water seemed darker and bluer because everything else at this time of night, when the shadows lengthened, seemed to be without color.

She looked farther, where rock walls bulged out over the creek and the waters tumbled through tortuous courses in the rocks.

Becoming unnerved by Iron Cloud's continued absence, Damita clung to her shawl and began to walk beside the creek, watching fish playing in the cool pools, some following the shelter of floating leaves, some darting between shadows. The water was so clear she could identify minnows and catfish and wondered why Iron Cloud could not have just caught a fish for their meal instead of going so far away to get larger game.

Fear building inside her, even though she had the pistol for protection should something happen to Iron Cloud, Damita returned to the campfire and sullenly sat down beside it again, gazing at Timothy.

He was her responsibility!

How could she have made such a mistake as bringing him to live with Jonathan in this wild country? Even though she had promised her father, she should have known that what he had asked was not the most sensible thing to do!

If she had remained in Boston, she could have used the money that she and Timothy had spent on their long journey to Nebraska to buy themselves a small dwelling just for the two of them. Once they had depleted their money, she could have found some sort of employment to help with her brother's schooling! She was quite skilled at doctoring—surely she could have found some sort of employment at a hospital, if only doing menial chores. At least she would be fending for herself and Timothy in surroundings familiar to them!

"How could I have been so careless in my planning for our future?" she fretted aloud. "Now Jonathan has most of my father's fortune, and what of me and Timothy?"

She shook her head slowly back and forth. Iron Cloud was offering her and Timothy futures as though they were Omaha, although that was perhaps not all that bad, especially since he would be a part of their future! No one could be as gentle—as compassionate!

Damita picked up her hairbrush and began pulling it in slow strokes through her hair to remove the windblown tangles. Catapulted into thoughts of Iron Cloud and what she truly thought about having been abducted by him, she could not help but admit to herself that she was better off with him than with Jonathan.

A thrill swept through her at the memory of what he promised her—Not only stability for herself and her brother in his village, but the life of an Omaha princess, should she decide to accept what he was actually forcing upon her.

Although she had been raised with the highest

Boston society, the thought of living away in the wilds with a man such as Iron Cloud did not offend her in the least. His lips and hands and his gentle ways had awakened her to so much that she could not help but have feelings for him that she had never felt about any other man.

She knew that perhaps her attraction to all of this might be because of the forbidden aspect of infatuation with an Indian chief and because of the challenge that being with him and his people might bring. But she no longer abhorred the thought of having been abducted, for she no longer felt like a captive.

She felt like a woman revered by a man!

She glanced over at Timothy again, realizing that even for him her worries were less. She had seen how Timothy had quickly taken to Iron Cloud—how he, in fact, idolized the powerful Indian chief.

Yes, she thought to herself, nodding—Iron Cloud had done them a favor. Damita had been searching in her heart for a way to get away from Jonathan, almost from the moment she had set foot in Fort Calhoun.

Now such an escape had been offered her!

She smiled into the dancing flames of the fire, wishing she could have been a fly on the wall of her cousin's cabin, to see Jonathan's reaction when he found his two cousins gone!

"Yet after he gets over the initial shock, I'm sure he'll be glad to be rid of us," Damita whispered to herself, reaching her arms over her head and yawning. "He's managed to get most of my father's money. That's all he was concerned with, anyhow."

She grew resentful again, realizing that she was now penniless. She and Timothy were truly at Iron Cloud's mercy. And Damita hoped and prayed that everything he had promised was true, and not just a way to make her travel with him without protest.

Unable to fight sleep any longer, Damita put her hairbrush aside and stretched out beside her brother on the blanket. Snuggling close behind him, she placed an arm over him and soon fell into a deep sleep.

Sometime later, a hand on her cheek drew her awake.

Afraid to move, afraid that someone besides Iron Cloud had ventured into their camp, Damita lay there, scarcely breathing, her eyes wide and wild.

"White Willow, it is good that you have slept," Iron Cloud said, reaching his hands to her shoulders and turning her to face him.

A rush of relief swept through Damita, and so glad was she that it was Iron Cloud that she moved quickly into his arms and clung to him.

Then, embarrassed, she drew away from him, her face hot with a blush. "I'm sorry," she murmured, rising slowly to her feet. "I guess I was more frightened than I realized. I didn't mean to..."

"There is no need for an apology," Iron Cloud interrupted, his eyes momentarily locking with hers. Then he turned abruptly away, troubled by his intense feelings for her. The more she was with him, the more he knew that he would never let her go. Not under any circumstances. Though he had not abducted her for this reason, he now knew that she would be his woman—in every sense of the word.

The word captive would soon be cast into the wind, as though never spoken between them.

"I have brought food," he said, bending to one knee before the fire and placing the skinned rabbit on a spit over the flames that he had readied before his departure. "We will eat rabbit tonight. Fish tomorrow."

Damita moved to the fire and sat down beside him as he eased down onto his haunches. "You were gone for so long," she said, eyeing the rabbit hungrily as the flames were already browning its skin. She glanced at Iron Cloud. "I didn't hear any gunfire. How far did you travel before you found this rabbit?"

"Not so far," Iron Cloud said, slowly turning the spit so that the rabbit would be browned evenly on all sides. He smiled at her. "And you did not hear any gunfire because I fashioned a spear from a stick and this is how I killed the rabbit. A spear is silent. A gun's blast is loud. It could attract unwanted travelers to our campsite."

"Oh, I see," Damita said, looking over her shoulder at the forest that was deep in shadows. She swallowed hard, suddenly aware of just how vulnerable they were out there in the vastness of this untamed land. How foolish it was for her to have fallen asleep. Anything could have sneaked up on her and her brother. Iron Cloud could have returned to two dead captives!

Iron Cloud gazed at Timothy, who still slept soundly, his freckled face touched with signs of a pleasant dream. "Your brother is a fine young man," he said sincerely. "He is a trusting young man. Sometimes that is good. Sometimes that is bad. Back at your cousin's cabin, had I been a Sioux going to Timothy's bed to abduct him—and the Sioux would have lied to him to capture a false trust from him—your brother could be dead even now, his scalp, the color of the morning sun, blowing in the breeze on a scalp pole. It is my duty to teach him when to trust and whom!"

"My brother has never known anything but a peaceful existence in his life, nor has he had much cause to mistrust anyone," Damita said, sighing deeply. "Perhaps my parents were too protective. They did not prepare us for the harsh realities of life, such as we have found in Nebraska."

"You are speaking of now? Of being with Chief Iron Cloud?" Iron Cloud said, his jaw firming tightly, his eyes growing darker with feelings.

Damita nervously shifted her legs beneath the skirt of her dress, crossing them at the knees. "No, I was not exactly referring to you, or that we have become your—your . . ."

Iron Cloud turned to her and placed a hand to her mouth, stopping her flow of words. "Do not say the word captive," he urged quietly. "I would like to think that you no longer see yourself or your brother as my prisoners. Did I not give you the chance to leave before? Did I not even tonight leave the firearm and horse at your disposal? Both times you chose to stay. So do not speak of being a captive again."

Seeing her eyes wide over his hand, and afraid of frightening her again, Iron Cloud dropped his hand away. "You have proved to me that you do not feel animosity toward me for taking you from your cousin's cabin," he said. "You even asked me to return there for your brother. These things, as other things you have said and done, tell me that you are with me now willingly. Does that not prove that you have no cause now to continue calling yourself a captive?"

"All of that is true," Damita said, her heart pounding as he continued to look at her with those piercingly large, dark eyes, as though he were looking clean into her soul. "And, truly, I did not mean to imply that you are the cause of my uneasinesses for being in this—this wild land. It is only because of what I found after arriving here. As I told you before, it is my cousin. He is not at all what I expected. Yes, as a child I knew that he was perhaps going to be a scoundrel once he grew into adulthood, but, because of my father's wishes, I had to come to Nebraska, and I hoped that my fears about my cousin were not well founded."

She dropped her eyes. "And because they were exactly what I did fear, I can only say that I am grateful to be away from him," she murmured, then slipped her gaze up again to meet his. "I truly appreciate your kindnesses to me and my brother. And I will never refer to ourselves as captives again."

"And you will stay with the Omaha without regret?" Iron Cloud said, gently touching her cheek with the palm of his hand. "It is still true that I can never let you return to live with the white people. No matter what you say, I will never allow you to return to the way of life that I have taken you from."

He took her hands, and as he rose to his feet, he drew her up before him. "White Willow, you are to be my woman, and in time—my wife," he said softly. "Now do you still say that you have made the right decision not to fight this that I have forced upon you? Will you, in time, stand at my side, be the adored wife of this powerful Omaha chieftain?"

Damita's throat became suddenly dry, rendered speechless by the fact that he was actually asking her to marry him! Although she knew that strange, wondrous feelings had been exchanged between them, she had not thought that they had meant so much to him. The thought of giving herself to him totally sent a thrill through her, yet it was frightening. Only hours ago he had forced her from her bed!

Now, he was asking her to share his, as his wife.

It was too much, too quickly, and she could not honestly give him an answer. How could he even expect her to?

"Please," she murmured, easing her hands from his. "My head is spinning. This is too much for me, too quickly. Please let me have time to think this all through. I . . . just don't know what to say, or to think!"

Iron Cloud released her hands. "This I understand," he said, bending to turn the meat again. He then rose back to his full height. "I will leave you alone for a while. I will go sit by the water. I will return shortly."

Damita reached a hand out to him as he left, fearing that she had offended him, although she had not heard any hurt in his voice. She watched him until he was lost in the darkness. Sighing heavily, she crept down onto her knees, truly not knowing what to say to him.

Going with him was one thing. Marrying him was another!

Oh, yes, she was very much infatuated with him, even gloried at the thought of being his princess. Yet it was something that had to grow on her!

She sat for a few moments stewing over this newest predicament in her life, and the more she thought about it, the more the prospect of being married to him thrilled her—through and through!

Yet, there was Timothy. What would he think about this new twist in their lives?

Then she recalled Timothy's excited talk of living with the Indians, of having young Indian braves as his own personal friends. He seemed to have accepted their new lot in life well enough.

Surely he would accept Iron Cloud as Damita's husband!

And truly, did either of them have a choice in the matter? Their futures had been changed and etched out the moment Damita's and Iron Cloud's eyes had met on the day of her arrival in Nebraska. It was then that he had surely started making plans to abduct her.

The rest had happened like pieces of a jigsaw puzzle being fit together.

With weak knees and a trembling heart, Damita rose to her feet again and began walking toward the rushing sounds of water in the creek, knowing that was where she would find Iron Cloud.

She was not sure, just yet, what she would say to him.

Chapter Nine

Damita stopped and leaned her ear toward the sound of a low voice wafting through the night air toward her. She listened closely, touched deeply when she realized that Iron Cloud was praying. Among all of the other wonderful qualities that she had discovered about him, she now knew that he was also a religious man. She could not help but wonder what else she would find out about him the longer she knew him?

She already knew that he was proud of his heritage, and he had also proved to be a man with a high sense of honor!

Not wanting to interfere in his private moment with his Great Spirit, yet wanting to hear the words of his prayer, Damita inched closer, then stopped when she saw the moon outlining his kneeling figure against the backdrop of night, his eyes and outstretched hands reaching up to the heavens.

She placed a hand to her mouth and sighed. The picture was so wonderfully serene, so beautiful! Tears sprang to her eyes as she heard the sweetness of his words and the sincerity with which he spoke them.

"Moon, there on high, have pity on me," Iron Cloud said softly. "Give me and my people the good road. Pity and help us, whatever we do. We desire only the good. Sky-father above, you seated there, I pray you to understand that whatever I do, I desire only good."

He turned his eyes down and leaned over, splaying his hands flat on the ground. "Earth, there, I pray you, Mother," he continued. "Pity me. Good is what I desire."

He raised his eyes and gazed slowly around him. "Winds of the four quarters," he said, again stretching his hands into the air. "Give me the good road. Whatever I do, I desire good."

Damita was surprised when he then rested his powerful hands on a large rock in front of him and began offering a prayer to it.

"Rock, old grandfather seated there," Iron Cloud murmured. "Keep me firm and straight."

Damita took a shaky step backward when Iron Cloud rose suddenly to his feet, turned, and discovered her there.

"I'm sorry," she said, placing a hand to her throat. "I did not mean to . . . to spy on you. I was coming to talk with you and found you praying.

It was such a lovely sight, I could not turn away."

Iron Cloud reached a hand out to her. "Come," he said kindly. "Come and sit beside me beneath the moonlight."

"You are not angry at me for having listened to your prayer?" Damita said, moving slowly toward him, her eyes wide. "I know that I shouldn't have. Truly, I am sorry."

Iron Cloud moved toward her and met her approach, taking her by the hand, then walked with her to the creek embankment. "Do not be sorry," he said, smiling down at her. "My prayers are not a secret thing. When I speak aloud while praying, it is for anyone or anything to hear that wishes to. It is a way of sharing. And Wakoda is pleased when others besides the one who is praying is touched in some way by the prayers."

"*Wakoda*?" Damita said, looking up at him quizzically. "Who is this Wakoda?"

"That is the name given to the Omaha's Great Spirit," Iron Cloud said, urging her to the ground beside him. "Wakoda is the Source of all Things." He placed a gentle hand to her cheek. "Even you are here because of Wakoda's blessings."

"I see," she said, smiling awkwardly at him.

"You said that you had come to me to talk," he said, now running his fingers through her long and flowing hair. "This that you have to say to me. It is something I will want to hear? It will make my heart sing?"

"I'm confused about so many things," Damita said, turning her eyes away from his steady stare.

"My feelings, especially."

"Let me help you discover the truth of your feelings, and then you will no longer be as you say—confused," Iron Cloud said, framing her face between his hands and lifting her eyes to his. He moved his lips closer. "My kiss will help your mind become clear."

"No, your kiss will only cloud my reasoning more!" Damita said, becoming filled with passion as his lips brushed against hers.

Everything within her thrilled at the prospect of the kiss, and she could not fight the desire which led her into accepting it—and even the fact that Iron Cloud was lowering her back to the ground.

As he kissed her long and sweetly, she was filled with such a wondrous rapture that she no longer thought about why this could be wrong—this love for a powerful Omaha chief.

And his kiss was not stealing her reason—it was clearing her mind so that she knew that she *did* wish to be with him, forever!

Iron Cloud drew his mouth only a fraction away from hers, his breath still hot on her lips. "My heart beats like many drums inside my chest," he whispered, his dark eyes gazing deeply into hers. "Its message to me is that you are here to share more than talk with me. The way you returned my kiss proves it."

"I am here because I could not stay away, that is true," Damita whispered back, reaching a hand to his copper cheek, relishing the touch of its smooth softness. "I cannot stop these feelings for you that are overwhelming me. I have never been in love before. I have never experienced such feelings before. Not until now, Iron Cloud. Not until you."

"And, White Willow, you can accept this?" he asked softly, placing a hand over her hand that still rested against his cheek.

He twined his fingers through hers and brought her hand to lie over his pounding heart, so that she could experience the wondrous beatings herself.

"My skin color does not match yours," he said thickly. "Our beliefs differ as night and day differ. Can you love me forever, or will your love turn to a bitter sorrow over losing your way of life?"

"I realize that much will be different," Damita murmured, disbelieving that she was actually discussing such things with him! Not long ago, she had been in Boston, with aspirations of being a doctor. She had anxiously awakened each day looking forward to working with her physician father, assisting him. She had gone to bed each night content with her life!

All of this had been reality until the terrible tragedy that had taken her mother and father away.

Now everything had changed. Everything . . .

"Yes," she continued after her brief moment of silence. "Everything will be different, but it is already for me. When my parents drew their last breaths, my life was instantly changed. So being with you, my love, is just a part of the change that has become a part of my life."

"I will make this change you speak of easier?" Iron Cloud questioned, smiling softly into her eyes.

"Being with you is like nothing else I have ever experienced before in my life," Damita murmured, returning his smile. "And, yes, because of you, everything has become easier for me. How could it not be? While with you, embraced by you, I feel as though I have found heaven on earth."

"Your words please me," Iron Cloud said, placing his cheek to hers and speaking softly into her ear. "Now let me please you. Let me teach you feelings of bliss, of joy."

Not recognizing this side of herself that had been awakened to sensual feelings, Damita stroked his thick black hair as she whispered back to him. "I do want to marry you," she said, her heart pounding as his hands crept up the skirt of her dress, the tingling sensation this caused making her suck in a wild breath of air. "I do want to marry you, Iron Cloud. I do."

"A marriage ceremony will come later, after we get settled in our new village in Illinois," Iron Cloud whispered back, his hand now caressing her throbbing center through her undergarment. "But beneath the moon and stars, and in the eyes of Wakoda, we will be joined as one tonight."

She fought the feelings of shame that tried to surface, knowing that in the eyes of *her* God what she was ready to share with this wonderful, gentle man was wrong. She fought off the memory of how she had felt when she heard Jonathan and Yellow Dove making love in the loft in his cabin, thinking that since they weren't married they were living in sin.

What she felt did not feel sinful—it felt right!

She would not let anything take away from this moment. She would soon be Iron Cloud's wife. He was the only man she would ever share such intimacies with. It was not as though she was going from bed to bed, man to man.

It was only one man, the man she would soon marry.

And Jonathan did not revere Yellow Dove. He was using her, the way animals used one another only to fulfill their carnal needs.

Damita knew that Iron Cloud loved her.

He wanted her only because he loved her!

Having settled this all in her mind to her satisfaction, Damita entered into the shared moments of loving with Iron Cloud without reservations. It was as though she were floating, so quickly undressed she was not aware of when or how.

And that Iron Cloud was also nude and kneeling over her, his dark and finely chiseled face very close, his lips moving toward her, seemed somehow unreal, as though she were someone else experiencing this forbidden pleasure.

When Iron Cloud's lips pressed hard into hers, his hands on her breasts gently kneading them, pleasure spread through her body in hot flashes. He kissed her with a fierce, possessive heat, causing a strange sort of hunger to invade her senses.

But as his hands swept over her body with a silent, urgent message, touching her every sensitive spot, she understood what was beckoning her from deep within herself. She wanted him with a fierce desire. She wanted everything that he was introducing her to tonight, every truth of a girl changing into a woman that he was awakening in her.

As his lips moved to the hollow of her throat and he kissed her gently there, she drew a ragged breath. Then when he rose away from her and she got a full view of the strength at the juncture of his thighs, his hand circling it as he led it closer to her body, she swallowed hard, fighting off the urge to be afraid, knowing that surely her fear would soon change to ecstasy. She had heard the groans of pleasure wafting down from the loft at her cousin's house. Although it had disgusted her then that they would be so bold, it had proven to her that being together in such a way had given them much pleasure. Already filled with rapture, she felt that the ultimate of pleasure was about to be taught her.

A part of her cried out to run away, yet a part of her cried out to stay!

She closed her eyes when Iron Cloud knelt lower over her and placed a knee between her thighs, gently parting them. She scarcely breathed when she felt his hardness probing, then opened her eyes wide when his hands framed her face, and his lips brushed softly against hers, his words soft and sweet as he peered into her eyes.

"White Willow, it is only natural that I see fear in your eyes at this time and hear an anxiousness in your breathing," he murmured, again softly kissing her.

He eased his mouth from her lips again, gazing at her with much gentleness. "It is not easy for a woman the first time," he whispered. "But trust me when I say that the pain will be brief. Then, White Willow, you will share the ecstasy with me." He smoothed some fallen locks from her brow. "Trust me?"

"Yes," she whispered, again swallowing hard. "I trust you." She beckoned with her arms to him. "Kiss me, my love. Kiss me."

Sweet currents of warmth flooded her senses as he kissed her with gentleness and love. She twined her arms around his neck and found herself lifting her hips to meet his soft probing, anxious to be one with him.

And then she cried out against his lips as he entered her in one thrust, the pain soon changing to something wonderful and sweet. He cradled her close as his lean, sinewy buttocks moved, his strokes within her flooding her with emotions never felt before. She clung to him as his tongue brushed her lips lightly and his hands again kneaded her breasts, causing her nipples to grow dark and tight in his palms.

Again he kissed her with an easy sureness, now moving slowly within her, then faster, causing her to go almost beyond coherent thought—only feeling intense pleasure, and a growing, fiercer love for this handsome, wonderful man.

Iron Cloud was finding it hard not to let go and reach that plateau that he was seeking, where he and his White Willow would soar, as though on the wings of an eagle. His body trembled as she clung and rocked with him. A blaze of desire fired his insides, and he knew that he was much too close now to deny what his body, mind, and soul cried out for.

He locked Damita in a steely embrace, his lips crushing hers as he let the euphoria tumble through him, beginning at the base of his skull, working its way down to his toes.

His strokes speeded, deeper and deeper, happy that she was responding to his every nuance of lovemaking, her body meeting his every thrust.

His body shook into hers, his mind momentarily filled with only pleasure, smiling when she responded, glad that it was he who had introduced her to the sensual side of life that she would only share, forevermore, with him!

Damita felt as if she were floating, and then, as though answering the call of Iron Cloud's body that seemed suddenly taken with trembling, his gasps of pleasure filling the cool, night air, she felt the pulsing crest of her own passion. She abandoned herself to these joyous feelings that were washing through her, the pleasure so intense that for a moment she felt as if she might faint!

And then it was over and they were lying quietly still in one another's embrace. Iron Cloud nestled

Damita close, breathing hard against her cheek.

"You are all right?" he finally asked, leaning away from her so that he could look down at her flushed face. Her eyes glazed with the aftermath of passion gave him the answer that he was seeking.

"I am fine," she said, smoothing her hand down his perspiration-laced back. "I am more than fine. Iron Cloud, I am still quavering inside from the pleasure." She lowered her eyes, blushing again. "Perhaps this is wrong? Is it right that I should feel so much? Is it the normal thing for a woman? I thought that only men experienced . . ."

Iron Cloud placed a finger to her chin and brought her eyes back up to lock with his. "If you love the one you share lovemaking with, the pleasure is right, and it is something a man is proud of—making a woman enjoy the lovemaking so much," he explained softly. "Had you not felt your pleasure as intensely as I, I would have felt that your being with me was for the wrong reasons."

"What wrong reasons could there be?" she asked, her eyes innocently wide.

"Some women use men," Iron Cloud said sullenly. Then he smiled down at her when she gasped. "I knew for certain before you lay down with me that you were not that sort. So do not think further about it. We have a long future together, White Willow. I will give you many pleasurable moments. I will teach you all the ways of loving!"

He leaned away from her and scooped her

clothes up from the ground. "I smell cooked rabbit," he said, chuckling. "My hunger is twofold now, my woman. Let us go and eat."

Damita's stomach growled as she took her clothes, slipping her petticoat quickly over her head. "I had forgotten just how hungry I was," she said, giggling.

Just as she had her dress halfway over her head, a gunshot rang out from the direction of the campsite.

Everything within Damita went weak, and the blood rushed from her face as she jerked the dress on down her body.

"Timothy!" she cried, guilt splashing through her as she realized that, while floating to paradise with Iron Cloud, she had forgotten all about her brother.

She bolted to her feet and, with Iron Cloud half-dressed beside her, began running barefoot toward the campsite.

"My Lord, Timothy!" Damita screamed, frantic at the thought of anything happening to him while she had been making love with Iron Cloud. "Timothy! Please be all right!"

She knew that she would never forgive herself if Timothy had been harmed in any way during her absence!

"Timothy!" she cried again. "Oh, Lord, let him be safe."

Chapter Ten

The distance from the creek to the campsite seemed miles for Damita as she ran breathlessly toward the camp to see if Timothy was all right. The campfire was now visible through a break in the trees ahead and Damita searched wildly with her eyes through these trees, trying desperately to get a glimpse of Timothy.

Her heart was thudding out her fear that something terrible had happened to him—and it was all her fault!

Iron Cloud's face revealed his own concern as he ran beside her. She didn't want those wonderful moments with him to be clouded over, yet she could not help but feel the wrong that she had done her brother by forgetting about him while she lay in Iron Cloud's powerful arms.

In truth, they were both to blame if Timothy had been hurt in any way!

Turning her eyes back in the direction of the campsite, she now saw Timothy standing beside the fire, clutching a rifle and peering downward at something that Damita could not yet see. Surges of relief flooded through her, and she felt as though she had been forgiven some terrible, unspoken sin.

Her brother was safe!

She saw no one else with Timothy, so the threat had apparently come from something else. She could not help but conjure up thoughts of wolves or bears!

Her brother had surely been stalked by some beast of the night. He could have been devoured, while she had been ...

Her heart seemed to drop to her feet as she jerked to an instant stop, seeing exactly what the intruder in the night had been.

"A bobcat!" she gasped, seeing how close it had gotten to the camp before Timothy had taken up the rifle and shot it.

Timothy turned and smiled at Damita. There was nary a trace of fear in his dark eyes—only pride. "Well, sis? What do you think?" he said, looking just as proudly at Iron Cloud as he stood beside Damita, a keen amazement etched onto his copper face.

"Timothy, I don't know what to think, except—except that I'm so glad that you are all right," Damita said, rushing to him and hugging him to her so abruptly that he dropped the rifle. "When I heard the shot, I thought someone had come along and had seen you alone and had shot you for what little provisions they could get from you." She stroked her fingers through his thick hair. "And then I began fearing it was an animal, and that you had managed to shoot it. Thank God you're safe. Thank God."

Iron Cloud went to the bobcat and knelt down beside it, studying the one, clean wound in its side. Timothy had felled the animal with only one shot. He rose to his feet and turned to Timothy, who had eased from Damita's arms.

"You are a courageous young man," Iron Cloud said, his eyes gleaming with admiration. "And an accurate shot. There are many young braves of my village who cannot even aim a rifle accurately, let alone make a kill with one shot."

He went to Timothy and placed a hand to his shoulder. "It will please me to work with you, to teach you the ways of hunting," he said. "You have the skills—the courage—it takes to become a great hunter. Soon, Timothy, you will rank among the best of my people, accepted as one of us. Does that please you?"

Timothy stared in awe up at this powerful Omaha chief. He had always fantasized about coming face to face with an Indian and making friends.

Never would he have thought this sort of friend-ship possible!

What Iron Cloud was planning for him made him feel as though he were in a dream, and he hoped that no one would pinch him and wake him up. He was going to be able to act out, in real life, what had once been played out only in his imagination.

"Nothing could please me more," Timothy said, stumbling over his words in his eagerness to answer Iron Cloud, and to please him. "When will we reach your people? How many days before we reach Illinois?"

Iron Cloud chuckled and drew Timothy to him for a bear hug. "Don't worry about the length of travel," he said, easing him out of his arms and peering proudly down at him. "Just become a part of it. Soon the journey will be over, and you can help erect wigwams through my village of Omaha. You have the muscle to build many."

"Wigwams?" Timothy said, his eyes wide, in awe again of this that was being mapped out before him. "I've studied about Indians and I've seen both wigwams and tepees in pictures. Will I be living in a wigwam, Iron Cloud?"

"Seems so," Iron Cloud said, going to Damita and peering into her eyes, realizing how quiet she had become and not having to venture a guess as to the reason. He was aware himself of being half-dressed, and that thus far, Timothy had been too excited to notice.

But when he settled down and began asking more questions, this time not about the travel plans, but about where his sister and Iron Cloud had been while the bobcat had been lurking about, there had to be answers to these questions.

And Iron Cloud had to make sure that Damita

was not embarrassed by them. There was much to lose if she was. He just might lose *her*. If she began to feel guilty, she would never turn to Iron Cloud again, to share in such wondrous embraces as they had just experienced.

He looked from Damita to Timothy, realizing that he had never resorted to lying before. He had always been straightforward and honest at all cost.

But now the price to be paid by honesty was too much! He had to fabricate a story that would fit their being only half-dressed and keep Damita's reputation intact in the eyes of her brother.

"Your sister and I are sorry that you were left alone. We were down by the creek," Iron Cloud said slowly. "Not knowing that I was there already, your sister went there because she felt the need to wash the dust of the journey off. I was already through with my bathing. I then stood guard as she splashed water on her face, arms, and feet. We will never again be so careless as to not stand guard over you while you sleep."

Damita's mouth opened in startled surprise that Iron Cloud told an untruth so easily, yet the more she thought about it, the more she knew that it was a most honorable thing for him to do, to lie in her behalf. She would never want Timothy to know why she hadn't been with him. He was too young. He wouldn't understand. She could not take a chance of his opinion of her becoming tarnished!

Timothy shrugged as he looked from Damita to

Iron Cloud. "That's all right," he said cheerfully. "I proved that I can take care of myself."

Damita went to him and hugged him, looking past his shoulders at Iron Cloud and smiling a silent thank-you to him. "If anything had happened to you, I wouldn't be able to stand it," she murmured. "Timothy, you are so precious to me."

Embarrassed by her treating him as a child, especially now that he had proven his ability to perform as a man to Iron Cloud, Timothy wriggled free. "Sis, you're making too much of this," he boasted. "You know that things are different here than in Boston. There will be many times when I'll have to fend for myself. You can't be with me every minute of the day." He went and stood over the bobcat. "I heard some sort of noise. It woke me up. I guess it was the bobcat sniffing around the camp."

He glanced over his shoulder at the rabbit that was crispy brown over the fire, its juices still dripping into the flames, setting off a pleasant odor. "I'm sure it was after the rabbit," he said. "I guess it was as hungry as us."

He knelt over the bobcat, now full of pity over the slain animal, seeing it as a handsome creature, long-legged with large paws and a rather short body and tufted ears. Although its fur was stiff, it was pretty with its pale, reddish-brown coloring and black spots.

He stroked its spotted fur, still feeling warmth in the body. "I truly didn't want to shoot it," he said softly. "But when it came eye to eye with me and hissed, revealing a mouth full of sharp teeth, then got into a leaping position as though ready to pounce on me, I had no choice but to grab up the rifle . . . and . . . and shoot."

Iron Cloud went to stand over Timothy and the slain animal. "No one wants to kill a defenseless animal unless forced to," he said, placing a firm hand on Timothy's shoulder. "Since the white man came to the land of the red man, there have been too many senseless killings. But what you did tonight was an act of courage, Timothy. Your life was in danger. You defended yourself as though you were a man. Feel pride, not shame, over having shot the animal."

Timothy looked up at Iron Cloud. "At first, I did feel proud, Iron Cloud," he said, his voice breaking. "But now . . . seeing the animal lying so still, so defenseless, I feel sorry for it."

"That is because you are a person of heart—of compassion," Iron Cloud said, nodding. "That is good. Were more white people like you, the destruction of the buffalo would not have happened and would not have brought the Omaha's industry of hunting buffalo in Nebraska to a close. It is too late for the buffalo, but never for the Omaha. My people will not be stopped by the evil mistakes of the white man! We will again hunt wild game once we reach Illinois."

Damita walked over to Iron Cloud and stood beside him as she gazed down at the bobcat. "What should we do with it?" she asked softly, shivering at the sight of the bobcat's green eyes seeming to stare holes through her, although it was sightless in its death sleep.

"I shall go and gather our clothes by the creek and return to the campsite," Iron Cloud said, turning to her, finding it hard not to reach a hand to her hair and run his fingers through the long golden tresses. But in front of Timothy, much caution must be paid to his outward actions of loving and desiring his sister!

"Then," Iron Cloud continued, "while you dress and take the meat from over the fire and prepare it for us all to eat, I shall take the slain animal far away and bury it beneath a heavy covering of leaves and twigs. It is best to get its scent away from our camp, if we want to get a full night of sleep. We do not want other animals following the scent of the slain animal to us. We need a full night of rest before we move on tomorrow."

He left and returned soon with their clothes. Damita accepted her shoes and slipped into them quickly, and while Iron Cloud was gone with the animal, she busied her hands by taking the meat and stripping its bones, placing equal amounts in three small wooden plates that Iron Cloud had removed from his buckskin travel bag, all the while Timothy rattling on about the day's adventures, and the fact that he had shot so accurately when placed in danger.

"I feel like a grown man," Timothy said, plopping down on a blanket beside Damita as they sat there, waiting for Iron Cloud's return. "Wouldn't Papa have been surprised to know that I actually shot something? He didn't allow us near guns, you know. He just didn't know that I practiced often with my friend Peter in the forest, close to his house. We practiced every time he could sneak the pistol from his father's desk. I could always out-shoot him."

Damita paled as she looked aghast at Timothy. "Timothy, that was a dangerous, sneaky thing to do," she scolded. "Mama and Papa trusted you, and you were actually handling and shooting fire-arms? Mama would have fainted, had she ever found out. Papa would have whipped you with the razor strop until you begged for mercy! You are so lucky you were never found out."

Again Timothy shrugged. "But they didn't," he said, laughing softly. "And here I am, without a scratch." He gazed into the dark forest, where Iron Cloud had entered. He frowned. "And had I not practiced firing a gun then, who knows if I would be alive now? The bobcat would have pounced on me. I did not have time to study a gun, trying to figure out how to fire it. I knew. And I *did*."

"Yes, I am sure you are right about that, but you should have never gone behind our parents' backs," Damita scolded.

Timothy frowned. "Damita, you know how strict they were," he said sullenly. "They were treating me like a girl instead of a boy. Had they had their way, I would have worn dresses instead of breeches! I had to do what I did, or lose respect for myself and never be a man in the eyes of my friends."

Damita leaned over and drew Timothy into her arms. "I know," she murmured, stroking his thick head of hair. Then she flinched when he drew away, scowling at her.

"See what I mean?" he said sourly. "Sis, most times you treat me like a girl, too. Please quit hugging and petting me in front of Iron Cloud. I don't want him to think I'm a sissy!"

Damita was speechless. "Timothy, by your bravery you have just proven that you are anything but a sissy," she murmured. "And an occasional hug will not make you look less a man in anyone's eyes. Everyone needs hugs and affection from time to time. If not, the person would become empty and embittered, just like cousin Jonathan. I am sure he never had his share of love while he was growing up. If I recall, his father was a distant sort of man, and his mother died when he was young. I would think that he yearned for what you are now denying!"

A noise in the brush to their right drew them into a quick silence. They knew that it was not Iron Cloud arriving, for they would have seen him quite clearly at this distance.

It had to be another animal, dangerously close again to the camp!

"Lord, Timothy," Damita whispered, paling. She watched Timothy pick up the rifle, knowing that perhaps again, much too soon, his bravery and ability to fire a firearm accurately would be put to a test. "What if it's the mate to the slain bobcat? It could be filled with hate over the loss of its loved one."

"If it's another bobcat threatening us," Timothy whispered to Damita, his heart throbbing from a mixture of excitement and fear. "I'll have no choice but to shoot it."

Both gasped and stood with wide eyes as a tiny bobcat kitten came into view, sniffing the ground, stopping where the slain bobcat had lain only moments ago, its blood a red splotch on the ground.

Timothy lowered the rifle to his side. "It's a kitten!" he said, watching the small bobcat, no larger than a housecat, continue to sniff the ground. When it lay down on the spot of the slain animal, as though finding comfort in the scent, Timothy crept over to it. He lay his rifle aside and reached a hand to the tiny animal, melting through and through when the kitten curled out its tongue and licked him.

"My goodness," Damita whispered, falling instantly in love with the kitten. She knelt beside Timothy. "That must have been its mother." She reached a hand and stroked the animal's stiff fur. "Now it's orphaned, just like us, Timothy."

"And hungry," Timothy said, gently picking the kitten up into his arms. "Don't you bet its mother had come into camp to try and steal the meat from over the fire for her kitten?"

"Perhaps," Damita said, rising to her feet and following Timothy back to the fire, where the meat lay on the wooden plates. She eased down on the ground beside her brother as Timothy took some meat from his plate and began feeding it to the kitten. Her heart was stolen even more severely as the kitten ate eagerly from Timothy's hand, so trustingly, so hungrily....

"I want to keep the kitten for my pet," Timothy said, begging Damita with his eyes.

"A kitten soon grows up to be an adult," Damita said, again reaching over to stroke the tiny animal with the trusting eyes and a purr similar to a cat's.

"Until then, I would like to care for it," Timothy said softly.

Tears came to Damita's eyes, glad to see the gentle side of Timothy surface when only moments ago he had been trying to prove that he was tough and untouchable. She started to reach a hand to his hair, to weave her fingers through it, then stopped and laid her hand on her lap as she smiled at him.

"All right, you can keep the animal, if Iron Cloud agrees," she said softly.

Iron Cloud stood only a few feet away, watching the touching scene, his eyes and heart absorbing it all. He watched a moment longer, then walked into camp. He knelt down beside Timothy and stroked the small animal's stiff fur.

"The *waho-the-ge*—orphan—is yours as long as it does not cause trouble for my people," Iron Cloud said, nodding. He turned the kitten over, then set it back to the ground. "It is a she. When she gets larger, be prepared to say goodbye. No animal should be without those of its own kind."

"Thanks," Timothy said, beaming up at Iron

Cloud. "Thanks so much." He stroked the kitten's fur, looking adoringly down at it. "Since you are hardly more than a baby, I will name you Baby."

Damita rose to her full height alongside Iron Cloud, and while Timothy was so absorbed in his new pet, they stole a quick kiss.

They then sat down and started eating, their hearts joined as though one.

Chapter Eleven

They had slept soundly for a full night and half of the next day, and then had resumed their travels without stopping. In the early dawn hours that next morning, as they rode their horses through a forested land, the day birds were just awakening, the nighthawk's "peent" was dying down, and the whippoorwill had just ceased its chorus.

A long-winged silhouette moved silently across the grass tops, and a short-eared owl settled down. A pair of cowbirds squeaked in a tree above, and a meadowlark gave the morning's first sweet song.

It was this time of morning, when the world seemed coated in grey and the sky lacked definition, at the period when the morning light refused to disclose whether the sky was cloudy or clear, that they finally caught sight of the Omahas' camp. The aroma of food wafted through the air from the large outdoor campfire.

Iron Cloud edged his horse close to Damita's. "Yonder are my people," he said, reaching to gently touch her cheek. "Now *your* people, White Willow."

Touched by Iron Cloud's continued gentlenesses to her, her heart almost melted into his, and her pulse raced as he, for a moment, caressed her face with his fingertips. She was beginning to accept her newly assigned name, in truth thinking that it was quite beautiful, and she had begun to drop her guard about her feelings about Iron Cloud around Timothy. There was no way on God's earth that she could hide her feelings for this wonderfully handsome Omaha chief. Timothy could not have helped but see it in her eyes when she looked at Iron Cloud, or heard it in her voice when she spoke his name.

A sudden fear came to her, making her eyes waver. "You see me and my brother much differently than your people will," she murmured. "What if your people don't accept us? What if they purposely make life hard for us?"

"My word is law among my people," Iron Cloud said firmly, his jaw tightening. "What I say, they do."

"But Iron Cloud, you are moving your people from their homeland because of people whose skins are white," Damita fretted. "Timothy's skin and mine are white. Surely they will resent us because of what the corrupt white people have done to them."

"Some will," Iron Cloud said, dropping his hand

to his side. "But they also will conform, in time. They must, for I will instruct them to do so!"

He looked past Damita at the hustle and bustle of his people's camp. He was proud to see that they were already discovering that life was more than answering to the white agent at Fort Calhoun. They had searched and found much game for food. They were even enjoying preparing it, it seemed, for he could hear much laughter among those who were cooking and talking. Even the children, as they romped and played around the fire with their dogs, seemed more gay and filled with anticipation.

Damita followed his gaze and her apprehensions lessened, for everyone seemed content enough with their move from Nebraska. She scanned their faces to see if she could find one among them that wore a brooding expression, and found none. Perhaps they had been so miserable under the government's rule that anything was better than continuing that sort of life.

Her thoughts were catapulted back to Jonathan, wondering how he had taken her and Timothy's absence. Had he sent out a scouting party to search for them? Or had he just shrugged off the fact that they were gone, and was glad to be rid of his responsibility for them?

He had to know that they had not left on their own. Jonathan knew Damita well enough to know that she would not have left her trunks of clothes behind unless forced to. All of her favorite dresses were in her trunks. All of the mementos of her parents were in the trunks.

A strange sort of emptiness assailed her, to think of what would happen to those mementos now. They would mean absolutely nothing to Jonathan. He would either sell them, to get what monies he could from them, or he would burn them.

Either way, they were no longer close by to cherish whenever Damita became lonesome for her parents.

"Let us go now to my people," Iron Cloud said, snapping his horse's reins to urge his appaloosa into a soft trot on through the forest. "It will be good to be with them again. I have feared for them while gone for so long from them. I thought I had weeded out those who have spoken against my cause, but there could still be some among my people who kept their viewpoints hidden until I was gone. It is those who could have spoken against my cause, causing discouragement among those who have already lost too much at the hands of the white people. Those people who have so little now are the ones who sway easily to words spoken greedily to them. They hunger for a decent life. I have promised them that. It is my hope that they do not become discouraged before we reach the land of our hopes and dreams."

"You seem to expect so much from Illinois," Damita said, worried that he did. "How can you be sure that you will find peace and solitude there?"

She was aware that there were scarcely any lands left, in any sections of the country, that were not ruled by the white man's law. She did not see how it could be any different in Illinois.

"My scouts traveled to Illinois and saw for themselves that in the southern part of that vast land, there are no forts, or agents close by, to create the same sort of problems that have been created for my people, and all Indian tribes, in Nebraska," Iron Cloud said. "We will not be assigned to a reservation. And the headquarters of the Superintendent of Indian tribes, to whom the subordinate officers, called agents, are to report, is at Saint Louis, far enough away from the land of Illinois to give us cause for comfort. He hired your cousin for Fort Calhoun. This makes him no better a man. I do not wish to deal with him, nor anyone like him. In Illinois, it seems I do not have that worry to burden my shoulders!"

"I hope it works out for you," Damita said softly. "I totally sympathize with your cause, Iron Cloud."

As they drew closer to the Omaha camp, the barking of the dogs grew louder. Suddenly there was a commotion beside Damita, on her left side where Timothy rode on his horse with his bobcat kitten secured in a makeshift sling that Iron Cloud had made for her out of a buckskin hide.

Damita looked quickly around and her mouth dropped open in surprise as she watched Baby finally manage to squeeze from the sling and jump to the ground. Soon she was bounding clumsily toward the sound of the barking dogs.

"No!" Timothy cried, waving his hands in the

air. "No, Baby! Come back! The dogs will tear you to pieces!"

Damita flashed a quick look at Iron Cloud. "Iron Cloud, do something!" she shrieked, her voice filled with desperation. She could not deny how attached she had become to the kitten herself.

Iron Cloud frowned and sighed heavily, then sank his heels into the flanks of his powerful steed and galloped toward the kitten that had now attracted the dogs from the camp, all of them heading toward her.

As Iron Cloud reached Baby, he leaned low over the side of his horse and grabbed her just as the dogs made great leaps toward Iron Cloud's horse.

Timothy and Damita rode up beside him. Iron Cloud shoved Baby into Timothy's arms, then grabbed his rifle from the gunsling on the horn of his saddle and fired several shots into the air. He lowered his rifle to his side as the dogs retreated, yapping and howling from fright.

Thrusting his rifle back into its gunsling, Iron Cloud gave Timothy, then Damita, an agitated stare. "Now you see the complications of having a pet bobcat?" he grumbled. "It is playful. The dogs are not!"

With that small, determined speech, he rode away from them and met his people, who had heard the shots and the excited, frightened dogs and had come with their firearms and bows and arrows to see the cause. Now that their view was not impeded by the trees, and they saw Iron Cloud, they ran up to him as he wheeled his horse to a shuddering stop.

"You have made a safe journey!" one said, reaching to touch his hand, as though they were touching one who was worshipped. "We will give much thanks to Wakoda for his blessings!"

Iron Cloud dismounted and shared many hugs and kisses, and then he realized why there was a sudden silence among his people, and why they were slowly backing away from him.

He turned and watched as Damita and Timothy came closer on their horses, soon stopping to dismount. Stepping between them, he locked an arm around their waists, Timothy holding on to Baby with all of his might as the dogs came into view again, lurking and sniffing.

Iron Cloud walked Damita and Timothy to where his people stood silently watching, much distrust in their eyes.

This, he also understood.

"My people, there will now be two living among us whose skin is not the color of ours," he said loudly, his gaze raking over the crowd of sullen faces. "But their hearts are good—are as one with you. Welcome them into your lives without hesitation, for, my people, they will now be sharing everything with you, as though born on this earth kin to the Omaha tribe!"

There were many gasps of disbelief and faces etched with shock, yet this soon faded as Iron Cloud began mingling among them, so that they could touch Damita and Timothy and get a closer look at them.

Iron Cloud looked proudly on, having known all along that Damita's smile had a way to melt anyone's heart—even those of his people, who had grown used to resenting and hating all white people.

He looked knowingly down at her as she turned a quick gaze in his direction. When their eyes locked, the message exchanged between them made Iron Cloud certain that their future together was sealed by sharing and loving.

He watched, then, as several young braves went to Timothy and gathered around him, each of them wanting to take turns touching and petting the bobcat kitten.

Iron Cloud saw the relief in Damita's eyes, as she also saw how quickly her brother was accepted by the young Omaha boys his age, the pet easing the awkwardness between them. This would make things much easier for Iron Cloud when he began training Timothy in the ways of the Omaha!

The strain of the presence of white people among them lessening by the moment, the Omaha women returned to their cooking pots to prepare the morning meal before they all resumed the long journey to Illinois.

Damita soon found herself sitting comfortably on blankets beside the communal outdoor fire, devouring an assortment of food from a wooden plate.

Iron Cloud sat beside Damita, eating just as vigorously, while Timothy sat away from them, sharing his meal with his bobcat kitten. Many young braves sat with him, each trying to talk to Timothy at the same time in the English that Iron Cloud had taught them, bombarding him with questions. Timothy seemed proud to be the center of attention, anxiously answering everyone between quick bites of meat and duck eggs that had been found on the banks of the river and boiled hard for eating.

And then suddenly Baby bounced from Timothy's lap and scampered away, and the children dropped their plates, laughingly running after him.

When the dogs began to follow, barking and snarling, Iron Cloud rose quickly to his feet and ran after the kitten himself, hoping that the dogs would soon accept the bobcat as part of the expedition to Illinois, or the kitten would have to be taken far away and left. He needed no more complications in his life. Getting his people to Illinois had to be his main concern—not a bobcat that riled the dogs from morning till night!

Shooing the dogs away, gently slapping their rumps to get their attention, Iron Cloud was glad to see them scatter in many directions other than that taken by the bobcat. He looked ahead, noticing that the young braves and Timothy had stopped, venturing to go no farther. He wondered why, for it was apparent that none had caught the bobcat. Timothy adored the kitten and would stop at nothing to have him in his possession again.

Yet, he still stood, just staring ahead.

Iron Cloud scratched his brow as he came upon the gawking boys, now seeing what they were looking at—a travois attached to one of Iron Cloud's warriors' horses. With all of its might, the bobcat kitten was tearing into a bear pelt wrapped around something long and narrow, hissing as its claws slowly uncovered something.

When the bear pelts finally fell away, revealing exactly what the kitten had smelled and had caused him to go into a frenzy, Iron Cloud paled and found himself staring in disbelief.

He grabbed up the kitten and thrust her into Timothy's waiting arms, then stared down again at the object on the travois. "The Sacred Pole!" he gasped, a strange sort of foreboding overwhelming him. "How can it be? The ... Sacred ... Pole!"

A presence at his side drew his head around and he found himself eye to eye with Black Coyote, his most troublesome warrior. "You? Why did you do this, Black Coyote?" he said, his voice rising. He clasped his fingers tightly to Black Coyote's bare shoulders and gave him a shake. "Tell me. Why did you do this unholy thing? You stole that which is the most sacred to our Omaha people. You took this, the emblem of the Omaha's governmental authority, from the Tent of War. Tell me! Why? It is not our right to have it. And how? Did you kill the Keeper of the Sacred Pole to get it? Did you?"

Iron Cloud's face was hot with anger, and his breathing was shallow as he awaited an expla-

nation that he knew would not be enough to make
up for the wrong one of his warriors had done to
the Omaha people.

Black Coyote defied Iron Cloud with a set jaw.
"I took the Sacred Pole so that our people would
be able to take their hearts and gifts to it," he said.
"You know that if it remained in Nebraska, none
of our people would ever be blessed by it again.
It is not right that our people are forced to sacrifice
so much. We are giving up our homeland. Why
must we also give up the rights to the Sacred
Pole?"

Iron Cloud stared in disbelief at Black Coyote,
then tightened his fingers on his shoulders and
leaned his face closer into his. "It was understood
by all of us that the Sacred Pole would be left
behind where it belongs, in the Tent of War, and
everyone but you, it seems, accepted this," he
growled. "How did you steal it? And did you kill
the Keeper? Did you?"

"Stealing it was easily done," Black Coyote said,
gritting his teeth with pain as he tried to jerk free
of Iron Cloud without success, only causing Iron
Cloud's fingers to bite into his flesh more severely.
"And, no. I did not harm the Keeper. I stole it while
he was sleeping."

"You were wrong to do this thing," Iron Cloud
said in a low hiss. "And you will have to be punished. But first, you will have to return the Sacred
Pole to its rightful place." He dropped his hands
away from Black Coyote, shaking his head slowly
back and forth. "You put me in a bad position.

Your foolishness will cause me to have to leave my people again, when they need me the most." He glared at Black Coyote. "To be sure you take the Sacred Pole to its proper resting place, I will have to accompany you there." Again he leaned close into Black Coyote's face. "When we return, you will receive your rightful punishment."

Damita crept close and gazed down at what she now knew was the Sacred Pole. From what she could gather, it was made of cottonwood, the bark having been removed and the pole shaved and shaped at both ends so that the top, or head, was rounded into a cone-shaped knob, the lower end trimmed to a dull point. Upon the top of the pole was tied a large scalp. About one inch from the head was a piece of hide bound to the pole by bands of tanned skin. This wrapping covered a basketwork of twigs, now shriveled with age, which was filled with feathers and the down of the crane.

She looked up at Iron Cloud as he stepped to her side. "What is a Sacred Pole?" she questioned softly. "Why is there such a fuss about it?"

He took her by the arm and led her away from the throng of people behind a thicket, where he took her hands, holding them tenderly. "I do not have time to explain now, but upon my return, I will tell you the history of the Sacred Pole and why it is so important to my people," he said.

"When you return?" she questioned, her eyes beseeching him.

"I have no choice but to return to the reservation

with Black Coyote," he growled out. "I must see that what has been stolen is returned."

"But—but that could be so dangerous," Damita said, not telling him that not only was she worrying about him, but also herself. A keen apprehensiveness swept through her at the thought of being left among his people without him. Except for her brother, she would not have a friend among them to whom she could confide, or with whom she could seek comfort.

"Yes, it is very dangerous," Iron Cloud confirmed. "When it was discovered that the Sacred Pole was missing, I am sure word was sent far and wide among the Omaha, to find the one responsible and kill him. Because I will be with the one accused, I could be blamed as well. But what I hope is that we can sneak in and replace the Sacred Pole without any disturbance, and leave just as quickly, so that I can bring Black Coyote back and hand out his punishment as I see fit!"

"But Iron Cloud, when you left, it was a secret parting from the reservation," Damita further said, worry furrowing her brow. "Each return will chance your discovery and perhaps lead to your death!"

"Or perhaps to much persecution of my people," Iron Cloud said, nodding. "But it is a chance I must take. The Sacred Pole must be returned to its proper place at all cost. That is the way it is. If it is Wakoda's wish that I return to you and my people unharmed, then so be it. If not, then a new chief will be appointed and his dreams and desires will be fulfilled, not mine."

Damita paled. "But what of me and Timothy if you don't return?" she said, her voice quavering. "We are here only because of you, Iron Cloud. Without you, what could we expect?"

"You would be free to return to Nebraska, of course," Iron Cloud said matter-of-factly.

He looked intently down at her for a moment longer, then swept her into his arms and gave her a long, meltingly hot kiss. Something told her then that she had nothing to fear. He would return. She had only just found him and the paradise they shared, and it was their destiny to be together forever.

He left her and went back to his people, directing them as to what they should do while he was gone again.

Then he mounted his horse, Black Coyote on his horse ahead of him, his wrists bound behind him, and the Sacred Pole again tightly bound to the travois that was now attached to Iron Cloud's horse.

Just as Iron Cloud started to ride away, he turned to Damita and locked eyes with her. Her heart almost melted into his when he leaned over and reached a hand to her face and for a moment caressed it with his fingertips.

"White Willow, I *will* return," he whispered, then rode away, his shoulders squared, his chin held proudly high.

Damita stifled a sob behind her hands, then turned and walked back with the others to the large outdoor fire. She sat down beside Timothy, who still held Baby in his arms. Damita and Timothy huddled closer together and looked slowly around them, both realizing their aloneness.

Chapter Twelve

It grew dark rapidly. As the night came over the valley, a faint silvery mist appeared above the water; the frogs began to boom and croak, and soon the forest was alive with the calls of insects.

Damita sat beside the communal fire, having passed her first day among Iron Cloud's people without any problems. Everyone had gone on their way, doing their chores, and at the end of the day were passing their time in an assortment of activities as they awaited their chief's return, treating her kindly enough as an occasional smile and nod came her way.

Timothy had become the center of attention again among the young braves of the tribe. They had fashioned a ball out of thin strips of leather and were laughing and crawling on the ground as they rolled the ball back and forth among themselves, teasing the bobcat kitten as she tried to capture it from them.

The women sat around the fire. For the most part, they were busying their hands, some sewing fancy beadwork onto moccasins or dresses. The young women of the group sat sidewise, their legs drawn round closely to the right. The older women sat with their feet stretched out in front of themselves. The younger girls, who stayed together in clusters, talking softly among themselves, seemed to have been taught to move noiselessly, creeping around almost too timidly, their hair neatly braided, some wearing buckskin garments, others cotton acquired at Fort Calhoun.

The men were sitting away from the fire and the women, most resting their backs against the trunks of trees. Their day at a close, some were leisurely smoking their long-stemmed calumet pipes, others carving what appeared to be bows. They were talking in their Omaha language, with a few English words scattered here and there, and they seemed content enough, apparently having forgotten the confrontation over the Sacred Pole and that one of their warriors had stolen it.

Damita had to wonder if they were concerned at all about Iron Cloud's welfare and whether or not he would return alive. It gave her a sick feeling at the pit of her stomach to think about the danger he was placing himself in by trying to return that which had been stolen.

Damita turned away from the men and groaned faintly. The headache that had begun earlier in the afternoon had worsened. She looked down at the plate of food on the ground beside her, which she had felt too ill to eat.

She swallowed hard, realizing how dry her mouth had become only during these past several minutes. She placed a hand over her mouth and coughed into it, the effort causing her head to ache even more.

Fear mounting inside her that she might be coming down with measles, she shot her brother a troubled glance, and then the young children that surrounded him.

Measles?

Oh, Lord, she could give the disease to everyone in the camp!

Her thoughts went back to that day she had held the Sioux baby—the moment of discovery that it had the measles. At that moment, she had become exposed to the disease herself.

So much had happened so quickly after that— her abduction, her flight from Fort Calhoun with Iron Cloud—that she had forgotten about the measles, and that she might get them. Even the day they had found the slain mother and child it had not come to her to worry about herself.

A wave of heat swept suddenly over her, and the skin at the back of her neck and shoulders prickled with a chill. Her eyes widened, realizing that she now had a temperature!

A quick panic seized her, knowing that she must separate herself from everyone, even her beloved brother! She stared at him with a beating heart, knowing that to separate herself from him, she must leave him with total strangers—not only strangers, but a tribe of Indians. If Iron Cloud were there, that would be different. She knew of his affection for Timothy. But without Iron Cloud, Timothy would be alone.

Torn with what to do, Damita clasped her shawl more tightly around her shoulders as another chill raced across her flesh. She felt a presence at her side and turned her head to see who it was, then rose quickly to her feet to step back from the woman who was approaching her, afraid of exposing her to what she now knew for sure was the beginnings of the dreaded disease.

The woman gave her a startled stare, then spoke softly. "I did not mean to frighten you," Girl Who Laughs said. She carried a blanket thrown over her left arm. "I have come to offer you this blanket. I saw you shiver twice. Although it is a warm night, if one is not used to the forest, she can experience a chill easily."

Another chill scourging her flesh, her brow growing hotter as her temperature mounted, Damita took another quick step back from the beautiful Omaha maiden. She clutched her arms across her chest. "Thank you for being thoughtful of me," she murmured.

As Girl Who Laughs held the blanket out for her, Damita reached out and took it, quickly placing it around her shoulders. "I do appreciate the blanket. And please know that I didn't move away from you because I was frightened."

She moved back another two steps from the woman, so fearing for this sweet person who had offered her the blanket out of the kindness of her heart. "It is not that I was frightened by you," she tried to explain. "It is—it is because I am ill. Please don't get any closer. I do not want to spread the illness to you."

Timothy came suddenly running up to Damita, Baby now leashed with a rope. "Sis, see what Lean Elk gave me?" he said, smiling from ear to ear. "A rope made from nettles gathered in the fall. The rope is for Baby, so she can't get away from me and get into trouble again. Wasn't that nice, Sis? Lean Elk and I have become fast friends!"

Lean Elk stepped up next to Girl Who Laughs, and leaned into her embrace as she wrapped an arm around his slim waist. "Mother, do you see? Timothy is my friend forever," he boasted. "We will learn much about life together."

"That is good," Girl Who Laughs said, smiling down at Lean Elk. She gazed at Damita, pride in her smile. "My son is a good boy. His heart matches that of his father, who is no longer with us. Gray Elk was a man of compassion. It is a trait that makes his son liked by all youths of our tribe and admired by the elders."

Seeing Girl Who Laughs' pride in her son made Damita step even farther away from her and Lean Elk, and to make sure that she made a distance between herself and Timothy. "Timothy," she murmured, suddenly realizing exactly what she must do to keep others from the harm of measles, if they had not already been exposed by her being among them. "Don't get any closer. I'm ill. Remember how Father taught us about the danger of measles? And that it was highly contagious?"

Timothy paled and stared wide-eyed up at Damita. "Yes, Sis," he said, swallowing hard. "I remember."

"Timothy, we both were exposed the other day, at the fort, by a Sioux baby that had the disease," she said, her mounting fever causing her to feel lightheaded. "You may have passed the incubation period without contracting the disease. I am not as lucky. I am certain that I am coming down with it."

Damita turned her head away and coughed into her cupped hand. She cleared her throat, then turned back to Timothy. "I must leave the camp for a while," she said, fear gripping her heart at the mere thought of going away, alone, to fend for herself totally, in order to keep her brother and the Omaha safe from the disease. "You must stay here, away from me. I will stay away until my crisis is past."

Timothy started to rush to her, but Damita saw him just in time to hold her hands out before her. "No," she said, a sob lodging in her throat. "You must understand the dangers, Timothy. I must leave. You have no choice but to stay behind."

"But, Sis, maybe you're wrong. Maybe it's not measles," Timothy said, choking back the urge to cry, not wanting to behave like a girl and be shamed in the eyes of the Indians, especially Lean

Elk! He did not want to jeopardize such a friendship by appearing to be a sissy, or worse yet, a coward!

"I'm not going to stay around here any longer to wait and see if the red blotches appear," Damita said, dying inside to take Timothy into her arms and hug him tightly to her, both needing comforting from the other.

"But . . . where will you go . . . ?" Timothy stammered, twining the rope so tightly around his fingers in his fear that it cut off the blood flow from them, numbing them. He quickly loosened the rope, yet continued staring up at Damita, hoping that she would change her mind. He was afraid, not so much for himself, but certainly for his sister!

"Since we left Fort Calhoun, I have learned many ways of survival in the wilds from Iron Cloud," she murmured. "I will go just a short distance away. I will make camp. I will build a fire as I have seen Iron Cloud start so many. I will return as soon as I feel it is safe for me to do so."

"Let me go with you, Sis," Timothy said, trying not to sound as if he were begging. "You will need someone to care for you. You will need someone to protect you. You saw how accurate a shot I am with the rifle. Let me stand guard. It is only right that I do this for you. You must allow it!"

"No," Damita murmured. "I can't. I'm sorry, Timothy. I just . . . can't."

Damita turned her watery eyes to Girl Who Laughs. "My brother and your son have become friends," she said, again coughing behind a hand. She took a deep breath. "Would you be so kind as to look after Timothy in my absence? It would lessen my burden so much if you would."

Girl Who Laughs looked cautiously from Damita to Timothy, then back at Damita again. "Your brother is welcome at my camp," she said softly. "And do not fear. I will treat him as though he were my own son." Her dark eyes softened with sympathy. "I will pray to Wakoda that you will be among the healthy again soon."

"Thank you," Damita said, grateful tears coming to her eyes. She started to say something else to Timothy, but he had turned and had gone to where his blankets were rolled neatly beside hers on the ground, back from the communal fire. She watched as he stooped and picked up her belongings for her. Then he clasped his hand tightly around the rifle that Iron Cloud had given to him to keep, after he had proved that he was capable of handling one.

Timothy went back to Damita. He did not get any closer to her than she allowed. Placing her belongings on the ground between where they stood, he also motioned with his rifle for her to see, then lay it with the rest.

"You take the rifle, Sis," he said thickly. "You may not feel like killing an animal for your supper, or may not even feel like eating for a day or so, but you will at least have the firearm for protection."

Damita felt much pride for her brother at this

moment, for she knew that inside himself he was battling the same emotions as she over this newest dilemma they had been catapulted into. She tried to be just as brave while finding it hard not to rush to him and grab him to her, and never let him go. She wasn't sure how long she would be gone. There were two types of measles. One was more severe. One lasted longer. Only time would tell just how ill she was going to be, or whether she could cope alone.

Or if Timothy was going to be sick, also. They had been inseparable, day and night, since their exposure to the disease.

"Timothy, soon things will be all right," Damita said, bending to gather the blanket roll into her arms, picking up the rifle with her free hand. "Please don't worry."

"How can I not?" Timothy said, his eyes revealing tears at their corners that he could not will to stay hidden. He glanced at the grazing horses, and then back at Damita. "Your horse. Should I get it?"

"No," Damita murmured. "The horse would be an added burden. I will walk as far as I feel I must, then make camp. That means, Timothy, I won't be that far away. Knowing that, surely you can feel better about my leaving."

Girl Who Laughs went to Timothy and took his hand, urging him to stand beside her. "Come," she said softly. "Come with me and Lean Elk."

"Do what you must," she said to Damita. "And thank you for being so thoughtful of my people. I

155

know of the disease measles. Some years ago, many of our people died because of it."

"Then it would be best not to speak too openly to your people of my leaving, or why," Damita said. "There is no need to cause alarm among them."

"You will be missed," Girl Who Laughs said, her eyes wavering. "How could you not be? It is obvious that you are Iron Cloud's woman. Many eyebrows will lift when they realize you are gone. But I will try and explain, without causing undue alarm. My people listen well to me. My name was given to me because I love life and laugh often. I cause my people to laugh. It has brought me very close to them. They depend on me to lift their spirits. Now, when they discover why you are gone, they will lean on me again, to assure them that none will get the disease from you."

"I pray that none will," Damita said softly. She smiled down at Timothy, then turned and walked away, feeling her brother's eyes on her back, as though he were willing her to return to him.

If only she could!

If only she did not have to flee into the night, alone, like a lost soul!

Who was to say what she would come face to face with? And once she was truly taken by the illness, would she be able to defend herself?

Knowing that she had to plan well her path to where she would take refuge, she chose to walk beside the river. That way, she would be able to find her way back to the Omaha camp—and Timothy.

The forest was ever a thing of mystery at night, standing stately and untroubled. Vines clung to Damita's feet as she made her way slowly through the darkness. Lightheaded, she seemed to glide through the bushes as noiselessly as a shadow, her eyes intent on the ground before her. The wind among the branches was like a whisper wafting through the air toward her, frightening her. The night was ghostly with a kind of queer luminous darkness, like velvet, soft and heavy, yet with a sheen of light so that she could dimly see objects ahead of her.

Then she found what she considered the best campsite possible. Not far back from the river was a wall of rock, rising tall above her, above the treetops of the valley. She knew that on this one side she would be protected from sniffing animals in the night. In the front she would make a fire. The flames would protect her on all three opened sides. And what the flames would not protect, the rifle would!

"Except when I am asleep," she fretted to herself, almost too feverish to gather up wood for the fire.

She eyed the rock wall again, recalling a lean-to that Iron Cloud had built against a wall. If she could manage to get a lean-to built, that would give her a roof over her head. With a wall to her back, a roof over her head, and a fire sending out flames into the night, she could then perhaps fall to sleep with some semblance of peace.

She worked steadily until she dropped, exhausted, to the blanket spread before her fire, yet proud of her achievements. This was the first night of seeing to her own survival, and thus far she had succeeded.

"And just in time," she murmured, drawing a second blanket over her as chills completely wracked her body. She closed her eyes wearily. "Lord, I'm so tired. So very, very tired."

She snuggled more deeply into the blankets. "And so very, very sick," she mumbled, her throat so parched that she found it hard to swallow. She opened her eyes and gazed at the shine of the moon in the river, thirsty, yet too weak and tired to get herself a drink.

She closed her eyes again. "Tomorrow," she said to herself. "I must drink a lot of water starting tomorrow. I recall Papa saying that was important." She began to drift off. "Yes, tomorrow. I must drink ... a lot of water...."

Damita was lulled to sleep by the liquid notes of a whippoorwill, and roused awake again by the mournful complaints of what she surmised had to be a starving wolf; then she was startled by the "Who! Who! Who!" of the winged monarch of the dark, an owl.

She reached for the rifle and placed it close to her side. She stared into the flames of the fire, tears streaming across her flushed, hot cheeks.

"Iron Cloud," she whispered. "I miss you, Iron Cloud."

Her eyelids began to flutter closed again. "Iron Cloud, I . . . *need* you," she whispered again.

Chapter Thirteen

The night was bathed in moonlight when Iron Cloud and Black Coyote arrived at the outskirts of the Omaha village, in which was housed the Tent Of War, where Omaha people from wide and far came to offer gifts and their prayers to the Sacred Pole.

With Black Coyote always a few feet in front of him, giving him no easy way to escape from the punishment that was due him, Iron Cloud had ridden his horse upward to the crest of a great ridge. At the top, he came out on a bare cliff, where he could scrutinize the land and village below him. He wanted no interference while returning the Sacred Pole to its rightful resting place.

Down below, like a giant carpet, the forest clothed the hills and swept down to the level ground that reached into the Omaha village. Iron Cloud rested a hand on the pistol that was thrust into the waistband of his fringed breeches, not wanting to be forced to use it. To do so would mean killing his own people.

He cast Black Coyote a sour look, silently cursing him for having placed his chief in such an awkward position. Iron Cloud was revered by most who knew him, but this vision of him could change if he was suspected of having stolen that which was most sacred to the Omaha!

Iron Cloud saw no signs of movement in the village below or on its outskirts.

"Dismount and come to me," he said in a feral snarl at Black Coyote. "I will remove the ropes at your wrist, and then you are to remove the Sacred Pole from the travois. But keep it wrapped! It must be kept from view should we be accosted while taking it to the Tent of War."

Black Coyote squinted angry eyes at Iron Cloud as he slipped easily from his saddle. He stared at him a moment longer after his feet hit the ground, then with a grunt of dissatisfaction stepped close to Iron Cloud's horse and held up his bound wrists. He glowered at Iron Cloud as he cut the ropes; then as his hands fell loose to his sides, he went to the travois behind Iron Cloud's horse, uncoiled the rope that held the Sacred Pole in place on it, and lifted it easily into his arms. He turned to Iron Cloud, who had dismounted, and held the blanket-wrapped Sacred Pole in his arms as he would a child.

Iron Cloud nodded toward the slight path that led down from the butte to a straight stretch of

Cassie Edwards

land that led on to the village.

"You go before me," Iron Cloud said in a harsh whisper. "It is the best of times to enter the village. This time of night even the dogs sleep soundly!"

Black Coyote offered no response. Iron Cloud kept his distance behind him as they began their descent, the rocks on the path slippery beneath their moccasined feet. Iron Cloud sucked in a startled breath as several small rocks scattered and tumbled noisily down the hillside. In the still of the night, they sounded to him like distant thunder!

When the rocks reached the level land below and stopped, and the night was still once more, Iron Cloud surveyed the village and land again, sighing with relief when he still saw no signs of movement.

Even at this vantage point he could get a good look at the Tent of War, which sat back from the others on a slight rise of land, and saw that there were also no movements there.

He quirked an eyebrow when he saw a whisper of smoke rising from the smokehole. He had thought that Blue Wind, the Keeper of the Sacred Pole, would have been banished from the tribe for having failing in his duties—in allowing the pole to be stolen!

Instead, it appeared that all looked well with the Tent of War, and more than likely with the keeper. Everything seemed calm and serene.

Perhaps the people of this village had accepted their loss. Or, he wondered, were the Omaha warriors even now scarring the land with the hoofprints of their horses, looking day and night for the thief?

Iron Cloud had never had much trust in Black Coyote, yet he had never had proof of any crime of his. It had mainly been his attitude—his ways of stirring up trouble—that made Iron Cloud distrust him. He was always challenging someone for something, yet always being the loser in the end! As now he was the loser.

And perhaps even himself this time, Iron Cloud thought regretfully.

He gritted his teeth angrily together, planning to make an example of Black Coyote once they returned to their people. But what would his punishment be? He had not yet decided how Black Coyote would pay for his crime. But Iron Cloud knew it must be severe!

No one else must gamble with his status of chieftain by involving him in heinous crimes!

This was the last time!

The flat land finally reached, Iron Cloud went to Black Coyote's side. "You stay close beside me," he whispered harshly. "If you try and run, afraid to face Blue Wind, I will not hesitate to shoot you."

"I am a proud Omaha," Black Coyote hissed out. "I do not run. I face my crime with a lifted chin! Remember, Iron Cloud, I stole the Sacred Pole with only good intentions inside my heart. I did not want our people to be without it! I still see it as not fair to them, this decision of yours to travel far from our homeland, away from the Sacred Pole!"

163

"Before we began our long journey to Illinois, I asked those who did not agree with me to leave our village and not turn their eyes back to us!" Iron Cloud gritted out between clenched teeth. "You should have left then! We have no room among our people for discontentment! It is like a sore—it spreads among the people, contaminating their minds and happinesses! You have interferred too much, Black Coyote. You will pay dearly for this!"

Black Coyote offered no response, just gazed at Iron Cloud with squinted, angry eyes as their eyes met and momentarily held.

Not ever having had such disrespect from one of his warriors before, Iron Cloud was shaken within, yet he turned away from Black Coyote and nodded toward the village. "We must get on with our chore," he grumbled. "It is not far from the Tent of War. Come. We must do this thing and leave before the skies begin to lighten with morning. It is my desire to return quickly to our people and resume our journey to Illinois."

Iron Cloud's heart and soul reached out to his camp, where not only his people awaited him, but also his wondrous White Willow! She surely felt alone and misplaced. He could not allow her to feel that way for long. The word 'escape' might cloud all the memories of what he had promised her, and what they had already shared!

If he lost her, he would lose a large corner of his heart!

Not wanting to allow himself to think of anything but the problem at hand, not even the woman he loved, Iron Cloud moved stealthily on through the night and stiffened when he came to the Tent of War, not knowing what to expect once he entered it. If Blue Wind was there, he could be reasoned with. If someone else had been put in charge, Iron Cloud's fate was questionable.

Never running away from danger, always facing it straight on, Iron Cloud gave Black Coyote another nod, indicating that he should go inside the large, highly decorated tent first. Iron Cloud lifted the entrance flap for Black Coyote, then stepped inside behind him.

The soft glow of a central fire inside the tent mutely revealed everything to Iron Cloud as he raked the room with eager, questioning eyes. When he found the platform on which Blue Wind slept, he breathed somewhat easier, yet he knew that the hardest part was yet to come—placing the Sacred Pole on the floor and fleeing without Blue Wind being the wiser!

Again he nodded silent instructions to Black Coyote, who followed them by taking a step farther into the tent, then bending low to release himself of the blanketed Sacred Pole. Just as he placed it on the floor, a gasp surfaced from across the firepit.

Black Coyote straightened his back and jumped back to stand beside Iron Cloud. Iron Cloud found himself staring down at Blue Wind as he rose slowly from his sleeping platform, drawing a long, bearskin robe around his stooped shoulders. When

Blue Wind stepped around the fire and gazed with alarming disbelief down at the bundle on the floor, and then up at Iron Cloud, Iron Cloud took a quick step forward and placed a hand on Blue Wind's shoulder.

"I have come tonight to right a wrong," he said thickly. "What you see lying at your feet beneath wrapped blankets is the Sacred Pole." He glanced over at Black Coyote, his eyes narrowing. "He is the one who is responsible for its disappearance. He, who was trusted, turned traitor." He turned soft eyes to the Keeper. "But I have returned it. Now I will leave you to your duties as Keeper. And I offer you my most humble apologies before departing. Are you accepting of them?"

Blue Wind, his eyes filled with wisdom, his face lined with time, let his robe fall away, revealing a frail body clothed in only a brief breechcloth. His knees shook from weakness as he knelt beside the Sacred Pole. His lean fingers shook as he unveiled the sacred object, tears filling his eyes as he peered with what could be nothing less than total relief at seeing the Sacred Pole. He stroked his fingers down the full length of it, then gazed up at Iron Cloud.

"How can I, one who is filled with so much gratitude, say no to your apologies?" he said, his voice breaking. "Not another day could pass before I was forced to reveal the thievery of the Sacred Pole to the Omaha people. It was not something that I wanted to admit to them—that I was negligent in my duties. I did not want to tell them that they no longer had the sacred object to which they could direct their prayers. But tomorrow— yes, tomorrow, I would have been forced to, for I have put off too long already those who wished to kneel before it."

Iron Cloud was stunned to hear that the Keeper had not yet told anyone about the theft. Yet he could understand why. And it was true, that Blue Wind alone possessed the authority to perform the ceremony, to recite the rituals over the Sacred Pole, and to deny or accept anyone's request to view it.

"You have been put through much agony because of my warrior," Iron Cloud said, kneeling down beside the Keeper. "Again, I apologize."

Blue Wind turned to Iron Cloud and placed one of his hands on his shoulders. "It is because of you there will be no successor of my duties assigned tomorrow," he said thickly. "I will not be banished from the tribe because of my failure. I will always remember this, Iron Cloud. Always."

"I regret deeply that this happened," Iron Cloud said, rising slowly to his feet as Blue Wind pushed himself up to stand beside him. "And I will leave you now to return to my people."

"Before my death, it is my duty to assign my successor," Blue Wind said, bending to pick up his robe and drawing it snugly around his shoulders again. "I will assign someone of your village to be the Keeper so that you can have the Sacred Pole close by at all times. Iron Cloud, no one deserves this honor more than you."

Iron Cloud's eyes wavered, realizing that Blue Wind surely had no idea of Iron Cloud and his people's exodus to lands far away. Soon the word would spread, and then Blue Wind would know the impossibility of Iron Cloud's village being in charge of the sacred object. It would be too inconvenient for the rest of the Omaha for it to be placed in a village so far away.

"Do not speak of your death as though it will be tomorrow," Iron Cloud scolded, escaping any further discussion about the Sacred Pole becoming a part of his village, envied by all who did not have it. He wanted it no less than anyone else, yet he knew that he would have to learn to live without it, as would his people!

"I grow more frail each day," Blue Wind said, smoothing a hand across his lined brow. "It will not be long, Iron Cloud. One as aged as I feels these things. It seems written on the stars and clouds each day as I gaze up at them."

"Wakoda will bless you with many more winters." Iron Cloud folded his arms around the aged man and gave him a gentle hug.

Then he eased away from Blue Wind and turned to Black Coyote to tell him to apologize to Blue Wind, but to his astonishment, Black Coyote was gone! While he was so absorbed in trying to say the appropriate things to Blue Wind, Black Coyote had slipped away, escaping not only the blame in Blue Wind's eyes, but also Iron Cloud's punishment!

"He is gone!" Iron Cloud said, doubling his

hands into tight fists at his sides. He turned to Blue Wind. "He is not only a thief, but also a coward! I must go after him!"

Blue Wind walked with Iron Cloud out of the tent. "Go with care," he said, patting Iron Cloud on the back. "And thank you, Iron Cloud, for being a man of honesty and compassion. You have not only saved this old man's life, but also my honor and ability to face our people again."

"Peace be with you, forever," Iron Cloud said, again hugging Blue Wind. He then turned and began to run through the village and across the straight stretch of meadow, praying to Wakoda that Black Coyote had at least enough respect for his chief to have left his horse for his return to his people. He gazed ahead, seeing the first signs of daybreak along the horizon.

Puffing hard, he ran faster, moving swiftly and silently up the steep hillside, his smooth muscles rippling. When he reached the top of the butte, it was in the shining mist of morning and he was stunned to find that not only his horse awaited him there, but also Black Coyote's! Black Coyote had not taken the time to return for his horse and was even now on foot, or as Iron Cloud quickly surmised, hidden somewhere among the wigwams in Blue Wind's village.

His jaw set, his eyes peering downward at the village, he saw that Black Coyote was a clever Omaha warrior, indeed. He surely knew exactly what Iron Cloud would have to do when he discovered Black Coyote missing—exactly what Iron

Cloud *had* done! Gone to the horses, expecting both to be gone!

Instead, Black Coyote had stayed in the village, realizing that night was quickly changing to morning and that Iron Cloud would not want to enter the village again so that everyone would see him. He knew that Iron Cloud would not want to draw undue attention to himself and that Iron Cloud was too anxious to get back to his people to chance getting involved elsewhere.

"Yes, he is a clever man," Iron Cloud said, swinging himself into his saddle. He reached for the other horse's reins and tied them into his own, then started to leave, but stopped when he felt compelled to take one last look at this land that he loved—and already sorely missed!

Far across the gray expanse of valley below, the sun was turning to ruddy copper as it rose slowly into the sky. The air was crisp, a sweet breeze sweeping down over the pine-covered hills. As the white clouds sailed overhead, their shadows rippled over the treetops in the valley below. At times it seemed as though the tip of a great ridge caught the bottom of a flying cloud and sent the fluffy white mass rolling over and over again to the bottom of the valley. He could hear the distant hoots of an owl returning from the hunt and the cheeping of birds awakening in the trees.

The sound of a horse approaching him from behind made Iron Cloud stiffen and his hand go instantly to the pistol at his waist, pulling it out and cocking it. He wheeled his horse around and just as quickly slipped the pistol back into his waist-band.

"Iron Cloud?" Brian Davis said, reining in beside Iron Cloud. "My God, ol' buddy, I've been looking all over for you. And I find you here? What have you got up your sleeve? I went to your village and found only the skeletal remains of your wigwams. Where are your people? What are you doing here?"

Iron Cloud sighed deeply. He had not wanted to bring Brian in on his secret exodus, but it seemed that he now had no choice. Yet he would tell him only what little was necessary to satisfy his curiosity. And Brian was a friend. If he was asked to keep things quiet, he would. Unless he had already spread the word.

"Have you told anyone about finding my people gone?" Iron Cloud said, his voice strained.

"Not a soul," Brian said, frowning at Iron Cloud. "I figured you had a reason for not telling. And for leaving. I respect your judgment in all things. Everything that you do is for the bettering of your people."

Brian glanced down at Blue Wind's village, then back at Iron Cloud. "Why are you here?" he said, cocking an eyebrow. "Where are your people?"

"You say you respect my judgment," Iron Cloud said. "Then, my friend, you must trust me now, when I tell you that I cannot confide in you what I have chosen to do with, and for, my people. Why I am here, even, is something I do not wish to share with you."

Iron Cloud reached a hand to Brian's shoulder. "In time, my friend, I will tell you everything," he said softly. "But this is not the time. I must go. My people await me."

"I'd give my left arm to know what's going on in your mind, but I won't press you for answers," Brian said. "Go, Iron Cloud. And if you ever need me, you know where you can find me."

"I always remember that," Iron Cloud said, smiling warmly at Brian. He looked overhead at the sun that was now rising too quickly. "I must say a goodbye now, my friend."

"Ride with care," Brian said, giving Iron Cloud a mock salute as Iron Cloud turned his horse away from Brian's. "Oh, and another thing, Iron Cloud. Do you remember Jonathan Jacobs' beautiful cousin? The one I bought to the fort from the railhead? Her name was Damita."

Iron Cloud's spine stiffened and his insides splashed cold as he drew his reins tight and stopped again. He turned and stared at Brian. "Yes, I remember her," he said, his voice flat and even.

"Well, it seems that both she and her brother were abducted," Brian said matter-of-factly. Then he chuckled. "That Jonathan is as mad as a wet hen. Pity the person who abducted them. Jonathan won't rest until he sees the culprit hang."

"Yes, a pity," Iron Cloud said, then rode away, now realizing just how quickly he had to get back to his people—and his White Willow! Should Jonathan's soldiers search and find White Willow with them, his people would suffer for what he alone had chosen to do!

He sank his heels into the flanks of his appaloosa and lay low over its flying mane, forcing his steed into a hard ride across the land, filled with a sudden fear. Black Coyote! For vengeance, would Black Coyote stoop so low as to lead Jonathan and the soldiers to the village where his sentencing awaited him? To keep from being sentenced, would Black Coyote turn on his people to save his own neck? The thought of this happening caused Iron Cloud's heart to beat like claps of distant thunder.

His White Willow!

He had to get to his White Willow!

Chapter Fourteen

The morning mist was vanishing as the sun cleared the horizon. Damita had gathered up twigs from beneath the trees and had just placed them on the fire. Her whole body aching, she stretched out on the blanket beside the dancing flames.

She drew the blankets up beneath her chin; her eyes were glassy and her brow hot. Yesterday her temperature had fallen, but when she had awakened this morning, the fourth day of the dreaded illness, the fever had crept up again and the rash had appeared on her body as small, dull red, slightly raised spots. They were spreading and getting bigger now, joining together.

She was relieved that the rash had finally appeared, for she now knew that she did not have to fight the disease much longer.

Perhaps even tomorrow the rash might begin

fading. Or it could last for two more days, as she knew because of her studies to be a doctor.

These past days she had fed mainly on berries and wild grapes that she had found close to her campsite, and had drunk an abundance of water from the river. She had made sure to keep herself bathed with the cool water to help keep her temperature down. She had done all that was within her power to help herself through the disease.

And she knew that God was looking down from his Heavens, keeping a close watch on her, for no animals had come lurking anywhere near her while she had been alone.

Her fingers circled around the rifle at her side, should God's eyes momentarily stray elsewhere.

Lightheaded and miserable with the fever, Damita moaned. She tried to get more comfortable beneath the blankets and was tempted to shed them because of the heat of her body. But she kept them on, not wanting to catch a cold along with the measles!

Through the feverish haze of her eyes, something caught her attention in the grass only a few feet away. A web, spun intricately and beautifully by a busy spider, sparkled with the morning dew and took on the appearance of a fine jewel that one could pluck from the grass and place on one's coat.

Only a short distance from the lovely web were tiny mushrooms growing in a ring, and close beside this a circle of moss, with delicate purple flowers growing in it.

"Faeries visited me in the night," she whispered, smiling as she closed her eyes and became lost in thought of something quite pleasant in her memory.

She was recalling how Amy, her best friend in Boston, who was a student of faerie lore, had told her many tales while sipping tea together in her friend's lush flower garden behind her house. Amy would have become quite excited on this morning's findings, calling such discoveries authentic 'faerie rings', where faeries dance and sing by night.

"Traditionally," Amy had told Damita, "faeries are thought of as nature spirits in near-human form. Each tree, each flower, even fruits and vegetables, has its own beloved faerie."

Damita recalled, with another soft smile, how she had listened so intensely over her cup of tea as Amy had told her that many sightings of faerie shelters dating back to the turn of the century had been found in journals, actually stating the exact location and time of the sightings.

Even now Damita could envision faeries sipping tea from tiny seedpod cups while sitting on the leaf of a hydrangea blossom.

"There are many kinds of faeries," Amy had told her. "There are water faeries, garden faeries, moss faeries, and forest faeries. They have many shapes and names—elves, gnomes, dwarves, and brownies. They can be bad or good, hateful or helpful, forgiving or judgmental, serious or playful."

Damita had been immersed in the tales of faeries so often with her friend that they had become as real to her as breathing.

"I wish a wee family would appear on a leafy bower beside me right now," Damita whispered to herself, giggling. Then her smile faded, and she truly wished someone was there with her. She was so alone, so miserably alone!

Timothy!

Iron Cloud!

Oh, but for just one look at them, one touch from them ...

She soon found herself drifting into a fevered sleep. Her thoughts seemed to float from dreams to reality and back again. In her sleep, she was transported to the land of faeries.

She was in a mossy glen surrounded by fragrant herbs. She was nibbling on a faerie cake the size of a small coin with the little people, sitting beneath an umbrella of tiny hydrangea blossoms at a miniature grapevine table, a rose petal serving as the chair.

Soon she joined with them to hold their hands and dance in circles. As her feet left the ground with the faeries, she felt herself flying, soaring weightlessly through the air, feeling wondrously happy!

Iron Cloud rode relentlessly onward on his mighty steed, the days turning to night and then to day again, stopping only long enough to rest himself and his appaloosa, and to eat.

To pass the days more pleasantly on his journey

back to his people and the woman he loved, he entertained himself by listening to the wind singing through the grasses. Some days it had been the wind winding through the needles of the pines that had soothed his weary senses. The drumming of a woodpecker, water tumbling over gravelly streambeds, and moments of pure silence in the black depths of a cave had given him brief moments of peace.

And now he was finally able to see his people through a break in the trees a short distance away, and a keen relief flooded him to see that nothing had happened to them—that Jonathan and the soldiers had not searched this far yet for Damita and Timothy.

And, apparently, neither had Black Coyote told anyone of their location. Or if he had, Iron Cloud had beaten them there.

Iron Cloud knew that he must nevertheless make haste to move his people onward. They must reach Illinois before anyone tried to stop them!

Once there, they could lose themselves in the haunts of the mighty forests where no one could find them.

Riding on into the camp of his people, Iron Cloud was greeted with much rejoicing as the children rushed toward him as he dismounted, and the women and men came to him, their eyes eagerly wide and relieved.

He accepted many hugs, then quirked an eyebrow when he saw Timothy standing at the edge of the crowd, his pet bobcat on a leash at his side.

But he saw no sign of Damita anywhere! Did she care so little for him that she did not come to greet his return with at least a smile? She had openly feared for his safety before he left to return to his homeland.

Had her affection for him lessened while he was gone?

When his warriors began questioning him about Black Coyote and where he was, and why he had not returned with Iron Cloud for punishment, Iron Cloud explained the events at Blue Wind's village.

With everyone's curiosity satisfied, Iron Cloud turned his attention elsewhere. Gazing intently at Timothy, he strolled square-shouldered and with a proud chin through the crowd toward him, the people stepping aside to make way for him.

When he reached Timothy, Iron Cloud placed his hands on the young man's shoulders. "Your sister," he said, his voice steady, yet his heart pounding hard against his chest. "Where is she? I do not see her."

Iron Cloud looked past Timothy, toward the river, where the low-hanging tree limbs impeded his view. "Perhaps she is gone to the river to get water?" he said tentatively, then turned troubled eyes back to Timothy. "White Willow did not join my people to show her gladness for my arrival because she does not yet know of it?"

Timothy gazed wide-eyed up at Iron Cloud. "She is not at the river," he said, swallowing hard. "I do not know where she is, Iron Cloud."

Iron Cloud's jaw tightened and his heart leapt

with horror. "You ... do not know where she is?" he said gruffly, dropping his hands from Timothy's shoulders. "What do you mean you do not know? How can that be?"

"She became ill," Timothy said, his voice breaking. "She left so that no one would become contaminated with measles. She ordered even me to stay behind." His gaze dropped to the ground. "I had no choice, Iron Cloud. I had to do what she said." He lifted his eyes slowly back up to meet the anger in Iron Cloud's. "I'm so worried, Iron Cloud. She has been gone for several days now. What if ... ?"

Iron Cloud's anger raged within him as he stared at Timothy for a moment longer. Then he turned and glared at his people, realizing that even they had allowed her departure!

His woman!

His White Willow!

How could they have allowed it? She was a tiny creature, ill, surely unable to fend for herself.

A quick dread grabbed him at the pit of his stomach, as he realized that she could now even be starving to death, or—or lying dead, a victim of the animals that stalk in the night!

Without uttering another sound to his people or Timothy, afraid of what he might say during his tongue-lashing that he might regret later, Iron Cloud went back to his horse and swung himself into his saddle. He slapped his reins and rode up next to Timothy, gazing down at him with a forced voice that did not reveal his disappointment in this young man whose future he was going to shape and mold. It now seemed that it might be harder to put the values into this young man's heart that he himself had been taught by his father.

"Which way did she travel?" Iron Cloud asked, his fingers tight on his reins.

Timothy pointed in the direction that he had last seen his sister walking. "That way," he mumbled, feeling shame for not having gone to check on her, yet knowing that was not what she wanted. "She went by foot. She said she wouldn't be far, Iron Cloud."

Iron Cloud hesitated no longer. He sank his heels into the flanks of his horse and thundered away, realizing that what he had planned upon his first arrival was going to have to be delayed again. He could not continue his journey to Illinois until he had White Willow safe with him!

He realized that it was a gamble—delaying the departure—now that too many people were possibly hunting for him.

Yet he could not turn his back on his White Willow. She was now a part of him, as though when she breathed, it was an extension of his own breath!

Iron Cloud tried to place his thoughts where hers might have been while searching for a place to make camp during her illness. She was not familiar with the forests, so he concluded that she would stay beside the river, following it as a guide for her return to his people. He edged his horse through the trees until he came to the river and then rode in a slow lope beside it, his eyes ever searching ahead of him for any signs of her, or perhaps smoke from a campfire.

He did not have to go far, even though his horse covered the distance she had walked in perhaps twice the amount of time it had taken her. His heart leapt into his throat when he caught sight of a fire through the break in the trees up ahead, and as he drew closer, he saw the lean-to built adjacent to the wall of rock.

And then he saw her, where she lay so quietly between blankets beside the fire, only a portion of her face exposed, revealing her eyes closed in a deep sleep.

"She is safe," he whispered harshly to himself. "My woman, she is *alive*."

He drew his horse to a shuddering halt and slid quickly from the saddle, securing his reins to a low-lying limb of a tree. He hurried to Damita and knelt down beside her, studying her, seeing the red splotches spoiling her lovely face.

Without much forethought, he reached a hand to her face, flinching when he felt the heat against the palm of his hand and jerking his hand away from her when he suddenly found a rifle aiming up at him as she jerked the weapon from beneath the blankets before he was even aware that she was awake.

Having heard the sound of a horse approaching and the footsteps coming and stopping close beside her, Damita had pretended to be asleep. But when the hand had touched her face, she could no longer pretend. She had been forced to act!

Before she had turned her eyes to see who the intruder was, she had jerked the rifle from beneath the blankets, and at the very moment she turned her eyes around, she had placed the rifle barrel in the ribs of none other than the man she loved!

Eyes wide, gasping, Damita stared up at Iron Cloud, dropping the rifle to the ground. "Iron Cloud?" she murmured, then slid quickly away from him, leaving her blankets in an empty huddle beside him. "You must go away! You can't stay here! Please, Iron Cloud. Leave! Can't you see the splotches on my face? I have measles! I don't want you to get them!"

He rose to his full height and went to stand over her, sighing heavily as she scampered to her feet and moved shakily away from him.

"Iron Cloud, didn't you hear me?" Damita cried. "I'm ill. I have measles! I left your village so I wouldn't expose any of your people to the dreaded disease. I especially wouldn't want to contaminate you!"

Not to be dissuaded by anything that she said, Iron Cloud took a quick step toward her, too quickly for her to move farther away from him, and drew her into his arms. "My woman," he murmured, stroking her long and tangled hair. "You are most kind-hearted and courageous to put the welfare of my people before your own. That I found you here, unharmed, is a blessing sent down from Wakoda. Did you not know the dangers of living

183

alone in the forest? And how did you survive? You are from the city! You know not of the ways of the wilderness."

He eased her from his arms and held her away from him, seeing that except for the splotches, the blood-streaked eyes, and her obvious weakness, she had survived her quarantine quite well!

Although she was finding paradise in Iron Cloud's arms, and relished his being there with her, Damita tried to squirm free of his grip again, but found herself too weak. "You shouldn't be here with me," she said, suddenly sobbing. She implored him with wide, tear-filled eyes. "Iron Cloud, if anything happened to you, and I were responsible, I would want to die! Please leave. I will follow at least by tomorrow. I will return to your camp. Go now! Please?"

"It is not necessary that you worry so much about Iron Cloud, or that I should leave," he said, taking her gently by the hand and walking her back to the fire. He eased her down onto the blankets. "You see, White Willow, many winters ago when many of the Omaha people died from measles, I was one of those who did not. My body was ravaged with fever and the red splotches, and then just as suddenly, I was well again." He placed a comforting hand to her cheek. "So you see, I am in no danger while with you." He sat down beside her and drew her into his arms. "Let me hold you for a while and then we must return to my people."

Damita melted against him, so relieved to know that she could be this close to him and not endanger his health. "It may be too soon for me to return to your people tomorrow," she murmured. "I am sure that by tomorrow my splotches will begin fading. But even then I must keep my distance from everyone for awhile."

"We must return to my people today and leave quickly," Iron Cloud said, leaning his cheek against hers. "You see, Black Coyote escaped. I fear that he, the traitor that he is, might lead the white pony soldiers here. Also, your cousin has search parties looking for you and Timothy. Should they come this far, there could be much bloodshed among my people. I did not bring them this far to see them die needlessly!"

"Cousin Jonathan?" Damita said, leaning away from him and looking fearfully into his dark eyes. "He's looking for me and Timothy?"

"That is what my friend Brian told me," Iron Cloud said in a low rumble.

"Of course you told your friend nothing about me and Timothy," Damita asked, yet realizing the foolishness of the question just as the words were slipping across her lips. She understood this was why Iron Cloud only looked at her and did not answer.

Then Iron Cloud bolted to his feet and began cutting long branches from trees. "I will make a travois," he said, his hands busy tying these branches together with long tough strands of grass. "On our continued journey to Illinois, you will travel on the travois behind my horse, far back from my people so they won't be exposed. I will guard you, my woman, with my life."

Damita turned grateful eyes up to him, feeling safe and very, very blessed.

Chapter Fifteen

Several Days Later.

It was early evening, the time of violet twilight. Feeling strong again, the splotches having long faded from her skin, Damita proudly rode beside Iron Cloud on her horse. She cast Timothy a worried look, realizing that he was not as spirited this evening. His shoulders were even slightly slouched.

She studied his eyes as he gave her a sidelong glance, quickly concluding that the cause of his subdued attitude was simple weariness. They had traveled the long day almost without stopping. And when they had paused, Timothy had busied himself, along with the other young braves, in watering the horses and searching for food in the thickets.

She did not want to think about the possibility

of her brother coming down with measles. Yet she knew that the chances were good that he had been with her long enough during her first hours of the disease to have been exposed.

She hoped with all of her heart that enough time had elapsed since his exposure to indicate that he would no longer be stricken.

She gazed at Iron Cloud. Just looking at him made her insides warm up deliciously. She was hopelessly in love with the handsome Omaha chief, and there was no doubt how he felt about her.

He treated her so gently, so wonderfully!

It had been such a relief for her to know that he had already had measles, and she would not have to worry about him becoming stricken.

But if he had, she would have put her doctoring skills to full use, caring for him night and day, proving to him her intense love for him.

Now she would show him in other ways much more pleasurable. That she soon would be his wife was something she still could not believe. It was as though she were living a fantasy, one that she now knew for certain that she hoped never to awaken from. While ill with measles, she had feared for a time that she had awakened, and that her future with Iron Cloud was an impossible thing.

But now she knew! And it thrilled her through and through to see herself soon as his wife!

Smiling contentedly, Damita looked away from Iron Cloud, aware now that they would soon be making camp again. The late sun was flashing its red needles of light through the foliage in the west, and darkness was quickly filling the woods. The mosquitoes were now buzzing around her head. She could hear the peep of frogs along the river-bank, and fireflies were just rising from their resting places beneath the trees, blinking their golden lanterns into the thickening darkness.

And soon they had halted, and a great fire had been built beside the river and the meat of rabbits was browning, dripping its tantalizing juices into the flames. At the edge of the coals fish were baking and wild potatoes were steaming.

The women and men had taken turns bathing in the river and now the men of the camp were sitting together, smoking and talking. The women were clustered around the fire, working on their needlework as the food cooked. Damita sat with Girl Who Laughs, laughing softly as they watched Baby scampering around the camp, its leash momentarily removed.

But when Damita's gaze moved to Timothy, her smile faded, and she began worrying all over again. He was not joining the others playing with Baby. He was stretched out on his stomach on a blanket, resting his chin in his hands, only watching. This was not at all like Timothy. He had become fast friends with Lean Elk and they had become almost inseparable.

Until now.

Lean Elk was running after Baby, grabbing her up, hugging her to him, while Timothy watched with only a bare trace of a smile on his freckled face.

Pushing herself up from the ground, Damita went to Timothy and sat down beside him. She recalled how he had so recently begun to complain about her fussing over him, not wanting the young braves to see him as weak, needing to be coddled by a sister, so she hesitated at even touching his brow to see if he was feverish.

But she set aside her worries of how he would react to her questioning him about his behavior and determinedly placed the palm of her hand against his brow.

She ignored his frown as he looked up at her, so relieved to find his brow cool to the touch. She drew her hand away, feeling foolish that she was so needlessly worrying about him. Children were allowed to have moods!

Yes, that was all that it was. Timothy was being moody. Yet, she could not help but wonder why.

"What's wrong?" Damita blurted out, her stare unwavering as Timothy moved quickly to a sitting position beside her.

"Sis, there's nothing wrong," Timothy said, his voice edged with irritation. "I'm just tired. Now please don't begin fussing over me again. The guys will see."

Herself irritated, Damita sighed heavily. "I have seen Girl Who Laughs fuss over Lean Elk many times and he offers no complaint about it," she softly argued.

"She's his mother," Timothy argued back. "You're my *sister*."

"That makes no difference," Damita said, angrily flipping her long, golden hair back from her shoulders. "I love you the same as she loves Lean Elk. And Timothy, you are my responsibility now, as though I were your mother. I believe I should be allowed to coddle you just a bit, don't you?"

Timothy lowered his eyes. "I'm sorry," he murmured. "I don't mean to hurt your feelings." He looked up at her again with weary dark eyes. "It's just that I have been catapulted into a new way of life. I have much to prove to myself, you, *and* my new friends." He glanced over at Iron Cloud. "I've much to prove to *him*." He looked at Damita again. "He was disappointed in me over my allowing you to leave the camp alone. He did not say it, but I know that he felt that I should have gone with you. I did disappoint him, Sis. And perhaps he was right. I should have gone with you. I should have stood guard while you fought the disease. I should have kept you in food and water."

Now Damita saw what was truly causing her brother's sullen behavior. He was worried about Iron Cloud and the Omaha chief's feelings for him. There had been an instant bonding before. Now she realized how it had been lacking on these last few days of travel. Until now, she had not thought much about it.

"I'm sorry, Timothy, if I am cause for any awkwardness between you and Iron Cloud," she said, patting him on the arm. "But if it makes you feel any better, you were right not to go with me. And in time, Iron Cloud will come to realize this and treat you as special again. If you had gone with me, you would even now perhaps be as ill as I was, or worse. As it is, I believe enough time has elapsed since you were exposed to the disease to almost be certain that you are not going to get it."

She so badly wanted to draw him into his arms, to comfort him in the way she always had until he had begun to display the independent streak that he had found of late, but she refrained from such a show of affection to further spare him humiliation.

"Now, Timothy, if I were you, I would round up Baby, secure her, and get ready to eat, and then go to bed soon after," Damita murmured. "You look tired. And, remember, tomorrow is another day. Things always look better when the day is fresh and new and filled with promise."

Timothy gazed at Damita for a lingering moment, then lunged into her arms. "I'm so lucky to have you for a sister," he said, his voice breaking. "I'm sorry for being mean to you. Honest, Sis, I am."

Damita sat there, stunned that Timothy had suddenly opened up to her, then grateful, returning his hug. "You haven't been mean to me," she whispered, stroking his thick crop of reddish-golden hair. "You're just growing up. It had to happen sooner or later. I just didn't expect it to be this soon."

"I never want to do anything to make you unhappy," Timothy said, awkwardly easing from her arms. "Please tell me if I do."

"I will," Damita said, smiling warmly at him.

"Promise?" Timothy said earnestly.

"I promise," Damita said, crossing her heart as they always had done when sealing promises with each other.

Timothy jumped up and chased down Baby and secured her with a leash, then sat back down beside Damita. After they had food on their wooden plates, she noticed there was still something different about her brother. He just picked at his food, and when Iron Cloud sat down with him with his plate of food, Timothy did not have much to say, which was odd for her brother.

Yet, she tried to believe that Timothy was still worrying about Iron Cloud's disappointment in him, and that was the reason behind his strained silence.

After their meal, and when Timothy had gone to his blankets and snuggled into them with Baby, Damita went to sit beside Iron Cloud. After she had remained silently thoughtful for several moments, he lifted her chin with a forefinger and asked her what was wrong. She did not know quite what to say.

"It's Timothy," she murmured. "His behavior puzzles me. I hope he's not ill."

"He is fine," Iron Cloud tried to convince her. "My concerns are for you. Is your strength back? Did it tire you too much to ride so long?"

She laughed lightly and brushed a lock of hair

Cassie Edwards

back from her brow. "I must admit that riding a horse all day is not my idea of fun," she said. "And, yes, it did tire me. But I am sure no more than it would have had I not been recently ill. If you will remember, I am from Boston, where the only horses I was acquainted with were those that were attached to fancy carriages and buggies. I am surprised that I am able to even sit in a saddle, much less ride the horse."

"You adapt quickly to changes," Iron Cloud said, offering her a hand and encouraging her to her feet. "As does your brother. Whatever is bothering him now will pass. Tomorrow you will see that he is back to his adventurous self."

Damita wanted to confide in Iron Cloud and explain that Timothy was worried about Iron Cloud's feelings toward him, but she felt that that was something they had to work out between them, man to man.

Instead, she said nothing and let him lead her through the campsite, away from the fire and into the calm, melancholy stillness of the forest. They walked along the serene river, trees bent above it like lovers, the moon casting their shadows into the water.

When they stopped and Iron Cloud drew Damita into his arms, it was like the first time their lips came together. Damita's knees almost melted beneath her. Her breath quickened with yearning, and she twined her arms around his neck and returned the kiss. Her pulse raced when he drew her so much more closely that through her dress she could feel the hardness of his risen manhood against her body. She was reminded of her last time with him—the intimacy they had shared and the incredible sweetness that had swept through her while within his arms, experiencing the ultimate of bliss.

She moaned throatily as he began gyrating his body into hers, his one hand slipping up the skirt of her dress, soon finding her pulsing mound at the juncture of her thighs. As he caressed her there, she opened her legs more to him, so that he could have total access to her, and felt passion quickly drugging her. When he thrust a finger inside her, she almost fainted from the exquisite sensations it aroused within her.

And when he urged her to the ground to lie on her back, she accepted him atop her, sucking in her breath as he pushed her dress up to her waist and removed her undergarment. She was breathless while waiting for him to lower his breeches, her face on fire with the excitement of the moment, wanting this between them as badly as he.

With a pounding heart, she watched his hand encircle his velvet shaft, moving his fingers slowly over it. As though bidden, she moved one of her hands to replace his fingers around his hardness, and the mere touch of him sent her heart to racing.

His eyes locked with hers, the bright moon giving her full access to his handsome face, and the sight of her hand working on his tightness made Damita forget everything at this moment but the pleasure that she was giving him. She could tell by the way he sucked in his breath each time she moved her fingers up and then down, and by the way his body had tightened, that she was pleasing him.

She did not know how to react when he moved and now knelt over her so close to her face that she saw what he wanted, yet was too shy to quickly comply.

When he placed his hands gently to her head and urged her lips closer to him, she saw this as something that he wanted badly, and not to displease him, she took her first taste of what she thought was most surely forbidden!

His hands moved her head, which sent her tongue, mouth, and mind into a different sort of lovemaking, but which caused the excitement to mount within Damita.

And then he switched his position again, and she found his mouth and lips pleasuring her in the same way that she had just pleasured him. She had to cover her mouth to stifle a cry of pleasure as his tongue plunged inside her, thrusting over and over again, until she felt that she was close to that brink of sheer bliss.

She was glad when he shifted his position again and this time mounted her in the way that they had made love before. She lifted her hips to receive him inside her. She trembled with readiness as he drove into her. She arched and moved with him, their bodies straining together hungrily.

The sensations were searing, his lips drugging her again with a fiery kiss. When he unbuttoned her dress and put a hand inside the bodice for her breast, she whimpered with pleasure against his lips. His fingers stroked her flesh with an exquisite tenderness. She clung to him and let herself become lost in the ecstasy.

He held her more tightly. His body hardened and tightened. And then they shared the explosion of bliss, their bodies fusing as though one, their hearts taking flight together. . . .

When it was over, Iron Cloud rolled away from her and lay at her side, nestling her close.

"I do love you so much," Damita whispered, stroking her fingers through his long sleek hair. "You are everything to me. Everything!"

"I will sing you a song—the song of an Omaha warrior in love," Iron Cloud said, stroking her tender flesh at the juncture of her thighs, arousing her again, slowly but deliberately. "It is a song joyous in feelings."

Damita closed her eyes as his fingers worked magic on her again, his voice no less magical as he began to sing to her so softly that not even the birds nesting in the trees overhead could hear. She thrilled at the words, at his nearness, and at his ability to send her to paradise with the mere touch of his hands and voice.

"Dadu, I have made myself known, the!
Dadu-na, I have made myself known, the.
Last night when you sang I uttered your
    name, the!

Dadu-na-, I have made myself known, the!
  Hi!
Who is it that sings? The!
They said, and I sitting there, the!
Wagu-tha is passing; I said, the!
It was your name I uttered, the! hi."

"Lovely," Damita whispered, feverish from her renewed desire for him. She sucked in a wild breath as he pressed his hardness into her again. This time they made love in a slow and leisurely passion.

Afterwards, after getting fully dressed, they lay and talked, and Damita finally learned why the Sacred Pole stirred such feelings among the Omaha.

"Long ago," Iron Cloud began softly. "The son of an Omaha chief was hunting alone in the forest at a time when the tribal elders were in council trying to devise a way to save the tribe from extinction. He came upon a tree that was totally luminous but was not being consumed by its light. The tree was cut down, trimmed, adorned with a scalplock and called a human being. It was placed in a crotched stick. When the people gathered, the chiefs said: 'You see before you a mystery. Whenever we meet with troubles, we shall bring all our troubles to him. We shall make offerings and requests. All our prayers must be accompanied by gifts.' The pole is called *waxthe-xe* and has become an emblem of governmental authority among the Omaha."

Damita found herself confused by this custom, yet took great care to pretend to see the reasoning behind it. "It is a beautiful story," she murmured, twining her fingers through Iron Cloud's as he drew her to her feet before him.

They embraced, and as Damita's eyes sheened with moonlight, they kissed again.

Then, hand-in-hand, they strolled back to the campsite, seeing that most were asleep, except for small babies being nursed by their mothers. Damita looked for Timothy among those who were asleep, and an instant fear grabbed her at the pit of her stomach when she did not see him anywhere.

Panic-stricken, she broke away from Iron Cloud and began running from blanket to blanket, searching the faces for Timothy's.

When Iron Cloud came to her, she looked up at him, pale with anguished fear.

"He's gone!" she cried. "My brother. Iron Cloud, he isn't here!"

Chapter Sixteen

Not knowing which way to turn—where to begin searching for Timothy—and frantic to know why he was gone, Damita stifled a sob behind her hand, her eyes wild as she gazed into the dark depths of the forest. She started to run one way, then stopped and started going another, and stopped again when Iron Cloud came to her and grasped her by the shoulders.

"Do not fret so," he said. "I will find your brother. I know the art of tracking well. Come. We, together, will find him."

"But it's so dark," Damita cried, wiping torrents of tears from her eyes. "We'll never find him."

Iron Cloud stepped away from her and knelt beside the fire. Damita had noticed unlit torches lying there, but had not thought much about it. Now she breathlessly watched Iron Cloud pick one up and light its tip with flames, then she followed

him in a half run as he trotted softly across the
camp, holding the torch low so that he could
search for Timothy's tracks.

When he found the path of crushed leaves and
grasses that had not been made by himself and
Damita when they had departed and returned to
the camp, he smiled.

"Though a young man of only fifteen winters,
your brother's weight and that of the bobcat kitten
which I am sure he carries within his arms is
enough to create a path for us to follow," he said
reassuringly. "Follow my lead. We will soon find
your brother and return him to camp with us."

The commotion had awakened the others. Several warriors were quickly following behind Iron
Cloud and Damita.

Knowing the dangers in so many being away
from the camp, Iron Cloud stopped and gave them
a steady gaze. "It is good that you care enough for
the white boy to join the search for him," he said,
holding the torch high, lighting the eager faces of
his men. "But it is not good that you leave the
camp at this time. Stay behind. You best serve
your chief tonight by staying with your women
and children, protecting them. There are those
who are even now a threat to our journey to Illinois. We must be ready, should they find us."

A spokesman for the warriors stepped forward.
"What you ask, we will do," he said, then looked
at Damita. "Your brother is a fine young man.
Wakoda will guide you to him."

"Thank you," was all that Damita could say,

choking back a sob of gratitude. She was very touched by these Indians and their feelings for her and Timothy, when in truth she had expected to be hated by them all.

She was kin to the man they all hated. She had thought that every time they looked at the color of her skin, eyes, and hair, they would be reminded of all that they had lost because of the arrival of the white soldiers and settlers in their precious homeland.

She would have expected a keen resentment from them, not an utter, heartfelt kindness!

"White Willow, let us resume our search," Iron Cloud said as the warriors turned and returned to the camp. "I do not expect that Timothy got far. The forest is dark. The owl lurks in the trees, a frightening thing in the dark, when all one sees are the large, penetrating eyes of the owl. Unless you are Indian, raised with the knowledge of the owl, it could be a frightening experience for someone of Timothy's age and inexperience."

Damita lifted the skirt of her dress, stepping high and low over fallen branches and clinging vines. "Why did he leave?" she fretted aloud. "Why, Iron Cloud?"

"A foolish notion, I am sure," Iron Cloud said, peering ahead, his eyes scanning the ground beneath the trees and beside the river. "But do not worry yourself so. We will soon find him. Then you will know why he has fled our camp."

"At least he took his blankets with him," Damita said, sighing heavily. "And Baby. So he is not altogether alone, and he won't be cold. But he did not take anything else of value with him." Her eyes widened. "The rifle," she said in a rush of words. "I wonder if he took the rifle that you gave him."

"He is an intelligent young man," Iron Cloud reassured. "You can expect that he took the rifle with him for protection."

"I truly hope so," Damita said, then her footsteps faltered when, through a break in the trees a short distance away, she saw something beside the river.

She broke into a hard run, tears splashing from her eyes. And when she reached Timothy, who was bundled up in a blanket asleep, Baby snuggling asleep beside him, she flew to her knees and drew them both into her arms and clung to them.

Timothy awakened with a start. He gasped, then looked sheepishly up into Damita's eyes. "Sis," he said, his voice quavering. "When you found me gone, did I frighten you too much? I didn't mean to. Honest."

Iron Cloud knelt beside Timothy and Damita. He crammed the end of the torch into the ground so that it stood up, its flames waving in the breeze. He leaned close over Timothy. "You say that you did not mean to frighten your sister?" he said in a growl. "Then why did you do this that you knew would upset her?"

Timothy turned wavering eyes up to Iron Cloud. "I did it for your people," he said thickly. He turned his head and coughed into his cupped hand while Baby yawned and scratched her ear with her paw, as though nothing was wrong.

"What do you mean?" Damita asked, waiting for Timothy to stop coughing, then framing his face between her hands and forcing his eyes to meet the questioning in hers. "What do Iron Cloud's people have to do with your running away?"

"Sis, don't you know?" Timothy asked faintly. "You're practically a doctor. Surely you know that I am in the first stages of measles. Didn't you see how listless I was all day? Then when the dry cough started tonight, I knew that I had to get away from Iron Cloud's people—like you, Sis, when you became ill."

"Measles?" Damita said, paling. She touched his brow and flinched, realizing that he did have a fever. She felt a quick panic rising within her. "Oh, God, I had hoped you would be spared." She clutched him to her chest, looking past him at Iron Cloud. "Iron Cloud, what can we do? Now Timothy is ill! You can't delay your journey—not even one day—for my brother! The dangers are many in your doing so. What can we do?"

Iron Cloud reached his free hand out to place it on Timothy's shoulder. "First let me say that your brother is courageous for this that he chose to do tonight," he said, feeling that Timothy had just rectified in Iron Cloud's heart the wrong that he had done by allowing his White Willow to leave the camp alone.

This young man, whom he would train to be

Omaha, had the courage of many warriors. He had entered the forest alone. He had risked his life, to perhaps save many of Iron Cloud's people!

Yes, Iron Cloud decided, all wrongs had been righted now by Timothy's courageous escape into the forest tonight.

"And as for our travel plans," Iron Cloud said, moving away from Timothy and folding his arms across his chest, "it will be the same as with you. He will travel by travois a distance from my people. There will be no cause for any delay."

Damita left Timothy and went to Iron Cloud, clutching her hand to his arm. "Iron Cloud, even though Timothy will be traveling separate from your people tomorrow, what about yesterday?" she said softly. "He was with them then. Surely many are exposed!"

"You were with my people also before you became ill," Iron Cloud said, taking her hand and folding it affectionately within his. "None of my people are ill, are they?"

"No," Damita murmured. "Only Timothy. But perhaps they won't be as lucky a second time."

"And if that is the way it is, then we shall do our best to live with it," Iron Cloud said, not offering her a smile, for within himself he was filled with many doubts and concerns for his people. Each day was a gamble with their lives, it seemed, If not as a result of the evil plans of the white men, then because the scourge of diseases that could claim them!

Yet, as he looked past Damita and down at Timothy, in his innocence, he could not blame him or his White Willow for this new dilemma they all faced. There was no way to hide from it.

If it was meant to be, so be it.

"I feel so at fault," Damita said, glancing over her shoulder at Timothy. "My brother and I have put your entire tribe in jeopardy because of our presence among them!"

Iron Cloud placed a finger to her chin and turned her face around so that she was eye to eye with him. "You do not remember that it was I who brought you and your brother among my people?" he said, scowling. "If anyone is to blame, it is myself. But I lay blame nowhere, except on fate. Now let us return to the camp. We can settle Timothy at the farthest edges away from our people and warn them of his illness. Early tomorrow he will be placed on a travois. He will travel far from the others, at the rear. You will ride with him. You will care for him. I will be there, to see that you are safe."

Damita gazed up at him for a moment, awestruck by his continuing kindnesses to her and Timothy. Then she crept into his arms and hugged him tightly. "Thank you for everything," she murmured. "How can I ever repay you?"

Iron Cloud ran his fingers through her waist-length hair, placing a cheek to hers so that he could speak in her ear, his words meant only for her to hear. "I abducted you and forced you to ride with me, and now you are thanking me for so much?" he said, chuckling. "White Willow, you have changed the meaning of the word captive. It is I who should be thanking you and asking how I can repay you." He paused, his breath hot on her ear. "There are many ways of repayment for both you and me."

"There are?" Damita whispered back, blushing as she caught Timothy looking at them.

"Each night I shall show you the many ways," Iron Cloud whispered back. "As tonight. Did I not show you new ways of making love?"

"Yes," Damita said, closing her eyes as just the thought of being with him so intimately made her head swim with ecstasy.

"And so tomorrow night I shall show you another way," Iron Cloud whispered huskily. "Now, before we have urges that we cannot act out, we should return to our camp. The night is half over. Tomorrow will come quickly, and tomorrow we will ride for a long time—from the time the sky becomes streaked with dawn until the moon is high in the sky!"

Iron Cloud eased her from his arms and went and stood over Timothy. He looked thoughtfully at Timothy and the bobcat kitten, then over at Damita. "I will carry Timothy," he said. "You can carry the torch with one hand, and with your other hold fast to the leash and lead the kitten back to the camp."

"Be sure and hold tight, Sis," Timothy said, handing Baby to Damita as she knelt over to take her into her arms. "She is getting feistier each day. One jerk and she could be gone." He swallowed hard. "Don't let her get away, Sis. Please don't let her get away."

"I promise," Damita said, cuddling the kitten close before setting Baby to the ground. She then took the torch in her other hand as Iron Cloud handed it to her. Her heart swelled with a wondrous warmth as she watched Iron Cloud grab Timothy and his blankets up into his arms, and Timothy so trustingly placed an arm around Iron Cloud's neck.

"I truly didn't mean to upset you, Sis," Timothy said, looking over Iron Cloud's shoulder at Damita as she fell into step behind him, the torch blaring brightly into the treetops. "But I didn't want to expose the Omaha people. I had no other choice."

"You had one other choice as I see it," Damita said, frowning at him. "You could have told me what you planned."

"I wanted to do it my own way," Timothy said soberly. He glanced over at Iron Cloud, then back at Damita. "It was important to me that I did it that way, Sis. Please try and understand."

Damita suddenly did understand, more than her brother felt free to explain. She could only believe that he had done this to impress Iron Cloud, especially after Iron Cloud had become disillusioned about him over having allowed her to go to the forest alone. Somehow, Timothy felt that this might change Iron Cloud's mind about him, and as far as Damita was concerned, her brother's scheme had worked. Iron Cloud was treating Timothy as special again—as though he were his own son!

As they came close to the camp, Iron Cloud veered to the right and carried Timothy to a cottonwood tree and set him down beneath it. Damita followed and quickly made Timothy a pallet of his blankets, then released Baby into her brother's arms again as he settled himself between the blankets.

While Iron Cloud rustled together enough wood to make a fire, Damita sat down beside Timothy. As she tried to reach her hand to her brother's brow, Baby hissed and batted a paw at Damita's hand, causing Damita to flinch and quickly draw her hand back.

"She's protecting me," Timothy said, laughing softly as he hugged Baby to him. Then he closed his eyes, and just as the fire was taking hold close beside him, he was asleep.

Seeing that his face was flushed, Damita reached over to touch his brow, and again Baby spat at her.

Determined not to let the bobcat kitten take charge, knowing the dangers in that, Damita caught the paw and softly slapped it, then set it aside and once again reached her hand to Timothy's brow, finally able to touch it.

Damita recoiled, feeling how hot her brother's flesh was, yet somehow feeling relieved at the same time. If his measles were coming on this abruptly, he was not going to be ill as long as Damita, and it would not be as severe. In a matter of two or three days he would be back on his feet, again facing the young Omaha braves in all sorts of challenges.

He did seem to fit in so well with them! This was making her own transition easier, for their futures depended on a mutual understanding of their new way of life.

Feeling a strong arm around her waist, Damita turned to Iron Cloud. "He's quite feverish," she murmured. She tore a portion of her petticoat away. "I'm going to the river to dampen this cloth and bathe his brow. Iron Cloud, you don't need to stay with us the full night. We're going to be all right."

"I will take the time to go and tell my people that Timothy has been found and explain where I will be, and then I will return," Iron Cloud said, rising to his feet. "I have promised to look out for you and Timothy. I never break promises."

Damita walked with him a short distance, then her breath was stolen as he swept her against him. His eyes were as dark as all midnights as he gazed down at her. "My White Willow," he murmured. "Oh, how you have complicated my life!"

Damita smiled devilishly up at him. "I'm sorry," she murmured. "But, Iron Cloud, would you have it any other way?"

His mouth coming to hers in a fiery kiss was all the answer that she needed.

Chapter Seventeen

Two Days Later.

Beside a low-burning fire, Damita looked down upon her brother, who had drifted into a peaceful sleep, Baby cuddled against him, purring in her sleep. Damita stroked her brother's brow with a damp cloth one last time, his fever having broken only moments ago. He had not been all that ill, only enough to gladly accept the travois for travel instead of his horse. He had lain there playing with Baby, letting the kitten run free alongside the travois as far as the leash would allow.

Damita smiled to herself, remembering how thoughtful Iron Cloud had been to add more rope to Baby's leash, allowing the bobcat kitten to scamper much more freely, to explore further into the untraveled forest, even to scamper after a squirrel now and then or a forest mouse.

Damita ran a hand across the stiff fur of Baby's head, laughing to herself as this caused the kitten's ears to twitch yet did not awaken her. The kitten was becoming more used to her and she to the kitten, and a mutual love was being formed.

"The kitten will have to be returned to its habitat one day," Iron Cloud said, bending to his haunches beside Damita. He stroked his fingers through Damita's long hair as she turned sad eyes to him.

"Perhaps not," she murmured. "She will surely be tame enough to stay with us. She is such a dear. She has captured such a large corner of my heart."

Damita reached a hand to his cheek. "And also yours, my darling," she said, smiling up at him.

Her gaze raked over him, seeing how the fire reflected on his copper skin in a pleasant glow. As he was dressed in only a brief breechclout, she could not help but stare at his sinewed shoulders, which tapered to narrow hips, a hard flat stomach, and long, firm legs.

He smelled clean, like the river and the pine scent of the forest, for always after Iron Cloud's baths, he dried himself off with the needles from pine trees.

She looked up at his finely chiseled bronze face and at his night-black eyes, and his raven hair hanging wetly over his shoulders, the headband now removed.

"You have bathed already?" she murmured, a question she knew the answer to. But she felt awkward at this moment, for her desire for him was so strong, it embarrassed her.

But she loved him so much, how could she not desire him with such a passion?

His nearness was causing her heart to pound, her belly to take on a strange sort of queasiness.

"Had you not been here, awaiting my return, I would have bathed with much more leisure," Iron Cloud chuckled. He nodded toward the river. "And, my White Willow, did you not return quickly from your bath? Was it because you were afraid in the river alone, or because you wished to hasten my own bath? Tell me you are not eager to crawl beneath the lean-to with your future husband."

He bent low so that his lips were brushing against her ear as he spoke. "My love, did I not promise to show you many ways of making love?" he whispered huskily. "In the lean-to, we have the privacy that is required for my further teachings. Your brother is asleep. We have bathed. We have eaten. Let us go now and soar together, you and I, on the wings of an eagle again."

Swept away by rapture, Damita lay the damp cloth aside and let Iron Cloud lift her up into his arms. She clung around his neck, his mouth sweet on her lips, as he carried her to their makeshift home for the night. As he bent low to carry her inside, she snuggled close to his bare chest, kissing first one of his nipples and then the other, drawing a groan of blissful agony from deep inside him.

Once inside, when she was lying on a thick pallet of furs that he had spread for her earlier, she watched him drop the blanket at the entrance, so that they were now enclosed within their lovenest on all four sides by blankets. Feeling as though they were the only two people on the earth, she welcomed him into her arms as he moved over her. His arms snaked around her waist, drawing her tightly against him, his mouth devouring her lips in a savage kiss.

And then he leaned away from her and his deft fingers began removing the buckskin dress that Girl Who Laughs had lent her, all the while gazing down at her with eyes lit with points of fire, smoke-black with passion.

When she was lying long and shapely and fully unclothed below him, Iron Cloud looked at her as though it were the first time he had seen her silkenly nude. Her pale skin was vibrant and glowing as the campfire lighted the blankets surrounding them in a soft, golden light. He feasted upon the sight of her liquid curves—her well-rounded breasts, her slim, white thighs, the supple broadening into her hips with their central muff of golden hair, and her long, beautiful, tapering legs.

Iron Cloud twined his fingers through the golden hair spilling over her shoulders, partially hiding her breasts and smoothed it aside. His hands moved over the glossy skin of her breasts and down over her ribs until he was gently massaging the soft flesh of her belly, and then lower, where his fingers found her wet and ready to be caressed at the juncture of her thighs.

Damita closed her eyes, sighing pleasurably

with sensual abandonment, and sucked in a wild
breath of joy when his mouth covered her lips
again with a lingering, deep kiss. He plunged his
tongue through her lips. Her mouth opened to receive him.

And then he slithered his lips down her neck
and his lips brushed the skin of her breasts. Her
head rolled as he then pressed his lips against a
breast, moving them over her abundant nipple. A
cry of sweet agony leapt from the depths of her
throat as he kissed the nipple, sucking it, his
tongue warm against her cool skin.

She drew in her breath sharply and gasped with
delirious pleasure as he suddenly thrust his manhood within her softly yielding folds, pressing
more deeply as she wrapped her legs around his
waist to give him more access to her.

Her gasps of pleasure became a long, soft whimper, as again he kissed her and thrust his tongue
into her mouth, flickering it in and out, then moving it along her lips.

Wanting to touch him, to feel the satin hardness
that was sending her into a world that knew only
the wonders of bliss, Damita ran her fingers down
his smooth, tautly muscled back to his smooth,
hard buttocks. She splayed her fingers against the
flesh, urging him faster, deeper.

And then her fingers moved around, where she
could get an occasional touch of his shaft as it
came in and out of her. Suddenly she had full
access to it as Iron Cloud leaned away from her,

taking her hand, to encircle her fingers around his pulsing hardness.

"Move your hands on me," Iron Cloud said huskily, his eyes hazed over with a building passion. "You give me much pleasure."

Damita leaned up and circled his shaft, feeling its heat against the palm of her hand and amazed at how it pulsed, as though Iron Cloud's heartbeat was centered there. She moved her hand over him slowly at first, then faster when she saw how much he enjoyed it.

His eyes were closed. His jaw was tight. His breathing was hard. . . . Recalling the one other time that she had been taught the forbidden way to love him, she lowered her mouth over him and gave him pleasure that even she felt, and then realized why. He had positioned himself so that his mouth and tongue were caressing her pulsing mound, as her mouth and tongue continued pleasuring him.

She closed her eyes and let herself enjoy the ecstasy, the floating lethargy that had claimed her.

A few moments later, Iron Cloud drew away from her and moved so that he was lying next to her. He framed her face between his hands as he pulled her lips to his. As they kissed, he moved over her and spread her legs apart with a knee. Soon he was thrusting within her again, this time in a more fevered fashion. Damita strained her body up to meet his, their naked flesh fusing as though one, flesh against flesh in a frenzied pressure....

His hands seemed to be everywhere at once on her body. She was delirious with wild sensations, ecstasy welling within her.

Iron Cloud felt the last vestige of rational thought float away. He kissed Damita's eyes, her nose, every place that he could reach. He could feel the melting energy flowing through his veins, the spinning sensation flooding his whole body.

His body hardened and tightened, and then the explosion of bliss overcame him, glad that she welcomed and absorbed his bold, hard thrusts as he spilled his warm liquid into her womb, clinging to him, her body also wracked with spasms of pleasure.

His lips trembling with the aftermath of pleasure, Iron Cloud kissed her, a soft yet lingering kiss as she clung to him.

Then he leaned away from her, their eyes meeting and holding in a mutual understanding.

"I love you so," Damita murmured, reaching a hand to the smooth copper skin of his face. "Had I not come to Nebraska, had I lived my life out in Boston—oh, how dull it would have been! Never would I have met anyone like you there, Iron Cloud. You are so special. So very, very special!"

"As are you special, my White Willow," he said, taking her hand and kissing its palm.

"Had I not come along, you would have married one of your own kind, wouldn't you?" Damita said, drifting toward him as he held his arm out for her.

She leaned into his embrace, savoring the moment.

"I have had many women to choose from in my lifetime, but none have made my heart beat as quickly as when I am with you," Iron Cloud said softly. "It is not the color of the skin that has caused the difference. It is the woman. It is the way her heart responds to the man. With you and me, the magic was there. It will be always."

"At first I resented being called by another name than my own," Damita whispered, as he gave her a brushing of a kiss on her nose, making her shiver with delight. "But now? I have grown accustomed to it. I love it, Iron Cloud. It is such a gentle name."

"You resented the name only because you felt you were losing your identity by being given another name," Iron Cloud said, turning her to face him. "But as you see, you are the same, except that you have a second name—one given to you by the man who loves you. And did you not notice? I have not ordered Timothy to call you White Willow. To him, you are Damita. To me you are White Willow. Does that satisfy you, my lovely woman?"

"It seems that everything you do satisfies me," Damita said, moving to her knees so that she could lean against him.

She twined her arms around his neck, her breasts crushed against his chest. "Satisfy me again, Iron Cloud?" she whispered, feeling brazen with the suggestion, yet filled with longings that only he could fulfill.

And what of tomorrow? Who knew of any tomorrows?

Tonight, the world was theirs!

His fingers ran down her body, caressing her, making her shiver. She placed her hands to his shoulders and urged him down on the pallet of furs. Straddling him, she eased his manhood inside her and began to ride him, gently at first, and then moved more quickly so that he had nothing to do but lie there and absorb the feelings that she was arousing in him.

Her golden hair fell away from her shoulders as she held her head back, her eyes closed in ecstasy. Her breasts bounced, then were captured within his warm hands, his fingers tweaking their nipples into a taut erectness.

And then Iron Cloud had her turned over so that she was beneath him. Too close to reaching the ultimate of pleasure, he probed with his hardness until he found entrance, then surged inside her, his teeth biting into her lips as he kissed her, his hands gripping her breasts. The familiar spinning sensation rose up and flooded Damita's whole body as Iron Cloud stiffened and then spasmed into her. . . .

Moments later, they lay side by side, breathing hard, their hands clasped together tightly.

"I shall never forget tonight," Damita said, smiling softly over at him. The fire burned so low now that she could only make out his silhouette against the blanket behind him. "Being with you alone like this is so wonderful. Each day when I awaken,

I fear what might happen that day to get in the way of our happiness. Such a happiness surely can't go on and on. It is as though I am someone else, looking down on myself from the sky. It is hard to believe that this can actually be happening to me. I . . . I have never thought myself beautiful, and since I was a child, I have been teased about being so tall and lanky."

She turned to him and placed her hands on either side of his face, peering into his eyes. "Do you see me that way? Or do you see what others cannot see, and perhaps see me as beautiful? Do you, Iron Cloud? Do you?" she asked anxiously.

"You are the heaven, the universe, the stars, the moon to me," Iron Cloud said, taking her by the wrists, drawing her against his hard body. "Do you think the weeping willow is beautiful?"

"Yes," Damita said, her heart pounding.

"Is not your name White Willow?" Iron Cloud said, kissing the tip of her nose.

"Yes," Damita said, closing her eyes as Iron Cloud kissed one and then the other, so gently that she could scarcely feel the press of his lips against them. But she could feel the heat of his breath. She could smell the forest smell of his flesh.

"Then, as I do, you see yourself as beautiful," Iron Cloud said, winding his arms around her, the press of her breasts against his chest causing his heart to thrill.

A sudden wet warmth on Damita's ankle made her freeze, as she realized that something was licking her! She jumped out of Iron Cloud's arms and turned around, her eyes wild as she looked to see what had entered the lovenest with them. She laughed when she discovered what it was. She moved to her knees and crawled to the bobcat kitten, giggling when the kitten placed its paws on her shoulders and stood on her hindlegs to lick Damita in the face.

"Do you see?" Iron Cloud said, chuckling. "The kitten also sees you as beautiful."

Damita swept the kitten into her arms and cuddled her close, Baby's purring proving that the tiny bobcat was happy. "I had forgotten about the longer leash," she said, kissing the kitten's nose. "I guess she got lonely."

Damita gazed at Iron Cloud, her face serene with love. "Darling, because of you, I shall never be lonely," she murmured. "And I will make sure you never have cause to be lonesome, either. I will be there, always, for you, my darling. Always."

Iron Cloud moved to her side and kissed her softly, and then they enjoyed Baby's company by playing with her until they all three tired from it.

Stretching out together, Damita and Iron Cloud made room for Baby between them. Soon they were all asleep, Baby's purring filling the night air with a lazy, contented sound, matching the contentment of Damita's dreams.

Chapter Eighteen

Two Weeks Later.

Southern Illinois.

Damita had awakened early and was taking a stroll to explore this new land that Iron Cloud had brought his people to. A shawl was draped snugly around her shoulders, and she lifted the fringes of her buckskin dress from the dew-dampened undergrowth as she made her way through the trees. A creamy fog that only moments ago had clung to the land like a fallen cloud was now fading quickly as morning suffused the sky.

Damita inhaled deeply, enjoying the fugitive scent of pine perfuming the air. Many cottonwoods were taking shape around her in the dim, pewter light, spreading shade and scattering on the wind their winged, cottony seeds, while their silver-lined leaves made a constant noise similar to rain.

Where the trees were more scarce, wild flowers exploded and retreated in masses of gold and scarlet, pink and purple. Momentarily startled, Damita watched as a streak of yellow moved quickly from pines to cottonwoods, singing a fluid tanager song in the leaves.

A pair of cowbirds squeaked in a tree above her, and a meadowlark gave the morning's first sweet song.

Smiling and feeling peaceful in her discoveries of nature this morning, Damita walked farther away from Wolf Lake, Iron Cloud's choice for his new village. She made her way through the trees and up an incline until she stood on a high bluff which overlooked the Missouri River, able to survey what else God had blessed this land with.

From this vantage point, she could see for miles and miles, and the wondrous sight nearly stole her breath away. Beyond, the whole face of the country seemed covered either with a luxuriant growth of grass or great reaches of forest. The magnificent bluffs studding the sides of the river gave her a peculiar pleasure, from the deep, soft green in which they were clad up their broad sides, to their extreme tops with a carpet of grass and clusters of timber in a deeper green.

Below her, the river bent into countless fascinating forms, reflecting in its depths the sun that was now shining out of a platinum sky.

"Was my choice of land wise?" Iron Cloud

asked, suddenly stepping up beside Damita.

Damita turned with a start, almost losing her footing in the loose gravel beneath her feet. She was glad when Iron Cloud's powerful hands were there, on her waist, drawing her away from the edge of the cliff and next to his strong bronzed body.

"I didn't hear your approach," she said, looking up at him, always in awe of how his very nearness made her heart beat faster. It was a most delicious feeling, one that she hoped would never become ordinary to her.

"Which proves to you, White Willow, that you must not go so far alone in a land that is yet a mystery to you," Iron Cloud said, his voice touched with annoyance. "It is not wise. Though my scouts explored this land carefully, that does not guarantee that evil ones have not come from another direction and are even now camped just beyond yonder hills. This is a beautiful land. In time it will lure more than the Omaha to it!"

"It seems too peaceful, too serene, to worry about the dangers of it," Damita said, touched deeply by the beauty of the land. "But I will heed your warning, Iron Cloud. I'm sorry I worried you today, when all of your concerns should be centered on getting your village established. I . . . I guess I was a bit selfish, wasn't I?"

"No," Iron Cloud said, brushing her lips with a gentle kiss. "Not selfish. Just swept into the magic of the new land. And that is good, White Willow, that you have warm feelings for your new home.

It is not going to be easy for you to adapt to living the life of an Omaha, much less to adapt to a new land as well."

"Around and near Boston, we had beautiful scenery," Damita said, a pang of homesickness plaguing her heart. "But it was not as hauntingly beautiful as Illinois." She touched his cheek gently with her hand. "And do not fret about my adapting to your way of living. I will be with you, won't I? That makes the difference in my world today, my darling. You *are* my world. If I am to keep house in a wigwam, so be it. I shall make the best of it. I will prove to you to be a most capable wife."

Iron Cloud held her close, and as he looked across her shoulder and into the far distance, he was suddenly caught up in that which could destroy their happiness.

Black Coyote. Where was he? And White Willow's cousin, Jonathan. Where was *he*?

Both were threats, always, as long as they were alive!

If Iron Cloud was a warring chief, he thought bitterly to himself, he would send warriors out and search far and wide for these two enemies and have them slain!

But since he was a man seeking only peace, he would not be forced to such extremes to guarantee a peaceful existence for himself, his woman and her brother, and his people!

But if they sought *him* out, he thought bitterly, there would be no pity shown them!

"What are you thinking about so hard?" Damita

asked, gazing up at him, seeing his tight jaw and firm chin, and a distant, troubled look in his eyes. "This is a time for hope, Iron Cloud, not doubt. Finally you have reached the land where you can make a new beginning. None of your people came down with measles, and thank God, neither Timothy nor I was harmed by it. There is so much to be thankful for, Iron Cloud."

She framed his face between her hands, forcing his gaze to meet hers. "My darling, we, you and I have so much to be thankful for," she murmured. "We have each other. Surely no one can love as fiercely and devotedly as you and I."

He took her hands and held them to his bare chest, drawing her closer to him. "Today, tomorrow and forever, our love will be as true—as dedicated—as it is today," he said thickly, then lowered his mouth to her lips and gave her an all-consuming kiss.

Damita's mind swirled with ecstasy, and she moved with him to the ground, a bed of moss soft to her back as he stretched her out beneath him.

Pebbles scattered down the side of the bluff as Iron Cloud busied his hands at disrobing her, his lips preparing her for the promise of what lay ahead, only heartbeats away.

Damita had only faint doubts about being alone with Iron Cloud like this in broad daylight, on a high bluff, as though wedded to the sky, for his hands were now working magic on her nude body, the soft breeze a sweet caress to her heated flesh.

And it was early morning. There would be only

a faint stirring of people back at the camp, and they would not be in the mood for exploring.

Now it was only the two of them, the sky, the wind, and the birds soaring overhead.

It seemed only right that they should start their new day—their new life—by furthering their commitment to one another!

And how better a way than to again show each other the depths of their love for each other?

It seemed there was truly never enough time for this that they shared privately between them.

Iron Cloud swept his arms around her and molded the shapely contours of her body into his, parting her thighs with a knee. As he reverantly breathed her name against her cheek, he plunged his hardness inside her.

Adoring him, she gripped him lightly and met his steady thrusts as he moved within her, his lips brushing her throat, and then seizing her mouth again for another drugging, hungry kiss.

Her whole body quivered as she clung and rocked with him in the soft light of early morning. She could feel his body tightening, the air heavy with the inevitability of the completion of a sought-for blissful joy.

Her throbbing center enlarged against him as each of his strokes brushed against it. And when his mouth eased from hers and he looked down at her with his passion-heavy, dark eyes, she felt herself going over the edge into total ecstasy.

She twined her arms around his neck and drew his mouth back to her lips and kissed him hard and long as their bodies rocked and swayed and quivered into the other, the explosion of their rapture finally claiming them....

Satiated, they moved apart and lay on the moss, staring up at the puffy white clouds floating past. When an eagle swept into view, its wings shadowing the ground beneath it, they gasped in unison with delight.

"Wakoda blesses our union," Iron Cloud said, reaching for one of Damita's hands, clasping it gently. "He sent the eagle to relay the message of acceptance. Wakoda will bless us with many children." He moved to his knees over her, straddling her. His hands tenderly cupped her breasts. "Your breasts will fill with much milk for our children. They will suckle contentedly from them."

He bent low, his lips covering one of her nipples, and sucked the tight nub between his teeth.

Damita closed her eyes and felt her desire rising again, yet knew that enough time had been spent in their own selfish desires. His people waited. She did not want to be the cause of their feeling neglected!

She placed her hands to his cheeks and encouraged his face away from her breasts. "I want you so badly," she said, feeling wicked for having such continued desires for a man, no matter if he was going to be her husband. It just didn't seem natural for a woman to have such insatiable needs as this!

Yet it was too hard to deny herself these needs with Iron Cloud there, as needy of her as she was of him. If she didn't love him so much, she would then see the wrong in having given in to her feelings for him.

But she did love him. Without him, she would not want to go on. Life would be meaningless....

And then she suddenly remembered her brother. She could not allow herself to neglect her brother's needs. Before Iron Cloud, Timothy's needs had come before her very own.

She must never forget his importance to her!

Iron Cloud took Damita's hand and helped her to her feet. She laughed softly as he began dressing her, insisting that she let him do this for her, since it was he who had undressed her. She giggled when he purposely allowed one of his hands to touch a breast, or perhaps her stomach just above her hairline, where she was so ultra-sensitive.

And when he drew her undergarment up her legs, allowing a finger to slide up inside her and linger there momentarily, circling within her, her face became flushed and she swayed in her passion against him.

"That's not fair," she whispered, placing a cheek on his bare chest. She kissed his copper flesh, then sucked one of his nipples between her teeth when he continued to thrust his finger inside her. The intense feelings building, she shuddered, closed her eyes, and held her head back, her hair tumbling in a golden sheen down her back.

One last, maddening thrust with his finger and she was lost again to the world and its surroundings, blinded by the waves of rapture that were soaring through her....

Almost collapsing from the pleasure, Damita wrapped her arms around Iron Cloud and clung to him, then offered him her mouth. He enfolded her within his arms, and when he kissed her, it was sweet and soft and beautiful, reminding her again of exactly why she loved him.

He was ever so gentle, ever so loving....

Then their lips parted and, both fully dressed again, they began walking hand-in-hand down the hill, soon entering the dark cover of the forest.

"I scolded you before for leaving the camp for a stroll alone," Iron Cloud said, giving her a wicked sort of glance. "Perhaps I was too hasty. I would like to be given cause to search for you every morning if this is my reward for finding you."

"I believe that could be arranged," Damita said, her eyes smiling into his. She was half skipping along, so content was she. She didn't see how anything could ruin their happiness—ever! It seemed so complete, so untouchable.

Yet she realized that she should never allow herself to ever become that comfortable—that assured—about anything. She had taken her life as much for granted before her parents had been taken so suddenly away from her.

She knew that Iron Cloud could be taken as quickly.

She tightened her hand on his and inched closer to him. Their bodies touched as they walked, and then he laughingly swept her up into his arms and carried her through the thickest of the under-brush.

Soon they reached the edge of the land that had been cleared yesterday for their dwellings. The women were preparing food over the large out-door communal fire, and the young girls were car-rying water from the lake. The men were in the forest cutting cedar poles for the tipis, others strips of birch for those who chose wigwams in-stead of tipis for their dwellings.

"I should hurry on and join the women in their chores," Damita said, giving Iron Cloud a quick glance when he did not relinquish her hand all that quickly. "Iron Cloud, I feel guilty for not hav-ing been there to help the women with the fire. I must go and help them prepare the morning meal."

"The women of my village have prepared many meals without your assistance," Iron Cloud said, chuckling. He turned her to face him. "And, White Willow, you will do your share of work. The women of my village work hard. Upon them de-pends much of the livelihood of our people—the preparation of food, of shelter, of clothing, and the cultivation of the garden patches. In return, our women are regarded with much esteem. Their wishes are respected and while women hold no public office, many of the movements and cere-monies of the tribe depend on their timely assis-tance. In the family, the mother is the center of much affection."

He drew Damita into his arms and held her for

a moment before leaving her for his own daytime activities with his warriors. "My White Willow, no one is so near, no one can ever be so dear as a wife," he whispered into her ear. "When she dies, her husband's joy dies with her. My White Willow, although we have not shared the wedding ceremony of my people, I look to you as my wife. Take care, my woman, that nothing happens to you. You are my joy, my life."

They clung to one another for a moment longer and then Iron Cloud led her on into the village, where he left her. Before entering the activities with the women, Damita stood aside to try and find Timothy among those busy with their tasks. She was amazed at how quickly the dwellings were being erected. The tipis were constructed in a conical form by the use of buffalo skins tanned on both sides. The tipi poles were of cedar, up to sixteen feet in length.

The setting up and making of the tipi seemed to be the women's task. Four poles were first erected and tied with a rawhide thong about three feet from one end. Other poles, ten to twelve in number according to the size of the tent, were arranged in a circle around the central four posts, the entrances facing the west.

The wigwam was a circular dwelling made of bent saplings covered with mats, with high walls, a dome-shaped roof, and a central opening for the escape of smoke and to allow light to enter. This was the sort of lodge in which Damita and Iron Cloud, and Timothy, would make their residence.

Still not seeing Timothy, Damita found herself watching instead the women who had children to care for who were too small to walk. Their mothers' robes were tied by a girdle around the waist, the upper part placed over the clinging child and the end crossed in front and tucked into the girdle. The mother gave an occasional gentle but decided shrug when the child loosened its arms and settled itself into its bag-like bed, from out of which it winked and peered at the world. It was an adorable sight to Damita, the children soon falling asleep as their mothers trudged along.

Finally Damita found Timothy among the young braves who were busy carrying strips of wood into the camp from the depths of the forest, Lean Elk beside him and Baby trailing along behind them both on her long leash. Damita could not help but see that her brother was changing before her very eyes. As each day passed, he seemed more Indian than white, especially now that Lean Elk had lent him a breechclout to wear instead of his breeches and shirt, and on his feet were colorfully beaded moccasins.

Damita smiled behind a hand as she watched Timothy talking with several of the young braves, for he had soon learned many Omaha words!

She looked to the heavens, thanking the Lord for giving her a brother who accepted changes instead of one who might brood and fight her every inch of the way against this new life they had been catapulted into.

She also said a silent prayer of thanks that Timothy had gotten well and that none of Iron Cloud's people had come down with the measles. It was now long past the incubation period, and she no longer watched for signs among the Omaha each day which might mean they would soon be downed with the disease.

Filled with peace, she soon entered into the day's activities, amazed at herself and how she was learning the ways of the Omaha women, and not resenting it. She felt strangely at home with these people.

And then a troubling thought came to her. For so long now, she had not allowed herself to think about Jonathan or to wonder when he would find her and Timothy—wondering why he hadn't yet....

The thought sent a paralyzing chill through her.

Chapter Nineteen

Sunlight brushed the tops of the gentle Illinois hills, but shrouds of mist still lingered in the shadowed fields, caressing the grasses with sparkling dew. Jonathan Jacobs rode stiffly in his saddle, urging his horse into a soft canter. His head was pounding, his throat dry, his face hot with fever.

But nothing would stop his determined search for Damita and Timothy, the search that had taken him to Illinois on the trail of Iron Cloud and his people.

After discovering that Iron Cloud and his people had fled the reservation at almost the same time that Damita and Timothy disappeared, Jonathan had concluded that Iron Cloud was their abductor, although not truly understanding why.

Unless to settle a score.

If Jonathan allowed himself to recall Iron

Cloud's last visit to his office, and remembered Iron Cloud and Damita coming face to face, seemingly instantly attracted to one another, it made his blood boil. Iron Cloud had probably at that very instant begun his plans for the abduction—for his act of vengeance.

Jonathan's brow furrowed. He couldn't help but wonder why Timothy had been included in the abduction, for the boy had surely by now proven that he was a hindrance.

Jonathan wiped a bead of cold sweat from his brow; his shoulders slouched like dead weights with his worsening health. He had heard rumors that Iron Cloud had chosen Illinois for his destination. Black Coyote, a renegade Omaha brave, was responsible for the rumor, but when Jonathan had tried to find Black Coyote to ask him to lead the search, he had disappeared into thin air.

Jonathan cast weary eyes over at Brian Davis who, of all the soldiers at Fort Calhoun, had been the best choice to be assigned the duty of finding Iron Cloud. It was no secret that Brian and Iron Cloud had ridden together during the War and were still friends. It would seem a twist of cruel fate for Iron Cloud if his friend uncovered his secret flight path.

That, above all else, was why Jonathan had requested Brian for this particular journey into parts unknown.

He would enjoy seeing Iron Cloud's admiration for Brian turn to a seething hate.

The pleasant stretch of land left behind, the entourage of soldiers and Jonathan crossed a stream that debouched through a swampy place thick with saplings, scrub, and reeds, where mosquitoes began swarming around Jonathan, attacking his face. He swatted and cursed, then rode on into a region that was a pathless maze of marshy bottoms, thickets of briar and thorns, great mats of vines, and acres of tall cane whose leaf edges sliced skin like razors.

And then that was left behind, and he was riding across a stretch of meadow where bluebonnet flowers bloomed in erect clusters, bonnet-shaped flowers with white-streaked upper petals.

Brian had stayed his distance from Jonathan, still fuming inside from having been chosen to search out his good friend. Friends did not deceive one another. And finding Iron Cloud would be the worst deceit of all. If Iron Cloud had wanted him to know his plans for the abduction and the details of his secret departure, he would have told him. They had confided in one another for years.

As it was, Iron Cloud had not felt free to tell Brian, and Brian now understood why. Iron Cloud had had enough insight to realize that perhaps Brian would be forced to tell of his whereabouts, if he knew.

Except, of course, that Brian, being the masterful tracker that he was, might find Iron Cloud.

At first Brian had tried to lead Jonathan in circles, taking longer to reach Illinois than it should, to discourage him and cause him to turn back to Fort Calhoun.

But once his deception was discovered, he had been forced to go in earnest in Iron Cloud's direction.

Disgruntled, Brian rested a hand on a pistol holstered at his waist, knowing that whatever Iron Cloud did, it was for the good of his people. Yet, his decision to abduct two white people, if he had really done it, puzzled Brian, for this had never been Iron Cloud's way of dealing with revenge. If it had been just the woman, that would have made more sense, for Brian had realized quickly that Iron Cloud had been captivated with her.

But to also take the boy? That did not make sense, unless it was done entirely as a vengeful act.

Having watched Jonathan carefully these past two days and having noticed how flushed his face was and how he seemed to sway sometimes in the saddle, as though ready to fall from it, Brian nudged the sides of his mustang with the heels of his boots and rode up beside him.

"You don't look so good," he said, gazing at Jonathan with troubled eyes.

"Never you mind with how I look," Jonathan grumbled, casting Brian an angry glance. "Just do your duty. Earn your pay the government is so generous to hand over to you. Get me to Iron Cloud's village."

Brian's eyebrows forked as Jonathan coughed

raspily into a cupped hand, and then noticed for the first time a rash on the agent's neck above the collar line. "Good Lord, man," he said, a sudden fear gripping him. "Why didn't you tell us you had measles? Or do you want us all to catch it and join you in your misery?"

Jonathan's mouth went agape and his eyes widened in sudden fear as he stared at Brian. "What do you mean—I have measles?" he said throatily. "Damn it, I've got a cold. That's all."

"I've never heard of anyone with a cold breaking out with a rash," Brian said. "You're obviously ill and feverish. I'm relieving you of your command. I will be taking charge of the men. For everyone's best interest, I believe we should return to the fort."

Light-headed, Jonathan weaved in the saddle, his hand reaching to his neck, and then his hot face. "It can't be," he mumbled. "I . . . can't . . . have measles."

He paused, feeling too ill to remain in the saddle. He stopped his horse and slid to the ground, his knees crumpling beneath him in their total weakness. He held his head in his hands for a moment, then suddenly recalled what Brian had said about returning to the fort and pulled himself back to his feet as he clung to his saddle.

"I'm not going anywhere except to the Omaha village," he said raspily. "You've been ordered to track down Iron Cloud. No one has rescinded that order."

"I have," Brian said, waving down the others,

stopping them. "I've got to get you back to the fort where you can receive proper medical attention."

"I don't need a doctor," Jonathan said, slowly reaching for his holstered pistol. His fingers shook so violently that he could hardly remove it from its holster, but finally he managed to do so.

Resting the pistol barrel on the back of his horse, Jonathan aimed it at Brian. "I order you to continue the mission," he said, placing his finger on the trigger. "If you don't, I'll shoot you."

"And get arrested for out-and-out murder when you return to Fort Calhoun?" Brian said, laughing sarcastically. "I think not. Or perhaps you're crazed even more than normal from fever?"

Dazed from illness and not truly comprehending the results of his actions, since he was not capable of thinking clearly, Jonathan fired off a shot at Brian. The bullet just missed Brian's left shoulder and frightened Jonathan's horse into galloping away in a frenzy, leaving Jonathan standing shakily, his pistol now dropped to his side.

Brian was stunned for a moment, then in a flash of anger wheeled his horse around and kicked the gun from Jonathan's hand.

"You sonofabitch, you deserve to die out here alone," Brian growled. "You've been nothing but a thorn in the sides of all the Indians in Nebraska. No other agent could be as vindictive, cruel, and greedy as you. I don't know what President Grant was thinking by appointing you."

"You'll . . . be . . . sorry," Jonathan panted out,

his eyes glassy with fever. "Damn it, Brian, you'll pay for this. When I return to Fort Calhoun, I'll have your head in a platter!"

"If you don't have the sense to return to the fort with us now, we have no choice but to leave without you."

Brian gave Jonathan a pitying look, then turned his horse around, thundering away, the soldiers following.

Brian had heard about Jonathan ordering the soldier to kill the woman and child to rid himself of worry about their spreading the disease to others of their tribe.

"He has no gun pointed at his head, but he is no less a doomed man than those he ordered to be shot," Brian murmured to himself, bitter that proof had not been found of the murders.

He had searched for days for the bodies and had not found them. Had he, the world would have been rid of a madman, for Jonathan would have been hanged.

But without proof, there had been no way to convince Washington that he was guilty, and so he had been free to remain at his post at Fort Calhoun, continuing to wreak havoc among the Indian population.

Brian's thoughts went to Iron Cloud, wondering exactly where he was and if he was safe. Also, he could not help but wonder about Damita and Timothy, and if they were with Iron Cloud. If not accompanied by many soldiers, Brian would have been tempted to go on searching for Iron Cloud, if only to satisfy his curiosity about all of this.

But he would do nothing to endanger his friend, now that Jonathan was not among them. He would not lead the other soldiers to him, for who was to say who was Iron Cloud's enemy or friend among them?

He rode on, comforting himself with the hope that one day he would see his friend again under more pleasant circumstances.

Jonathan tried to get up from the ground, but his knees were too weak. His head pounding, his mouth so dry it felt as though it were lined with cotton, soaking up his saliva, he began crawling on the ground toward the shine of water through the bushes a short distance away.

God, he despaired to himself, not seeing his horse anywhere. His horse, as well as the soldiers, had deserted him!

An emptiness assailed him, and fear gnawed at his consciousness. Too weak to go any farther, he stretched out on his stomach and wept into his hands. "What am I going to do?" he sobbed. "Lord, what have I done to deserve this?"

He wept a moment longer, then resumed crawling until he came to the embankment of the lake. Grunting, he shoved his body along the ground until he was able to dangle his hands down into the water. Cupping them, he brought out two handsful of cool, refreshing liquid and gulped it down thirstily, then sighed heavily and moved to his side.

Lying in a fetal position, hard chills ravaging his body, Jonathan drifted off into a lethargic sleep, filled with nightmares of Indians surrounding him, each taking turns firing arrows into his body.

Chapter Twenty

Several Days Later.

The drums were beating, the rapid tapping creating a steady, rhythmic pulsing sound, accompanied by gourd and deer-hoof rattles fastened by thongs to a beaded stick.

It was the night to celebrate the completion of the Omaha village in the forested haunts of Illinois, and to give thanks to Wakoda for having blessed them with such a new and wondrous land of plenty.

The air was filled with the tantalizing aroma of various foods cooking over a great outdoor fire. Several poles, called *who-uthugashke*, were set on the edge of the fire, slanting toward it. From these kettle poles the pots were hung.

The scent was of the ground nut called *nu*, which was boiled, then peeled and eaten as a vegetable, as was the root of the great yellow water lily, *te-thawe*. The tender shoots of the milk weed were added to corn and meat, and mushrooms were fried in deep fat. Shoulders of game roasted over the flames, alongside several ducks thrust on a stick, standing up before the fire.

Damita was sitting with Iron Cloud and his people at the far edge the village, clustered around this outdoor fire, the firelight shedding a ruddy glow on the faces of those who made the wide circle around the fire. In the distance, the tents and wigwams stood pale and specterlike. Overhead, the stars were brilliantly white in the clear, dark sky, and as the drums and rattles stopped their musical cadence, no sound but the snapping of the burning wood broke in on the flow of an elder's words as he began delighting everyone with a tale which drew from his store of memories, myths, and fables.

Damita glanced over at Timothy, Lean Elk close beside him, their faces intent on listening to the adventures of the pygmies, and of the *gajazhe*, the little people who played about the woods and prairies who led people astray.

Smiling to herself, Damita noticed how Timothy had learned to sit steadily on his heels like the young Indian braves his age. Slowly, but most surely, he was changing, becoming more like those he played and rode with each day. If not for the color of his skin, he would most definitely pass for a young Omaha brave! Even tonight he wore a beaded headband and strips of fur around his upper arms.

He never wore his breeches and shirts and shoes anymore. He mingled with his friends barechested, his breechclout looking more and more natural on him as each day passed.

Damita herself was clad in a soft new buckskin dress embellished with colorful beads. On her feet were intricately designed moccasins, and her hair had been drawn back and braided, a spray of flowers over her left ear fastened into the strands of her hair.

Again the dry sound of puffin beaks, used as rattles, and the insistent beating of drums filled the night air with steady, rhythmic sounds. Damita turned her head to see that the elder Omaha brave had finished speaking and that the people were joining together, singing various songs in time with the beats of the instruments. Damita had been told that songs were an integral part of the life of the Omaha, that through songs they approached the mysterious Wakoda; through songs they voiced their emotion.

They sang in their native tongue only, beautiful to Damita even though she could not understand what they were saying. She listened closely, enjoying this time of camaraderie with people who had welcomed her as one of them with open hearts and arms.

"Uho-thete-nide-tho," they sang.
"Uho-thete-nide-tho.

I-dakutha-nide-tho.
Uho-thete-nide-tho-he.
I-dakutha-nide-tho-he-tho."

And then Iron Cloud turned to Damita, and as everyone listened, their eyes on Damita and Iron Cloud, he sang the song to Damita in a translation that she could understand.

"The feast awaits you—come eat,
The feast is awaiting you,
Members, comrades, come and eat.
The feast awaiting stands before you, come,
Members, comrades, come and eat! *He tho."*

Without further words to Damita, Iron Cloud, dressed in a brief breechclout only, rose before his people and, along with several other warriors, went to the food that several women were placing on wooden platters.

Damita had been told earlier that at a formal feast like this one, the men served the food. The offering to Wakoda was made by the man of the highest rank present, which meant that the honors went to Iron Cloud, their chief.

Very soon everyone had been served. Damita observed their politeness, each having said thank-you as they were given their meal.

Along with Damita, they now watched silently, almost breathlessly, as Iron Cloud stood beside the roaring fire to make his people's offering to their Great Spirit. He lifted a small portion of meat,

Cassie Edwards

then dropped it into the flames in recognition that all food was the gift of Wakoda.

After that, everyone smiled, chatted, and ate, some using horn spoons, others metal spoons, which most Omaha referred to as metal buffalo horn.

"You are enjoying the celebration?" Iron Cloud asked, leaning close to Damita as they lay their empty plates aside. "Your alliance with the Omaha feels stronger because of it?"

Damita sighed leisurely, fearing this happiness that she was feeling, thinking that it surely could not last forever. Everything seemed perfect in her life, so satisfying. When she was with Iron Cloud, a sense of peace always settled over her. When he touched her, she turned into sweet, quavering jelly!

"Yes, I'm enjoying myself," she murmured, smiling at him. "Immensely."

Great whoops and shouts directed their attention elsewhere, their gaze stopping at several young boys and girls who had quickly eaten and were now playing amongst themselves.

Damita's gaze found Timothy and Lean Elk among the older children, standing by as observers instead of participating in the game among the children. Damita turned her eyes back to those who were playing, noticing that a string was tied around the waist of one of the young boys, the same string then being attached to a long line of children.

There was much merriment and laughter as the

children began singing and running, making their merry way through the village, each one repeating an innocent prank of their leader—perhaps tossing a pebble at the door of a wigwam or knocking over an unsteady pile of wood. The line was kept by each child holding to the string about the waist of the boy in front.

"What they are playing is called *uhe-basho-sho*, or crooked path, known also as follow-the-leader," Iron Cloud explained, his eyes straying occasionally to Timothy, proud of how he was dressed and how he seemed to be one with the other young braves his age. He was proud that he had so quickly accepted his new life. Iron Cloud could feel his bond growing stronger and stronger with Timothy each day, and nothing could please him more. He had not only captured the heart of the woman he loved, but also the one person in her life that meant so much to her—her brother.

He smiled to himself, thinking that yes, this made him comfortable, very comfortable....

The line of children broke away, and they became quickly involved in another game. The boys who played warrior wore war bonnets made from corn husks, and the girls were carrying blankets.

"They are now playing going-on-the-hunt," Iron Cloud softly explained. He then nodded toward some smaller children who stood by, watching. "See the smaller girls yonder? They are carrying dolls made from corncobs. See the smaller boys? They have with them hobby horses which are their make-believe ponies. They are made from sunflower stalks, with one nodding bloom left on the end. They will soon race these ponies. They will ride one stalk, and trail two others as fresh ponies."

"How cute," Damita said, laughing softly. "And, Iron Cloud, they all seem so content. Surely that makes your heart swell with pride, to know that your plan has worked—that you have moved your people and they are happy with the move."

"They are happy, yes," Iron Cloud said, frowning down at her. "Yet, again, a part of them is sad. They will never stop missing their homeland. The reservation they do not miss. But the land of Nebraska, the Nebraskan sky, the Nebraskan birds— yes, they miss it all, but they are not the sort to complain. They learned long ago to make the best of what Wakoda gives them. It was *I* who could not sit still for the little my people had. Wakoda understood my misgivings—my unhappiness, or I would not be blessed today with so many smiling faces on my people."

Damita cuddled close to him, slipping one of her hands into his. "I feel so blessed myself," she whispered, gazing rapturously into his eyes. "My darling, you have given me such happiness. How can I ever repay you?"

"By being my wife," Iron Cloud said, squeezing her hand affectionately. "Soon. We will give my people more time to adjust to the idea, and then we will become as one, for eternity."

"Nothing could make me happier," Damita murmured, then accepted another plate of food as one of the braves brought it to her. She laughed loosely as she eyed the food, her eyebrows lifting quizzically as she tried to figure out what it was.

"My people consider that a delicacy," Iron Cloud said, seeing her hesitate to eat the new offering. "It is made from the marrow from the foreleg and hind-leg bone of the deer. A bread is made from this by pounding the end of a sprig of the wild cherry, used in serving the marrow. This cherry stick is called *wazhibe ibagu-de*."

Iron Cloud lifted it to her lips. Damita took a small bite, tasting the rich sweetness, then eagerly took it from him and ate the rest as he ate his own portion.

The rest of the evening was filled with more food, games, and song. Damita listened intently to Iron Cloud as a hush fell over the village while he told a group of small children, who sat wide-eyed before him, how it was at the very beginning of time—about the mysteries of creation.

"In the beginning," he said, smiling from child to child, "Wakoda, the Great Spirit, made this world for his pleasure. He piled up the mountains, scooped out the lakes, traced the rivers, planted the forests. He created the insects, the fish, the reptiles, the birds, the beasts, and man. All of our flesh and all the breath of life is a measure of the Great Spirit. All are his children, and man is but a little higher than the animals; he is better only in having a better understanding and better Knowledge of the Great Spirit...."

Afterwards, Iron Cloud received big hugs from

each of the small children, and then it was time to retire for the night.

Timothy came anxiously to Damita, his bobcat in his arms. "I would like to spend the night with Lean Elk," he said, his eyes wide. "May I, Damita? We have so much to talk about."

"Did Girl Who Laughs give Lean Elk permission to ask you?" she asked, repositioning a lock of his hair back beneath his beaded headband, thinking he had never looked so sweet.

"Yes," Timothy said, looking anxiously over his shoulder as Lean Elk waited for him, a few other boys with him. He turned begging eyes back to Damita. "Please, Sis? Please?"

Damita eyed the boys carefully, then looked over at Iron Cloud who gave her a slow smile and a nod of approval. She gave Timothy a hug. "Yes, go on," she said softly. "But go directly to Lean Elk's dwelling. Don't get into any mischief."

"We plan to sit around the fire and tell stories," Timothy said over his shoulder as he ran away from Damita, the gang of boys quickly clustering around him as he reached them.

Damita watched him walk away with them, finding it refreshing to see Timothy happy with his new friends. He had been forced to leave many friends behind in Boston. But he had found substitutes, it seemed, and perhaps even better friendships among these boys whose every word and movement seemed to be that of sincerity. Back in Boston, so many of the boys were spoiled, causing their mothers many a sleepless night with their antics.

Here, in the forested hills of Illinois, everything seemed so right—so perfect!

Arm-in-arm, Damita and Iron Cloud went to their own shared dwelling, where the fire in the firepit in the center of the wigwam had burned down to softly glowing embers. For a moment, Damita stopped and gazed around her, at her new home, finding it adequate and surprisingly refreshing after the elaborateness of her house back in Boston, where her mother had made sure every fancy thing had its place, and no one dared to touch or move them.

Here, in the simplicity of the wigwam, she felt more alive—more free.

The furniture was simple. Robes used for bedding were of hide taken from the bear in the winter when the fur was the heaviest. The pillows were of soft deerskin stuffed with the long winter hair of the deer.

Except for a few willow seats, there was nowhere to sit in the wigwam.

The cooking utensils were few, but adequate. The women made pottery of a rather coarse type, ornamented with incised lines. A pottery kettle always hung or set over the fire. Bowls of pottery and wood were used.

At the far end of the wigwam, a blanket had been hung on a rope that separated Timothy's sleeping area from Iron Cloud and Damita's. Most nights, Iron Cloud and Damita took a long stroll in the forest, to find privacy enough for sharing their wild embraces.

"Tonight, my White Willow, we have the dwelling all to ourselves," Iron Cloud said, slipping the flowers from her hair and tossing them aside.

"So that is why you gave me such an eager nod when Timothy asked if he could stay all night with Lean Elk?" Damita asked, her heart thrilling as he slipped her dress over her head, the warmth from the coals in the firepit reaching her flesh, caressing it.

"Perhaps?" Iron Cloud said, tossing her dress aside, then bending low to a knee, lifting one of her feet to remove a moccasin, and then the other.

"Do you not see the same opportunities as I?" he asked, looking up at her with a devilish sort of grin.

Damita moved to her knees before him and placed her fingers to the waistband of his breechclout and began slowly lowering it over his hips. "My darling, my scheming started early this morning, before you even gave me my first kiss," she murmured.

Iron Cloud sucked in a wild breath and closed his eyes to the ecstasy when Damita circled his hard shaft with her fingers, moving them over him, slowly, then faster and faster.

"Scheming?" he said between gritted teeth. "My woman knows how to scheme?"

"Only because of you, my darling, and my need to be with you," Damita said, tossing his breechclout aside.

"And what did you do?" Iron Cloud said, his hand on hers, stopping the pleasure that she was giving him, for it was too much, too soon. He placed his hands to her shoulders and eased her down onto a thick layer of pelts. He moved over her, his teeth nipping one of her breasts, drawing a leisurely sigh from deep within her.

"While bathing in the river with Girl Who Laughs, I hinted that she should ask Lean Elk if he might want Timothy to spend the night with them," she said, laughing softly. "It seems Girl Who Laughs saw the suggestion as good."

"Good for you and me," Iron Cloud said, sliding her thighs apart with one of his knees. "My White Willow, my schemer . . ." he said, then crushed his mouth to her lips and gave her a wild kiss as he plunged his hardness inside her.

Damita choked out a cry of pleasure and locked her legs around his waist, again lost in a reverie of need. He splayed his hands against the rounded flesh of her bottom, molding her against him. His body plunged to hers, whispering fierce words of love to her against her hot, wet lips.

And then they made love slowly. Every part of their bodies awakened to delight and pleasure, and each lazy caress brought them closer to the ecstasy they sought.

And then the explosion claimed and rocked them, the spinning sensation rising up and flooding their whole bodies.

And then they lay next to one another, pressing themselves tightly together, Iron Cloud's hands roaming slowly over Damita's exquisite creamy flesh.

"I could make love to you all night, if you would allow it," Iron Cloud whispered against her cheek.

"I allow it," Damita whispered, sighing and closing her eyes as his lips slithered down her neck to her breast. . . .

Chapter Twenty-one

Iron Cloud's birch canoe glided noiselessly through the water, his paddle rising and sinking in the river, dripping and flashing in the sunshine. The air was filled with freshness. Being introduced to another way of Indian life, Damita and Timothy sat next to each other behind Iron Cloud, enjoying moving beneath the low-hanging trees that lined this river that snaked through the forest, still and tranquil.

Along one side of the river, trees were void of their leaves, standing knee deep in the water like grotesque skeletons beckoning to them. Damita turned her eyes from these strange trees, not wanting anything to spoil her outing today. Iron Cloud had promised to teach Timothy many things, and she had been invited to be a part of the lessons.

She smiled to herself, thinking that she understood why she had been included so heartily.

Iron Cloud seemed not to be able to get enough of her, which was just the way she felt about him. They both cherished every waking moment, as though there would be no more. Life was a gamble, it seemed, and one needed to take advantage of every heartbeat!

She gazed at Iron Cloud's bare back, admiring the rippling of his muscles as he continued drawing the paddle through the water, the effort causing beads of perspiration to glisten on his copper skin, like raindrops during a gentle spring rain. She hoped that Timothy would not glance her way, for she knew that within her eyes her deep feelings for Iron Cloud were revealed. The memory of their many hours of lovemaking filled her cheeks with a heated blush to match the heat that was troubling her at the juncture of her thighs.

She had never known that love could be like this—so totally consuming!

But of course, she had concluded long ago that there were no other men like Iron Cloud on this earth. When God made him, he had surely thrown away the mold!

Damita clutched to the sides of the canoe when Iron Cloud suddenly changed its course and began taking it toward shore. After beaching it on a spit of sand, he went to Damita and lifted her into his arms and carried her to dry land.

Timothy hopped out of the canoe and hurried his steps until he was trudging along beside them, his bare chest puffed out with pride that Iron Cloud was taking this special time with him to

teach him more ways of his people. That Damita
had come with them did not spoil it for Timothy.

Timothy gave her a shaded glance, thinking that
he would not mind that she was there as long as
she did not treat him like a baby in front of Iron
Cloud. To him, that would be worse than death,
especially now that he had succeeded at regaining
Iron Cloud's admiration, as well as that of many
others of his village.

His new friends seemed to look up to him and
catch onto his each and every word.

Of course, he thought to himself, smiling, they
did not see that he did the same with them. Each
word, each movement of his friends were new lessons to him. Each day he arose with the hopes of
learning more.

He never wanted to stop learning. He could even
now envision himself as a great warrior!

One day, he *would* be an Omaha warrior, for he
would have earned the title by his honorable actions and deeds!

His thoughts were so filled with fantasies that
he stumbled in a hole and suddenly found himself
flat on his face on the ground. Iron Cloud went to
Timothy's aid, placing a gentle hand to his arm
as he helped him back to his feet.

Humiliated, Timothy could not hide the blush
that suffused his face as he brushed dirt and pieces
of dried leaves from his chest and breechclout.

"Timothy, you must be ..." Damita began, but
stopped in mid-sentence when she saw the instant
look in her brother's eyes that revealed to her

again that he did not want her babying him.

She smiled awkwardly and took a step back from him, then turned and walked beside Iron Cloud as they moved farther away from the river, with Timothy now at Iron Cloud's other side, obviously watching his feet so that another mishap would not occur. Baby had been left behind for this outing, Lean Elk having been more than eager to care for the kitten.

Iron Cloud walked a while longer, then stopped when he found what he considered a comfortable place to sit and talk beside a pond of quiet water, where water lilies bloomed in masses, and water spiders skipped across the water beneath occasional splashes of sunshine as it poured through the breaks in the foliage overhead.

"Sit," Iron Cloud said, gesturing toward Timothy, and then Damita. He took Damita's hand and sat down with her on the ground where moss was spread like a large, spongy cushion.

Timothy sat down on the ground and looked devotedly up at Iron Cloud. He drew his bare knees to his chest and hugged them with his arms, crossing his feet at his ankles.

"Timothy, there are many sayings of our elders that have been carried down through generations after generations of Omaha that I would like to share with you," Iron Cloud said, stretching one long, lean leg out and folding the other up before him, encircling it with his arms. He took on the appearance of one that was now elsewhere, lost in time.

"The path of the lazy leads to disgrace," he began. "When a boy uses a knife in cutting his meat, the old men have always said, 'The knife eats more meat; you should bite it.'" He looked at Timothy with eyes filled with wisdom. "The meaning behind this saying is that the use of the knife makes one lazy. A man should rely on his own resource; the one who so trains himself is ready for any emergency."

Timothy's eyes widened, anxious to hear more.

Damita looked from Iron Cloud to Timothy, feeling as though she were in the presence of a husband, a son and father, the father teaching the son! In a sense, she *was* Timothy's mother, and once she was married, Iron Cloud would become Timothy's father, even if he wasn't so by blood.

She listened earnestly, so filled with pride and a strange sort of melancholy peace.

Iron Cloud continued, "If a boy borrows a kettle for his mother, it is customary never to return a borrowed kettle entirely empty—leave a little of the last portion that was cooked in it. If a lad should help himself to that which came home in the kettle, old men would say, 'If you eat what is brought home in the kettle, your arrows will twist when you shoot; they will not go straight.'"

Iron Cloud paused and smiled at Timothy, reaching a hand to Timothy's thick hair and tousling it playfully beneath the beaded headband. "The meaning behind that saying," he said softly, "is that the youth who thinks first of himself and forgets the old will never prosper. Nothing will go straight for him."

Iron Cloud shifted his position. He folded both legs beneath him and picked up a blade of grass, sucking it for a moment between his teeth, then tossed it away as he once again began talking.

"Young men are forbidden to smoke," he said, looking firmly down at Timothy. "Smoking makes young men short-winded, and when they go into battle they will be quickly overcome. And you must learn to make arrows. Old men have said that if one does not make arrows, he will borrow moccasins, leggings, and robes, and be disliked by the persons from whom he borrows. The teaching behind this is that one must be industrious in order to have things of one's own. If a boy does not make arrows for himself, and a young man who is industrious shows you his arrows, you will be tempted to steal from him."

"And what of warring?" Timothy anxiously asked. "Of becoming a warrior?" He leaned forward, awaiting an answer.

"Although warring has been required to preserve my people through the years, and it is true that I rode with the white pony soldiers during the war of the white man called the Civil War, my heart is one of peace. My desire is never to have to raise a firearm against anyone, except those who make themselves my arch enemy, or while in defense of my loved ones," Iron Cloud tried to explain. "But I will teach you some important aspects of warring, for, my child, before you die, you will also see many useless deaths. It is the way of men, to find reasons for fighting and hating one another."

Timothy went to Iron Cloud and knelt down before him. Iron Cloud reached a hand to his shoulder and clasped his fingers into his flesh.

"There are two classes of warfare, Timothy," Iron Cloud said. "Defensive and aggressive. *Ti-adi*, the defensive class of warring, is when one is fighting for the protection of the home, the women and children. *Nuatathisho*, aggressive warfare, meaning war with men, is caused by the quarrels and schemes of ambitious men whose idea it is that war is allied to the cosmic forces and under their control. The storm, with its destructive lightning and deafening roars of thunder, was regarded as a manifestation of the war phase of the mysterious Wakoda, our people's Great Spirit."

Iron Cloud then added, "Our young warriors are taught that it is Wakoda, not man, who decrees death on the field of battle," he said, then leaned away from Timothy as Timothy sat down on the ground before him.

"Tell me more," Timothy said anxiously. "I must know everything of your people. I wish to one day be a warrior!"

"A warrior, yes, in time, but I hope you will never be forced to enter battle," Iron Cloud said, gazing into the pond wistfully.

He glanced at Damita, then looked at Timothy again, seeing and admiring all over again the need of the young man to have his head filled with the knowledge of a way of life that he had not been born into. It seemed that he was more hungry for this sort of learning than even some of the young Omaha braves.

And Iron Cloud could see why. Timothy wished to stand with the others and speak of these things as knowledgeably as they.

"I will speak now of horses and ownership of them," Iron Cloud said. "A warrior must not be envious and maim the horse of another man if it is a fine horse to look at. If one is not industrious, he will borrow a horse from a young man who may be insignificant, of no position in the tribe, and he may be proud that he rides a horse even if it is not his own. He will borrow a bridle, too, and he will be disliked by all other men, for he has stolen. Also, one must not take another's robe or blanket, or his moccasins. You will be tempted to do these things if you are not industrious, and if you yield to temptation you will be shunned by all persons. All persons dislike a borrower. Also, stolen food never satisfies hunger."

Iron Cloud paused, then started to talk, but a sound like someone crying in the brush behind them drew them all quickly to their feet. Iron Cloud drew his knife as he moved stealthily toward the sound, Damita and Timothy trailing along behind him.

When Iron Cloud separated the bushes and peered downward, he gasped and quickly slipped his knife back into its sheath.

"Baby!" Timothy gasped as he rushed on past

Iron Cloud and fell to his knees beside a dripping wet bobcat kitten that lay on its side, its front right paw swollen and bloody.

He drew Baby up into his arms and held him close to his chest, crying as he gazed questioningly up into Damita's eyes, then Iron Cloud's. "How did she get here?" he sobbed, no longer concerned about whether or not he looked like a child, with a child's emotions. "And look at her paw! She's . . . hurt!"

Iron Cloud eased Baby from Timothy's arms. The kitten's eyes were hazy with pain as it looked pleadingly up at Iron Cloud, its meows sounding like a baby's soft whimpering. "As you can see, her leash is broken," he said as he smoothed his fingers over the bloody fur, separating it enough to study the wound. "She must have been following us all along. Even while we were in the canoe she must have been behind us in the water, swimming after us."

"I thought all cats were afraid of water," Damita said, her heart going out to the wounded, soaked kitten. She reached a hand out to Baby and stroked its wet fur lovingly. "Poor Baby. Poor little baby."

"She apparently loves Timothy more than she hates water," Iron Cloud said, placing the kitten on the ground, moving to his knees beside it. "And while following Timothy, she was bitten by a snake."

"A snake?" Timothy said frantically, falling to his knees beside Iron Cloud, his heart pounding out his fear for his beloved pet. "No. Oh, please no!"

"I hope we've found her in time," Iron Cloud said, slipping his knife from its sheath again. He gave Damita and Timothy stern looks. "Which one of you want to hold her down while I cut into her flesh, so that I can try and suck the venom out?"

Timothy swallowed hard and quickly volunteered by taking the kitten into his arms again. "Do it, Iron Cloud," he said bravely. "I've got a good grip on her."

"She may bite and scratch you," Damita worried aloud as she knelt down beside Timothy. She held her arms out to her brother. "Let me hold her, Timothy. I'll give her to you as soon as Iron Cloud is through with her." She smiled wanly at Timothy as he cast her a doubtful glance. "Timothy, remember that I am a practiced doctor. I have helped Father many a time when people have brought their injured pets to his office."

"Baby is my pet," Timothy said, his voice breaking. "I will hold her."

Damita gazed into her brother's eyes, seeing his tears flooding them again, then nodded slowly. "All right," she murmured. She gritted her teeth and clasped her hands on her lap as Iron Cloud eased the knife into the kitten's bloody paw. The kitten's whole body lurched quickly, then calmed again as Iron Cloud placed his lips to the opened wound and began sucking and spitting.

Soon the ordeal was over. Iron Cloud washed his mouth out thoroughly; Damita cleaned the kitten's wound and wrapped it with a strip of her buckskin dress that she had ripped from the hem; and Timothy hugged and rocked the kitten in his arms, crooning a lullaby to her.

"We should return to the village now," Iron Cloud said, placing an arm around Damita's waist as they looked for a moment longer at Timothy and his devotion to his kitten. "Tonight will tell whether or not there will be a tomorrow for Baby."

Timothy looked wildly up at Iron Cloud, tears flooding his eyes again. "She won't die," he sobbed. "She . . . she can't. If so, it'll be my fault. I shouldn't have left her behind. I . . . I should have brought her with me. She depends on me for her existence." He swallowed hard. "I've become her parents—both mother and father." He lay down over her, his cheek against her dried-out fur, feeling Baby's eyes on him. "And I let her down. I . . . I neglected her!"

A heavy hand on his shoulder drew Timothy's head up again and found Iron Cloud's dark eyes on him.

"You blame yourself unjustly," Iron Cloud said softly. "You have no control over Baby's destiny. When Baby dies was planned the day the kitten was formed in its mother's womb, the same as your destiny and mine was formed. Now we must wait and see what the plan is for Baby. Blaming yourself is not going to change a thing. So let us leave now. When we are back at the village, your time and emotions will be better spent in making your pet more comfortable."

A burden seemed to have been lifted from Timothy's heart, and again he saw the wisdom of this man, this Omaha chief. Smiling, stifling a sob in the depths of his throat, he rose to his feet and welcomed Damita's arm around his waist as they began walking back to the canoe, Iron Cloud carrying Baby.

Timothy leaned closer to Damita. "I didn't mean to be such a baby," he whispered so only she could hear.

"You weren't a baby," Damita whispered back, smiling down at him. "You were a person filled with much compassion. That trait is quite admirable, little brother. Quite admirable."

A wide grin spread across Timothy's face. His steps were proud and his heart was light as he continued walking through the forest until the beached canoe came into sight.

Damita gazed over at Iron Cloud. They exchanged knowing looks, which said so much that did not need to be spoken aloud.

Half-starved and half-crazed from the raging temperature, Jonathan crawled through the forest, desperate to find someone that would help him. He had heard hoofbeats in the distance, but no one had ventured close enough for him to yell at them.

His thoughts were muddled now as to how he had gotten there, and with whom—even why. But he had enough sense to know that he needed quick attention, or he might die.

"Help!" he cried, his voice parched from lack of water, having crawled in a direction opposite the river, hoping to find a trail that would lead to civilization. "Please...help...me!"

Totally exhausted, Jonathan rolled over on his back and peered up at the sky. The afternoon was ebbing. The distant hills were shaded in purples and grays. The sunlight was liquid gold, pouring across a landscape of bronze and green.

A chill wind sighed in the grass. When Jonathan saw the horizon fading off in the distance, a quick panic seized him.

"Oh, God, let someone find me...before...it gets dark," he prayed, then went limp as he drifted off into semi-consciousness.

Chapter Twenty-two

Absorbed in her quill work, Damita was sitting on a willow seat beside Timothy behind the privacy blanket in their wigwam, glad that Timothy was finally drifting off to sleep. Baby was snuggled close beside him, breathing more easily now, its pain seeming to have lessened. Iron Cloud had prepared a poltice from herbs and had applied this to the kitten's swollen paw. Now the swelling, as well as the fever, had lessened.

Damita had chosen to stay with Timothy to-night behind his privacy blanket to keep an eye on Baby while Timothy slept. Damita loved the kitten as though it were a child. She had said many silent prayers tonight that Baby would pull through and be as feisty as ever, the joy of all of the children in the village, and even the elders.

Lean Elk and Girl Who Laughs had apologized over and over again that Baby had found a way to escape their care. They had left Baby tied just outside their wigwam while they went for wood in the forest. The kitten had chewed its rope in half and had been gone when they returned.

"I'm sure that you are the cause of many a sleepless night tonight," Damita whispered to Baby, as Baby opened her green eyes and gave Damita a shy glance. "As for Timothy, I believe he was too exhausted from emotion to be able to stay awake any longer."

Damita lay her quill work aside and stroked Baby's stiff, spotted fur. "And he knows that I am here to care for you. He knows that I love you very much."

Damita leaned her face down and rubbed her cheek against Baby's face. "Nothing could be as sweet as you," she whispered. "Nothing."

Damita's heart soared with relief when Baby emitted its first purr since its mishap. "Why, listen to you," she whispered, tears pooling in her eyes. "That's the most beautiful sound I've heard in ages." She stroked Baby behind the ears, causing Baby to lean into her hand, purrs now more steady and louder.

"Yes, my dear kitten, you are going to be fine," Damita murmured.

Damita resumed her work, using the quill of a porcupine and a wild turkey's tassel for her very fine embroidery work tonight on a soft doeskin blanket.

Iron Cloud had taught her that the quills had to be plucked as soon as possible after the porcupine was killed, for if the skin became dry, the quills were liable to break. The quills were sorted as to length and size and laid in bladder bags, the outer or black ends being placed together.

The largest quills, those in the tail, were kept by themselves and were used in ornamenting comb cases and workbags. The long ones of medium size were reserved for fine work. The fine quills were used in embroidering the line on the middle of the upper part of the moccasin.

Too tired to continue with her decorative work, Damita laid it aside and stretched out beside the kitten, lodging Baby comfortably between herself and Timothy. Closing her eyes, snuggling close to the kitten, Damita felt that it was safe now to go to sleep, yet she did not want to give up her vigil yet. By morning she would resume her normal activities.

Her eyes opened momentarily as she glanced toward the privacy blanket, knowing that beyond it lay her beloved Iron Cloud. When she heard a faint snoring, she smiled contentedly to herself, her eyes drifting closed again. She was just feeling the lethargy of sleep when a slight noise on the other side of the blanket drew her abruptly awake again, her eyes wide, her heart thumping.

She scarcely breathed as she listened more closely, feeling somewhat foolish for letting herself be afraid when all along Iron Cloud was so close.

Her heart skipped a beat and her eyes grew wider. "Iron Cloud!" she whispered, but there was no response.

Knowing that she would not rest again until she was sure Iron Cloud was all right, Damita rose quietly to her knees and crawled the short distance to the blanket and slowly lifted a corner.

What she saw made her almost faint with alarm.

The fire's glow was bright enough for her to see the face of Black Coyote as he crept closer to Iron Cloud. He held a knife grasped tightly in one hand, the blade picking up the shine of the fire, making it gleam menacingly and cast dancing reflections along the walls and ceiling.

Damita's heart thudded wildly within her chest, knowing that she had to do something, and quickly. Her gaze swept around her, just outside the blanket, and her heart seemed to leap into her throat when she discovered Iron Cloud's rifle leaning up against the wall only a fraction away from her.

Unpracticed with firearms, she swallowed hard, but when she saw out of the corner of her eye that Black Coyote was starting to lean over her beloved, she threw the blanket aside and lunged for the rifle.

Grabbing it, she aimed it at Black Coyote, who was already stopped in mid-step, with disbelieving eyes and mouth agape over her sudden appearance from behind the blanket.

"Drop it, or by God I'll shoot," Damita said, her voice as steady as she could hold it.

Iron Cloud awakened with a jolt and bolted to his feet when he found Black Coyote standing over him, a knife in his hand, and with a shifting of his eyes found Damita standing with a rifle aimed at the renegade Omaha.

"Drop the knife, Black Coyote," Damita said, taking a step closer. "Drop it *now*." She was afraid to take her eyes off him to look at Iron Cloud, but she could feel his eyes on her, admiring her. This made her warm with pride—pride that she had had the courage to protect the man she loved!

Iron Cloud stood still for a moment, mesmerized by the sight of his White Willow standing there with a firearm, protecting him. In so many ways she had proved to be a valorous woman. And she could not prove her heroism nor how much she loved him any more than at this moment. His heart was filled with much at this moment for his woman.

Then he turned glaring eyes at Black Coyote, this renegade warrior who was not only a man of deceit, but too shameful ever to be called Omaha again! He went to Black Coyote and yanked the knife from his hand. "You have made a fatal error in judgment again," he said, his eyes squinting angrily into Black Coyote's. "You do not only want to be labeled a thief, but now a murderer? I never trusted you, Black Coyote, yet I did not think that you were this untrustworthy. What do you have to say for yourself?"

Black Coyote offered no response or explanation. He pursed his lips tightly together, squared his lean shoulders, and dared Iron Cloud with a stern stare.

Iron Cloud moved to stand beside Damita, and

as Timothy crawled from behind the blanket, all wide-eyed and stunned, Iron Cloud leaned the knife down and gave it to him.

Iron Cloud then eased the rifle from Damita's hands. "Would you not say that I have a brave woman?" he said, chuckling low as he gazed with contempt at Black Coyote. "Or did you think that she was still a captive, one who would assist you in your killing should she discover you standing over me, knife in hand?"

Black Coyote still made no response, yet his gaze shifted slowly from Iron Cloud to Damita, then slowly back to Iron Cloud again.

"And so you have nothing to say?" Iron Cloud said, setting aside his rifle. He went to Black Coyote and placed a hand at his throat, half lifting him from the floor. "That is good. What you would say would be meaningless. But what our people have to say should interest *you*. I am going to stand you before them and let them decide what your punishment should be. I think that you will wish for death, for anything less would be less than honorable."

Iron Cloud jerked his hand away from Black Coyote's throat, grabbed him by a wrist, and turned him so that his back was facing him.

Iron Cloud then turned to Damita. "If you wish, if you would be more comfortable with the situation, stay in our dwelling while sentencing for Black Coyote is being handed down," he said. "If the sentence calls for the renegade's death, it will be done quickly, immediately after the sentencing.

Perhaps you would not want to see this."

Damita's eyes were wide. She swallowed hard, not truly knowing what was expected of her. She wanted to be involved in everything Iron Cloud and his people did, to totally become as one with them—yet did that mean that she would have to witness an execution?

Yet, she knew that once she was married and was the chief's wife, everything—even taking part in the sentencing of those who had wronged the Omaha—would be expected of her. Her word would be as valuable as anyone else's in the village, especially since she was married to their chief.

"I will go with you," Damita said, her heart pounding, not knowing what to expect. If Black Coyote was killed by a violent means, she was not sure if she could stomach it.

Yet again, she reminded herself, that also would be a part of her future—having to accept any and all customs of the Omaha people.

Even sentencing one of their own to death.

Timothy rose to his feet and moved to Damita's side. He gazed intensely up at Iron Cloud. "I also wish to go," he said, squaring his bare shoulders. "If I am to be a warrior, I must be taught all ways of a warrior. That must include being able to witness punishments of those who have wronged . . . our people!"

Damita was taken aback by how her brother so readily included himself among Iron Cloud's people. He had more than adapted himself to their ways, he actually saw himself now as one of them.

This was surprising to Damita, yet she did not see any wrong in it. Wasn't she as dedicated—as determined—to make this work for herself, her brother, and Iron Cloud?

It was just that Timothy, in his innocence, had found it in his heart to adjust more quickly, more deeply.

Damita knelt beside Timothy and spoke up into his face. She took one of his hands and squeezed it affectionately. "Timothy, this time I think it would be best if you stayed with Baby," she encouraged him, not wanting her brother to be exposed to too much too soon that might color his vision of his future, since at this time, to him, it was one of magnificence and grandeur.

"Remember?" she tried to explain. "We decided, you and I and Iron Cloud, that if Baby made it through the night, we could expect her to totally recover. It would be best, Timothy, if you are there for her should she awaken and need something."

She paused, and quickly added, "Perhaps a drink, or more salve rubbed into her paw," she murmured. "We've had cats for pets before, while growing up in Boston. You know that a cat has a tendency to lick anything that gets on its paws. If Baby awakens and is troubled by the herbal salve, she might lick it and get ill from it."

Timothy cocked his head, his thoughts deep and serious. Then he nodded. "Of course, you are right, Sis," he said. "I'll see the next sentencing." He gave Iron Cloud a quick glance, then leaned his lips to Damita's ear. "I truly don't want to see any punishment tonight. It's not because I'm a coward, though. You do understand, don't you, Sis?"

"Yes, I understand," she whispered back, then patted Timothy on the knee and rose to stand beside Iron Cloud. "Timothy will stay behind. I'll go with you."

Iron Clad gave her a long stare, his pride in her showing in his warm smile. "Then, my White Willow, come," he said, giving Black Coyote a shove toward the entrance flap. "Our people must be awakened from their sound sleep for the sentencing. Black Coyote's fate lies in their hands. They do not debate for long. When they see the wrong done, they know what punishment matches the crime."

Damita gave him a wan smile, knowing that he already knew the punishment, since he knew which punishments matched which crimes. She wanted so badly to ask him what she could expect, yet she did not want to look apprehensive in her decision to be a witness to this custom of the Omaha. She knew the crimes were severe, yet she hoped with all of her heart that the punishment would not be as severe. She did not want to waver in her admiration of Iron Cloud and his people. She had heard Indians referred to as savages. She hoped that she would not have cause to say that after tonight.

Her chin held high, her heart pounding, Damita followed Iron Cloud and Black Coyote outside, where the moon was only a sliver of white in the sky, and the stars were like tiny candles glowing against the dark heavens.

The great outdoor fire had burned down to glowing embers, and in the distance a wolf bayed at the partial moon.

Damita almost jumped out of her skin when Iron Cloud let out a loud shriek that seemed to have the power to split the heavens.

She gasped as she questioned him with a blank stare, then became aware of a hustling and bustling around her as men, women, and children rushed from their dwellings, clasping bows and arrows, rifles and spears, in their hands.

Iron Cloud shoved Black Coyote in among his people, who began making a wide circle around them.

"Black Coyote has returned to us," Iron Cloud shouted, stepping around so that he could look Black Coyote directly in the face. "Black Coyote, would you care to tell why you returned?"

Black Coyote firmed his jaw, not giving so much as a hint of his humiliation, or that he was ready to humble himself before his chieftain and his people. He folded his arms tightly across his chest and spread his legs, glaring back at Iron Cloud.

Damita found herself becoming a part of the proceedings before she even had given it much thought. As though willed to by an unseen force, she stepped to Iron Cloud's side, turned and faced his people, and lifted her voice into the night.

"This man came tonight to kill Iron Cloud," she shouted, hearing her voice echoing through the trees around her. "He came into your chief's wigwam with a drawn knife."

She stopped there, not wanting to brag about being the one that had stopped Black Coyote. She didn't have to. Iron Cloud had her by the wrist and was raising her hand high in the air.

"This woman that you all now know as White Willow is responsible for your chief being alive!" Iron Cloud said in a booming voice. "She bravely went up against Black Coyote and kept him from sending the knife through my heart. Again she has proved to be courageous—worthy of your praise and acceptance! Let me hear your praises now for my woman! Lift your voices to the sky! Let your praises reach far and wide!"

Damita's face became hot with a blush as the Omaha people let out several whoops and shouts, their weapons dancing in the air over their heads as they thrust them over and over again in a show of acceptance. She smiled awkwardly and uttered frail thank-yous, and was glad when everything became quiet again.

Iron Cloud placed an arm around Damita's waist and drew her back to stand at his side. "It is now time for Black Coyote's sentencing!" Iron Cloud shouted. "Some might say that he deserves punishment. Some might say that he deserves to be flogged. Some might say that . . . he deserves to die! Think now about what he has done before passing judgment. He stole the Sacred Pole from the Tent of War. He fled from me, knowing that upon his return to our village, he would be punished. He has probably led the agent to us! And now, for whatever twisted reason, he has tried to kill me, your chief! So his guilt is great. So should his punishment match the crimes!"

Damita scarcely breathed when everyone became quiet and lost in thought, still worrying about how Black Coyote would be put to death, should they choose the death penalty.

But she didn't have long to ponder over this. It seemed that everyone spoke in the same breath, at the same time, shouting, "Death! Death! Death!"

Without further hesitation, Iron Cloud went to his wigwam, then came back to the circle of people with a small vial of liquid and a stick that had been whittled to a sharp point.

Iron Cloud stepped up to Black Coyote and looked him square in the eye. "Lie down on the ground," he ordered, void of emotion.

Damita watched, wide-eyed, as Black Coyote did as he was told, lying flat on his back, staring blankly into space as Iron Cloud knelt over him. She watched the solemn ritual, yet not understanding exactly what was happening, as Iron Cloud dipped the point of the stick into the white, murky liquid in the vial, then quickly jabbed the stick into the vein in Black Coyote's neck.

Black Coyote's body began twitching, and spittle began running from the corners of his mouth. He looked up at Iron Cloud and emitted a throaty, vengeful laugh. "Do not look so smug, my chief," he taunted raspily. "What I failed at tonight, others will do. The agent from Fort Calhoun and many soldiers are near. They are coming for the white woman and her brother. They are also coming for you. You...will...die, Iron Cloud. Die!"

His threat made fear spread through Damita like many sprays of ice flooding all the corners of her body. She knew that no matter what she said to her cousin, it would not be enough to keep him from punishing Iron Cloud and his people for having taken her and Timothy with them and for having fled the reservation!

But then her fears were banished for the moment when Black Coyote's body lurched one last time, then subsided into a nothingness, his eyes locked straight ahead in a death trance.

"It is done!" Iron Cloud said, shouts of victory filling the air. "And do not let his threats bother you." He turned to Damita, their eyes locking. "None of you fear his threats. Before the agent and his soldiers arrive, we will find them first. You will be protected, at all cost! All of you, my people." He leaned down into Damita's face. "And you and your brother, my woman."

Forgetting her audience of many, Damita flew into Iron Cloud's embrace. She hugged him tightly. "I can't help but be afraid," she murmured. "Iron Cloud, everything we have shared could be torn asunder by my cousin! He just can't. Please don't let him."

"Nothing will spoil what we have found together," Iron Cloud whispered. "Nothing."

Damita's gaze fell on Black Coyote, shivering at

the sight of him lying there so still, yet relieved that his death had not been unnecessarily violent. She leaned away from Iron Cloud, imploring him with her eyes. "How did he die?" she murmured. "It was not entirely painless, yet more merciful than most would have assigned him."

"Rattlesnake poison," Iron Cloud said matter-of-factly.

Damita was taken aback. "That was what you used?" she gasped.

"That is the way of the Omaha," he said. "And so are the ways of punishment handed down. Quick and absolute."

Chapter Twenty-three

Apprehensive over leaving Damita and Timothy back at the village, although they were well-guarded, Iron Cloud rode through the forest with his warriors, their eyes ever searching for signs that would indicate where Jonathan and the soldiers might have traveled. Thus far, there were no indications that anyone had been in this area except for those who were now traveling through the thick layer of decaying leaves beneath the trees. There had been no paths made before them. There were no signs of campfires, or horse dung anywhere.

Somewhat discouraged, and growing suspicious of the tale Black Coyote had told him just before dying, Iron Cloud raised a fist in the air, stopping his men. He and his warriors had ridden the rest of the night and a portion of the morning.

It was time for decisions.

Should they continue? Or should they retreat and return to their loved ones?

It was not a pleasant thought to believe that perhaps the soldiers and Jonathan had gone another way and were at Iron Cloud's village even now, wreaking havoc and destruction!

"My warriors, what do your hearts and instincts tell you?" Iron Cloud shouted, as the warriors made a wide circle around him. "Do we continue? Or do we return to our village?" He moved his gaze from man to man, awaiting their response.

A warrior broke away from the circle and inched his horse closer to Iron Cloud's. "You are a man of wisdom," he said, stopping his steed beside Iron Cloud's. He placed a hand on Iron Cloud's muscled shoulder. "You are our leader. We follow you. What you say, we will do. Your decisions are always for the best of our people. No one wishes to speak above you."

The warrior held his hand in place on Iron Cloud's shoulder a moment longer, then dropped it to his side and returned to those who devotedly awaited Iron Cloud's decision.

"It is my decision, then, to ride for an hour longer, then if we still do not see warning signs of the agent and the soldiers, we will make a fast retreat back to our people," Iron Cloud said, hoping that no one heard the growling of his stomach.

They had not stopped to eat. To him that would be a foolish waste of time. Each warrior had learned well the art of restraint, even when it came to feeding their hunger.

Of this, he was proud. There were no other warriors like his. They were disciplined, strong, and trustworthy.

He smiled proudly and squared his shoulders as he wheeled his horse around and traveled on through the dark shadows of the forest, then drew his reins tight and stopped suddenly when through a break in the trees ahead he saw something that looked like a body stretched out beside an azure streamlet.

He raised a hand in the air, stopping his warriors' approach. He yanked his rifle from the gunsling on the horn of his saddle and slid easily from the saddle, always fearing a trap. He gave his warriors a nod for them to follow his lead.

They dismounted, their rifles clasped in their hands, and began moving stealthily behind Iron Cloud.

Before they reached the unconscious man, they paused behind trees and scanned the land around them for as far as they could see.

With Iron Cloud at the lead, they rushed onward when they had made sure that no one else was there.

Iron Cloud was the first to reach Jonathan. For a moment, he stared down at the whiskered man, who was emaciated, his jaw and eyesockets sunken.

Then Iron Cloud fell to a knee beside him. He lay his rifle aside and reached a finger to the vein in Jonathan's throat to see if there was a pulsebeat. When he discovered one, he checked the man over for signs of bites or blood, finding none.

"What is wrong with him?" one of Iron Cloud's warriors asked. "Has he lost his way? Is he unconscious because of lack of food?" He looked guardedly around him. "Where are the soldiers?"

"I know none of these answers," Iron Cloud said, rubbing his chin thoughtfully. "Black Coyote did say that he was traveling with soldiers. Why did they abandon him? Where is his horse?"

"What are you going to do with him?" another warrior asked.

Iron Cloud's first thought was to leave the man there to die. He deserved no more than that!

Then his thoughts went to Damita. What would she expect him to do? Although she despised Jonathan, she would surely not want Iron Cloud to be heartless enough to leave her cousin to die in the wilderness.

As Iron Cloud saw it, he had no choice but to take the evil agent back with him to his village, and at least be thankful that he was alone.

Alone and ailing, Jonathan was no threat.

"Quickly put together a travois!" Iron Cloud said, rising to his feet, frowning at his warriors. "We will take the agent to our village. I shall allow White Willow to determine his true fate. Should she wish to see him cared for, then I will give her permission to tend to him. If she wants nothing to do with him, we shall return him to the depths of the forest and let him die a slow death, alone!"

Although no one seemed too happy to follow this direct order from their chief, a travois was soon put together and placed behind Iron Cloud's horse.

Begrudgingly, Iron Cloud lifted Jonathan on the travois and secured him with a rope, marveling at how slight in weight the agent was, as if it had been days since he had eaten. But *why*? Why *was* he alone? Why had the soldiers abandoned one of their own kind, of their own skin coloring?

Of course, Iron Cloud had seen many habits of the white pony soldiers that he had not understood while riding scout during the Civil War—the killings, maimings, burnings, rapes . . . It had all been senseless!

When the Omaha had killed, it was always for reasons of survival!

Iron Cloud had been more than eager to return to the peaceful life of the Indian, and upon the death of his father, he had assumed the role of chief. The Omaha had fought long and hard to keep a civil tongue with the white man.

Even now, Iron Cloud was fighting to keep this same relationship with them, yet knowing that flight had been the only way. He would not have been able to tolerate much more from the United States Government.

Just as Iron Cloud swung himself onto his saddle, a moan from Jonathan made him step to the ground again. He knelt at Jonathan's side and held his head up from the layer of pelts. He watched as Jonathan's eyes slowly opened, yet seemingly not focused on Iron Cloud or anything else.

"Jonathan?" Iron Cloud said, leaning down closer to Jonathan's face. "Do you hear me?"

Jonathan licked his parched lips and stared up at Iron Cloud, obviously not realizing who he was, or where.

"Jonathan, I was told that you were traveling with soldiers," Iron Cloud prodded. "Is that so?"

Jonathan's lips parted to speak, but it was obvious that his throat was too dry, for only a slight hiss slid across his lips.

"Bring the man a drink of water!" Iron Cloud shouted, gesturing toward his men. "He apparently did not have the strength to bend over the stream to get a drink. He is as thirsty, it seems, as he is hungry."

A buckskin flask was brought to Iron Cloud. Iron Cloud took it and tipped it to Jonathan's lips, letting the water pour slowly into his mouth so as not to choke him. When he felt that Jonathan had had enough to drink, he handed the flask back to his warrior, and questioned Jonathan again.

"Jonathan, it is Iron Cloud," he said, drawing his words out. "Do you recognize me?"

Jonathan blinked his eyes, then slowly nodded. "Iron...Cloud...?" he whispered raspily. "Where...am I?"

"You don't know?"

"No. I don't remember."

"Then you don't recall any soldiers that were traveling with you, either?"

"Soldiers?"

Jonathan's jaw tightened and a trace of fire

emerged in the depths of his bloodshot eyes. "Yes, I recall . . . soldiers . . ." he said, his voice breaking. "The sonsofbitches. They . . . deserted me."

"Why would they?" Iron Cloud persisted.

"Measles," Jonathan said, closing his eyes wearily. "The god-damned measles. The cowards. They left me . . . to . . . die alone."

He opened his eyes in a flash and reached for Iron Cloud's arm. "Are they gone?" he gasped. "Are the splotches gone? Am . . . I . . . well? The measles didn't kill me?"

"The splotches are gone, and no, the disease did not kill you," Iron Cloud said stiffly, recalling the small baby and her mother he had found on the trail, murdered. "It seems you survived much better than those you have sent to their death because they were diseased with measles. Now that I think about it, perhaps I should cut the travois from my horse and leave you to die alone, after all."

He grabbed Jonathan by the throat and lifted his head partially from the pelts. "You would not die from measles, but from lack of food," he said. "Or would you prefer that I put you out of your misery right now? Of course you know of Black Coyote. I am sure he told you that I led my people to Illinois. Only yesterday I put that traitorous warrior to death by injection of rattlesnake poison! Perhaps that is how you should die?"

Jonathan's breathing was coming faster, his eyes wild with fear. "You wouldn't," he said, his voice quavering. "Have mercy, Iron Cloud. Have . . . mercy."

"Did you have mercy when you ordered the Sioux mother and child killed?" Iron Cloud said, his teeth clenched. "And when you gave my people only part of their rations? Where was your mercy? It is only because of Damita that I will spare you. She will be given the chance to name your fate— whether you will live or die!"

Jonathan reached a hand to Iron Cloud's arm and clutched it as Iron Cloud released his hold on his throat. "Damita?" he said. "You know where Damita is? I was right all along? She is with you? And what of Timothy? Did you abduct him also?"

"Yes, both were abducted," Iron Cloud said, rising tall over Jonathan, shadowing him. "And both are with my people, awaiting my return."

"Are . . . they well?" Jonathan asked weakly.

"And do you truly care?" Iron Cloud hissed.

"They are my kin," Jonathan said, inhaling a shaky breath. "Of course I care."

"Then we shall see if Damita cares as much when I give her the opportunity to either look after you until you are well, or tell me to take you away and leave you alone to die," Iron Cloud said, smiling coldly down at Jonathan.

"I don't . . . understand," Jonathan said, frowning. "Why would you give her any say in the matter? She's a captive."

"Soon you shall see how much a captive she and Timothy are," Iron Cloud said, chuckling.

Iron Cloud swung himself into his saddle, sank his heels into the flanks of his appaloosa, and sent his steed into a soft lope across the land, feeling

Jonathan's eyes on his back. He laughed to himself, knowing that he had puzzled the agent. Right now, Jonathan must be filled with many questions about his cousins—and he would get quite a surprise to find that they were now more Omaha than white!

Damita was cutting up potatoes and wild onions for a rabbit stew, dropping the chunks of vegetables into boiling water that hung from a kettle over the fire inside her and Iron Cloud's dwelling. Timothy was outside, cleaning the rabbit for the stew. It was hard for her to fathom that her brother had actually gone on a hunt with the other young men and had killed something for their supper.

Every day, it seemed, he was becoming more of a man than a boy.

But, of course, she thought to herself—this was the difference in raising a child out in the wilderness, rather than in the city. In the city, everything was handed to children on a silver platter. In the wilderness, they had to learn to fend for themselves and their families.

Timothy was obviously happier with this life.

Damita leaned an ear toward the entrance flap, catching the slight sound of horse's hooves in the distance, making her heart skip a beat.

"Sis!" Timothy shouted and stuck his head inside the wigwam, through the flap. "Iron Cloud is coming. And he's got someone with him on a travois. Do you think it's Cousin Jonathan?"

Startled, Damita dropped the knife. Moving quickly to her feet, she wiped her hands on the sides of her buckskin dress and hurried outside with Timothy. Stiffly, she stood and waited for Iron Cloud's arrival, her eyes never leaving the travois that he was dragging behind him.

And when he stopped next to her, and she got a full view of the man's face, she gasped and paled. She recognized Jonathan beneath his thick facial whiskers, yet she was shaken by his gauntness. He had wasted away to almost nothing, the skin of his face drawn tautly over bone.

Jonathan turned his eyes up to Damita and he reached a shaky hand toward her. "Damita?" he said, his voice quavering. His gaze moved to Timothy, shock registering in his eyes when he saw Timothy's attire and the Indian headband.

Damita knelt beside the travois and placed a hand to Jonathan's brow. "Timothy and I are fine," she murmured when Jonathan's eyes searched over her, seeing that she was also dressed in Indian attire. "But how about you? What happened?"

Iron Cloud stood over her, placing a gentle hand to her shoulder. "He was abandoned after the soldiers discovered he had measles," he said. "He is near to starving, I would say."

"Help me, Damita," Jonathan pleaded, his eyes wavering. "Don't let the Injuns do anything to me. Please . . . help me."

"His fate is up to you, White Willow," Iron Cloud said. "He is your blood kin. Should you wish to nurse him back to health, so be it. Should you wish to turn your back on the scoundrel, so be it. I will send him away. He can die a slow, lingering death alone." He paused then added, "What shall it be, White Willow? Life or death?"

A keen uneasiness overcame Damita at the prospect of being the one to say whether or not her cousin would be condemned to die or would have a chance to live.

Yes, she felt sorry for him. He looked as though he was at death's door!

Yet when she remembered why he was in the forest this close to the new Omaha village, her pity changed to a slow-burning anger and resentment. She had to believe that her cousin's search was not so much to find her and Timothy, but to find and punish her beloved Iron Cloud!

"If I do nurse him back to health, what then, Iron Cloud?" Damita said, rising to stand beside him. She implored him with her eyes. "He could bring the soldiers back and destroy your village."

"After he is well again and capable of riding, he will be blindfolded as he is taken away," Iron Cloud said matter-of-factly. "And he has to know that he would not be given a second chance if he showed his face in Illinois again."

Damita turned and stared down at Jonathan. She sighed heavily. He *was* her cousin—her blood kin. She could not hand down his death sentence. She would never be able to live with herself if she was responsible for a man's death—especially that of her cousin!

"I'll do what I can," she murmured. "But Lord help me if one day I regret this decision."

Jonathan smiled crookedly up at her.

Chapter Twenty-four

After seeing that Jonathan was made comfortable behind the privacy blanket where Timothy usually slept, Timothy took his belongings to the outer part of the wigwam to sleep beside Damita. Iron Cloud was rolling up pelts to take outside to sleep so that Damita would not have to answer Jonathan's embarrassing questions should he see her and Iron Cloud share his blankets and pelts.

Timothy, with Baby frolicking on her leash, scurried from the wigwam, eager to tell Lean Elk all about this cousin who had suddenly appeared in his life again. Iron Cloud positioned his thick roll of pelts beneath one arm and looked heavy-lidded down at Damita.

"You truly don't have to do this," Damita murmured, reaching a hand to his copper cheek, lovingly caressing its smoothness. "You don't have to sleep outside, away from me, just because of

Jonathan. I'm not ashamed of our relationship. And Jonathan will know soon enough of our marriage plans. I intend to tell him everything, Iron Cloud." She laughed softly. "It will delight me to see his expression when he realizes that his cousin is in love with an Omaha chief and is going to marry him. Jonathan will be truly shocked!"

"I know that you speak from the heart when you say that I need not sleep away from you for the duration of your cousin's stay here," Iron Cloud said, reaching his hand to bring hers to his bare chest to clutch it there. "And it is good that you are going to tell him all truths about us. But, still, White Willow, there is no need to allow him to share our togetherness. The wigwam is too small for such a man of large ears."

A blush suffused Damita's face, realizing what he was referring to. She shyly cast her eyes to the ground, her insides heating up at the mere thought of the wondrous moments with Iron Cloud—she was going to miss their lovemaking.

Her gaze lifted and she smiled half-wickedly at him. "Where do you plan to make camp?" she asked softly. "I will come to you. It will be no different than when we left the wigwam long enough to give us privacy away from Timothy. We need not go one night, my darling, without being together."

Iron Cloud chuckled, and his eyes danced down into hers. "My woman has turned vixen?" he teased. Then, with his free hand, he placed his arm around her waist and yanked her to his hard body, pressing her tightly against him. "My love, I will be down by the river. You can follow the light of my fire. I will have erected a small tent, yet large enough for you and I."

He glanced toward the blanket, making sure that Jonathan was not spying on them, then lowered his mouth to Damita's lips and gave her a lingering, sweet kiss.

When he drew away from her, he reached for his rifle that he had leaned against the curve of the wall. "You sleep with this at all times," he said sternly, handing her the firearm. "Your cousin may not be as ill as he seems. Should he feel too threatened here in our village of Omaha and decide to flee, you stop him, White Willow. If need be, shoot him."

Damita paled as she looked down at the rifle, then up at Iron Cloud. "I'm not sure I could," she murmured. "He . . . he is my blood kin."

"Only by an accident of birth," Iron Cloud reminded her. "Your hearts are not the same. Never trust him, White Willow. Never."

He glanced at the privacy blanket again, then down at Damita. "Perhaps it is not wise that I leave you with him without my protection," he said. "Perhaps I should sleep just outside the door so that should you need me, I would be quickly there."

"No," Damita said, gently taking him by the arm and guiding him toward the entrance flap. "It is not necessary that you stand guard over me. Jonathan is quite ill. And if he wasn't, I am very capable of taking care of myself."

Timothy came into the wigwam in a huff, Baby in his arms. He saw the rifle in Damita's hand, looked at the privacy blanket, and then at Iron Cloud. "I'll protect her, Iron Cloud," he said, proudly puffing out his chest. "I'll stay with her instead of mingling with my friends. They will understand."

Damita turned to Timothy, almost laughing at the sight of Baby, and how she was beginning to over-fill her brother's arms. Each day the bobcat was larger and clumsier. "You will do nothing of the kind," she said, smoothing a hand over Baby's spotted fur, her heart warming as Baby licked her hand with her rough tongue. "You and Baby need exercise and excitement. You wouldn't like being stuck inside the wigwam with me and your Cousin Jonathan."

Baby squirmed until she managed to jump from Timothy's arms, and when she ran to the pot that had not yet been replaced on the hook over the fire and began sniffing around it, Damita rushed to her and brushed her aside, giving Timothy an annoyed stare.

"Timothy, she's getting awfully hard for us all to handle," she said, yet regretting having to. She knew that in time, Baby would have to be set free. No one was ready for that—especially not Baby. The bobcat kitten would perhaps never know how to fend for itself in the wild, yet its teeth and its claws were growing sharper every day, unaware of the pain she inflicted when she teasingly nipped and slapped at those around her.

"I know, Sis," Timothy said, again capturing Baby into his arms. "But we'll manage, won't we?"

Damita sighed heavily, then nodded. "Yes, somehow we'll manage," she murmured.

Timothy left again with the bobcat kitten. Iron Cloud brushed a kiss across Damita's brow and also left.

Damita turned to the privacy blanket and stared at it for a moment, not looking forward to being with Jonathan for any length of time.

But because he was kin, she felt duty-bound to look after him. After he was well—that was a different story. . . .

She lifted the corner of the blanket and peered inside at her cousin. When she found Jonathan dozing, she went back to her chores at hand, knowing that more than anything else, food was the most important ingredient for nurturing him back to health. His prime weakness seemed to be lack of food, not medicine. He was no longer ill, just weakened from the illness and lack of eating properly these past several days.

The shoulder of a deer lay in the hot coals, roasting. Its thigh had been cut in thin slices and was in the pot that Baby had been sniffing, already boiled, its broth rich and yellow.

Damita went to her cooking utensils and chose one of her most colorful gourds which served as cups, and set it aside to use when Jonathan awakened.

Remembering the many roots that she had left outside for drying to slice later and store in bags like shelled corn, Damita left the wigwam to check on them, but stopped and smiled to herself as she watched some small girls at play not all that far from her wigwam.

They were mimicking their parents by playing house. They had put up miniature tents, their mother's shawls or robes having been seized to use for tent covers, the poles tall sunflower stalks. As the girls crawled into the tents and stretched out, their feet and legs protruded.

Damita giggled at how sweet the children were. She had seen this game often enough to know that if their heads were well under cover that was all that was needed to play make-believe.

As she checked on her roots, deciding to leave them out for a while longer, she became lost in thoughts of what it might be like to some day have children of her own, to raise among the Omaha instead of among white children.

She turned and scanned the village for Timothy, and when she found him, she shadowed her eyes from the sun with her hands and watched her brother at play.

Seeing him so happy made her know that she would never object to raising her own children as Indian instead of white. There were many advantages to bringing children into this more innocent world that wilderness life offered.

Yet, she also knew very well the disadvantages, for which her very own cousin was responsible!

She hoped that in time this would change, and that Indians and whites could live as one people, sharing everything equally.

"In time," she whispered, nodding. Surely in time things would be different, she thought. Right now, it was too soon after the Civil War to expect the country to find peace without suspicion and strain among its people.

She firmed her jaw, her eyes flashing as she went back inside the wigwam. "And the Indians *are* a part of our country's people," she said aloud, as she stood staring angrily at the privacy blanket. "But as long as there are people like my cousin in charge of things in the government, the Indians will never be recognized as anything more than— than savages!"

"Damita?" Jonathan said weakly from behind the blanket. "What is that . . . you are . . . saying? Damita, where are you? Where the hell . . . am *I*?"

Sucking in a quavering breath, Damita went to the pot of food and dipped out enough broth to fill the gourd cup. Balancing this in one hand, she went to the blanket and drew it all of the way open on its rope, then knelt down beside Jonathan where he lay on his thick pallet of pelts.

"Don't pretend that you don't know where you are," she said, lifting Jonathan's head with one hand and tipping the gourd to his lips with the other. Slowly he sipped the broth between his lips, his eyes never leaving Damita.

"What I would like to know is what would your plans have been had you not gotten the measles?"

she said dryly. "Would you have come and massacred Iron Cloud's people? Would you have killed him? What would you have thought if I had been the one to aim a rifle at you, with every intention of killing you, had you killed Iron Cloud? I would have shot you, Jonathan. Without even batting an eye. If you ever harm Iron Cloud, you will most definitely have me to answer to."

After half emptying the gourd cup, Jonathan coughed and eased it away from his lips. He wiped his lips dry, his eyes still on Damita. "That's all I can swallow now," he said. "And I don't just mean food. Damn it, Damita, what you're saying turns my insides cold. You—you are talking like a—a woman who loves a man. And not any man. An Injun!"

"Perhaps it sounds that way because that's the way it *is*," Damita said, setting the gourd cup aside. She smoothed the wrinkles out of the blanket spread atop Jonathan. "We are going to be married, Iron Cloud and I."

Her gaze shifted upward and her eyes locked with Jonathan's. "Soon, Jonathan," she said in a deliberate silken purr. "As soon as things get settled down around here. If you hadn't interfered and spoiled things, I am sure that Iron Cloud and I would have shared our marriage vows even *today*."

Jonathan gasped, his eyes registering a horrified sort of shock. "An Injun abducts you and—and you turn right around and agree to marry him?" he demanded. "How can you? Have you even bothered to think ahead to the consequences?"

"And what sort of consequences might you be suggesting?" Damita said, curling her fingers together on her lap, her back straight, her face innocently solemn.

"Like living poorly instead of like you're used to in Boston," Jonathan said, trying to lean up on an elbow, his weakness sending him back flat on his back. "And for Christ's sake—*children*! Do you want babies with copper skin hanging on the tail of your skirt? Don't you know the prejudices they will be faced with? And yourself? You would be the laughing stock of Boston should you ever decide to return to see your old friends. You would be shunned, Damita. No one would have anything to do with you."

"There are prejudices only because of people like you, Cousin Jonathan," Damita said, fighting to keep her anger at bay. "There are too many like you running the government. Sad to say, it's people like you whom too many others listen to when making their choices in life. Politicians! None are worth walking across the street to shake hands with, much less listen to. You are one of the worst, Cousin Jonathan. I pray that one day soon we will have a President who will weed out the bad and fill in with the good. Only then will the Indians have a chance at life in this country."

"Just listen to you," Jonathan scoffed, wheezing, the sparring with Damita wearing him out. "Just rambling on and on. You're like all women. You haven't got the slightest idea of what you're talkin' about. Your opinion counts for nothin', Damita. Absolutely nothing."

Not able to stand any more of the useless quarreling, or of Jonathan's outrageous insults to women in general, Damita scurried to her feet and didn't even stop when in her haste to get away from Jonathan she toppled the rest of the broth, spilling it on the mats spread across the floor.

Breathing hard, she jerked the blanket closed again, shutting Jonathan off behind her, then grabbed her shawl and headed for the river. When she got close enough to see Iron Cloud busy erecting his tent, she stopped and silently stood by, watching.

Jonathan's ugly words about Indians rang through her consciousness. She could not understand how anyone could look at Iron Cloud and think anything about him except that he was a dignified man, a man born of a proud heritage, a man with a high sense of honor.

It shamed her that her cousin could be such an arrogant, ignorant man. He deserved no kindness whatsoever from Iron Cloud, and Iron Cloud had even given up his dwelling to the bigot!

Breaking into a run, Damita hurried to Iron Cloud and tossed her shawl aside. "Let me help you," she said, picking up a pole and helping him tie it into the others.

Iron Cloud smiled at her, his dark eyes twinkling. "It is not night and yet you come to my camp?" he teased. The poles now standing freely, he began sheathing them with buckskin wrappings.

Damita blushed and laughed loosely. "Iron Cloud, stop teasing me," she murmured. "I came to help you put up your tent. That's all."

He swung the last of the covering around the poles, then went to Damita and took her hands in his, leading her backward into the entrance, where they both had to stoop to fit into the small space. "Your eyes and the beat of your heart tells me you came for other reasons," Iron Cloud said huskily.

Once inside he stretched her out on the ground that was not yet prepared for sleeping. A firepit had not even been dug.

"It is daylight," Damita said, yet unable to fight off the lethargy that was claiming her as Iron Cloud rained her face and neck with warm, wet kisses.

"Wakoda did not set down a rule which said a man and woman must make love only at night," Iron Cloud said, his hands pushing the skirt of her dress up to her waist. She no longer wore underclothing, the buckskin dress and moccasins her only daily attire now that she was being transformed into Omaha!

Feverishly, Damita lowered his breechcloth. All cares were cast aside as he plunged inside her and kissed her with a fierce heat. His steel arms enfolded her and cradled her close as she rocked and swayed with him, their bodies caught up in an unbearable, sweet agony of growing rapture.

And then they reached that joyous peak. They

clung and quaked together, their moans of pleasure mingling as Iron Cloud still kissed her.

Afterwards, Iron Cloud rolled away from her, then turned back and pressed his lips against her breast, his tongue moving around her abundant nipple.

Damita placed her hands to his head and drew his mouth closer, closing her eyes with the ecstasy. When she dropped her hands aside and his tongue and lips slithered away from her breasts and ventured lower, her heart pounded out the seconds until he was pleasuring her again, in what she still saw as the forbidden way of making love.

But she could not deny herself what he offered. Her head rolled as she emitted a cry of sweet agony as once again she felt the blissful joy claim her for that brief moment of paradise.

The sound of children laughing and giggling outside the tent drew Damita and Iron Cloud away from each other, quickly shifting their clothes back into place.

Damita crawled to the entrance flap and held it aside, relieved to find that it was a small cluster of young girls, and that they were nowhere near the tent, but instead down by the river.

Iron Cloud came to her side and looked out, then laughed quietly. "It is all right," he said, lifting Damita's hair and kissing the nape of her neck. "They have come to the river for clay. They will take it back to the village and make clay babies for themselves. Some of our children are very clever at modeling dolls."

Damita was touched by this, recalling what Jonathan had said while comparing life in the wilderness to that of Boston. It was true that she had been blessed with parents who gave her many dolls in her lifetime. But here were children who would never see a true doll, much less own one, and they seemed happy enough.

She turned to Iron Cloud and eased into his arms. "Hold me, darling," she murmured, sighing contentedly. "I love you so much. And I can hardly wait to have children by you."

"Children?" Iron Cloud said, forking an eyebrow. Then he smiled as he lifted her face so that their eyes could meet and hold. "Yes, that is something to look forward to. We will make a baby soon, my White Willow."

He lowered his mouth to her lips and kissed her gently, as though she were already carrying his baby within the protective shelter of her womb.

Chapter Twenty-five

Several Days Later.

Damita rode beside Iron Cloud through a mist lying over the ground that covered the underbrush like a layer of smoke. She clung to her horses's reins and squinted her eyes, peering through the shroud of mist, making sure that she never lost sight of the three horses riding ahead of her and Iron Cloud. One was carrying Cousin Jonathan, his hands tied behind him and his eyes blindfolded. The other two riders were separate from Jonathan, their happy laughter wafting back to Damita like a sweet melody.

She glanced at Iron Cloud, marveling at his continued kindess and consideration. He had not only agreed to let her and Timothy join this journey that would lead Jonathan far enough from his village to set him free, to return the rest of the way to Fort Calhoun on his own, but also Lean Elk. Timothy and Lean Elk had become inseparable, friends forever, as they both had announced time and again.

Damita's gaze settled on Baby. The bobcat was almost too overgrown now for her sling at the side of Timothy's horse. Yet even though so much of her body hung loosely over the sides of the sling, her paws squeezed up awkwardly beneath her chin, she did seem content enough. Her eyelids would drift closed, coming open again quickly when the sound of a close-by bird caught her attention.

Damita edged her horse closer to Iron Cloud's. "Thank you for letting me and Timothy come," she murmured. "And Lean Elk. Those boys are certainly enjoying the outing."

"It is good they wanted to come," Iron Cloud said, looking admiringly at Timothy. "It is a way for them to be alone for a while, as best friends should be. In the village, surrounded by the other young braves, it is only courteous of them to include others in their play or learning time. This way, alone together, they can learn each other's secrets and exchange knowledge of their different ways of life."

He frowned and cast a scowl at Jonathan. "It is good that Timothy holds no resentment over how his cousin is being treated by the Omaha," he said. "As you and I have, he has seen his cousin's evil ways. It will make him more astute when he comes face to face with those people who are like your cousin. He will be wary—suspicious of those who make offers while speaking with forked tongues."

"Timothy has no feelings for Jonathan one way or the other," Damita said, shrugging. "He is so young. But in time, he will understand."

"He knows more than you give him credit for," Iron Cloud said. "When he grows into adulthood, his wisdom may outmatch mine. In time, he might even become a chief. The color of the skin does not matter. It is the wisdom and courage of the man!"

He gave her a wistful stare. "If we do not have sons, then perhaps Timothy will be chief after Chief Iron Cloud," he said without hesitation. "And how would you feel about that, my White Willow?"

Damita swallowed hard, beginning to feel awkward with this conversation. She did not want to even think about Iron Cloud as an old man, and his eventual death, much less talk about it.

And she did not want to believe that she would not be able to give him a son.

And to think that her brother could ever be a powerful chief was not even comprehensible to her!

When she did not offer a reply, she felt Iron Cloud's questioning eyes on her for a moment longer, and then felt them drift away, locking on something else. She was content not to go into further discussions, anxious to get the chore of setting Jonathan free behind her. They had broken camp before daybreak. The morning light was just now growing in the forest, and the mist was drifting into the higher branches of the trees.

Nearby a woodpecker drummed at a dead sycamore, and then a sudden, strange sort of quiet filled the air, except for the faint patting of the mist drops that occasionally pooled together and fell as hardly a sound at all on the ground cover.

Damita jumped with a start when Iron Cloud suddenly reached over and grabbed her reins, stopping her horse. She questioned him with large, wide eyes, wondering if he was angry at her because she had not wished to talk further of chieftains and death. She could not understand this, when he had never been moody with her before.

She quickly discoverd that was not at all what was wrong. She had never seen the wary fear in his eyes that she was seeing now, and it sent spirals of dread throughout her, wondering what was causing this chief's courage to waver.

"We must all find a hiding place," Iron Cloud said in a low, urgent tone. "White Willow, come with me. I will alert the boys and Jonathan."

Damita sat stiffly in her saddle as Iron Cloud led her horse up to Timothy's and Lean Elk's. She was quiet as Iron Cloud gave warnings to the boys, and then Jonathan.

Leading their horses and traveling by foot, they followed Iron Cloud along a quiet stream until he found a wild, thickety hollow. Choosing a place where the erosion of years had eaten a little cave into the base of a short bluff, Iron Cloud beat down the brush and broom grass and made room for them all to stand. Soon they were hidden behind thick clusters of forsythia and lilac bushes, Iron Cloud clasping onto his rifle.

"Aren't you going to tell us why we had to go into hiding? Damita asked, sidling over next to Iron Cloud. She glanced at the boys, Baby snuggling in Timothy's arms, and saw traces of fear in their eyes as they peered through the bushes, awaiting their fate.

Jonathan stumbled over to Iron Cloud, still blindfolded. "What is this all about?" he asked, his hands trying to work with the ropes at his wrist behind his back. "If we're in danger, Iron Cloud, set me free. Damn it, can't I even defend myself? Or do you intend to let the intruders have their way with me to save your own hide? Take this damn blindfold off. Untie my hands!"

"Not intruders, Jonathan," Iron Cloud said in a hiss of a whisper. "There is only one intruder that I sensed by its smell and the alertness of my ears. It is not the sort of intruder I wish to come up against this early in the morning when it is searching for its first meal of the day. The unmistakable rank odor of a bear run is what alerted me to danger!"

Iron Cloud did not have to say any more. Damita, as well as the boys, caught sight of the huge bear at the same moment as Iron Cloud. Through an opening in the willows, several yards away, a bear emerged, walking slowly. Huge, black, and shiny, the sunlight spotting its coat, the bear's great shoulders moved with the lazy rhythm of its walk as it padded flat-footed beneath the trees, its jaw hanging open, panting.

Damita's heart skipped a beat. She swept an arm protectively around Timothy and welcomed Lean Elk at her other side so that, in the absence of his mother, he could seek some sort of solace from Damita.

"Good Lord!" Jonathan said in a frightened whisper. "What is it? I sense that something is near. You've all gone as quiet as church mice!"

"Jonathan, what would you know about church?" Damita found the courage to say in the face of approaching danger, for the bear was not aware of being observed, continuing on its way as though it owned the forest—the king of the woods!

"As a child I never missed a Sunday of church," Jonathan whispered back. "I can still quote scripture that I memorized."

"Then you'd best recall some of those scriptures and begin using them in a prayer right now," Damita whispered shakily, her gaze not leaving the bear.

The huge animal had now reared upright, obviously searching for insects. It clawed away a long section of rotten bark from an elm tree. Turning the bark over, the bear inspected its underside and began methodically eating the grubworms that had tunneled into the tree's pasty surface.

Iron Cloud lowered his rifle, feeling that the bear seemed to be no threat at all while it contented itself with the food at hand. But he knew that one wrong move from those observing the beast might change its choice of menu. He gave Damita, Timothy, and Lean Elk looks of assurance, ignoring Jonathan when he continued to grumble in a low whisper at his side.

And then the most unsuspected thing happened. Baby had caught sight of the bear, and its instincts moved into gear. She sprang from Timothy's arms and ran out of hiding into a clearing where the bear not only got a good whiff of her, but also a clear sighting.

Baby moved into a crouching position, ready to pounce on the bear. But when the bear curled its black-rubber lips away from a set of threatening teeth and growled a rumbling challenge from its belly and poised for a kill, the bobcat kitten was instantly startled and began crying like a human in pain. She fled into the forest, sending quail up into a frightful, thundering flight.

"No!" Timothy screamed, breaking away from Damita, going after Baby. "Baby! No! Come back!"

Iron Cloud stiffened, watching the bear and Timothy. Timothy was now the beast's target. He rushed from hiding and stood with his legs parted and a straight back and aimed the rifle. Then a loud blast echoed across the land.

"You missed!" Damita cried, dying a slow death inside as Timothy was now frozen in place, gazing eye to eye with the bear.

"It was my purpose to miss," Iron Cloud said, slowly lowering his rifle to his side as the bear stared at Timothy a moment longer, and then Iron Cloud, then turned and fell to all fours and lumbered off in the opposite direction.

Damita ran to Timothy and drew him into her arms, cradling his face close to her bosom. She looked wild-eyed up at Iron Cloud as he came and stood over them. "You didn't kill him," she said, questioning Iron Cloud with her eyes. "You could have. But . . . you didn't."

"It was not a necessary kill," Iron Cloud said somberly. "Did you not see? It was as frightened of us as we were of it. It took only the sound of the rifle to prove to it who was the most clever of us all."

Timothy inhaled a nervous breath, then jerked free of Damita. "Baby," he cried, his eyes wildly scanning the forest where Baby had last been seen. "I've got to go after her! I must!"

Iron Cloud placed a solid hand on Timothy's shoulder, stopping him. "We understand your affection for your animal friend," he said softly. "We shall search. But you must understand, once we have searched and we cannot find Baby, we must go on our way. You must learn where your concerns lie—with family and friends, not with bobcats turned pet."

"But the bear, Iron Cloud?" Damita fretted aloud. "What if it returns?"

"Its fears will take it far away," Iron Cloud tried to reassure her.

"We must find Baby," Timothy said, dancing

frantically in place in his eagerness to begin a search.

They all moved slowly through the brush, alongside thick blackberry bushes alive with blooms and beneath trees whose foliage was so thick overhead that no light penetrated, turning everything beneath it from day to night.

Timothy ignored the briars piercing his flesh as he tore through the bushes, his eyes ever scanning the land, glad when they came to a clearing so that he could stand and see some distance.

Damita's heart went out to him. She lifted the skirt of her buckskin dress and went to Timothy's side, and took his hand. "She's gone," she murmured. "The bear frightened her too much, Timothy. I'm sorry."

Timothy turned desperate eyes up to Damita, and then Iron Cloud, as he stepped to his sister's side. "We can't go on just yet," he said, a sob lodging in his throat. "Let's make camp here. Baby will come back to me. I know it!"

"Timothy, we just broke camp and had just begun traveling again this morning," Iron Cloud said, resting the barrel of his rifle in the crook of his left arm. "If we delay a full day waiting for Baby, that makes a full day longer away from our people. There are risks in that, Timothy. I am sure that you understand."

Timothy looked wildly at Lean Elk. "Lean Elk, stay with me?" he cried. "Let's stay here. You and I. Alone. Then we can rejoin Iron Cloud and Damita when they come back this way."

Lean Elk did not have a chance to answer, for Iron Cloud interceded. "That is not best," he said. "As you just saw, bears are always a danger. I will not leave you behind. Now go to your horse. Mount it. We will be traveling onward. Now."

Damita had never heard him be so firm and decisive with Timothy before, yet she understood, and agreed with his decision.

Timothy gazed in disbelief at Iron Cloud, then broke away from them all and ran blindly to his horse, but did not mount it right away. His gaze turned slowly to Jonathan as Jonathan stood alone, waiting for someone to assist him onto his horse. Timothy swung away from his horse and stomped to Jonathan. He doubled his fists to his sides as he glared at his cousin a moment longer. Then he began pounding Jonathan on the chest with his fists.

"It's your fault!" Timothy shouted, pummeling his fists over and over again against his cousin's chest. "If not for you, Baby would be with me! It's ... your ... fault. I hate you. Do you hear? I ... hate ... you!"

Damita grabbed Timothy's wrists and pulled him away from Jonathan. Again she drew his face to her bosom and cradled him close. She glared at Jonathan, also having the urge to strike out at him. But seeing his uneasiness and disbelief of what had just happened seemed enough for the moment.

She led Timothy to his horse and helped him into the saddle. "Perhaps she'll find her way back to the camp," she tried to encourage him. "Remember the one other time she followed you? Her love for you is strong, Timothy. Never give up on her. Never."

"Or perhaps this is the best way," Iron Cloud said, stepping up to Timothy and patting him on the knee. "In time you would have been forced to say goodbye to her anyway. Now it has already been done, and time will heal the loss. You will see."

Timothy wiped tears from his eyes and squared his shoulders, having for a few moments forgotten that he was supposed to be courageous, brave, and the noble young man in this chieftain's eyes. He swallowed hard, then nodded.

"Let us go on our way," Iron Cloud said, helping Jonathan onto his horse. He then swung himself into his own saddle and sent his horse into a canter. Yet as he rode, he found himself looking over his shoulder more often than not for the bobcat kitten.

Chapter Twenty-six

Several days had passed since Jonathan was set free far from the Omaha village. Iron Cloud had eagerly returned to his village to become involved in more pleasant things.

Their horses tethered, Damita and Timothy were now following Iron Cloud farther into the woods on foot. Iron Cloud's hand clasped a bow, and a quiver of arrows was slung across his shoulder and hung down his bare back. Timothy carried his own bow and wore his own quiver of arrows, this day having been chosen to teach Timothy more of the ways of the hunt.

Damita gave her brother a wistful glance. The outing had been planned for him to help get his mind off missing Baby so much. She and Iron Cloud had even delayed their wedding plans, putting Timothy before their own desires. They had seen Timothy's deepening remorse over the loss of his bobcat kitten, and nothing anyone said or did seemed to alleviate his pain.

Even today Damita could tell that his mind was not on the hunt.

His gaze was moving steadily around him, searching, ever searching, and not for game—for Baby!

Lean Elk had not joined this trek into the forest. Timothy had asked him to stay behind at the village, in case Baby returned home.

Damita had accompanied them on the hunt today with Iron Cloud's blessings, not only to help find a way to lighten her brother's spirits, but to be with Iron Cloud. She never missed an opportunity to be with him. She knew that she would even follow him into battle, if need be, to be at his side!

She loved him fiercely.

She feared, sometimes, that she loved him too much. If anything should happen to him, she did not think that she could go on. He was her every breath, her every heartbeat!

Now he moved silently through the forest, his smooth muscles rippling, his dark skin glistening. He was gliding like a fox through the bushes, as noiselessly as a shadow, his eyes intent as he looked around him.

The midafternoon sun stabbed through the opening in the dense leaf canopy of the hardwoods, in its rays the spider webs that had been woven in the early morning hours now fluttering their tatters in the soft breeze.

Larks sang, and grasshoppers whirred in the tall grasses beyond the edge of the forest. In these lush woods, springs and creeks could always be found in the low ground. Iron Cloud led Damita and Timothy to a cool spring, where they slaked their thirst.

Then they sat down on the embankment and took time to rest and talk in this place that was far from the sound of man. Damita blinked at the sunlight filtering through the trees to dapple the secret hollow. A blue jay dropped a nut, a crow called its alarm from far away, a squirrel rustled in the hickory trees above them. In the big spring hole, trout hung in the water at least thirty feet down, looking as big as logs.

"We had decided not to kill game today," Timothy said, smoothing his hands along the wooden curve of his bow. "Just to learn how to stalk it. When do we go on a serious hunt, Iron Cloud?"

Damita laughed softly. A serious hunt. That sounded like something her brother would say. And it was wonderful that he was speaking of something besides Baby. This outing *had* been well-planned. Timothy was remembering his desire to learn—his eagerness to be taught the ways of the Omaha.

"It is as important to learn how to be alert as it is to actually kill," Iron Cloud said, laying his bow aside. He stretched one leg out before him, bending the other comfortably at the knee, and leaned back on one elbow. "A man is not a desirable husband until he has proved his skill as a

hunter and shown himself alert and courageous."
He smiled at Timothy. "You have already proven
to be courageous. Today you learn to be alert. Soon
you will be a hunter."

"I'm not wanting to learn all that you are teaching me because of any woman," Timothy scoffed,
firming his jaw. "I doubt if I ever get married.
Women. Who needs them?"

Iron Cloud chuckled. He and Damita exchanged
glances that said more than words could say, then
Iron Cloud resumed his teachings.

"As you have noticed, Timothy, it is a rare thing
to see herds of buffalo today," he said sadly. "The
white man has depleted these sorts of hunts for
the red man. But when I was a young brave, my
teachings were mostly of the buffalo. I will teach
you the same now, for there may come a time,
perhaps when you are an adult, when the buffalo
will multiply again across our land."

He paused and seemed to become lost in the
past as he spoke in a monotone, his voice filled
with melancholy.

"If a young man is not industrious when a herd
of buffalo is slaughtered, he may come across another young man whom he might consider insignificant, but who has killed a buffalo by his
energy," he said softly. "The young man will look
longingly at the best portions of the meat, but the
young man responsible for the kill will give to
another who is known to be thrifty and generous,
and the young man who was not industrious will
go away disappointed."

Iron Cloud paused again, shifting into a sitting position, so that his legs were drawn up to his chest. As he began speaking again, he hugged his legs with his arms, his gaze now intent on Timothy. "There is a part of the intestine of the buffalo called *washna* that is very tender, so that old people who have no teeth, or but few, can eat it and chew and digest it," he murmured. "If a young man wants to eat this tender bit the old men would say, You must not eat the *washna*, for if you do, and go with a war party for spoils, the dogs will bark at you."

"Why would the dogs bark at the young man?" Timothy asked, his eyes widely innocent.

"Why the dogs would bark was left a mystery," Iron Cloud said, chuckling. "But the mystery would make the young people afraid to take the *washna*, and so the old people could enjoy it in peace."

Iron Cloud sighed and stretched his legs out before him again. "There are many sayings of the old people that I have memorized from my teachings as a child," he said, again staring into space and seeing distant scenes of his childhood. "When the marrowfat of the buffalo was dried out and a lad desired some of it with his meat, the old men would say, If you eat of the marrowfat you will become quick-tempered, your heart will become soft, and you will turn your back to your enemy— you will be afraid."

"Tell me more," Timothy said, moving to his knees before Iron Cloud, looking eagerly into his eyes. "It is all so interesting."

Iron Cloud placed a firm hand on Timothy's shoulder. "It is good that you wish to know things, even if some of these sayings might sound foolish to you, a white boy," he said.

"Nothing you say or do is foolish," Timothy said, then glanced at Damita who was sitting quietly absorbing everything. "Is he, Sis? Isn't he the smartest man you've ever known?"

Timothy ducked his head momentarily and swallowed back a quick lump in his throat. "Except for Papa," he murmured. "Except...for Papa."

Damita found herself choking up with that display of her brother's emotions, realizing at that moment just how well he had hidden his feelings of loss over his parents' deaths.

And now—he was facing another loss.

Of course, this new loss was not to be compared with losing a mother and father, yet the bobcat kitten was sorely missed. Damita suddenly realized that Baby had somehow mended the place in her brother's heart that had been severed by the death of his parents.

She now saw the importance of finding Baby, if ever at all possible!

"Yes, Timothy," she said, reaching a hand to his cheek. "He's very smart, and so was Papa. And so are *you*. You are learning so much so quickly. I'm very proud of you."

Beaming, Timothy looked up at Damita, and then at Iron Cloud again. "What else about the buffalo can you tell me?" he said, firming his jaw. "I will kill a buffalo one day and prove my worth to your people. There are some that still wander across the land from time to time. One of those will be mine, an offering to you and your people!"

"*Our* people," Iron Cloud corrected. "My people are now your people." He looked at Damita and their eyes locked in a silent understanding. "Both you *and* your sister's."

"My people..." Timothy said, seeming to test the words as they passed over his lips. He smiled and puffed out his chest. "Yes, *my* people. I like that. It makes me feel somehow more important."

"And that is how it is meant for you to feel," Iron Cloud said, fondly patting Timothy on the shoulder.

"Please tell me more," Timothy pleaded.

Iron Cloud looked overhead at the way the sun had shifted in the treetops. It soon would be dusk, and he wanted to be back at his village before night fell in its total blackness. Tomorrow was a special day for him and his woman. They were going to become man and wife. Nothing could stand in the way. Nothing!

"Just a few more sayings of the elders, and then we must head back," Iron Cloud said, patting Timothy on the shoulder. "The liver of the buffalo must be eaten raw—to make a man courageous and to give him a clear voice. The fat about the heart of the buffalo is given to children so that they might have strong hearts and courage. Also, young Omaha braves are taught that when a man wounds a buffalo, a lad must not shoot an arrow at it. He would be justly chastised if he did, as the buffalo belongs to the man who wounded it."

Iron Cloud rose to his feet. He offered Damita a hand and helped her up, as Timothy scrambled to his feet. Timothy knelt and swept his and Iron Cloud's bows up into his hands, then gave Iron Cloud's to him. Then they both hung their bows over their shoulders.

Iron Cloud positioned himself between Damita and Timothy, taking each of their hands as he walked them away from the spring. His eyes were gleaming as he glanced from Damita to Timothy. "There are some sayings of the old people that I have found amusing, yet I would never admit this to anyone but you," he said, chuckling. "There is one old saying—that when a young man attempted to drink the broth in a kettle, the old men would say, A young man must not drink the broth; if he does, his ankle will rattle, and his joints will become loose."

Damita laughed softly, feeling free to, since Iron Cloud had voiced his own amusement in the saying. She strolled hand in hand with him, wishing this innocent moment could last forever, yet she was beginning to have a sort of ache at the pit of her stomach, and she was feeling somewhat light-headed.

As a great stabbing pain grabbed her at the pit of her stomach, thankfully only lasting for a fraction of a second, she faltered in her step for a moment, glad that Iron Cloud had not noticed. She did not want to be the one to spoil the camaraderie that was becoming sealed between the man she loved and her brother.

"It is said that if a lad desired to eat the turkey's head, he was told, If you eat that, tears will come to your eyes when you hunt. You will have watery eyes," Iron Cloud said, looking amused. "And it is said that if a boy should wish to play with the turkey's legs after they have been cut off, the old men would say, If you play with turkey legs, your fingers will be cold in the winter and liable to be frostbitten. Then you can not handle anything."

Timothy giggled, then paled suddenly and gasped when Damita emitted a sudden shriek of pain and fell to the ground in a dead faint.

Iron Cloud moved to his knees and cradled Damita's head on his lap, stunned that she had fainted and wondering why. Only a moment ago she had been sharing and laughing with him and her brother!

"Go," he said sternly to Timothy. "Get the water flask from my horse. Bring it to me. Quickly, Timothy! Quickly!"

"What's wrong with her?" Timothy cried, seemingly frozen to the spot.

"Timothy, do as you are told," Iron Cloud said, giving Timothy a stern look. "And make haste!"

Fear gripping his heart, Timothy turned on a heel and ran to the horses that were now in sight through a break in the trees only a few feet away. With trembling fingers he jerked the water flask from Iron Cloud's horse, then turned and rushed back to his side.

Falling to his knees, he handed the flask to Iron Cloud. Wide-eyed and with a wildly beating heart, he watched as Iron Cloud poured some water into the palm of his hand and began gently patting it on Damita's flushed face.

"White Willow," Iron Cloud said, trying to hold down the desperation that had seized him. "Speak to me. What is wrong? Tell me, White Willow, my love. Speak to me!"

Damita stirred in his arms, and she could hear his voice that seemed to be speaking to her from the dark, deep depths of a well.

Then she began hearing him, as though he was drawing closer, and as her eyes fluttered open, she found that he was holding her, caressing her face with soft, cool water.

"What happened?" she said, blinking her eyes as she gazed wonderingly from Iron Cloud to Timothy, seeing the stark fear etched onto their faces.

"You fainted," Iron Cloud said, easing her up into a sitting position, then leaning her against him, holding her close.

"Fainted?" Damita said, and then a lightning bolt of pain at the pit of her stomach reminded her of why she had fainted. The pains that she had earlier felt had been too much for her to bear. As now, as she clutched her abdomen, she felt her senses drifting, the black void once again ready to claim her.

"White Willow!" Iron Cloud said, his voice rising in pitch as he gazed down onto a face twisted with pain. "What is it? Don't leave me again. Stay conscious. Tell me what is wrong so that I can help you."

A sudden gush of warm wetness at the juncture of her thighs made Damita regain her senses. She had helped her father enough in his office to know what was happening. She was not having the beginnings of a normal monthly period that was four weeks past due. The amount of blood, and the clots that she could feel passing from her, meant that she was having a miscarriage!

"No," she cried, clutching at her stomach as the pain seemed to subside as the blood flow lessened. She relaxed herself against Iron Cloud, weeping freely. "Iron Cloud, you'd best get me back to the village. I . . . I may hemorrhage. I may need the assistance of the women of your village."

Iron Cloud became shaken as he saw the blood begin to seep through her clothes.

When Timothy saw the blood, he became hysterical.

"There is no cause for alarm," Damita said, biting back the urge to cry again herself.

Oh, but, how was she to explain to Timothy the full truth without shocking him? There was a chance that he might even lose total respect for her. She had become pregnant before wedding vows had been exchanged with the man she loved!

Yet she had never lied to Timothy before, not even to save face, and she was not going to start now!

"What has happened here happens to women every day. I . . . I have miscarried a child that I was not even aware of carrying inside me. I . . . I have been too caught up in our daily life to even realize that I could possibly be pregnant." She placed a hand to Iron Cloud's cheek, and then Timothy's. "There will be more children. You'll see. Now please take me to the village."

"A child?" Timothy gasped, paling. He looked at Iron Cloud, torn with feelings, yet not so innocent that he had not been aware of his sister having gotten caught up in feelings for Iron Cloud that she had never had for men in Boston.

Timothy tried to understand, but everything in their new life was so far from normal as he had known it. He would not resent his sister for finding love in this, the most challenging time of her life. Although his sister was involved in a forbidden love, Timothy decided that he would never make her feel guilty because of it. Iron Cloud was special.

"Yes, Timothy, a child," Damita said, watching his expression change from shock to a silent understanding, making her sigh with relief. When he reached a gentle hand to her cheek and smiled, tears fell from her eyes onto his hand.

"I'm sorry, Sis," Timothy murmured, tears glistening in the corners of his own eyes. "Truly, Sis. I'm sorry."

"Thank you," she said, swallowing hard, glad that he was behaving like a man now when she needed it most, yet dying a slow death inside—

realizing that if she had had one miscarriage there could be another, and another, and another. She might not be able to bear children for her beloved.

And to a chief, that could be the kiss of death, for they depended on heirs to become the next chief in line!

Her gaze shifted to Timothy. Perhaps he would be the son that Iron Cloud would never have....

But, she wondered sadly, would that truly be enough?

Iron Cloud lifted her gently into his arms and carried her to the horses. "Timothy, tie your horse with your sister's," he said, looking devotedly down at her. "She'll ride with me."

Very gently, Iron Cloud placed her on the horse. He swung himself up behind her, then lifted her onto his lap, so that she could cling to him around his neck and rest herself against his body.

"I am sorry," Iron Cloud said, lifting her chin so that their eyes could meet and hold. "I shall make it up to you. You'll see."

"This isn't your fault," Damita murmured, holding back tears that she was dying to shed. "It is nature's way of telling us that this was not the right time for us to have a child. In time, my love, we will be blessed with a child. I promise you."

He gave her a lingering look, then nudged his appaloosa's flanks with his heels and urged his steed into a slow, easy canter through the forest. He held his head high, but inside, his heart was aching. He had seen the women of his village have miscarriages. Those were the ones who usually did not ever bear their husbands children. And tomorrow White Willow was to become his wife!

No matter, he thought stubbornly to himself. She still would be his wife. He would offer many prayers to Wakoda to help them through this newest crisis. Tonight, he would take his pipe and go alone to the hills; there he would silently offer smoke and utter the call, *Wakoda Ho!*

Chapter Twenty-seven

As dawn cast its soft mists of light down the smokehole in the ceiling, Damita stirred in her sleep. As she slowly awakened, she recalled everything that had happened the prior evening—its sadnesses and eventual sweetnesses.

The night had been long, but a bittersweet one for Damita as she lay curled up beside Iron Cloud, his strong arms holding her, his warm breath on her cheek as he had slept, comforting her.

He had helped vanquish all of her doubts and fears about her miscarriage, whispering to her over and over again that all that was important was that she was well, that his White Willow still had breath and life.

He had reassured her that she was young and that there would be many babies blossoming within her womb in their lifetime.

His Wakoda would make it so!

Throughout the night, when she awoke for moments at a time, she had prayed to her own Lord that what Iron Cloud had assured her would be true. She knew the importance of children to Iron Cloud—the importance of a *son*.

Damita's eyes opened with a jerk as she suddenly realized that she no longer felt Iron Cloud's breath, nor his powerful arms holding her. She turned with a start and gasped lightly when she found him gone. She squinted her eyes into the semi-darkness, searching the wigwam for him, a quiet fear touching her heart when she found that he was gone.

This was most unusual for him! Did it mean that his disappointment was just now settling in on him? Now that he had had a full night to think, and possibly to have nightmares about never having a son, had he decided against marrying her after all?

Was he out in the forest, meditating with his Great Spirit, asking how he could relay this message to Damita without totally destroying her?

Tears splashed down Damita's cheeks as she moved into a fetal position, staring into the glowing embers in the firepit. She sobbed as the tears flowed more heavily, wondering if anything in life would ever be fair to her. She had lost her beloved parents ever so tragically. And now she was to lose the man she adored with all of her being?

"I can't," she sobbed aloud. "Oh, Lord, please don't allow it. Please."

"Sis?"

Timothy's voice behind her made Damita stiffen. She immediately wiped the tears from her eyes and turned his way as he came to lie down beside her.

"What's got you up so early, honey?" she asked, smoothing his tousled hair back from his eyes.

"Sis, I'm worried about you," Timothy said, his freckled face etched with worry. "How are you? I ...I'll never forget seeing that blood."

Damita swallowed hard, knowing that the time to explain a few facts of life had arrived, and it would not be easy, especially in her present state of mind, when she did not know what her future held for her.

But her brother came first, above her own wishes and desires. She must remember that. She was totally responsible for him now.

"I'm fine this morning," she tried to reassure him. "Very weak. But fine." She paused, then placed a hand to his cheek. "And about that blood. Darling, it wasn't that much. My body will soon replenish it." She paused again, cleared her throat, then continued talking softly to him, explaining about babies, the love that shaped them within a woman's womb, and about the love that she shared with Iron Cloud.

She very awkwardly tried to explain about how it could have happened that she had been with child before wedding vows had been spoken between herself and the man she loved, never wanting her brother to think less of her for it.

"Things in the wilderness are much different than in the city," she murmured. "In the city, weddings are planned and there is much pomp and circumstance surrounding it. In the wilderness, rarely is there even a preacher for miles to perform a ceremony between two people in love. Also, Timothy, considering the circumstances under which Iron Cloud and I met, there have been no opportunities whatsoever, nor will there be, to be married by a proper minister of our church. There are none here. There were none on the trail. And we do not plan ever to go to a city where we could find one."

She took a deep, quavering breath, the effort of talking exhausting her.

Then she continued, glad that Timothy was the sort of child who listened well and learned from the listening.

"Also, Timothy, my circumstance is quite different than it would have been had I fallen in love with a white man," Damita said. "You know that most people see a marriage between a white woman and an Indian as forbidden. The marriage ceremony planned today would have been Indian. I knew that I could accept that. So should you be able to."

She wiped tears from her eyes, then drew Timothy into her arms. "Too many circumstances kept me and Iron Cloud from marrying earlier," she murmured. "But Timothy, in the eyes of God I knew that we were already blessed. God knew the circumstances. God does not sort out the colors of skins, nor is He partial to any one color. He sees my love for Iron Cloud as sincere and beautiful. He has blessed it as such. I . . . feel this in my heart, Timothy. I feel wed to Iron Cloud in every way. I just do not have a piece of paper to prove it."

Timothy snaked his arms around Damita's neck. "I understand everything," he whispered, gently hugging her. "Don't worry, Sis. I understand."

He eased out of her arms and their eyes locked and held. "Sis, I'm sorry about the baby," he said softly. Then his eyes lit up with a thought, and he smiled. "When you do have a baby, I will feel more like its brother than its uncle. Sis, you have become my mother, you know. And I love you so much."

He flung himself into her arms again and hugged her tightly.

"As I love you," Damita whispered, caressing his bare back. "And thank you for the compliment. Mama was special. I am honored by the comparison."

She looked past his shoulders at the entrance flap, again consumed with fears about Iron Cloud.

Where was he?

What was lying so heavily on his mind that he left her without seeing how she was this morning?

If he truly cared, he would have not gone anywhere until he saw that she was truly mending.

She could not hold down the hurt feelings that

were assailing her, realizing that he surely had never cared as much as she had thought! She could not stop the resentment that was building inside her—resentment for a man that she would have willingly died for!

Now she did not know how to feel about him anymore.

The entrance flap lifted and Iron Cloud was suddenly there, his eyes gleaming, a smile quavering on his sculpted lips as he gazed down at Damita, then at Timothy. "Timothy, I've come for your sister," he said. "We're going away together for today."

Iron Cloud knelt beside Damita and Timothy. "Timothy, in my absence will you take care of my chieftain duties for me?" he teased, chuckling when he saw Timothy's reaction in the widening of his eyes and the smile that brightened his freckled face.

Damita's heartbeat quickened, and a surge of relief flooded her senses. Only moments ago she had been doubting Iron Cloud, to the point of actually resenting him, while all along he had apparently been making some sort of special plans for her.

Shame filled her, and she hoped that he would never know that she had doubted him.

"I can be chief for the day?" Timothy said proudly, bolting to his feet. "What are my duties, Iron Cloud? Tell me. I will do them eagerly!"

"Your duties?" Iron Cloud said, rubbing his chin thoughtfully, still teasing Timothy. "Let us see now. What can you do as chief?" He grabbed Timothy and wrestled him playfully to the floor. "Play with the other youngsters, Timothy. Have a day away from learning. Just enjoy the day, as Damita and I plan to do."

Having enjoyed the moment of lightheartedness with Iron Cloud, Timothy laughed heartily, then rose to his feet. Then he brushed his hair back from his eyes and looked down at Damita, then back at Iron Cloud. "Where are you going?" he asked softly. "Damita is not strong enough to travel. Should she even leave the wigwam?"

Tears came to Damita's eyes, so touched was she that her brother would show such concern over her welfare. More and more he proved how much he loved her. This intensified her love for him, and her admiration of him, a young boy turning so early into a man.

"You do not have to concern yourself about your sister's welfare," Iron Cloud said, bending down on his haunches beside Damita. He touched her cheek gently, looking adoringly at her. "Everything I do is for her best interest. Today is no exception. I know that she is weak and she will have no energy to spare to go with me. I have a special place prepared for us. In this special place, we shall privately exchange our wedding vows."

A thrill leapt through Damita and she felt a blissful joy filling her. When Iron Cloud lifted her into his arms and placed a blanket over her, she snuggled close and twined an arm around his neck. As they looked into each other's eyes, they suddenly became the only two people on the earth. She did not even think of Timothy, or of saying goodbye to him, as Iron Cloud carried her from the wigwam into the early morning light. It was dawn and chilly, the pale air filled with reedy tree frog sounds and the cadence of the crickets.

Damita rested her cheek against Iron Cloud's powerful bare chest as he carried her through the village, away from it, and into the darker depths of the forest. She closed her eyes, never as sweetly content as now. Her beloved still loved her. No matter how she had failed him, his love was too strong for her to turn his back on her and what their future might *not* hold for them. Children!

She pinched her eyes more tightly together, trying to squeeze out that word that might plague her until her dying day.

Children!

Now was not the time to be plagued with regrets. Now was the time to be serene and happy. She was soon to become Iron Cloud's wife. Forevermore, she was free to love and adore him. He was going to be hers! Totally hers!

Iron Cloud held Damita gently within his arms and walked determinedly onward, carrying her far away from the village. Soon he began climbing steadily upward until he came to the top of a bluff.

Damita's eyes widened and she uttered a gasp of surprise when her gaze found a soft fire burning close to the edge of the bluff, and a few yards back from that, a tent that had wildflowers heaped on both sides of the entrance.

341

"How lovely," she murmured, her face flooding with a pleased smile as she turned her eyes up to Iron Cloud. "My darling, you do such wonderful, surprising things. How can I be so deserving?"

"My woman deserves more than anything Iron Cloud is capable of giving her!" he said, brushing a kiss across her lips. "I love you, White Willow. My heart would be empty without you. Tell me again that you want to be mine forever."

Damita gently framed his handsome face between her hands. "I want to be yours forever," she whispered, bringing his lips to hers and giving him a lingering, soft kiss.

He drew his lips away and looked solemnly down at her. "The ceremony we will share today is not the usual one for the Omaha," he said, his voice filled with emotion. "But due to your condition, I did not think it best to force a celebration upon you. You would not be able to share in the dancing and so many other activities of the wedding celebration. Today, as chief, and with the blessings of Wakoda, I will see that our vows will be plighted beneath the morning sky and the fading stars. Does that please you well enough?"

"Yes, that pleases me well enough," Damita said, choking back a joyous sob. "I love you. Oh, how I love you, my darling." Then her eyes became downcast. "But, my darling, we will not be able to share what most share on their wedding days. I . . . I am not well. I shan't be for a few weeks."

"And you think that matters?" Iron Cloud said thickly. "My White Willow, we have all eternity

342

to make up for this one night."

Again they kissed, as the wind blew soft on their faces and the aroma of pine scented the air.

Still holding Damita in his arms, Iron Cloud nodded toward the setting laid out before them. "Is this not a perfect place to exchange our vows, my love?" he asked, as he gazed across the blue, misty haze of distant hills. "This bluff overlooks woods that are wilder here, bigger, and with more of the smell of the wilderness about them than anywhere we have seen. It is a pleasant smell of uncut trees, huge and mossy, and the ancient odor of undisturbed and virgin forest, never burned, never planted or grazed. It is the edge of the wild land, the edge of all tomorrows." He turned his eyes to hers. "*Our* tomorrows, Damita. All of our tomorrows."

"Yes, my darling, all our tomorrows," Damita said, their lips again meeting in a tender kiss.

Iron Cloud eased his mouth away and held tightly to Damita as he moved to the tent and bent his back to take her inside. Her breath was stolen away when she saw what he had prepared for her all the while she had been lying in their wigwam, thinking that he had forsaken her!

Great, thick pelts lay circled around a lazy fire. Flowers were in abundance everywhere, filling the dwelling with a mingling of sweet and spicy scents. Fruit was piled high on trays. And a jug of *tabehi*, tea made from the leaves of a small shrub, was standing by the fire, two gourd cups beside it.

She turned misty eyes up at Iron Cloud. "It's so lovely," she murmured, touched deeply by his gesture to make everything right for her at this moment in her life when she had lost so much. She brushed his lips with many soft kisses. "Thank you. My darling, thank you."

Iron Cloud set her down beside the fire on the thick pallet of furs, drawing one over her lap. "We shall now be married in a beautiful way," he murmured, settling on his knees before her. He took her hands in his. "It is a ceremony without relatives and guests. The Gods will marry us."

He paused. "My God *and* yours, my love," he added, smiling down at her. "I will sing to you, and then we shall speak words of togetherness that will seal our bond as man and wife."

Damita wiped away tears, unable to stop their flow as she listened to him sing, his voice deep and emotion-filled.

"Let us see, is this real,
Let us see, is this real,
This life I am living?
This wife I am taking?
You, Gods, who dwell everywhere,
Let us see, is this real,
This life I am living?
This wife I am taking?"

When he was done, Damita smiled through her tears at him. "That was so beautiful," she said. He released his hold on one of her hands and smoothed his fingers over her face, wiping her tears away.

"My woman, the one who fills my heart with rushes of joy, do you take this man as your husband?" Iron Cloud said, unable to stop the heat of tears in his own eyes.

"Yes, I take this man as my husband," Damita said, her heart soaring with happiness.

She paused, then said softly, "My beloved, the one whose heart has melted into mine, and who has filled my life with such meaning—such a blissful joy—do you take this woman as your wife?"

"Yes, I take this woman as my wife," Iron Cloud said, his face marked with a beaming contentment.

Iron Cloud placed his hands at her waist and gently drew her up onto her knees and into his arms. He kissed her with quavering lips, their tears of happiness mingling.

Chapter Twenty-eight

Six Months Later—A new year.

The sun was a hazy orange disk as it rose slowly into the sky behind the savage mists of morning. The snow was crisp and white, the trees covered with its white, fine lace. The village was a silent place, where only an occasional dog barked, and smoke spiraling from the smoke holes filled the air with the gentle fragrance of burning wood.

Iron Cloud watched Damita contentedly stirring a pot of rabbit stew over the fire inside their dwelling. Her stomach was pleasantly round, swollen with child.

Timothy was busy carving a design on the new spear that Iron Cloud had given him for Christmas, a holiday never before celebrated by Iron Cloud or his people.

But Damita and Timothy had changed that.

They had cut a huge pine tree and had placed it in the middle of the village and had decorated it with all sorts of handmade things and pinecones found lying beneath the trees in the woods.

Iron Cloud smiled to himself, recalling how much he had enjoyed helping his wife and Timothy paint the many pine cones different bright colors and later attach them to the tree. He would never forget the squeals of the small children when Damita lit many candles on the boughs of the tree.

And then gifts had been exchanged.

It had been a wonderful day, a holiday that would now be repeated every December on the twenty-fifth, as Damita had taught them all.

Enjoying being alive, and silently counting his blessings, Iron Cloud again looked at Damita and how radiant she was in her pregnancy. This time she had not miscarried early on. If both of their gods allowed it, in four months she would give birth to their child.

And he had told her time and again that it did not matter if it was not a boy. He had Timothy. *He* was their son, and as Iron Cloud had decided, the next chief-in-line, after Chief Iron Cloud!

And a daughter in his wife's image was his true wish—his deepest desire.

Yes, a daughter.

He would concentrate hard on his White Willow having a daughter, and then perhaps it would be so!

"You're staring at me again," Damita said, giggling and blushing as she felt Iron Cloud's intent gaze on her—mainly on her stomach.

"You get more beautiful every day," Iron Cloud said, rising to go to her. He bent over her and brushed her hair up from her neck, kissing her nape. "And you even smell more beautiful. It is good how Girl Who Laughs taught you to mix rose petals in with your soap as you are making it for yourself. My love, you smell of the wild roses today. So sweet."

He bent to one knee and lent his lips to her ear, so that Timothy could not hear his flirting. "So tempting," he whispered. "Shall we send Timothy on an errand? Would not the pelts feel warm to your back, with me lying on top of you to warm your belly with my flesh? Would you not enjoy having my lips on your breast, suckling your nipples? They are enlarged, so tempting to your husband, my darling. I want them now, for soon they will only be for our child!"

"It's too cold to send Timothy outside," Damita whispered back, a sensual shiver riding her spine. "Perhaps if the snow begins melting later on this afternoon."

"The snow does not impede much," Iron Cloud said, settling down beside Damita. "Even this afternoon I must lead our warriors from the village to hunt for more game. The horses have been trained to serve the warriors well in all weathers, and the warriors also are trained to fend well in low temperatures."

He cast Timothy a smile as Timothy glanced up, listening when he caught the word warrior in the

conversation, seeing himself as a future leader—
most definitely a warrior!

"The snow would never stop me," Timothy
boasted, thrusting out his chest. Today he was
wearing a heavily beaded, fringed buckskin jacket
and breeches, and moccasins which laced to the
knee. "I wish to go today with you, Iron Cloud, to
hunt with my new spear. Will you allow it?"

"I will think about it," Iron Cloud said, his eyes
dancing, always admiring Timothy's challenging
nature. "Just continue making your spear even
more special than it is. Yours will be the most
decorated of all if you continue to work with it
day by day."

"Lean Elk's is nice," Timothy said, holding his
spear out to study his designs. He shrugged, casting Iron Cloud another smile. "But mine *is* better."

He resumed his carving while Iron Cloud
watched him admiringly. The spear he had given
Timothy was most deadly and efficient. Iron Cloud
had taken great care in its manufacture, especially
in the shaping of the flint point. The weapon he
had made for Timothy was beautiful as well as
functional.

Iron Cloud left Timothy to his carving and
placed more wood on the fire. Damita dropped
another slice of wild carrot into the pot.

Loud shrieks and the popping of gunfire close
to the village broke the serene, contented silence
of the morning. Damita screamed, Timothy bolted
to his feet, pale as a ghost, and Iron Cloud grabbed

his rifle. Before leaving the wigwam he turned concerned eyes to Damita.

"No matter what you do, or what happens, do not leave this dwelling!" he ordered her, then gave Timothy a stern glare. "You stay with your sister. Do not let anything happen to her. It is time for you to prove much to me, little warrior. Do you understand?"

Timothy swallowed hard, his eyes wide. "Yes, sir," he mumbled. "Whatever you say, sir."

Damita moved shakily to her feet, welcoming Iron Cloud's arm as he came quickly to her and gave her a reassuring hug, then hurried outside, stunned at what he found. His whole village had heard the first gunfire as it had been exchanged between some early-rising Omaha hunters and the early-morning invaders, and they all seemed to be out in the snow, ready to defend this land that was now their home.

Boys too young to hunt, whose bodies had never been toughened by the long journey of the warpath, whose hearts had not been made strong by the first fast, grasped the weapons that they had as yet used only on rabbits and ground squirrels, defending their people against the soldiers who were now riding into their camp, their rifles drawn and firing.

Even the women, taking what weapons they could—axes, hoes, and mauls—had marshaled themselves for the battle.

The sun glistened on polished lances and gleaming faces. But Iron Cloud's warriors were armed more with bows and arrows than any other weapons, and as they were discharged, there were so many that it was like a cloud of grasshoppers all above and around the soldiers.

The soldiers were shooting desperately, but not accurately. Their horses, terrified by the clamor of the Indian people and their assorted unconventional weapons, were rearing and plunging, spoiling their riders' aim. Several soldiers dismounted to steady their guns and make their shots more effective. But at that moment the large body of Indians closed in on them, making them withdraw.

The voices of women could be heard singing songs to inspire their men, and at the close of the songs the women gave the cry of the hawk to evoke the supernatural power of the bird, which was associated with the god of war.

It was at this moment that Iron Cloud recognized Jonathan among those who were cowering, trying to retreat as they wrestled with their horses to get hold of their reins. Iron Cloud went to Jonathan and yanked him away from his horse, knocking him to the ground. He placed a moccasined foot on the agent to hold him to the ground.

"And so I made a mistake by letting you return to your fort," Iron Cloud growled, pressing his heel more deeply into Jonathan's groin. "This time I will not be so careless. You will die like your friend Black Coyote—by the poison of a rattlesnake!"

Jonathan, panting, his eyes wild, moved so quickly it was like a blur as he grabbed hold of

Iron Cloud's ankle and gave a jerk, causing Iron Cloud to lose his balance. As Iron Cloud landed on the ground, his rifle discharged accidentally, causing all those who were near to scatter desperately in all directions, seeking cover.

Jonathan had the advantage. He jumped on Iron Cloud, straddling him. He quickly doubled a fist and hit Iron Cloud in the chin, but the blow did not even stun him. He knocked Jonathan off and leaped forward like a great cat, but Jonathan's knee caught Iron Cloud's thigh, causing him to stumble.

Jonathan quickly straddled Iron Cloud again. He reached for his knife that he had placed in a sheath at his waist. He yanked it free and raised it for its death plunge in Iron Cloud's chest. But Iron Cloud raised a knee and knocked Jonathan away from him.

Iron Cloud rolled over, wrestling with Jonathan, the knife still perilously close to Iron Cloud's throat.

Again Jonathan raised the knife. Iron Cloud grabbed his wrist and struggled to shake the weapon loose, but no matter how hard he tried, the knife came closer and closer.

Jonathan suddenly gasped, his body flinching and causing the knife to fly into the air away from Iron Cloud, as a spear and several arrows entered his back and came out the front of his chest.

Eyes wide, blood curling from the corners of his mouth, Jonathan clutched at the spear for a moment, then toppled over sideways, away from Iron Cloud—dead.

Stunned, Iron Cloud rose slowly to his feet. He stared at Jonathan and at the spear that was piercing his body. Quick recognition of the spear's design made him look suddenly over at his wigwam, seeing Timothy standing in the doorway, Damita beside him.

"Timothy?" Iron Cloud said in a gasp. "You used your new spear to defend me?"

Timothy broke away from Damita and ran to Iron Cloud and hugged him desperately. "He almost killed you," he cried. "My cousin almost killed you. I didn't see the other warriors aiming their arrows at him. I felt that I had no choice but to—but to kill Jonathan myself. It's horrible, Iron Cloud. So horrible that I had to kill my own kin!"

Timothy eased away from Iron Cloud. "But I love you much more than him," he said soberly. "I did what I had to do. And . . . and I don't regret it. Honest I don't."

A blanket wrapped around her arms, Damita moved carefully over the snow, and when she reached Iron Cloud, she leaned into his embrace. "My darling," she murmured. "Oh, my darling. Will these tragedies ever end? I thought that we had finally found peace. And now this. Oh, Jonathan. Poor Jonathan. He was such a lost soul."

"I wish you had not been witness to this, nor that Timothy had been forced to kill for me," Iron Cloud said sadly. He eased Damita from his arms and looked slowly around him at the soldiers who

had died and at those who were now prisoners of
the Omaha. He was proud to see that the Omaha
had prepared themselves well for the attack, for
none had died. Of his people, he was the only one
who had come close to dying today. If not for his
warriors, and Timothy and his courageous nature,
Iron Cloud would not be there now, breathing and
anticipating so many tomorrows with his people
and his beloved.

"Take the prisoners and tie them with the horses
in the corral!" Iron Cloud shouted to his warriors.
"Let them have a full night away from a campfire
and then set them free in the morning to find their
way back to Fort Calhoun by foot. Those who arrive alive will tell others that it is best not to come
to Illinois and torment the Omaha! If soldiers set
foot on our soil again, they will die—and quickly!"

A gunshot rang out in the forest a short distance
from the village. Iron Cloud hurried in the direction of the sound, stunned speechless when he
found Brian Davis leaning low in his saddle with
a bloody shoulder wound.

"Brian?" Iron Cloud said, hurrying to Brian to
help him from the saddle. He let his old friend
lean into him as he guided him toward his village.
"Why are you here? Were you planning to be a
part of this attack? You know that is what my
warrior thought when he saw you approaching
our village so soon after the white man's raid on
my people. That's why he shot you."

"Surely you know me better than that," Brian
grunted, clutching his wound, from which blood

seeped between his fingers. "Don't you remember how we often said to one another that to be false to a friend marked one as without honor? Iron Cloud, I was coming to warn you of the attack. I guess I was a mite too late. Jonathan was already here—that bastard. How much damage did he do? Is he gone? Did he escape with his hide?"

"Jonathan is dead, and none of my people died," Iron Cloud said, looking solemnly at Brian. "It is good that your friendship is still a solid one and that you came with the sole purpose of warning me. Jonathan must have known you were there and circled around ahead of you. He was a clever one, but not clever enough this time, it seems."

"He's dead?" Brain asked disbelievingly. "I didn't think people like him ever died."

"Their spirit never dies," Iron Cloud growled. "It is the restless spirit of an evil that searches forever for rest that is never found."

Damita and Timothy came into view, waiting eagerly for Iron Cloud to return to camp. When Brian saw them, his mouth opened in a slight gasp. He questioned Iron Cloud with his eyes, then looked at Damita and Timothy again.

"My God, you *did* abduct them. . . ." Brian said, his words trailing off as Damita broke into an awkward run, her belly bouncing, flinging herself into Iron Cloud's arms and hugging him with all of her might.

Brian leaned away from Iron Cloud, able to support his full weight now, and eyed Damita with wonder, seeing that she was quite pregnant, and it was obvious who the father was.

Iron Cloud was speaking softly to Damita, brushing an occasional reassuring kiss across her lips, his hands framing her delicate face.

Brian had never seen any two people so obviously in love.

Chapter Twenty-nine

Feeling intense eyes on her, Damita drew away from Iron Cloud and turned to gaze at a face vaguely familiar to her. Then her gaze lowered to the blood seeping from his shoulder wound. The doctor in her made her go to him and inspect the wound. She frowned up at him. "This must be seen to," she said softly. "Come with me. I'll tend to the wound."

Brian smiled awkwardly at Damita, then at Iron Cloud, still in awe of his discovery.

Iron Cloud saw his dismay and went to him. He placed a comforting arm around his waist to steady him and continued walking him toward the village. "You have many questions, do you not, about my wife who is heavy with child, and about my son Timothy?" he said, his proud eyes watching as Timothy saw to Damita's safety across the packed, slick snow, trusting him as though he were

357

there himself, caring for his wife.

"Your wife?" Brian said wonderingly, his eyes watching Damita waddle along through the snow, her brother anchoring her against him at his side. "Your son?"

He glanced at Iron Cloud. "Iron Cloud, this woman and the boy are the reasons Jonathan and the soldiers sought you out," he said, wincing when pain began stabbing his shoulder. "Jonathan came back to the fort and told everyone that they were being held captive. That is why the soldiers arrived prepared for battle."

Brian paused, then added, "And you call her White Willow?" he said. "Her name is Damita. What have you done, Iron Cloud—converted both her and the boy to the Omaha way of life and beliefs?"

"They are both Omaha in the eyes of my people, and within my heart," Iron Cloud said, proudly squaring his shoulders. But then he gave Brian a stern look. "Damita is White Willow to me and my people; Damita to the whites. She was abducted, but Timothy came on his own."

Brian paled. "If she was abducted, that has to mean that—you forced yourself upon her," he said. "She is with child—apparently yours, Iron Cloud." He frowned. "Iron Cloud, I rode with you for a year during the Civil War, and never once did you hunger for a woman. I never once recall you even being with one, much less forcing yourself on one to quench your hunger of the flesh. And now you raped this woman? It is not like you, Iron

Cloud. I find it very hard to believe."

Iron Cloud stopped suddenly and placed a hand to Brian's uninjured shoulder. "Did you not see the love my woman has for me?" he asked. "Did you not see the devotion of her brother to me? Does that come from being forced? Does it, my friend? Can you, after seeing such affection exchanged between me and my woman, say that I raped her?"

"But you said that you abducted her, Iron Cloud," Brian mumbled. "What else can I think?"

"She was abducted, but soon after decided to join me willingly," Iron Cloud said, his words slow and deliberate in his explanation. "She asked me to go for her brother. I did as she asked. We have now become family. Her brother is to me like a son. If no sons are born to me and White Willow he will succeed me as chief of my people. It is written into law already that this is how it should be! Now do you still doubt your old friend, Brian? Do you?"

Brian's face softened into a playful grin. "You truly haven't changed," he said, chuckling. "You have always had the talent to make things work out for your best benefit. Now it seems, even with women. And you say that Timothy has become your son? It proves that your heart is big, and that Jonathan was quite skilled at lying. He told everyone at the fort that you were using Timothy as a slave and that Damita was being handed around from man to man. Now can you see why the soldiers came, ready to fight with a vengeance?

Somehow they managed to forget all of your good qualities, wanting to believe that an Indian is only capable of being a damn savage."

With a growl, anger filling his heart in hot flashes, Iron Cloud jerked away from Brian. "It is good that Timothy was the one who killed him then," he said, his teeth clenched. "Such lies about my son Timothy and his sister, who is now my wife, and my people, were stopped quickly by my son's spear!"

Brian paled. "A spear?" he gasped. "Timothy killed Jonathan with a spear?"

"It was quickly done," Iron Cloud said, shrugging. "And now the world is rid of one more evil man with a dark heart." He placed an arm around Brian's waist and helped him into the village.

Damita had waited at the edge of the village. She took her blanket from around her shoulders and offered it to Brian. "You have already been chilled enough," she said, taking it upon herself to place the blanket around his shoulders. "Come now. Come to our dwelling. I will see to the wound. Once you are more comfortable and warmed through and through, you can eat a dish of my rabbit stew. It should be cooked enough to eat by now."

"Thank you," Brian said, smiling at Damita, transported back in time in his mind to the first time he had seen her at the railhead in Nebraska. Never had he seen such a lovely, proper lady. And although not beautiful, as most defined beautiful, she caught the eye instantly with her long golden hair and her unusual height for a lady.

Yet though tall, her walk had been filled with such grace—such poise. And her laughing eyes were so friendly! So captivating.

Yes, he could see why Iron Cloud had fallen in love with her that first day, when he had run into her as he had been fleeing Jonathan's office....

He started to follow them to their wigwam, then stopped, aghast at the sight of several soldiers lying across the land dead, and Jonathan lying in the snow in a pool of his own blood, the spear and many arrows piercing his body.

Then he saw in the distance how the surviving soldiers, wounded and well alike, had been herded into the corral with the horses and were being treated no better than animals.

"My gaze follows yours and what I see displeases me, also," Iron Cloud said gruffly. "But they must be taught not to enter Iron Cloud's village with warring on their minds. I no longer tolerate such behavior, even from those I rode with during the War!"

Brian turned to Iron Cloud and placed a hand to his shoulder. "My friend, this is not the way," he said. "Those men you have rounded up and placed with the horses are not at fault here. Jonathan was the one who spread the lies that made these soldiers enraged enough to fight you. Wouldn't you have ridden at their sides, if such lies had been told to you about an innocent woman and child? Let them go. They can deliver the message to Fort Calhoun that everything was a lie, and that you are an innocent man. I encourage you, Iron Cloud, for the benefit of your future relationship, should you need it, with the government—let them go."

Brian turned his gaze toward the men lying dead in the snow. "Let these men be returned to their loved ones for proper burial," he said, his voice breaking. "These were loyal, honest men, obeying orders. They had no choice but to do as they were told, Iron Cloud."

Iron Cloud rubbed his chin thoughtfully, his gaze raking over the dead men, recognizing at least two of them. They had joined in poker games together during the cease-fires during the war. One in particular made a stab of regret pierce his heart.

"Yes, the dead can be returned," he said at last. "And so shall those who are wounded and otherwise," he said thickly. He gave a wave of a hand to a warrior. "Release them, but as you do, check each one to make sure their firearms have been removed." He gazed down at the dead again. "Let those who have survived take the dead with them."

"Thanks, ol' buddy," Brian said, sighing heavily. He walked on alongside Iron Cloud, his shoulder heavy with pain, yet knowing that it was mostly a flesh wound. He was glad that a bullet was not imbedded in his body. This far from civilization, gangrene could set in before he could return to the fort, where proper care could be given to such a wound.

Damita had hurried on inside the wigwam, taking a brief moment to warm herself beside the fire, considering the safety of her baby before anything else. And once she felt deliciously warmed, she spread fresh blankets beside the fire for Brian atop a thick layer of pelts, and stood aside as Iron Cloud helped him to lie on them.

She went to Iron Cloud and spoke softly into his face. "Darling, the Buffalo Doctor is not needed here," she whispered. "I can take care of the wound. I have seen many in my father's office. Men were always accidentally shooting each other while hunting in the forest." She smiled sweetly up at him. "They were not as skilled as you—or Timothy."

Iron Cloud nodded, amused by her and her comparisons, then stood aside and watched proudly as she knelt down beside Brian and ripped his shirt away from the wound. She took much care at cleansing the wound, then used herbal preparations that Girl Who Laughs had taught her about and spread the white gummy matter across the wound.

Brian winced only momentarily as the pressure of her fingers applying the medicine pained him. But it seemed to be a miracle how quickly the strange sort of gummy substance began to soothe the pain away into nothingness.

Damita rose to her full height and stood beside Iron Cloud, watching as Brian relaxed on the blankets, breathing much more easily.

"My wife is quite skilled at doctoring," Iron

Cloud said, leaning over to brush her lips with a kiss.

Brian looked up at them, his lips tugging into a smile. "Thanks," he said softly. "But I hate to put you out."

"I want you to stay until you are well enough to travel the long distance back to Fort Calhoun," Damita offered, with Iron Cloud nodding his approval. "We will place our pallets with Timothy's behind his blanket, to give you privacy."

"That's asking too much of you," Brian argued. "I can travel with the soldiers back to the fort. I'm not a weakling."

"I insist," Iron Cloud said firmly. "Tomorrow, should you feel the need to travel, we shall see then how well you are faring. For tonight, you will share our dwelling, as though one of us."

A sudden outburst of gunfire echoing through the air outside the wigwam drew a quick silence inside it. Damita's heart seemed to plummet to her throat when she searched with wild eyes around the dwelling, realizing that Timothy was not there.

Grabbing a blanket and circling her shoulders with it, she was the first to flee the wigwam, quickly relieved when she saw Timothy at the edge of a crowd that was gathering in the center of the village, where the dead soldiers still lay.

"Timothy!" Damita cried, going to him. She wrapped him in her arms, softly crying. "My Lord, when I heard the shot and saw that you weren't

in the cabin, I thought—I thought you might have
been shot."

Timothy clung to Damita, hysterical with tears.
"It was not I," he cried. "It—it was Lean Elk!"

Damita paled and felt her knees grow weak. She
looked at the crowd, unable to see anything else.
"How?" she gasped, now holding Timothy from
her, searching his eyes for answers. "How did he
get shot? The soldiers' weapons had been removed. They were being given their freedom!"

"It was not one of those who had been released
from the corral," Timothy sobbed. "It was one of
the men everyone thought was dead. He...he
awakened long enough to fire one last shot from
his pistol. It...it hit Lean Elk!"

A heartrending wail soon rose into the heavens,
and Damita realized that Girl Who Laughs no
longer had cause to laugh. She had found her
wounded son.

"I must go to him!" Timothy cried, starting to
slip and slide in the snow, his eyes blinded with
the onrush of tears.

Damita reached out and stopped him. She drew
him to her side, holding him there as Iron Cloud
broke through the crowd and saw Lean Elk lying
in the snow, so still, the man who shot him now
certainly dead, a knife piercing his heart.

Iron Cloud knelt down beside Lean Elk, his fingers searching the young man's thick hair for the
wound and soon finding it. He grimaced and was
filled with sorrow, knowing that head wounds
were the hardest to heal. He gazed with anguish

up at Girl Who Laughs, who knelt on the other side of Lean Elk, wailing, beside herself with grief.

Iron Cloud embraced Girl Who Laughs, causing her wails to soften to soft whimpers. Then he turned from her and gazed up at the wide circle of his people. "Stand back! Make room for Buffalo Doctor!"

As the people stood aside, Damita got her first look at Lean Elk and his injuries. A sob lodged in her throat and she clutched at Timothy. Lean Elk looked so young and helpless in the snow, blood oozing from the wound at the back of his head.

Soon, through an opening in the crowd, she saw a tall man dressed in a huge buffalo hide pass through the space to where the boy lay. She had heard much about the Omahas' Buffalo Doctor, but had never seen him work his medicine. He wore the entire skin of a buffalo's head worn over his head, the skin and hair parted to expose his face from the eyes down, but leaving it hanging on each side of his chest and down his back. Buffalo tails were fastened in a belt at his waist. He carried a staff made from a red willow branch, the leaves left on.

Buffalo Doctor knelt down beside Lean Elk and felt his wrist, and then his heart. "He is alive," he announced, his breath steaming in the chilly air. "Warriors, come. Lift him on a robe and take him to his mother's house. Draw the sides of her tent up to let in the fresh air and to permit people to witness the operation I will soon perform."

Although cold and exhausted from the day's excitements and sadnesses, Damita went to Girl Who Laughs and placed a gentle hand to her arm to help her up from the ground, as Lean Elk was taken to his mother's tent.

"Let me help you," Damita said, leaning down into Girl Who Laughs' lovely copper face, now blotchy from crying. "Come. Let me take you to your son's side. I will sit with you, if you like."

Girl Who Laughs looked pityingly up at Damita, sniffling. "I will go alone," she murmured. "You must care for yourself and your unborn child. Nothing must happen to this second child, White Willow. Nothing!"

"At least let me walk with you to your tent," Damita insisted.

Girl Who Laughs nodded and went with Damita. Damita left her at the entrance flap and went around to the side, where the tent had been rolled up for viewing of what was to transpire inside. Iron Cloud came to her side and placed an arm around her waist. Timothy edged up close to Iron Cloud's other side and clung to him, his eyes locked on his best friend, wishing that it were he, instead of Lean Elk who had to endure this suffering.

His old eyes crinkling in the folds of his wrinkled face, Buffalo Doctor sat down beside Lean Elk, the fire in the firepit at his back. He began in a low tone to explain to Lean Elk how in a vision he had seen the buffalo which had revealed to him the secret of the medicine and taught him the song he must sing when using it.

As he began singing, he removed a skin pouch from inside his robe and began compounding the roots of wild anise and other herbs that he had picked before the snows had fallen. A warrior entered the tent and stood beside Buffalo Doctor and began playing a bone whistle, imitating the cry of the eagle.

After the song had started, Buffalo Doctor put the bits of roots into his mouth, ground them with his teeth and taking a mouthful of water from a gourd cup, bent low beside Lean Elk, bellowing and pawing the earth like an angry buffalo at bay.

Then he rose slowly, so that he was now hovering over Lean Elk. He drew in a long breath, and with a whizzing noise, forced the water from his mouth into the wound.

Lean Elk spread out his hands and winced as though he had been struck, startling Damita. She clung fiercely to Iron Cloud, finding it hard not to go to Lean Elk and offer her own sorts of services.

But she knew that was forbidden, now that their resident doctor was already involved in the healing process.

Buffalo Doctor uttered a series of short exclamations: "Hi! Hi! Hi!"

Girl Who Laughs lifted her outspread hands toward the doctor to signify her thanks.

The treatment was repeated three more times, and then the doctor sang a song which conveyed to the Omaha mind a picture of the prairie, the round buffalo wallow like a pool of water, and the wounded buffalo being healed near it by its companions.

Damita had been told that there was a belief among the Omaha that the buffalo cure their wounds with their saliva; therefore their doctors prepared the herbs in the mouth and blew the water into the wound.

Iron Cloud drew Damita around to face him. "This ceremony will continue for as many days as are required for Lean Elk to get well," he said softly. "It is best that we leave the doctoring to Buffalo Doctor." He turned to his people, and with a silent gesture of his hand, even they disbanded.

He ushered Damita into their dwelling, encouraging Timothy to stay there with her and Brian, then went outside and gave the orders that soon cleared the land of the dead and those that had been allowed to live and return home.

Broodingly sad, Timothy sat beside the fire opposite Brian, while Damita dipped rabbit stew in cups. When Iron Cloud came into the wigwam, his hand clasped onto Timothy's spear, Timothy rushed to his feet to take it, then stopped, remembering how it had only a short while ago been used. He turned his eyes away, then gulped hard when he felt Iron Cloud force the spear into his hand.

"It is yours," Iron Cloud said. "You have earned the honor of keeping it forever. You have proven again that you are a most courageous man. Thank you, my son, for saving my life."

Touched deeply by Iron Cloud's constant referral to him as his son, and by his approval of what he had done, Timothy willingly circled his fingers around the spear. "Thank you, Iron Cloud," he said, looking proudly into Iron Cloud's dark, mystical eyes. "I shall keep it. I am proud that it is mine."

Timothy gazed down at the spear, unable to hold back a shudder when he recalled the sound it had made as it entered Jonathan's body, yet relieved that Iron Cloud had cleansed it of any signs of blood before bringing it back to him. His eyes misted as he held the spear out before him, feeling that it was today, more than any other time before, that he had been truly transformed from a boy to man.

Chapter Thirty

Three Days Later, Late Evening.

Buffalo Doctor stood in the center of the circle of anxious Omaha people, giving them solemn stares. Damita stood between Timothy and Iron Cloud, waiting anxiously for the doctor's announcement. Brian stood back from them, clutching a blanket to fend off the cold, for he had not been strong enough as soon as he had expected to travel back to Fort Calhoun.

He had basked in the warmth of the sun for much of the day, but now it was dusk, the sun flashing its last light atop the trees like tongues of flame.

He looked toward the trees, whose limbs were no longer heavy and sheathed in white. The temperature was more agreeable now, the winds having shifted to the south, their gusts now carrying a trace of warmth. The snows were melting, which would give his horse a surer footing upon his return to Fort Calhoun.

His plans were to leave on the morrow, after sharing the morning meal with his adopted family. Damita, Iron Cloud, and Timothy had taken the place these past three days of the family that Brian had never had. He had been orphaned as a child and had been raised in an orphanage, from which he had escaped at fourteen.

The Army had been his life—and his family—ever since.

The army had even become his wife, he thought to himself. Until now, there had been no special woman in his life.

Until now . . . .

His gaze shifted, settling on Girl Who Laughs, who stood just outside her tent, the weight of worry seemingly lifted off her pretty shoulders as she stood with a soft smile, waiting for the doctor's announcement. When she turned her eyes slowly Brian's way, he nodded a silent hello to her and smiled, feeling as though the day's last sunshine were flooding his senses when she returned the smile, then cast her eyes down to the ground bashfully.

Brian had watched her coming and going from her tent these past few days as he had gone outside to walk to regain his strength. They had found themselves drawn to each other, finding ways to be at the same place at the same time, forcing them into dialogue with one another.

Brian had become quickly taken with her. She was not only mystically beautiful, but also sweet, and had her son not been lying ill, he would have been glad to share much laughter with her. Since her name was Girl Who Laughs, he knew that her laughter would surely be special—and musical to the ear!

This in truth was why he had not left the Omaha village any sooner—not because he was not altogether well enough.

When Girl Who Laughs turned her full attention back to Buffalo Doctor, Brian followed her lead, hoping that the doctor would make an announcement that would please everyone—especially Girl Who Laughs, which would in turn please Brian!

Buffalo Doctor raised his hands over his head and turned so that he faced the waiting people. Then he turned his gaze so that it was not focused on anyone, or any one thing. He spoke in a monotone, his arms now clasped to his sides.

"My people, it is good to tell you that Lean Elk is now out of danger," he said, drawing gasps of delight from those who were listening. "In the morning, he will be made to stand and meet the rising sun, and so greet the return of life."

Girl Who Laughs emitted a loud cry of joy, then disappeared inside her tent, where her son lay. In the distance, drums began to beat their steady rhythm. There was an instant celebration as singing commenced and there were many shared hugs, and even wild dancing around the communal fire.

Iron Cloud turned to Damita and ushered her

back to their wigwam. "But Iron Cloud, I want to celebrate also," she softly argued.

"You will celebrate quietly with your husband," Iron Cloud said, removing the blankets from around her shoulders. "Sit by the fire. Warm yourself."

Damita looked around the wigwam. The fire cast a soft glow on the walls and curved ceiling, but there was no one else in the wigwam. She turned concerned eyes to Iron Cloud. "Where is Timothy?" she asked. "Where is Brian?"

"I can only think of one place," Iron Cloud said, settling down beside her. He poured her a cup of tea and handed it to her. "Timothy and Brian are at Girl Who Laughs' tent. Timothy is there because of Lean Elk, and Brian"—He chuckled—"I believe he has his heart set on a certain lovely Omaha maiden."

Damita's eyes lit up with a smile. "Are you saying that while Brian has been here recovering, he has had his mind on more than getting well?" she asked, giggling.

"Exactly," Iron Cloud said, leaning back on his elbow and stretching a long, lean leg out before him. "You know that his wound is not a severe one. He could have returned to Fort Calhoun two days ago. He became afflicted with another wound before he could leave our village—an arrow piercing his heart!"

"My word," Damita said, then giggled. "I think it's wonderful. Just wonderful!"

"Finish your tea. Then I am going to see that

you are in bed early tonight," Iron Cloud said, waiting for her to empty the cup. "Everyone will want to be up early to see Lean Elk emerge from his sick bed. My woman, you and our child must have your rest before rising that early."

"Yes, you are right, as usual," Damita said. She emptied the cup and gave it to Iron Cloud. "But I won't go to bed unless you lie down next to me." After he set the cup aside, she crawled to him and splayed her fingers against his powerful chest. "I have missed our lovemaking. Perhaps we stopped too soon? Was I too concerned about our child to suggest we not make love after the fifth month, my darling? Should we make love tonight?"

"I was taught restraint as a child, so I do not need the lovemaking," Iron Cloud said, twining his fingers through her long, golden hair. "But if you need something, I can at least rub you and make you feel good. Would that please you, my woman?"

"Very much," Damita murmured.

She rose with him and leaned against him as they went behind the privacy blanket. Unable to shed her clothes, afraid that Timothy or Brian might come into the wigwam, Damita lay down on the pelts and lifted her dress up past her thighs. When Iron Cloud knelt down over her and kissed her throbbing center, then stroked her with his tongue, she melted inside and closed her eyes and let the joyous bliss claim her.

* * *

Damita was awakened the next morning by the sound of singing. She rose on one elbow and saw that Timothy and Iron Cloud weren't there: then she raised the blanket and saw that Brian was also gone!

Anger rose within her at the men for having left without her, yet her resentment faded when she felt the baby kicking within her womb and realized that when Iron Cloud had seen her sleeping so soundly, he must have been the one to forbid anyone waking her.

Their child. All was for their child.

Her rest was as important as food. No one wanted her to miscarry this time, and thus far, with everyone pampering her, it looked as though she was going full term with this baby!

Still dressed from falling asleep in Iron Cloud's arms, all that Damita had to do to make herself presentable was smooth her hair with her hands, then she draped a blanket around her shoulders and hurried outside.

It was quite early. The air was heavy with fog, yet she could see that the crowd of Omaha people had already gathered around Girl Who Laughs' tent. Damita sorted through the crowd with her eyes and found Iron Cloud, Timothy, and Brian. She waddled over to them and worked her way in beside Iron Cloud.

When he looked down at her with his midnight-dark eyes, she gave him a slight frown to scold him for having left her sleeping, then smiled sweetly up at him to let him know that she understood why he had done it and was not truly angry at him for it. When his arm slipped around her waist, beneath her blanket, everything became beautiful again, and she snuggled against him to await the appearance of Buffalo Doctor outside the tent.

As dawn drew nearer, the fog slowly disappeared, as if to unveil the great red sun that was just visible on the horizon. Slowly it grew larger and larger. As it cast its glorious light on Girl Who Laughs' tent, Buffalo Doctor appeared at the entrance flap. He moved out, and then there were many sighs of relief when Lean Elk was finally visible, being helped outside by two warriors on each side of him.

There was silence as Buffalo Doctor went to Timothy and told him to take four steps unassisted toward the east, while the doctor sang the mystery song which belonged to this stage of the cure.

The two warriors let go of Lean Elk and began to count as the young brave feebly attempted to walk—one, two three . . .

The steps grew slower, and it did not seem as if he could make the fourth, but he dragged his foot and took the last step.

"Four!" cried the men. "It is done!"

The doctor sang the song of triumph, and then there were many shouts and chants rising into the sky, and many gifts laid at the doctor's feet. There were robes, bear-claw necklaces, eagle feathers, embroidered leggings, and other articles of value.

Lean Elk leaned his full weight against his

mother as she came to him, her eyes filled with tears of pride. "I am not altogether well, mother," he said weakly, turning grateful eyes up to her. "But soon I will be back among my friends to learn the skills of our elders."

Girl Who Laughs drew him into her embrace and hugged him, then led him back inside the tent and to his bed beside the fire.

Timothy ran inside, carrying a flute that he had carved himself and gave it to Lean Elk. "This whistle will give you something to do while you are mending," he said anxiously. "I made it, Lean Elk. Do you like it?"

Lean Elk clutched the flute to his chest. "It is a gift I will always cherish, my friend," he said, smiling up at Timothy. "Thank you." His eyes wavered. "While I was so ill, did you find Baby?"

Timothy cast his eyes downward and swallowed hard, hating to disappoint his very best friend in the world. "No," he murmured. "Baby is gone, I guess forever."

Damita and Iron Cloud came into the tent, Brian and Girl Who Laughs following close behind them. Damita knelt down beside Lean Elk. "I'm so glad that you are better," she said, gently smoothing a raven-black lock of hair back from his brow. "Soon you will be playing and hunting with Timothy again. And you can stay all night with him as often as you wish. You can talk into the wee hours of the morning, telling each other tales only meant for best friends to hear. Does that sound nice, Lean Elk?"

"I am eager to do everything," Lean Elk said, laughing softly. "I do not like being away from all the excitement." His brow knitted into a frown as he cast a glance Brian's way. "*He* was one of the soldiers? Why is he here? And why is my mother so friendly to him?"

Damita and Iron Cloud exchanged troubled glances, then Iron Cloud knelt down beside Lean Elk and placed a hand on his shoulder. "He is a soldier, yes," he said, "but he was not among those who attacked our village. He is not responsible for your wound. And..." He glanced toward Brian and Girl Who Laughs, seeing that their conversation had taken on a serious tone, their gazes intent on each other's eyes.

He looked back at Lean Elk. "His name is Brian," he further explained. "He has become fast friends with your mother. And, Lean Elk, *my* feelings for Brian are the same as those you have for Timothy. Brian is my very best friend in the world. I would do anything for him. Even die, if it was necessary."

Lean Elk's lips parted in a slight gasp, and as his mother came to him, with Brian at her side, and knelt down beside him opposite to where the others were kneeling, Lean Elk scarcely breathed. His mother was behaving strangely. He had never seen her look so radiant, her eyes filled with a strange sort of haziness.

"My son," Girl Who Laughs said, taking his hand, gently holding it. "I am so happy you are going to be well. I prayed nightly to Wakoda, and he has blessed us both by making you well." She gave Brian a shy smile, then looked back at her son. "My son, Wakoda has blessed us a second time. She has sent this man to us. He offers to be my husband—and your father."

Lean Elk looked guardedly at Brian, then at his mother. "And what did you say?" he said softly, his heart hammering.

"I told Brian that the decision is yours, my son," Girl Who Laughs murmured. She kissed Lean Elk on the cheek, then gazed at him again. "Is it too soon after your recovery for such a decision?"

Lean Elk thought for a moment, then said, "It is too soon, yes." Then he turned his eyes away from his mother.

Damita placed a hand to her mouth, sealing a gasp behind it. She watched with pitying eyes as Girl Who Laughs rose to her feet beside Brian, her eyes wavering.

"I am sorry, Brian," Girl Who Laughs murmured, obviously fighting back tears. "My son has spoken."

Brian nodded, gave her a quick kiss on the cheek, and left.

Girl Who Laughs gave Damita and Iron Cloud a lingering, sad look, then sat down beside her son again and took his hand and held it. When he looked her way again, he gave her a weak smile. She reciprocated with a sweet kiss, then drew a blanket up to his chin.

"My son, the day has been a tiring one for you,"

she murmured. "Sleep now. I shall resume my beading."

Iron Cloud rose to his feet, helping Damita up. He nodded to Timothy to leave, and they all went back to their wigwam. They found Brian drawing on a heavy buckskin outfit that Iron Cloud had given him for travel.

"It is time for me to resume my duties at the fort," Brian said gruffly, not looking Iron Cloud's way. "I've been away too long as it is."

Damita went to Brian and leaned over to kiss his cheek. Iron Cloud gave him a bear hug. Timothy shook his hand. They all went outside and bid Brian a sad farewell as he mounted his horse and rode away.

Damita cast her eyes toward Girl Who Laughs' tent, seeing her tiny shadow at the entrance, watching Brian ride away with tears silvering her cheeks.

Chapter Thirty-one

The village was filled with merriment. The drums boomed. The people's feet stamped out the rythm of the music as they danced and sang around the large outdoor fire. The skin of the fox bounced about the legs below the knees of some warriors, the tail hanging as an ornament on the outside of the leg. Bells fastened about the waists of other dancers tinkled merrily, emphasizing the rhythm of the dance. Food was being prepared in the dwellings for the celebration of life—Lean Elk's life.

"At a time when Girl Who Laughs should be so happy, so thankful, I am sure her heart is heavy with the loss of Brian," Damita said, sitting beside the fire in the warmth of her dwelling beside Iron Cloud. She strung another bead on her needle. "But of course, I can understand Lean Elk's feelings." She looked slowly up at Iron Cloud. "His father died during a skirmish with a white man while on a hunting expedition, didn't he?''

Iron Cloud scowled into the fire, drawing his knees up to his chest. "I was also fired upon that day," he said moodily. "I still believe it was the doings of Jonathan. But it could never be proved. Those who did the firing escaped into the thicket. It was my duty to get Wise Elk back to the village, for medical assistance, not to go after those who had shot him."

He cast his eyes downward, silent for a moment, then glared at Damita. "He did not live long enough to say goodbye to his wife or son!" he growled out.

"How tragic," Damita gasped. She leaned her ear to the jubilant singing outside, the drums and rattles filling the air like the intensified pulsing of one's heartbeat. "I am sure that it was not easy for Girl Who Laughs to let herself fall in love with a white man, after . . ."

"Brian is white, but like you, his heart and his soul are Indian," Iron Cloud said, moving to his knees before Damita. He placed a finger to her chin and lifted her lips to his. He kissed her softly, then rose to his feet and lifted the entrance flap and peered outside. "In time, when Lean Elk sees his mother pining for Brian, the young warrior will open his heart also to the white man. He is a devoted son to his mother. He will want her to be happy, not sad."

Damita laid her beadwork aside. Placing a hand to the small of her back, she moved awkwardly to her feet, not understanding how she could be so large so soon! She felt as though she were carrying around an army of children inside her, not only one.

Her eyes widened and she gasped as a thought came to her. Could she be carrying twins? Was that why she was always so hungry, eating twice the amount that she deemed normal? Was that why she felt such pressure on her bladder that made her seek the forest more than once during the night to relieve herself?

Iron Cloud gave her a quick glance over his shoulder as she moved slowly his way. "White Willow, did you say something?" he asked, forking an eyebrow when she did not immediately reply, yet gave him a smile that seemed to hold secrets within it. Never had he seen her look so devilish! And he knew that it was not because she was about to approach him sexually, teasing him in the way that only she knew how!

Damita caught his quizzical glance, realizing that he saw something different in her smile, yet she had just decided not to tell him of her conclusions—that perhaps she would be giving him two children in one package on the day of her birthing! She could even now see his reaction! It would be that of a husband overwhelmed with praise and happiness! He would be able to take a child in each arm outside to show his people! He would look twice the virile man in their eyes than he was now!

Now, as never before, she had to take care that

nothing happened to this pregnancy. Just envisioning a child nursing at each breast thrilled her through and through!

"No," Damita said, finally reaching Iron Cloud. She slipped an arm through his and leaned into his side. "It was only my groans as I pushed myself from the floor. Lord, Iron Cloud, my stomach is so heavy!"

Iron Cloud patted her stomach, where it strained against the buckskin dress, drawing the fabric tightly across it. "Perhaps I was wrong to be calling this child a girl," he said, laughing softly. "Perhaps it is two boys!"

Damita's lips parted and she looked up at him with wide eyes. "Two...boys...?" she murmured, then laughed at how it seemed their minds always carried the same thoughts. She had only moments ago been thinking of twins!

"Or two girls," Iron Cloud said, shrugging. He leaned a soft kiss to her nose. "My darling White Willow, you know that it matters not to me what the child, or children, will be. Just stay healthy, my love. You are the most important one to me."

"Could anyone look any healthier?" Damita said, giggling as she gently pushed her stomach into his side. She then turned again and leaned into him as his arm snaked around her waist and held her close. She looked outside, her eyes scanning the crowd. "Do you see Timothy anywhere?"

"He is probably still with Lean Elk," Iron Cloud said, his one foot tapping out the rhythm of the drums and rattles. "He is a dedicated friend. He

Cassie Edwards

would not allow himself to go out and dance, sing, and play, while his friend is unable to—no matter if the celebration is because of the friend."

"I'm quite proud of that young man," Damita said, gazing up at Iron Cloud. "My Lord, Iron Cloud, if I hadn't allowed him to step outside to see what was happening the day Jonathan raided your village, you—you would have been killed."

"You must always remember that more than a spear killed your cousin," Iron Cloud said. "But it is true that Timothy was a hero on that day. And my people will never forget this. It is my life that is being celebrated today, my love, as well as Lean Elk's. Also, Timothy's heroism is being celebrated!"

He broke away from Damita and stepped outside.

"Where are you going?" Damita asked, holding the entrance flap aside, the chill wind whipping through her dress.

"Soon you shall see!" Iron Cloud said, giving her a mischievous smile over his shoulder. "Wrap yourself warmly in blankets, then come outside. There is something that needs doing!"

Filled with wonder, Damita watched him for a moment longer, then went and wrapped herself in a blanket and hurried outside. She walked slowly toward the celebrating Omahas, her eyes scanning the crowd for Iron Cloud, yet not seeing him anywhere.

Then suddenly she saw him. She stopped almost in mid-step when he came from Girl Who Laughs' dwelling, Timothy perched on his shoulders!

Damita placed a hand to her throat. "What on earth?" she gasped. "What is he doing?"

It did not take long for her to understand. The Omaha people broke away, to make space for Iron Cloud to mingle with them. As he held on to Timothy's legs, Timothy supporting himself by clinging to Iron Cloud's neck, Iron Cloud went to the center of the crowd and stood beside the roaring fire.

"We celebrate many things today!" Iron Cloud shouted. "Do not forget our young warrior Timothy! He has proven much to you. His act of heroism should never be forgotten! Now do you see, my people, that this young man whom I have adopted to be my own son is capable of the teachings of chieftain? That he deserves to walk in my shadow, and one day take my title as his own? Let me hear your acceptance, my people! Let Timothy hear!"

Touched by Iron Cloud's devotion to her brother, Damita choked back a sob that was trying to escape from the depths of her throat. She looked around, filled with pride and much gratitude, as the Omaha people began to raise their hands in the air, shouting their praises of Timothy high into the heavens.

And when some of the warriors took Timothy from Iron Cloud's shoulders and began passing him around from man to man, walking through the village with him on their shoulders, Damita could not help but let the mists in her eyes burst into full-blown tears.

The celebration suddenly ceased and a great silence fell. Damita watched the direction of their gazes as the people turned to stare, and she saw Brian Davis returning on his horse to the village, carrying something wrapped in a blanket on his lap.

She rushed to Iron Cloud's side and stood with him as Brian made his way through the crowd on his horse, his eyes filled with a strange sort of sadness. She scarcely breathed as he reined in just a few feet away and dismounted, walking toward her and Iron Cloud, the bundle now appearing to be much larger in his arms than it had appeared on his lap.

"What have you there?" Iron Cloud asked, his gaze on the bundle. "Why have you brought it to us?"

"I didn't get far before I came across two bobcats in a fierce battle," Brian said, bending to one knee and placing the blanketed bundle on the ground. "I wasn't sure if I should intervene, but when I saw that one of the bobcats was hardly more than a kitten and the other full-grown, I decided that I might even up the score for the smaller one. But before I could dismount and grab my rifle, the smaller bobcat was already the victor—she had ripped the other one's throat open, and it was bleeding to death."

Brian started to unfold the blanket. "But don't get me wrong," he mumbled. "She may have been the victor, but she didn't get away from the fight without some major battle wounds. She didn't fuss at all when I picked her up and wrapped her in these blankets. It was as though she was familiar with the smell and the kindnesses of a human."

"Bobcat?" Damita said, her knees weakening with the hope that perhaps the surviving bobcat might be Baby. Of course, she would be much larger now, and might not be even considered a kitten, as Brian had described this bobcat.

Having heard Brian's tale, Timothy fell to his knees beside Brian. "Let me unwrap her," he asked, pleading up at Brian with his dark eyes. "Please?"

"Go ahead," Brian said, arching an eyebrow. He glanced up at Iron Cloud, receiving Iron Cloud's approval by a nod of his head. When he looked at Damita, and saw such hope in her tear-filled eyes he was even more confused by their reaction to his having brought an injured bobcat to their village. Being a man who loved animals of all sorts, he had hoped they would see to its injuries. But he hadn't expected to find such anxiety for a stray animal—if, he suddenly thought—the animal was a stray! Perhaps it was a long-lost pet?

With trembling fingers and a heartbeat that seemed as though it might swallow him whole, Timothy curled one corner of the blanket away, then another. When only one layer of blanket remained, he clasped and unclasped his fingers, then in one jerk of the blanket discovered that his beloved pet bobcat lay there before him, her eyes closed in a deep, unconscious sleep.

Timothy's feelings were a mixture of happiness and horror, for after completely uncovering Baby, he was able to see the extent of her wounds. One of her paws was missing, a bloody stump all that remained. Gouges of her beautiful fur were ripped away, leaving bloody wounds on her stomach and sides.

Timothy turned his eyes away, feeling like retching, but when Iron Cloud's strong hand rested on his shoulder, he received from it the strength that it held.

Sweeping his arms beneath Baby's limp body, Timothy lifted her and held her to his bosom as he rose slowly to his feet. He turned sorrowful eyes to Damita, then Iron Cloud, and walked toward his wigwam, his eyes downcast, his heart bleeding.

"Thank you for bringing Baby to us," Iron Cloud said, placing a firm hand on Brian's shoulder. "You had no way of knowing what it would mean to Timothy. He has mourned long for the loss of his pet bobcat. That he has gotten the bobcat back is a blessing of Wakoda. Thank you for answering Wakoda's silent biddings by bringing her to us."

"No, I had no idea," Brian said, his gaze moving to Timothy as Timothy went inside his dwelling, Damita now at his side. "But anything that fought as valiantly as that bobcat was fighting deserved to live—and to have medical attention." He added thoughtfully, "It was as though she was fighting for her territorial rights."

"And so she was, it seems," Iron Cloud said, turning to gaze at his wigwam. "She was on her way home to Timothy. When she got that close, and the other bobcat intervened, she saw no other choice but to fight to protect those who were important to her."

"She's wounded, but I think she will live," Brian said, bending to pick up his blankets and folding them.

"She is a survivor, that is for certain," Iron Cloud said. "She has spent many months wandering alone, searching for her home. Now that she is home, she will fight even harder to survive!"

"I'd best hit the road again," Brian said, his gaze momentarily lingering on Girl Who Laughs' wigwam. "I've got my life to get back in order." He turned to Iron Cloud, his eyes suddenly dancing. "I've some ideas on the future that might include you, ol' buddy. Only time will tell, though, if they can hatch into something productive for both you and me." Again he gazed at Girl Who Laughs' wigwam. "And only time will tell about that lovely Omaha maiden I can't seem to get off my mind."

Iron Cloud swung an arm around Brian's shoulder and walked him to his horse. "My friend, Illinois is now my home, and my people's," he said. "If you wish ever to come and join us, you are welcome." He saw Girl Who Laughs step to her doorway then, holding back the entrance flap only enough for her to see Brian, her eyes heavy with sadness as she gazed at him.

"In time, my friend," Iron Cloud said to his friend as Brian placed his foot into the stirrup. "Girl Who Laughs will also welcome you."

"I'll court her to death 'til she does," Brian said, chuckling. He made a mock salute with his hand at his temple. "See you soon, ol' buddy. Soon!"

Iron Cloud wondered what his friend had on his mind, but then his own mind filled with concern over Baby, and he hurried back to his wigwam. When he stepped inside, he stood in the shadows and watched for a few moments, seeing the dedication of both his wife and son as they administered to the bobcat. The blood had already been washed from its paw and fur.

Timothy was the first to notice Iron Cloud there. He looked up at him sadly. "Even some of Baby's sharpest teeth are missing, Iron Cloud," he said, his voice breaking. "Poor Baby. She had to fight for her life, it seems."

Iron Cloud bent down on his haunches beside Timothy. "Not so much for his life, but for *yours*," he said thickly. "She realized that she was nearing home, and when she saw the other bobcat so near to your home also, she saw no other recourse than to fight it, to keep it from coming into the village, possibly harming you. So, my young warrior, your bobcat's bravery matches your own."

Damita was gingerly wrapping a sterile cloth around Baby's paw, hardly able to contain the tears that still threatened to spill from her eyes. Just looking at the bobcat lying there so injured made her feel miserably sad.

"Iron Cloud," she said, gazing up at him. "Will she recover? Truly, will she?"

Her heartbeat quickened when she felt a warm tongue on her hand. Her gaze shifted quickly downward, discovering that Baby's eyes were open, her tongue taking lazy swipes at Damita's hand. And when Baby began purring, her eyes looking trustingly up at Damita, Damita could not help but burst into tears and laughter at the same time.

Timothy fell onto his knees beside Baby. He gently eased the bobcat's head onto his lap and hugged her. "Baby," he crooned. "My sweet Baby. You're going to make it! You're not going to die!"

Damita rose slowly to her feet and welcomed Iron Cloud's comforting arm around her waist. She leaned into him now so peacefully, perfectly content, as she peered down at Timothy, so radiant in his love for his bobcat.

"You'll never leave us again, will you?" Timothy asked, directing Baby's gaze into his. "You've found your home again. You won't ever run away again, will you?"

Realizing the restlessness of such an animal, Iron Cloud and Damita gave each other sudden, questioning frowns, yet both knew that the chances were good that Baby would never leave them again, for she would have the foresight to see that she was no longer able to fend for herself. With only one paw, and most of her teeth missing, she had to rely on others than of her own kind.

Chapter Thirty-two

Two Months Later.

As the canoe sliced through the water, the faint dipping of paddles barely broke the stillness of the early morning hours. There was suddenly a great whirring sound as a startled grouse took flight when the canoe slipped onto the embankment, and Timothy quickly bounced from the canoe, beaching it.

He grabbed his buckskin bag from the canoe and slung it over his shoulder, then offered Lean Elk a hand. "You said that you know how to seek out turtles?" he asked anxiously. "I want to take back the largest of them all, Lean Elk, for all to see."

Lean Elk refused help as he stepped from the birchbark vessel, his strength having returned well enough from his accident so that he could fend for himself. "I must remind you that it is not the turtle itself that you will present to the warriors tonight as you take the final step to prove your worthiness to be called an Omaha warrior," he said, walking beside Timothy across the damp sand in his thin-soled moccasins.

"I know," Timothy said, trying to hide the reluctance in his voice at the thought of having to kill the turtle and remove its heart. He kept reminding himself that although this sounded like something required of a young man in the "old men sayings" of which Iron Cloud had told him so many, it was not.

This was a serious matter.

Each Omaha boy who wished to become looked upon as a true warrior had to partake in this ritual.

It would take much courage, he knew, to kill a defenseless turtle and cut into it to remove its heart. Perhaps more courage than ever before, for he did love animals with such a passion!

He had purposely left Baby home during this outing, not only to keep Baby safe, but to keep Damita company. They had grown closer than ever while Damita nursed the bobcat back to health. And that was good, Timothy had decided. Damita was now so heavy with child, she could hardly move! Baby was there, in Iron Cloud's and Timothy's absences, to be a companion during her time of waiting for her child to be born.

Timothy's thoughts shifted back to the present when he noticed that Lean Elk's legs almost gave out beneath him as he walked along the riverbank with him.

"Are you sure you are able to do this?" Timothy asked, grabbing for Lean Elk and placing a quick arm around his waist. "Although it's been two months since your injury, your mother warned that it is too soon to be doing anything as strenuous as this."

Lean Elk frowned. "Did I not prove my strength by doing my part paddling the canoe?" he asked, flecks of anger in his voice. He jerked free from Timothy's grip. "You should concern yourself over things other than Lean Elk. I am not helpless!"

"It is good to be with you again on an outing," Timothy said sincerely. "It is true that I now have many friends among those in our village, but none as true as you. I do not feel free to speak my mind to anyone but you. You are not only my best friend, but also my confidante. I withhold no secrets from you."

"True friends we are to one another," Lean Elk said, nodding. "Before my father died, he taught me that to be false to a friend, in either love or war, marks one as without honor, and especially to be shunned." He smiled mischievously. "Also friends act as go-betweens when love is awakened in one or the other's heart. A friend secures an interview for his friend with the chosen girl."

Timothy's steps faltered as he stared at Lean Elk. "Are you saying you have feelings for a special girl?" he asked warily. "Who? During the time of play and celebrations, I've never seen you single one out with your eyes."

"There is one, yes, who makes my heart seem

to quiver like a bowstring after an arrow's release," Lean Elk confided. "You have seen her, Timothy. Many times during my recovery period she brought me presents." He glanced down at the bear claw necklace that hung around his neck, bright as white diamonds glittering beneath the rising sun's reflections. "This is my most special gift."

"I thought you made that to keep your hands from being idle these past two months," Timothy said, giving the necklace a critical look. Then he frowned at Lean Elk. "Friends share. You didn't share this with me—the fact that you have a girl whose heart is warm for you!"

Lean Elk's face flooded with color. "It was not yet something I felt comfortable with," he said softly. "She is the first for me, Timothy. Never has a girl caused my heart to betray me!"

"And so *you* betray a *friend*," Timothy scolded, then saw the wrong in his behavior and forced a light laugh. "But you are forgiven. Tonight, allow me to take a message to her for you? That will make me a part of it. Can I? Can I tell her that you have special feelings for her?"

Lean Elk forked an eyebrow, seemingly in deep thought, then nodded eagerly. "Yes, you can tell her," he said, his face filled with a smile, his eyes twinkling. "You can ask her to sit with us."

"I will gladly do that for you," Timothy said, eagerly nodding his head. Then he stilled his head and his eyes got serious. "Who is she, Lean Elk? Tell me her name."

"Her name is Star Shining," Lean Elk said dreamily, sighing. "Is not the name beautiful? It matches her loveliness, Timothy. One day soon I hope to kiss her!"

Timothy gasped. "You would kiss a girl?" he said, disgusted at the mere thought of such an action. "I would rather kiss a snake!"

Lean Elk laughed throatily.

They proceeded on their way, their eyes watching the ground for turtles.

Timothy suddenly broke the silence.

"Late in the night, when I am thought to be asleep, I've heard Damita and Iron Cloud talking about how your mother loves Brian Davis," he said, giving Lean Elk a cautious glance. "They talk of how your mother is not free to love because of your feelings for this man. Is that so, Lean Elk? Did you actually forbid your mother to marry him?"

Lean Elk's copper brow furrowed into a deep frown. "I do not forbid my mother anything," he grumbled. "I told my mother it was too soon for another man to take the place of my father." He paused, then spoke in a low hiss. "And this man my mother's heart is warmed for is white!"

Timothy paled as he looked disbelievingly at Lean Elk. "My friend, you speak as though you hate white people," he said, his voice weak. "Must I remind you, my friend, that my skin is white?"

Lean Elk looked toward Timothy, but his eyes wavered. "I did not mean—" he said, his words cut off when Timothy interrupted.

"I know," Timothy said softly. "But it should give you food for thought, shouldn't it? You should learn not to compare all white people with the one who killed your father."

Lean Elk slowly nodded. "Yes, I guess that is so," he mumbled.

"Wouldn't it be better to have a step-father than no father at all?" Timothy asked, his thoughts filled with Iron Cloud and his camaraderie with him. He was glad to look to Iron Cloud as an adoptive father. No son and father could ever be closer!

"No one could ever take the place of my father," Lean Elk said moodily. "And I already know all that is needed to become a great warrior. I am already a skilled hunter! My father taught me that in hunting, the hunter is guided by the habits of the animals he seeks. He taught me that a moose stays in swamps, or low land, or between high mountains near a spring or lake, for thirty to sixty days at a time. He told me that most large game move around continuously except the does in the spring. It is then a very easy matter to find her with the fawn."

"I know all those things already and I have only been among the Omaha a short while," Timothy argued. "And I would not have known these things had it not been for Iron Cloud, whom I very gladly accept at my side as my adoptive father, since my true father is . . . dead."

"That is different," Lean Elk argued. "Anyone would accept Iron Cloud as their father."

Timothy's mouth opened, hearing jealousy for

the first time in his friend's words and seeing it in his attitude. Perhaps it was because Lean Elk had wanted his mother to become involved with Iron Cloud—something he now knew was never to be!

Their thoughts were taken quickly with something else as a turtle's head popped up out of the water, its slanted eyes looking back at them as they stopped and stared at it. Oblivious of the danger, it ambled out of the water, up the slight sand embankment, and began inching its way toward the taller grass.

"It's quite large," Timothy said, his heart pounding. He gave Lean Elk a questioning glance. "Is it large enough, Lean Elk? Is it? Do you think it will do?"

Lean Elk bent down and rested himself on his haunches as he took a stick and placed it in front of the turtle, stopping its slow amblings. Its head quickly retreated into its shell, its feet soon also withdrawing within its private shelter.

"I would say this turtle will do fine for the ceremony," Lean Elk said, tapping the shell, trying to get the turtle to peek its head out again. He smiled up at Timothy. "I shall grab it. You open your bag. I will drop it inside for you."

"But shouldn't I—I go ahead and remove its heart?" Timothy said in a stammer that quickly embarrassed him. He did not want to look a sissy in his friend's eyes. He had to pretend that whatever transpired from this moment on that dealt with preparing himself for the ritual tonight did nothing to cause him any uneasiness or squeamishness.

"The heart's removal will be done tonight at the ceremony for all to see," Lean Elk said, jumping with a start when the turtle's head and feet suddenly appeared and it turned and started going in another direction, away from the stick.

"Get it! Don't let it get away!" Lean Elk said, quickly rising to his feet. "Once it gets in the tall grass, you will have trouble finding it."

His heart thundering within his chest, as though many drums beat there, pounding out the dread of the moment, Timothy scampered toward the turtle. In one swoop of his hands he had the turtle between them, holding it by its shell, and in another heartbeat the turtle was in the bag, the drawstrings tied tightly at the top.

"There," Timothy said, wiping a bead of nervous perspiration from his brow. "It's done. Let's return home. I'm anxious to show Iron Cloud." He frowned and gave Lean Elk a troubled glance. "I doubt I should show Damita. She would not appreciate it. I doubt if she will even come to the ritual tonight. She loves all animals and she will not enjoy seeing her brother kill a turtle, then eat its heart."

"She will be there, for as you are, she is now a part of the Omaha and believes in our customs," Lean Elk said, shrugging. "Yes, she will be there."

Timothy felt the weight in his bag and looked at its movements as the turtle tried to escape its proposed end....

Swallowing hard, Timothy most certainly hoped that he, the young man who was to be honored tonight, would show up for the ritual himself. Suddenly he didn't feel all that courageous, and wished that this particular event *had* just been a part of the old men's tales, a myth only talked about, not actually lived.

The moon lay like a path of silver over the river beyond. A huge outdoor fire lapped at the darkness. Sparks hissed at the figures leaping into the air around the fire, twisting themselves into all assortments of dances. The celebration had just begun to reach its peak of excitement. Meat was broiling at the fire, filling the air with its savor.

Damita sat beside Iron Cloud, wrapping herself more closely into the folds of her shawl. Her hair was arranged in two braids, their ends bound together and brought up to the back of the neck so that they fell in a long loop behind her ears. Following the tradition of the Omaha women, the part of her hair had been painted red, and similar treatment had been bestowed on her cheeks, back to the ear, and she wore a necklace of sweetgrass.

Smiling to herself, she looked at Iron Cloud, his handsomeness enhanced tonight by his heavy buckskin jacket ornamented with bands of embroidery and fringe, and his *uto-to-ga*, "big leggings" with their fringed, large flaps at the ankles, which were worn exclusively by the chiefs. His hair was loose and flowing down his proud, straight back, an otter skin headband holding it in place.

Her smile wavered as she watched Iron Cloud begin nodding his head in time with the insistent beating of the moose-hide drums, his eyes revealing his eagerness. Damita could not share his feelings this evening. She had seen the turtle that Timothy had captured by the river. She did not want to linger in her mind over what her brother was going to do with it to further prove himself to the Omaha warriors and be proven worthy of the title himself. She thought that he had proven himself time and time again. Why did he have to go this one step further?

She tried to blot out her worries by watching the frenzied excitement of the Omaha people—men, women, and children, alike—dancing and singing. She searched with her eyes until she found Timothy. He was resting on his haunches beside Lean Elk, his and Lean Elk's eyes watching a beautiful young thing as she twirled and stamped her feet in time with the music in front of them, her eyes teasingly moving from Timothy back to Lean Elk, as though trying to captivate them both with her charms!

Damita knew the dangers in this! Friends could quickly become enemies because of jealousies!

Damita nudged Iron Cloud in the side. "Who is that young lady?" she said, nodding toward the dancing seductress.

"That is Star Shining," Iron Cloud said, his eyes showing their admiration in their depths. "She is eighteen winters of age. She has matured nicely, wouldn't you say? She could be married now, should a warrior desire her." He chuckled as he looked around the circle of warriors who were not dancing, seeing their eyes intently on Star Shining. "There will be a marriage soon. I am sure of it."

Damita inhaled a shaky breath. "I most certainly hope so," she whispered, not wanting her brother's mind to get shadowed with ideas about girls just yet—especially one that was older than he!

She was greatly relieved when one of the Omaha warriors went to Star Shining and took her by the arm, guiding her away from the light of the fire, her giggles following along after her.

Damita looked at Timothy again, and then at Lean Elk, seeing surprise and disappointment on both of their faces, knowing that they had just learned the first lesson about women, and what some were capable of—that they could be *very* fickle!

She smiled, glad the lesson was learned at such an early age. It was the time in their lives when their desires could be shifted quickly elsewhere!

And then what had been a time of merriment in the Omaha village turned to a serious affair. Everyone sat down in a wide circle around the fire, the warriors now passing among themselves a long-stemmed pipe, the ascending smoke carrying with it each warrior's appeal, voiced in the prayer to the invisible Wakoda.

With this rite, the opening ceremonies which included Timothy began. A warrior went to Timothy and took his hand and urged him to sit alone closer to the fire. His turtle was brought to him in his buckskin bag.

Another warrior brought Timothy a large rock on which to place his bag.

Another warrior brought him a knife and placed it on his lap.

Timothy sat timidly quiet as the people began to sing in fast time, and whoever was so inclined arose, dropped his robe on the ground, and stepped forth. Then, in a conventionalized pantomine, he acted out one of his experiences in war from which he had gained public honor.

The dancer was light of foot and agile. A variety of steps were taken. The foot was brought down on the ground with a thud, making a synchronous accompaniment to the resonant drum beat and the voices of the singers; the limbs were lifted at sharp angles; the body was bent and raised with sudden and diversified movements, as in a charge, or as if dodging arrows or averting blows from weapons.

In all this dramatic presentation of an actual scene there was not a motion of foot, leg, body, arm, or head that did not follow the song in strict time, yet keeping close to the story that was being acted out.

The throb of the drum beat time with the pulse of the spectator and held him to the rhythm of the scene as the eye followed the rapid, tense action

Cassie Edwards

of the dancer and the ear caught the melody which revealed the intent of the strange drama.

A rest song, slower in time, followed the dance, and then the dancer sat down, muffled in his robe, dripping with perspiration and panting to recover his breath.

And then everything became quiet, the full focus on Timothy.

Iron Cloud dropped his robe away and went to settle himself on his haunches before Timothy. He reached a comforting hand to the boy's bare shoulder and smiled at him.

"It is time to take this one last step to earn not only the title of warrior, but also an Omaha name," he said. "My son, I have chosen well a name for you. Cut out the turtle's heart, swallow it, so as to make your own heart stronger! In this act, you will prove yourself worthy of the new name and the title of Warrior!"

Timothy's eyes lit up. "I will have my own Indian name like everyone else?" he said, his voice lifting in pitch with each word spoken. He so badly wanted to fling himself into Iron Cloud's arms and hug him, but he was already learning the art of restraint and held himself back from this show of emotion. "That would be good, Iron Cloud. Very good."

"The name I have chosen for you is Spotted Eagle," Iron Cloud said, lifting his voice so that not only Timothy could hear, but the whole throng of people who were sitting quietly, their eyes and ears directed toward their chief and his adoptive son. "This name is derived from the spots on your bobcat, and the eagle, because of its powers over mankind! Spotted Eagle, it is time now for you to kill the turtle and swallow its heart!"

"The name is one of strength and courage," Timothy said, gazing devotedly up at Iron Cloud. His heart thudded wildly. His knees were weak with excitement. He no longer feared killing the turtle. He knew that it was something that every warrior who looked upon him this day had done. It was not a deed to look upon with fear and shame. It was to be looked upon with honor! With reverence! "Thank you for the name, Iron Cloud. I will never give you cause to regret it."

Iron Cloud moved to his haunches beside Timothy and lifted the bag from the rock and loosened its drawstrings so that the turtle could crawl from its prison. When it did not attempt to escape, Iron Cloud held the bag up and gave it a slight shake. The turtle fell out, its hard shell making a loud thump when it landed and rocked back and forth on the rock where it lay, upside down.

Glad that the turtle was not offering its head from the shell, so that its slanted eyes did not meet Timothy's, Timothy picked up the knife and began the dreaded ritual.

Damita looked away, swallowing hard, as Timothy plunged the knife into the bottom of the turtle's shell. She did not look again until she heard the low chantings beginning around her, which she hoped meant that Timothy was nearing the end of the ritual.

When she turned her head around, her heart lurched, seeing that the turtle was difficult to kill. Even with its heart now removed, the turtle still quivered. She had heard Iron Cloud warn Timothy earlier that even after the turtle's head was severed, it might still have the ability to bite.

Finally the turtle ceased to move, and Timothy sat with the heart lying in the palm of his hand. It was flat and about one inch in length. He stared down at the heart for a moment longer, thinking that swallowing it should not be any harder than swallowing raw clams, which he done often while living in Boston. He plucked it up between his fingers and raised it to his lips and dropped it into his mouth. Without giving himself a chance to taste it, he let it slide on down the back of his throat, the deed done—his heart stronger because of it!

There came a great pulsing of drums and chanting that filled the night air. Iron Cloud lifted Timothy to his shoulders and started prancing around the wide circle of his people, smiling proudly from one to the other.

"Spotted Eagle!" the younger braves chanted. "Spotted Eagle!"

Blushing, his pulse racing, Timothy looked around him, his gaze stopping at Damita. He could see her mouth the words, "Spotted Eagle, I am very proud of you." He nodded toward her, reveling in this moment that was his alone.

His gaze searched out and found Lean Elk, puzzled by an intense look of jealousy in his friend's eyes. Then he recalled Lean Elk's obvious jealousy earlier in the day! He tried to understand, yet found it hard to. It was not Timothy's fault that Lean Elk had not yet been accepted as a warrior in the eyes of his Omaha people! It was not Timothy's fault that Iron Cloud treated Timothy as special! It was not even Timothy's fault that he was there in the village!

But he was, he thought stubbornly to himself, and Iron Cloud was his step-father, and he would not let Lean Elk and his petty jealousies ruin any of this for him!

When Baby hobbled into sight through the circle of Omaha people, Timothy cast worries of Lean Elk aside and asked Iron Cloud to place him on his feet. Breaking into a run, he went to Baby and lifted the bobcat into his arms, then quickly placed her to the ground again. The bobcat's weight was such that even Iron Cloud could scarcely lift her any longer.

He knelt beside Baby. "You will not hear me called Timothy ever again," Timothy whispered into the ear of his bobcat. "My name is now Spotted Eagle." He cocked an eyebrow, looking at the size of his pet. "I think it's time we change your name, also, don't you think?" he said aloud. "To something more mature like ... like ..."

A sweet voice spoke up behind Timothy, interrupting him, jerking his head around toward the sound.

"Why not call her Three Paws?" Star Shining said, moving to her knees beside Baby to caress her stiff pelt. "It is not a pretty name, of course, but it suits her well. That is why anything or anyone is given a name—to match something of its character."

Timothy's face became hot with a blush, and he suddenly felt flustered in the presence of this girl, who was more woman than girl in the way her rounded breasts pressed snugly against the inside of her buckskin dress. He knew by the heady fragrance wafting from her that sometime during the day she must have pulverized columbine seeds and mixed them with water, then sprinkled this over her body, perfuming it, for never had he smelled anything as deliciously wonderful as Star Shining!

She was all that it took for him to feel less than a strong warrior at this moment, for just being near her made his heart do strange flip-flops. He knew that if someone handed him a bow and arrow right now, he would not be able to shoot it. He would be made a fool, and all because of a woman!

He turned his eyes away from Star Shining. "Go away," he mumbled. "I need no girls telling me what to do. Go away!"

Star Shining placed a hand on Timothy's cheek and ran her fingers down its full length in a gentle caress. "I will give you a kiss if you name your pet what I suggested," she whispered, slyly looking from side to side, obviously seeing if anyone had heard.

She then leaned her face close to Timothy's, her

breath hot on his lips. "Meet me in the forest soon," she softly encouraged. "I will show you how it feels to be kissed and touched by a girl." She leaned even closer. "You can even touch me, if you wish."

Shocked by what she was saying, even more shocked by how what she was saying was affecting his body, Timothy rose clumsily to his feet and turned away from her.

When he felt eyes on him other than those of the temptress, he died a slow death inside when he realized that they were Lean Elk's, and that in them was a silent anger.

Timothy smiled awkwardly at Lean Elk, ignoring Star Shining. He placed his back to her as he urged his bobcat around, away from her. He was stunned at himself when he addressed his bobcat as Three Paws, and Star Shining's soft, teasing laughter behind him told him that he had just begun something that might end in disaster.

Chapter Thirty-three

Morning came crisp and gray with frost. The fire's embers glowed in the morning light. The chill had awakened Damita. She shivered when she tried to scoot closer to Iron Cloud, giggling when she could not get close enough to take advantage of his body's warmth because her stomach got in the way.

Iron Cloud turned over and faced her, smoothing a lock of her hair back from her face, then shaped his hands around her tight ball of stomach, her doeskin gown soft against his fingers.

"And how are my wife and children this morning?" he asked, kissing the tip of her nose. "I hope last evening's rituals did not tire you." He gazed at the privacy blanket. "Spotted Eagle came in quite late. I did not question him. The night was his to do with what he pleased, and so I allowed it."

"I saw him tiptoe in very quietly," Damita said, frowning when she recalled how Star Shining had stayed close to everywhere that Timothy had gone all evening. She did not want to even let herself believe that Timothy could have gone off with her later.

He was only fifteen—to Damita, a mere child!

Damita placed a gentle hand to Iron Cloud's cheek, directing his gaze back to her. "Darling, when did you first experience sexual frustrations?" she whispered, in case Timothy was awake. "At what age did you start looking at women, wondering about them, desiring to experiment, to see what the mystery about them was?"

Iron Cloud's lips tugged into a playful smile. "What does that matter?" he said, cupping one of her milk-filled breasts through the doeskin fabric of her gown. "You are my woman. There is no looking back when a man has someone like you to warm his bed."

"Iron Cloud, it is not so much you that I am asking about," Damita said, sighing exasperatedly. "It is Timothy! Is he at the age when he sees women as women? Even girls who behave as women? Is he old enough to . . . to want to be with them, if they entice him to be?"

"Timothy?" Iron Cloud said lightly. "He is no longer Timothy. He is Spotted Eagle. Call him Spotted Eagle."

"Whatever," Damita said, moving quickly into a sitting position. "Whether he is Timothy or Spotted Eagle, he is the same person." She looked determinedly at Iron Cloud as he rose to a sitting position beside her. "I need to know these things, Iron Cloud. You saw how Star Shining flirted with . . . with Spotted Eagle all evening. It was utterly disgraceful!"

Iron Cloud chuckled beneath his breath. He gave Damita an amused smile, then busied himself at preparing the morning fire. "How Star Shining behaved was normal for her age," he said, keeping his voice low and steady. "As I told you last night, she is of marriageable age. She flirts to draw attention from all of the warriors, not only Spotted Eagle. She seeks a husband. She is more restless, perhaps, than most her age." He turned and smiled again at Damita. "She is more beautiful, also."

Pangs of jealousy stabbed at Damita's heart. She glanced down at her condition, at how large and unseemly she was. Even without a mirror to see herself, she knew that her face was puffy, her eyes sometimes almost swollen shut with the accumulation of water in her system.

"I am ugly in your eyes, am I not?" she blurted out, placing her hands on her hips as she looked hurtfully at Iron Cloud. "So much that you are even seeing girls who are eighteen years old as more beautiful! She wants a husband? Why not throw yourself at her like the rest of the warriors and take yourself a second wife?"

Iron Cloud's eyes widened, and his mouth fell open. He had never expected such a response from his usually sweet, quiet wife. He dropped the wood into the flames in the firepit and turned to Damita. He clutched her shoulders gently and urged her onto her back, then moved down beside her, drawing her next to him, his lips brushing hers with featherings of kisses.

"My beautiful, quite pregnant wife is jealous?" he murmured, his lips slithering down her neck, locking on the nipple of a breast through the fabric of her gown.

When she uttered a guttural groan of pleasure, he looked quickly at the drawn blanket, hoping not to have awakened Spotted Eagle. The young warrior had surely been shown many things last night. Iron Cloud had seen Spotted Eagle and Star Shining slip into the thicket. There they had remained until late into the night.

But this was not something that Iron Cloud had shared with White Willow. He did not want to alarm her unduly. It was time for Spotted Eagle to learn all the ways of manhood! Even the wonders of being with a woman!

But, Iron Cloud, also thought, Spotted Eagle did not need to learn it firsthand in the wigwam of his sister and adoptive father!

It was time for Spotted Eagle to have a lodge of his own!

"I miss being with you so much," Damita whispered, running her hands over Iron Cloud's smooth, hairless chest, reveling in the mere touch of him. "It has been forever, Iron Cloud. And there is still so much time left before I have the child.

I'm not sure if I can wait so long. I need you, Iron Cloud. I need you now."

"As I need you, my beautiful White Willow," Iron Cloud said, whispering in her ear. "Time will pass quickly now. You will see. Would you like for me to spread a blanket over you and rub you? Would you get satisfaction enough for now if I did this for you?"

Damita looked toward the drawn blanket, then back into Iron Cloud's eyes. "Perhaps later," she whispered. She trailed her fingers down his nude body and locked them around his swollen manhood. She heard him hold in a groan of pleasure as she began caressing him. When she heard a stirring behind the blanket she moved her hand away, watching Iron Cloud quickly slip his breechclout on, his face flushed with unfulfilled desires.

"I have things to do," Iron Cloud said thickly. "But first I must awaken Spotted Eagle. It is for him, this chore that I have chosen to do this morning."

Damita leaned up on one elbow. "What is it?" she murmured. "What are you going to do?"

"Soon our baby will be here," Iron Cloud said. "It is time for Timothy to live alone, in his own dwelling." He knelt beside Damita, his hand cupping her cheek. "And it would be nice for us to have our privacy, do you not agree?"

Damita giggled and blushed, then nodded her head. "That would be wonderful," she murmured. Then her smile faded, and she stared up at Iron Cloud warily. "But that would also give my brother the privacy he may *not* need. Surely it is too soon for him to have—to have women with him. He wouldn't do that, would he, Iron Cloud?"

Iron Cloud did not respond, just stared into her eyes a moment longer, then went and stepped behind the blanket. "Rise, young warrior," he said, gently shaking Timothy by the shoulder. "Today we build you a wigwam."

Timothy awakened with a start, his bobcat stretching and yawning as she awakened beside him. Then Iron Cloud's words sank in, and he bolted to a sitting position. "A wigwam?" he gasped. "For me? My own, alone?"

"Soon a baby will fill the space that is now yours," Iron Cloud explained softly.

Timothy's face became suffused with an excited flush. He grabbed his breechclout and slipped it on. He combed his fingers through his hair that was now past his shoulders and positioned his beaded headband.

Slipping into his moccasins, he was lost in thought—of the previous evening. He had felt guilty about being alone with Star Shining, knowing how Lean Elk felt about her, and feeling less than honorable about it, especially when Star Shining removed her dress and let him touch her all over.

At that point there had been no turning back. He had let her remove his breechclout and her fingers had performed what he still saw as nothing less than miracles on his body.

Even now, just thinking about the pleasure she

had aroused in him made him grow weak in the knees. He could never hunger any less for her than he did now, at this moment. He could hardly wait until they were together again.

He looked anxiously up at Iron Cloud. "Can I have anyone in my lodge that I want to?" he asked, his excitement peaking at the thought of sleeping a full night with Star Shining—which, in truth, would not be spent in sleeping at all. He would spend the night touching and exploring her body and she his.

"There will be no restrictions," Iron Cloud said. "You are your own man now. You must do what your heart leads you to do—but never forgetting friends and family in your decisions."

Timothy swallowed hard, again feeling guilty about Lean Elk, and what their vows of friendship had meant to him—until last night.

He said nothing to Iron Cloud, afraid that anything he said might some day turn into a lie, and Iron Cloud had given him too much to give him cause to lose respect for him. He would have to tell Star Shining to come after dark, when everyone else was asleep. They would have their own piece of paradise on earth.

Iron Cloud gave Timothy a lingering look, then went to Damita and started to give her a farewell kiss, but stopped and leaned his ear toward the entrance flap when he heard the distinct sound of many horses entering the village.

He and Damita exchanged troubled glances, then he stepped outside, seeing that Brian was at

418

the head of a procession of Omaha warriors not of his village, although there were many familiar faces among them.

Wrapped snugly with a bear pelt, Damita stepped outside with Iron Cloud and placed a robe around his broad shoulders. Brian and the Indians had now dismounted and were leading their horses through the village.

Iron Cloud stepped away from Damita and met the entourage halfway. Brian and Iron Cloud hugged generously, then Brian turned and gestured toward the Indians that stood placidly behind him.

"I did not think that you would mind that I have brought Sun Rising and his warriors to your village," Brian said. "Sun Rising had a desperate need to bring a message to you." He looked over his shoulder at Sun Rising, then back at Iron Cloud. "I will let him speak with you, to tell you why he saw an urgency in this meeting."

Brian motioned with a hand for Sun Rising to step forward. Brian stepped aside as Sun Rising came and stood eye to eye with Iron Cloud.

"Blue Wind is with his ancestors now," Sun Rising said solemnly. "But before he died he told me all about the Sacred Pole having been stolen by Black Coyote, and that you brought the Sacred Pole back to its rightful place in the Tent of War. Blue Wind gave the order before he died that because you proved to be loyal to Blue Wind, the Keeper of the Pole, that you should be allowed to name the new Keeper. He also said that you were

worthy of having the Sacred Pole in your village."
He turned, and with a swing of his hand, he gestured toward a horse that had a travois attached behind it. "Blue Wind's wishes are now fulfilled. The pole has been brought to you. You are now in charge of protecting it. You are given the honor of erecting a Tent of War and choosing the new Keeper."

Iron Cloud was too stunned to speak. Never before had he been rendered speechless! But this! This was something so beyond belief that he was humbled by the honor.

He watched as the travois was removed from the horse and laid aside. He started to give Sun Rising a sincere thank-you, but the solemn warrior was already walking back to his horse, the others having already turned back in the direction from which they had just come.

Soon Brian and Iron Cloud were standing alone, Damita at Iron Cloud's side, gazing with wonder down at the travois and the bundle tied securely onto it.

"What is that?" she murmured, placing a hand to her throat. "What did they want? Why did they leave?"

"I have been given one of the highest honors of my people," Iron Cloud said thickly, moving slowly toward the bundled Sacred Pole. "And I do not know what to say, or what to do."

"You will keep the pole in your village, of course," Brian said, placing an arm around Iron Cloud's shoulder. "And you will appoint a Keeper.

And soon, I hope. I understand the importance of the Sacred Pole to your people."

"That is what disturbs me," Iron Cloud said, stopping to stare down at the wrapped sacred object. "It is not good that the pole is so far from so many. It should be in Nebraska, not Illinois."

"Then, ol' buddy, go back to Nebraska," Brian said matter-of-factly. "I've cleared your name. No one holds you accountable for anything." He stepped away from Iron Cloud and puffed out his chest proudly as he widened his legs and placed his fists on his hips. "*And*, ol' buddy, I, personally, will see to it that your people will have their fair share of annuities."

Iron Cloud lifted an eyebrow. "And how can you do that?" he asked, seeing the smugness in Brian's smile.

"Because, Iron Cloud, I have only recently been assigned the agent's post at Fort Calhoun," he said, chuckling. "I went to St. Louis, asked for the position, and since I have proven myself as a trusted, loyal soldier for so many years, they did not have to think twice before accepting me."

Iron Cloud's jaw went slack, then he let out a loud whoop and grabbed Brian and hugged him hard. "That is good!" he shouted. "That is very good!"

Brian laughed softly as Iron Cloud finally released his hold on him. "Then you will return to Nebraska with me?" he said anxiously. "You know that for the most part this will make your people happy. Uprooting them had to be an upsetting experience for them."

"Everyone *should* have the opportunity to bring their offerings to the pole," Iron Cloud said thoughtfully. "It would be selfish of me to keep it in Illinois, so that only my people are blessed by it."

"Yes, that is true," Brian encouraged him.

Damita stepped forth and placed a comforting hand on Iron Cloud's arm. "It would be best for everyone," Damita murmured. "Even for you, my darling. Although Illinois is beautiful and has been a refuge, it is not your homeland, where your ancestors are buried. Let's return, Iron Cloud. Let's go with Brian."

Iron Cloud felt that he perhaps should take his pipe and go alone to the hills to ask for Wakoda's guidance and blessing, yet in a sense, the blessing was already his! And he knew that he could not run away from all mankind—from "progress", as the white man called it. The white man was closing in on him from all sides, it seemed. It was best for his people that he return to Nebraska. Perhaps in this one decision, to bring them to Illinois, he had been too hasty and headstrong.

He smiled. At least he could boast that his move to Illinois had eventually caused the demise of— had rid the land of the evil agent!

"Yes, we will go!" he shouted, thrusting a fist into the air. "Let us spread the word now! We shall take this one last night in Illinois, then tomorrow we shall begin our journey back home!"

Iron Cloud turned to Damita, his eyes dark with emotion. "Home," he said thickly. "We're going home, darling."

Tears silvered Damita's eyes. "Yes, home," she said, placing a hand to his cheek, touching it gently. "Our child will be born in your homeland."

Nodding, Iron Cloud turned back to the travois and stared with a wondrous heart down at it. He felt certain that the secrets of all happinesses lay there, beneath the wrapped blankets.

The fires had burned low, and the last dog had crept away and had fallen into a fast sleep. Brian went to Girl Who Laughs' wigwam and whispered her name ever so silently through the entrance flap. Girl Who Laughs responded quickly. She left the wigwam, a blanket robe thrown around her shoulders. They looked intently into each other's eyes for a moment, then walked quickly away into the darkness.

After finding a quiet nook beside the river, where the treetops were silvered with the moon, they moved together and trembled with a kiss they had saved up for this moment. There was some warmth to the air this night. Brian took her to a blanket that he had spread there for their secret meeting. In a matter of moments he had a fire built for them and they were sitting beside it, snuggled in one another's arms.

"You will marry me, won't you?" Brian asked, his voice quavering.

"Yes, enough time has passed," Girl Who

Laughs said, looking adoringly up at him as his fingers awakened her to desires she had not known since before her husband's untimely death. She leaned into his hand as he crept his fingers down the inside of her dress, then gasped with pleasure as his hand cupped her breast, then softly kneaded it.

"I need you," Brian said huskily, leaning her down onto her back, straddling her. His hand traveled slowly up her dress, soon hiking it up past her waist.

"I want you," Girl Who Laughs whispered, twining her fingers through his shoulder-length golden hair.

"I love you," Brian said, lowering his breeches to his knees and pressing his manhood into her soft, yielding folds.

"I shall never love anyone but you," Girl Who Laughs whispered back, a cry of sweet agony filling the night air as he thrust himself deeply inside her. She clung and rocked with him, her whole body quivering with rapture.

An incredible sweetness swept through Damita as she lay beneath the blankets beside the fire. Iron Cloud's fingers brushed over and over again against her soft, warm flesh at the juncture of her thighs. Her breath quickened and she welcomed his lips as he touched hers in a gentle and lingering kiss.

And then she began fighting the wondrous feelings, worrying about Timothy and how he might react if he came into the wigwam and found her face so flushed, her eyes so dreamy with pleasure.

She very gently shoved Iron Cloud away. "Where is Timothy?" she said, inhaling a quaking breath. "He should be home by now. He knows he has a lot of responsibility tomorrow. He has to help get everything ready for the long journey back to Nebraska."

"Spotted Eagle was excited about the adventure of it," Iron Cloud said, resting a hand on Damita's thigh. "He is perhaps making plans with his friends about what they might see and do while on the trail."

Damita frowned, thinking that might be true, yet knowing that he could also be with the seductress!

"Do not fret so over things beyond your control," Iron Cloud said, leaning his lips close to hers. "Let us enjoy our last night in our wigwam. We will not know such comforts again until we reach Nebraska."

"But what about Spotted Eagle?" Damita said, breathless as Iron Cloud ducked his head beneath the blanket and began lapping first one breast, and then the other, with his hot, wet tongue. "What if he should arrive home?"

"We are beneath the blankets," Iron Cloud said huskily. "If he looks at us, he will only see what we are doing by what he allows his imagination to conjure up."

Damita forgot all reason as he began loving her

with his tongue and lips in all of her secret places, giving herself up to the rapture of the moment.

Moving as quietly as a panther through the dark forest, Lean Elk followed the light of a campfire a short distance away, and the sound of laughter. When he came close enough to see who was making the sounds, his insides stiffened and he felt as though he might retch.

His mother and the white man!

They were making love!

He turned his head away, hardly able to stand the sight. He felt betrayed!

Betrayed!

Running away, blinded by tears, he sought another avenue of escape than that which he had just taken, not yet wanting to return home. He ran for a while, then voices through the break in the brush ahead caused his heart to skip a beat when he recognized them.

His heart pounding, a wave of dull anger sweeping through him, he glided like a fox through the bushes until he was close enough to see. What he witnessed made him feel like a fool for having been betrayed twice in one night!

"Spotted Eagle and Star Shining!" he whispered between gritted teeth. He could not help but watch the performance being acted out before him, having for so long wanted to be the one playing the role of the lover with Star Shining. His gut twisted and his hands rolled into tight fists as he watched Star Shining moving her hand over Spotted Eagle's body, stopping at his manhood to curl her beautiful, tiny fingers around his distended member. His body stiffened when he heard Spotted Eagle's guttural groans of pleasure as her hand speeded its movements.

Lean Elk almost fainted from the shock of it when Star Shining knelt down over Spotted Eagle and took his throbbing member into her mouth!

He turned away, gasping and holding his throat as a bitterness rose into it and caused it to constrict. Then he knelt down and retched until his stomach felt as empty as his soul.

Slowly he pushed himself up from the ground, vowing revenge.

One day.

He would make his friend pay—for now he was his arch-enemy!

His heart soaring with love for Star Shining, his body still throbbing from her teaching him all the ways of lovemaking, Timothy stole quietly through the forest to his wigwam. By the soft light of the moon, Timothy saw something lying just outside the entrance flap of the wigwam. He knelt and inspected the object, his heart skipping a beat when he discovered what it was!

"The flute that I gave Lean Elk to seal our friendship!" he whispered, paling as he stared down at the gift that was now broken in half. There could be only one meaning to this destruction—Lean Elk had severed their friendship forever! Lean Elk was now his enemy!

Yet Timothy quickly decided that he would not allow guilt to ruin the happiness he had found within Star Shining's arms. Lean Elk had been jealous of Timothy before he had paid any thought to the lovely Omaha maiden! This just made the jealousy worse.

But it did sadden him, this loss of friendship. He bowed his head and lingered a while longer outside before going into the wigwam.

Always, it seemed, there were adjustments to be made inside his heart.

Always, he was losing someone special to him!

But always, he survived the loss—as he would this one!

Chapter Thirty-four

Nine Months Later.
Nebraska

Damita had just helped with the delivery of Girl Who Laughs' baby, and since mother and son now rested comfortably as Brian sat proudly at their bedside, she returned to her own dwelling, needing some time to herself.

Iron Cloud and Timothy had just left for the hunt with many other warriors—but not Lean Elk. After returning to Nebraska, Lean Elk had organized his own group of young braves who had not yet reached the status of warrior for one reason or another, and had fled to the hills, now renegades dodging not only the white man's law, but also the people of their own village.

Going to her crib, Damita gazed down at her own piece of heaven on this earth. When God had granted her a full-term pregnancy, it seemed that he had planted a lily in her heart, for she had given birth to a most precious girl, who had her golden hair and her father's copper skin. Her daughter was truly something to look at—so beautiful, so unique.

Damita leaned over the crib and lifted Suzanne into her arms, laughing to herself at the times she had thought that she was carrying twins within her womb. It had not been twins.

Instead, it had been a nine-pound baby girl!

Yet the birthing had come quickly and easily. There were no scars to show that Damita had given birth to a child.

Laughingly, she thought back to the day when Iron Cloud had told her that if she wished to learn the sex of their coming child, there was a way. He had told her to take a bow and a burden strap to the tent of an Omaha squaw who had a child not yet old enough to speak and offer this child the articles.

If the bow was chosen, the unborn child would be a boy. If the burden strap was chosen, the unborn child would be a girl.

Being superstitious, Damita had taken neither bow nor burden strap. She had been afraid of jinxing the pregnancy that had been going too well to tamper with.

And she was glad that she had made that decision, for she had been blessed with a daughter, the light of not only her life, but also Iron Cloud's.

"And how are you this morning, my precious?"

Damita murmured, wrapping Suzanne in a doe-skin blanket embroidered by Damita's own hands in the design of kittens and dogs—and one lone bobcat!

She looked long and lovingly into the face of her child. At dawn those several months ago, when her daughter had been born, the women of the village had gathered around her, proud for their beloved chief, his wife, and their firstborn—even though it was not a son. Everyone had accepted Timothy as Iron Cloud's son, their next-chief-in-line.

Thick lashes fluttered over dark eyes and the tiny, perfectly sculpted lips quivered into a smile as Suzanne gazed contentedly up at her mother.

Damita kissed Suzanne's brow. "You have a new playmate," she murmured. "Girl Who Laughs just gave birth to a baby boy. His name is Lance. Like your name, it is not altogether an Indian name, but in time he will adopt one that will fit him well. But you, my sweet, will always be Suzanne."

Damita rocked Suzanne in her arms, humming softly a lullaby that she had heard the other Omaha mothers sing to their infants.

"Who is this?
Who is this?
Giving eye-light
On the top of my lodge?
It is I, the little owl,
Coming, coming.

It is I, the little owl,
Coming,
Down! Down!"

Damita sang another song, her voice soft and sweet.

"The earliest moon of winter time
Is not so round and fair
As was the ring of glory on
The helpless infant there."

Damita gave Suzanne one last kiss, then wrapped her baby and strapped her to a carved and curtained cradleboard. After fastening this to her back, she went out of her shadowed wigwam into the sunshine of morning.

She left the village and walked away from the river where the sun lay like a path of fire over the water, across dark, mossy places the sun seemed never to touch. The wet debris on the forest floor steamed in the heat. All about her was a sort of dim gray light, and the dark laurel stems made strange patterns on it. Flies buzzed sleepily in the muggy air under the trees, and locusts sawed endlessly against the fabric of summer heat.

Damita walked until she came through a clump of young trees. Before her lay a tiny open meadow, its borders a ring of thicket and tall trees. Here the valley stretched before her, like some vast spell of blue enchantment, an open land with its sea of waving grass and reeds.

Damita walked on until she found water dripping from a tinkling spring into a quiet pool. Hanging her cradleboard onto the low-reaching branch of a maple tree, she drank from the crystal-clear water, then looked out over the billowing fields and toward the savage mists that were being falsely created by the hazy streamers of sunshine falling from the heavens.

The breeze rocked her little bundle, in time to the merry songs of the birds overhead.

But suddenly the birds' lively calls were stilled. Damita's spine stiffened and the skin at the back of her neck and shoulders prickled as though with a chill. She crept back toward her cradleboard, wondering if the sound she had heard was Suzanne beginning to whimper, perhaps too hot all strapped in tight and snug on her cradleboard.

Or was it something else . . . ?

As she reached for the cradleboard to remove it from the tree, she heard another whimpering sound, and it was most definitely not Suzanne. The sound was coming from the farther reaches of the forest, beneath the thick canopy of trees!

Then the sound changed from a soft whimpering to a groan of pain, and then strange grunting noises.

Frightened, Damita was torn with what to do. She had been foolish not to have brought a firearm with her for protection.

She glanced at the cradleboard, and then toward the whimpering sounds that had begun again, and knew that no matter what danger she might be putting herself and her child in, she had to see who was in pain.

Perhaps someone was injured. Perhaps she could offer some help. She still recalled many teachings of her father. Had she not just performed wonderfully in helping Girl Who Laughs give birth to her child?

Lifting the cradleboard from the branch, she held it close to her bosom instead of fastening it to her back and crept toward the continuing sounds of someone obviously very much in pain. When she stepped into a clearing, she saw a tiny woman all swollen with child lying beneath a tree a short distance away. Her dress was hiked up, her legs widely spread, and her hands clutching two low-hanging branches of a tree as she grunted and pressed down in an effort to release the baby from her body. Damita grew pale and gasped, recognizing the young woman.

It was Star Shining! Star Shining was pregnant and was even now giving birth to a child!

Now Damita realized why Star Shining had disappeared many weeks ago. When she had begun to show her condition, she must have fled the village, not wanting anyone to know!

Damita felt a dizziness sweep through her, for she had found out about Timothy and Star Shining's love affair many months ago. She felt nausea rising within her, to think that this child might be her very own brother's!

She could not help but be sickened at the thought. Her brother was sixteen now, yet still a child more than a man! And of course, Star Shining knew this and knew that he would not marry her. It seemed her only other recourse was to run away, have the child . . .

"Then what?" Damita whispered to herself, aghast at what her mind was conjuring up. Was Star Shining going to have the child and abandon it in the forest, to die alone and motherless?

"No, I can't let that happen," Damita whispered to herself, yet knowing that her interference at this time would mean many complications for her family—especially Timothy.

She set her jaw, blaming her brother as much as this little vixen. He had not been forced to have intimate relations with her! He had gone with her willingly into the forest. If the child was his, he was responsible for it!

Damita looked to the Heavens. "Please, God," she prayed. "Let me do the right thing." She prayed, too, that the child would have all traits of an Indian. Then perhaps it could be proven that it was not Timothy's. It was well-known that Star Shining was a seductress. Surely she had bedded others besides Timothy.

Her mind made up, Damita hurried to Star Shining and stood over her, seeing fear in the younger woman's eyes as she looked up at her.

"You!" Star Shining gasped. "Go away! I not want you here!"

"If you think I want to be here, you are quite mistaken," Damita grumbled, hanging her cradleboard onto a branch. "I did not come looking for you. I found you by accident."

Star Shining tried to inch away from Damita, but the tree was at her back, stopping her escape. "No one but my parents know of the child," she wailed, tears splashing from her eyes. "I have been living alone, fending for myself, so that no one else would know. I can have the baby by myself. Leave. It is not of your concern!"

"I'm afraid it is," Damita said, falling to her knees beside Star Shining. "I would rather it wasn't, but I can't just leave you lying here, alone, having a child. It seems you are having difficulties. How long have you been in labor?"

"Much time," Star Shining said. Sweat poured from her brow, and her hair hung in wet ringlets around her lovely face, which became grotesquely twisted when she began groaning and pushing down as another pain wracked her body.

Damita placed her hands on Star Shining's belly and gently pressed her fingers along her clammy flesh, feeling nothing out of the ordinary in the way the baby was lying. She then knelt between Star Shining's legs and crept her hands up inside the birth canal until she could place her hands on each side of the baby's head.

"Push again, Star Shining," she encouraged. "I'll help you."

After what seemed like an eternity to Damita, the child slipped out into her arms, and everything that she had prayed for seemed to have vanished into thin air, for the child was an exact duplicate of Timothy, from the color of its thick hair and eyes to the shade of its skin. She wanted to retch, her disappointment was so keenly etched within her soul, but she knew that from this moment on she had to learn to accept fate and what it handed her—good or bad.

"My baby," Star Shining said, sobbing. "I don't want to see my baby. Place it in the bushes! Let it die!"

Damita paled at the thought, and at the cold-heartedness of the young woman, yet not believing that she truly felt that way. It was in the way she looked at the child that she hungered to hold it.

Taking the time only to cut the cord and wipe some of the birthing debris from the body with her hands, Damita made sure that the mother held the baby very quickly, so that all ideas of abandoning her child would be forgotten.

Laying the small child into Star Shining's arms, Damita saw the quick bonding between mother and child, and tears came to her eyes. She no longer resented anyone for anything. The child was beautiful. The love for the child in the mother's eyes was beautiful. The way Star Shining knew to open the bodice of her dress and offer her breast to the child was beautiful!

Damita turned her eyes away, tears flooding her cheeks. This child was her nephew. No matter how anyone looked at this birth, he was her nephew and she would never allow anything bad to happen to him!

She waited for the afterbirth to be dispelled, then busied herself cleaning up both mother and child. She was surprised to find that Star Shining had the strength to walk along beside her, carrying her child, as they headed in the direction of their village.

"I did not want this," Star Shining said solemnly. "I do love Spotted Eagle. That is why I did not want him to know about the child. I know his age and what a burden I will be. I do not want to be a burden! I truly love him!"

Star Shining turned her eyes away, ashamed. "My parents sent me away so that no one would know that I was with a child," she sobbed. "They no longer claim me as their daughter!"

Damita was stunned by Star Shining's seriousness. She was very convincing in her love for Timothy, and Damita felt pity for her for having been banished from her family. There was nothing much anyone could do about Star Shining's parents and their decisions.

But as for Timothy, Damita knew that his feelings for her were sincere. He had moped around, seemingly only half-interested in life, since her absence. Only recently, after Timothy had celebrated his sixteenth birthday, had Iron Cloud succeeded in pulling him out of his shell and bringing him into their daily activities again.

"Things will work out," Damita reassured her, reaching over to take Star Shining's delicate hand. "You'll see. Things will work out."

When they reached the village, Star Shining was near exhaustion. Damita helped her to Timothy's wigwam and made her comfortable on his sleeping platform, the child lying snugly beside her. Damita took Suzanne from her cradleboard and laid her on a soft pallet of furs away from the warmth of the firepit.

"I have a pot of stew cooking in my dwelling," she said, smoothing Star Shining's hair back from her eyes. "I shall go and get it. You need nourishment if your milk is going to be healthy for your son."

Star Shining smiled gratefully up at Damita, then grabbed her hand and smothered it in kisses. "I shall watch your baby while you are gone," she murmured. "And thank you so much for everything." Tears flooded her eyes again. "But what of Spotted Eagle? What will he think? What will he do?"

A sudden shaft of light told Damita that someone had lifted the heavy bearskin at the door. A sudden shadow filling the spaces of the entranceway made Star Shining pale and gasp. Damita turned and her heart skipped a beat when she discovered Timothy standing there, a most stunned expression on his freckled face.

"I didn't know you had returned from the hunt," Damita said, rushing to Timothy. She took his hand and led him into the dwelling. "I have quite a surprise for you."

Timothy and Star Shining's eyes met and held for a moment. Unspoken words were exchanged between them, and then Timothy's gaze shifted to the child.

"Ours," Star Shining said, sobbing as Timothy

knelt down beside the sleeping platform, softly touching the baby's face. "He is our son. Do you like?"

"Our . . . son . . . ?" Timothy said, his voice breaking. "Is this why you left? You were . . . pregnant?"

"Yes. I did not want to worry you with it," Star Shining said.

"I found her in the forest having the child," Damita offered. "I helped her with the delivery, then brought her back where she belongs." She placed a hand to Timothy's shoulder. "She and the child are your responsibility, Timothy. You are now a family."

Timothy sat there for a moment, motionless, his breath escaping in short rasps. Then he leaned over and swept his arms around Star Shining, almost swallowing her whole with happy kisses.

Damita picked up Suzanne and crept from the wigwam. Outside, she stopped and inhaled a quavering breath, thankful for blessed favors from God above! The day had been long, yet filled with deep emotion. She sighed and looked to the dark sky, a soft prayer of thanks inside her heart.

She sighed and walked slowly away from Timothy's wigwam, the blackness of the summer night as tangible, as warm as the breath of an animal. When she saw Iron Cloud coming from the corral, several rabbits slung over his shoulder, she hurried toward him.

Damita stepped up beside him and walked with him toward their dwelling. "I see you had a fruitful day, darling," she said in a teasing fashion. "So did I."

"Oh?" Iron Cloud said, forking an eyebrow.

"My doctoring skills came in quite handy today," she boasted. "I delivered not one child, but *two*."

Excitedly, she told Iron Cloud everything. His reaction was almost the same as hers—hesitant at first to accept Timothy's new status in life, then somewhat elated, for he realized that this would enhance Timothy's prowess as a virile warrior.

"I want to see the child," Iron Cloud said, turning to walk away, but stopping when Damita reached a hand to his arm. He turned to her, an eyebrow lifted quizzically.

"I wouldn't go now, darling," Damita murmured. "Spotted Eagle has only moments ago realized he has a child, and that Star Shining has returned, deeply in love with him. They need time to talk things out, and to be alone with their child."

"I will go later," Iron Cloud said, moving on to their wigwam, dropping the skinned rabbits just outside the entranceway. He washed his hands thoroughly in a basin of water that Damita always had ready for him after a hunt on a stand just outside the wigwam. He turned passion-heavy eyes to her.

"All day I thought of nothing but you," he said huskily.

He dried his hands on a towel, then wove his fingers through her unbraided hair and drew her mouth close to his. "My White Willow," he murmured. "My beautiful White Willow. How lucky I am to have found you. You fill my every want and need."

He brushed his mouth across her lips with a kiss. "I want you now," he whispered. "The hunt filled me with excitement. Let us not waste such feelings that still linger within my soul. Let us put them to good use by making love!"

Her skin tingled with the thought of what he was offering, and it was wonderful to be able to experience these moments with him now that she had given birth to their child. She was proud to show off her newly slim body to her beloved.

"That sounds beautiful," Damita murmured, then laughed softly when Iron Cloud took Suzanne into his arms and nuzzled her neck with a kiss.

"Did my sweet Suzanne miss me?" he crooned, gently carrying her into the wigwam. He bent over the cradle and laid her in it, laughing boisterously when Suzanne gave him a wide grin, followed by a contented gurgle.

"Both of your women missed you," Damita said, surprising Iron Cloud by how hastily she was able to shed her clothes. When she stepped around in front of him, her skin was vibrant and glowing, the golden fronds of her hair spilling over her shoulders and tumbling down her back.

His gaze burned her flesh. With a pounding heart he once again enjoyed the sight of her slim, white thighs, her long and tapering legs, and her well- rounded breasts with nipples hard and peaked, seemingly waiting for his lips to caress them.

Damita smiled seductively up at him as she began slipping his breechclout down past his hips, his hardened readiness springing in sight as she pushed the breechclout on down to his thighs, then gave them a shove until they landed around his ankles.

"I love you," Damita whispered, twining her fingers around his manhood, slowly working them up and down, as the vein begin to pound in his neck. She leaned against him, her breasts pressing hard into his chest. "You smell so good. Like the scent of pine, and the wind." She placed her tongue at the hollow of his throat and licked him hungrily. "And you taste just as good, my darling."

Hardly able to hold back the passionate energy building within him, Iron Cloud swung Damita up into his arms and carried her to their sleeping platform. He kissed her savagely as he laid her down and crept over her, parting her legs with a knee. In only one thrust he was inside her, her whole body quivering into his.

As his lean, sinewy buttocks moved, Damita rode with him, the euphoria blossoming within her. Her pulse raced when his lips made a descent downward across her throat. Then he cupped a breast, his fingers kneading its softness, his teeth nipping the nipple, until she wanted to scream with the pleasure this was evoking within her.

Iron Cloud felt the nerves in his body tensing, then a familiar tremor began deep within himself.

He placed his hands on Damita's buttocks, sinking his fingers into her flesh as he lifted her more snugly against him. His heart pounded and he emitted a thick, husky groan, burying himself deeply inside her with each added thrust until the flames of passion burned too high and he was not able to hold back the pleasure any longer.

He felt it growing, growing to the bursting point, and then felt the final thrust that brought him to the brink of the pleasure he had been seeking.

Damita strained her hips up to him, crying out at her own fulfillment.

And then they lay together, breathing hard, their hands clasped.

"I see and feel your happiness," Iron Cloud said huskily, leaning a soft kiss to the tip of her nose. "It matches mine, my White Willow."

"Our love is so strong, it would endure all hardships," Damita said, tracing his handsome facial features with a finger. "Are you glad that you returned to Nebraska? Are you content living on the reservation?"

"No chief wants to see his people forced to live on reservations," Iron Cloud grumbled. "And had it not been for Brian, and the fact that I owed it to all Omaha people that the Sacred Pole be available to them, we would still be in Illinois." He roamed his fingers over her body, touching her as though it were for the first time. "And wherever you are, my White Willow, I am happy. You are here in Nebraska? I am happy. When you were in

Illinois, I was happy. You *are* my happiness, my darling."

"So much seems perfect, yet there are some things that make me sad," Damita said, cuddling closer to him as he enfolded her within the muscled strength of his arms. "What of Lean Elk? He has fled into the hills. Girl Who Laughs never sees him or hears from him. And what of Spotted Eagle? He and Lean Elk were the best of friends. And now the young woman who caused their separation has returned with a child—with Spotted Eagle's child. Lean Elk will never be Spotted Eagle's friend now. He will be my brother's enemy forever!"

"Those problems are not yours," Iron Cloud said, placing a finger to Damita's chin, directing her eyes into his. "Let the young men work them out between them. Perhaps in the future they will meet and settle their differences. As for the woman, she now has more of a bond with your brother than Lean Elk could ever have. She has borne him a child. One must never forget that, White Willow. That child is more important now than a friendship between two young men who have drifted apart."

He gazed more intently into Damita's eyes. "As for the child, we will interfere if interference is needed, for that young warrior born to Spotted Eagle today is a future leader of our people," he said. "After Spotted Eagle, he will be chief!"

Damita looked away from Iron Cloud toward the crib bearing their own child. "You really don't

445

resent me for not giving you a son, do you?" she murmured. She looked slowly back at him. "You have truly adopted Timothy into your heart as a son, haven't you? It does seem enough. Is it?"

"You called him Timothy," Iron Cloud said. "You did not call him Spotted Eagle."

"Darling, he was Timothy to me for too long for me ever to forget the name that my parents gave him at birth," she said, placing a hand to his cheek. "But I will remember, when we are around others, the importance of calling him by his Omaha name."

"That is good," Iron Cloud said, nodding. He framed her face between his hands and drew her lips close to his. "And, yes, Timothy has become my son in every sense of the word. And how could I resent you for anything? You are everything that is good on this earth!"

A wondrous peace settled over Damita as Iron Cloud kissed her. He was the promise of all her tomorrows! Through the savage mists of time, their love had endured. And it would, for always and always.

SAVAGE Persuasion

CASSIE EDWARDS

**Winner of the *Romantic Times* Award
for Best Indian Series**

Fleeing from an Indian attack, lovely young Brietta was
captured by a Cherokee brave, whose dark, smoldering eyes
urged her to surrender. But Brave Eagle was not the only
Indian to lay claim to the beautiful white woman. Brown
Cloud, leader of the Osage tribe, swore she belonged to him.
Blinded by a fierce love, each brave pledged he would have
Brietta for his own—or he would set the Ozarks aflame with
burning arrows of desire and destruction.

__3140-X $4.95 US/$5.95 CAN